AN ENEMIES TO LOVERS ROMANCE

If You GIVE A CEO A Chance

ANN EINERSON

Paperback ISBN: 978-1-960325-11-2

Cover Design by @okaycreations
Dev Edited by Jeannine Colette, @bryannareads, @probablyalovestory, @bookswithkaity
Edited by Rebecca @Fairest Reviews Editing Services, Sisters Get Literary Author Services
Proofread by Judy Zweifel @Judy's Proofreading, Courtney DeLollis
Formatted by Champagne Book Design

For those chasing a dream that feels just out of reach—keep going, don't stop believing, and never give up. The sky is your limit.

PLAYLIST

Nice To Meet You – Mylee Smith
Good Luck, Babe! – Chappell Roan
Please, Please, Please – Sabrina Carpenter
Welcome to New York (Taylor's Version) – Taylor Swift
do I ever cross your mind – sombr
not friends, not enemies – Isaac Levi
Us. (feat. Taylor Swift) – Gracie Abrams
I Wish You Would (Taylor's Version) – Taylor Swift
we can't be friends – Ariana Grande
i like the way you kiss me – Artemas
Constellations – Jade LeMac
Make You Mine – Madison Beer
Good Days – SZA
Ordinary – Alex Warren
her – JVKE
Stargazing – Mylee Smith
Home – Good Neighbours

AUTHOR'S NOTE

Hey, Reader!

Thank you for picking up *If You Give a CEO a Chance*. From the moment readers met Harrison in *If You Give a Grump a Holiday Wishlist,* they've been asking for his book, and I knew early on that I had to give him the happy ending he deserved. This is an interconnected standalone and was written to be read on its own.

If You Give a CEO a Chance is an enemies-to-lovers, second chance love story between a retired hockey player and his live-in private chef, in a banter-filled spicy romance.

Harrison was diagnosed with celiac disease as an adult. I've done extensive research on the subject, including common symptoms, gluten-free diets, and allergy-free cooking. I also worked with multiple sensitivity readers who have celiac disease. However, please note this is a work of fiction, and I did take liberties to enhance the storyline.

If You Give a CEO a Chance contains explicit sexual content, profanity, mention of a parent's death, mention of an absentee guardian, and emotional/verbal parental abuse.

Reading is meant to be your happy place—choose yourself, your needs, and your happiness first!

Xoxo,
Ann Einerson

If you give a CEO a private chef, he may be tempted to have her move in with him. And if she moves in, they may start a prank war, which will lead to playful banter and flirting, and then he'll start to have feelings for her. He'll send her surprises just to see her smile and invite her to watch him play at a hockey game where he'll kiss her on the ice and be determined to find a way to make her his...

If You Give a CEO a Chance

CHAPTER 1

Harrison

THE FALL AIR IS COOL AGAINST MY SKIN AS I STEP OUT onto my parents' patio. Fairy lights hang above, casting a soft glow over the space, and the sound of laughter and conversation fills the air. Tonight, we're celebrating Cash and Everly's wedding after their surprise Vegas elopement a few months ago. Since our family wasn't there, my mom was overjoyed when they agreed to a vow renewal so we could all share in the moment.

Everyone's mingling on the back deck and sampling appetizers while we wait for dinner. I approach Cash, who's leaning casually against the railing. Everly must still be inside changing into something more comfortable.

Cash is one of my younger brothers and has always been the easygoing type, drifting through life without a purpose. I used to worry he'd never settle down, but then Everly came back into his life, and everything changed.

He flashes me a grin before popping a stuffed mushroom into his mouth. "This is incredible," he mumbles, barely pausing to swallow. "Fallon really outdid herself. Have you met her yet?"

I shake my head. "No, but I'd like to. My assistant interviewed her last week and thinks she'll be a good fit as my new private chef."

Everly's brother Theo, a world-renowned chef, spoke highly of Fallon, his protégé who specializes in allergy-friendly cuisine. I was diagnosed with celiac disease after years of battling unexplained abdominal pain before a particularly agonizing episode landed me in the hospital, leading to my diagnosis.

I quickly learned that outsourcing household meal prep not only made it easier to stick to a strict gluten-free diet but also allowed me to focus my attention and energy on Stafford Holdings, our family business. It's the largest real estate firm in the country, which requires constant oversight to ensure every project stays on track and meets our high standards.

When Cash told me Fallon was moving to New York to work as a private chef, I had my assistant contact her since my last chef retired recently. Theo arranged for Fallon to fly to Aspen Grove to cater tonight's dinner for his sister's special day, but I haven't had the chance to introduce myself yet since Fallon's been tied up in the kitchen all afternoon.

Plus, business doesn't take a break, even on my brother's big day. Stafford Holdings is in the final stages of another major acquisition, so while we're waiting for dinner to begin, I'm reading through an email from our legal team when a voice I never thought I'd hear again interrupts my concentration.

"Is everything to your liking, Cash?"

"Yeah, the food is fantastic. You really outdid yourself, Fallon," he says with enthusiasm.

"Thank you," she replies.

"I want to introduce you to my brother Harrison," Cash says.

The sound of my name pulls my attention away from my phone, and I look up.

My breath falters before setting my mouth into a tight line when I'm met with the gaze of a woman I know all too well. It's not just those ocean-blue eyes that invade my dreams or the way her tongue grazes her teeth when she's lost in thought. It's the fact that I have every curve of her body burned into my memory, even though I only had her for a fleeting moment. Her presence stirs up a memory I'd rather leave buried.

I shove open the double doors to the kitchen, my heart pounding as I glance over my shoulder. A wave of relief sweeps through me when there's no sign of the puck bunny who was following me. Looks like I lost her when I cut through the service hall. The team invited a group of them to join us tonight, but I wasn't interested in anyone.

Apparently, being the son of a billionaire real estate mogul and playing professional hockey is enough to make the women chase me like I'm a prize to claim. Granted, at first, I liked the attention. It made the grueling traveling schedule more fun early on in the season, but the novelty wore off quickly, and playing hockey has been my sole focus. Winning the Stanley Cup made it all worthwhile, and better yet, we beat our rivals, the Stormbreakers.

Although the final game was two days ago, the team is still in celebration mode. My family flew home yesterday, but I stayed behind, booking a suite at the hotel for the weekend.

Tonight, the team is hosting a party at one of the event rooms before hitting up a club.

Unaware of my surroundings, I stumble back when I realize I've bumped into someone, or should I say a silver tray pressing into my stomach. I glance down at the champagne glasses teetering on the edge, threatening to spill over, and grab the server's wrist to steady it.

"Are you…" I trail off as I look up and lock eyes with a woman.

Her blonde hair is styled in soft waves, falling to her shoulders, framing her delicate oval face and piercing blue eyes. The scent of vanilla and oranges infiltrates my nose as I take her in.

She's beautiful.

Her skin is soft under my touch, and an electric jolt races down my spine. She shivers when I let my hand linger, the air between us crackling with unspoken tension. Her breathing quickens as she tips her head to get a better look at me.

She readjusts the tray, raising an eyebrow. "Could you watch where you're going? I'd hate for you to take a champagne shower and ruin that fancy suit of yours."

"I don't mind getting wet, but at least let me buy you dinner first." I wink.

She snorts. "You're just lucky it wasn't the Dom Pérignon, or you'd be footing a hefty bill if it had spilled. They serve the expensive champagne at the top of the night and then switch to the cheaper stuff once everyone's hammered. No one knows the difference."

"Except you, right?" I quip.

She sets the serving tray down on a nearby counter and shakes out her wrists. "Sure, if reading labels on bottles is considered a talent."

A smile lights up my face. I'd be lying if I said her comment doesn't have my body standing at attention.

"Any chance there's another bottle of the good stuff in the back? I'd like to share a drink with you," I say, unabashedly.

She runs her hands down to smooth the wrinkles in her apron. "Depends. Care to explain why you were busting through the door and nearly toppled me over?"

"Wanted a moment to myself," I answer vaguely. "I'm Harrison, by the way." I hold out my hand.

She doesn't appear to know who I am, which is unusual. I'm used to everyone recognizing me, so this is a refreshing change.

The woman stares at me, her teeth skimming her lower lip.

"This is when you tell me your name," I nudge playfully when she doesn't answer.

"Elizabeth," she answers boldly, accepting my hand.

The way her name falls from her lips is soft and inviting.

"A name as pretty as the woman it belongs to." I smile softly.

She scoffs, rolling her eyes. "How original. I'm guessing that line works wonders with the ladies, huh?"

I frown. Anyone else would be swooning by now, but Elizabeth just stares at me, unimpressed. Oddly enough, her resistance is captivating.

"So, this is what it's like to meet someone immune to my charm," I say, clutching my heart like I'm wounded.

"Charm? I must have missed it. Was it hiding behind that terrible line?" she quips.

"Guess I'll have to rethink my strategy." I playfully tap my chin. "This could be fun."

"As amusing as it is watching you dig yourself deeper, I really have to get back to work," she says, tapping her foot on the floor.

I might be pushing my luck, but I can't let the chance to get to know her better slip away. Even if all I get out of it is playful banter, I'll take every second. Especially since she's the first woman I've been interested in this past year who's not after me for my family's wealth or my status as a hockey player.

"Why don't I take you out after your shift, and you can help me brainstorm a new strategy?"

Elizabeth raises an amused brow. "Did I give you the impression I was interested? What if I'm seeing someone?"

I stuff my hands in my pockets and rock back on my heels, a smug smile on my face. "If you had a boyfriend, you wouldn't be flirting with me."

Her mouth falls open before she snaps it shut. "I'm not flirting with you," she says, defensively. "If anything, I'm just trying to get through this conversation without dying of boredom."

The corner of my mouth twitches up as my smile widens. "Whatever you say, Elizabeth."

A faint blush rises on her cheeks. "Does this non-date include fries and a Diet Coke, because I could go for both after my shift."

"You'd choose Diet Coke over Dom Pérignon? I don't know whether to be impressed or concerned."

"Don't judge. We all have our vices."

"I promise you'll get your Diet Coke. Hell, I'd bring you a whole truckload if that's what it takes."

She chuckles. "Unfortunately, my shoebox apartment doesn't have room for that, but I admire the enthusiasm."

"Then we'll settle on a six-pack for tonight. It's a date," I state.

She laughs softly. "Why do I get the feeling I was just played?"

I shrug, feigning innocence. "What can I say? When I see a shot, I take it."

"Okay, Mr. Hotshot," she retorts, biting her lip to keep from laughing, but the sparkle in her eyes gives her away.

"That has a nice ring to it. Guess I'll have to get my name swapped out on my jerseys for next season," I say, flashing her a crooked grin.

"You're really that full of yourself, aren't you?"

I give her a cheeky nod. "It's a gift."

She glances around as she steps around me. "I really do have to get back to work. I'll meet you in the hotel lobby in two hours," she says as she heads toward the banquet hall.

"See you soon, Elizabeth," I call out after her.

As she walks away, another smile stretches across my face. What started as a brief encounter turned into a lasting impression, and I'm counting down the minutes until I get to spend more time with her.

A light tap on my shoulder brings me back to the present.

When I glance over, Cash is staring at me, worry evident in his eyes. "You okay?" he asks.

I nod, unable to find my voice. I'm frozen in place, grappling with the reality that Elizabeth, the woman who's haunted my dreams for the last ten years, is none other than Fallon Hayes, the private chef from London. I never thought I'd see her again, much less in my parents' backyard.

My mind is racing with questions. Why does she go by a different name? Did she know I'd be here tonight? And the one that still keeps me up at night: why didn't she ever call?

Fallon raises her chin, straightening her shoulders. "Hello, Harrison," she says in a clipped tone.

"It's *you*," I state coldly.

She narrows her eyes at me. "Cash, you forgot to mention your brother's charming ego," she says.

I scoff. "Is sarcasm part of your standard approach with all of your potential clients? No wonder you had to move to another continent to start your new business."

Cash mentioned that Fallon recently moved from London, where she worked for Theo. I was told she spent the last few years mastering allergy-friendly cooking, skills that would rival elite chefs. And I can't help but wonder why she'd give all that up to work as a private chef for a handful of clients in New York.

She scowls, putting her hands on her hips. "At least I'm not the one suffering from a case of superiority complex," she quips.

Cash's eyes dart between us. "I take it you two have met before?"

Our heated stares remain locked on each other. "Yes," we say in unison. Her voice carries a trace of bitterness, which leaves me perplexed.

Fallon breaks the silence first, clearing her throat. "Tell your assistant thank you for the interview request, but you'll have to find another private chef, *Mr. Stafford*. I don't work for boorish narcissists," she states flatly. "Now, if you'll excuse me, I have to get back to work." She marches across the deck, her hands clenched at her sides.

Cash turns toward me. "What the hell was that all about?"

"Nothing," I mutter.

He raises a brow. "That was definitely something."

"Don't worry about it. You heard her. She doesn't want to work for me, so case closed."

If only it was that easy to erase her from my memory. Believe me, I've tried.

Cash taps me on the shoulder. "Uh, Harrison. I'm not so sure you'll have a choice in the matter."

"Why not?"

He nods toward the back door where Mom has managed to corner Fallon, casting us an amused glance every now and then with a mischievous smile. "I'm pretty sure Mom's already plotting how to get you two hitched next."

I rub my temples and let out a heavy sigh. "Jesus Christ, she's relentless," I mutter. "She's wasting her time. Even if Fallon was the last woman on earth, I'd never date her, let alone marry her."

Not after she… I shove the thought aside. Today is about Cash and Everly, and I'm not letting Fallon take up any more space in my head than she already has.

"Welcome to the mom meddling club," Cash says, clapping me on the back. "Now, if you'll excuse me, I need to go find my bride."

Fortunately, my phone rings before I can respond. As I answer the call, my mind keeps circling back to Fallon and her icy reaction to seeing me. It stings, realizing I was right all along. She played me the weekend we met and never actually cared about getting to know me.

After taking another work call following dinner, I stumble upon Fallon alone in the kitchen. She's at the counter, leaning over a tray of crème brûlée, her brows furrowed in concentration as she caramelizes the tops with a small torch.

She hasn't noticed me yet, so I linger in the doorway, taking her in. She's wearing a gray long-sleeved T-shirt and black pants with an apron tied around her waist. Her blonde hair is tied back in a messy bun, a few strands falling loosely around her face, and freckles dot the bridge of her nose. There's a smudge of almond flour on her cheek, and I ball my hands into fists, resisting the urge to wipe it off.

She's even more beautiful than I remember.

The faint smell of vanilla and caramel fills the air, taking me back to the night we met. It's been a decade since I last saw her, and I remind myself that what happened between us is in the past, and that's where it should stay.

Her jaw tightens as she moves the flame over the final set of ramekins.

"Is there something I can help you with, Harrison?" she asks, barely giving me a glance.

"Nope. Just craving something sweet that doesn't leave a bitter aftertaste for ten years."

"Still as charming as ever. I guess some things never change," she mutters.

I cross my arms, leaning against the doorframe. "I can't be all bad. Seeing as we barely left the hotel suite all weekend."

Fallon slams the torch on the counter, shooting me a fiery glare. "Trust me, it wasn't all that memorable," she snaps.

I exhale sharply, anger clawing its way to the surface. "Believe me, the feeling is mutual, Elizabeth. Or should I say, *Fallon*." I push off the door and approach her. "Why did you lie about your name when we met?"

"Already jumping to conclusions about my character. Why am I not surprised?" she taunts, taking a step closer, her chin tilted upward to meet my gaze.

Being in the same room as Fallon again might make my blood boil, but there's no denying she's got courage for standing her ground. That's more than most people can say when dealing with me. I'll give her credit for that.

"If you don't want me to make assumptions, then explain," I demand, my patience wearing thin.

"Elizabeth is my first name," she retorts, wrinkling her nose as if the name tastes bitter in her mouth. "When I enrolled in culinary school, I wanted something that felt more me. Elizabeth was too stiff, so I started going by Fallon, my middle name." She chews on her bottom lip, and I know she's not telling me the full story, but I'm not interested enough to press further, so I let it go.

"I see. And what's your excuse for being here tonight? Am I supposed to believe it's a coincidence that you're catering at my parents' house?"

"How dare you insult my motives." Her voice grows louder, despite the gap between us growing smaller. "I never would have taken this job if I knew you'd be here. Trust me, you're the last person I wanted to see tonight. Believe it or not, the world doesn't revolve around you," she grumbles.

The bite of her words ignites another flash of fury, and I resent that she can still provoke a reaction when she means nothing to me. The fiery woman I met ten years ago is just as bold now—if not more. Whereas, I acknowledge that I'm no longer the carefree hockey player that she met. I'm the man who grew an empire through discipline and control with no time for distractions, especially ones that come wrapped in trouble and a sharp tongue.

I place my hand over my heart. "I'm wounded, truly." I lean in, her breath grazing against my neck. "Just be sure not to skip out early tonight. That would be unprofessional."

Fallon shakes her head. "You're the only one here who walks away without considering how it'll affect someone else," she says, venom dripping from every word.

I recoil, dropping my hand from my chest. "What the hell is that supposed to mean?"

"You're kidding, right?" A fleeting shadow of sadness crosses her face before she masks it. "Never mind. It doesn't matter. You're just another guy who couldn't see past his ego, and that's on you. Lucky for me, I dodged a bullet."

She might as well have slapped me. How dare she put the blame on me when it falls squarely on her shoulders. I thought she was someone capable of earning my trust, but now it's clear she was stringing me along and is scrambling to save face now that we've crossed paths again.

"Consider my offer for employment rescinded." I take out my phone to send an email to my assistant.

Fallon can't work for me. Period.

"You can't take away an offer that I already turned down," she fires back, pointing at my chest.

"Unbelievable," I mutter, throwing my hands in the air.

"At least we can agree on one thing," she says, a touch of amusement in her tone.

"What's that?"

"Working together would be a recipe for disaster."

She's got that right.

Fallon might be the most stubborn woman I've ever met, and for someone so goddamn beautiful, she has the uncanny ability to push my buttons. That's not a compliment.

I tuck my phone into my pocket, and as I glance up, I notice a piece of hair that's fallen across her face, resting above her mouth. There's something mesmerizing about the curve of her lips, the way they press together in frustration.

Fallon's tongue darts out, tracing the edge of her plump bottom lip as her eyes flicker up to meet mine, defiance warring with an unspoken pull that I wish didn't exist. We're locked in a standoff neither of us wants to lose, yet the tension crackles like a live wire.

"Fallon, is there anything I can do to help—" I spin around to see my mom standing in the doorway. Her eyes widen momentarily before a mischievous grin tugs at her lips. "Am I interrupting something?"

"No," Fallon and I say in unison as I take a step back.

My mom's gaze flickers between us, her eyes sharp with interest.

Dammit.

She's taken it upon herself to play matchmaker for her kids, and now that I'm the only one still single, I can't escape her well-meaning meddling. I'm afraid she's misread my close proximity to Fallon as mutual attraction and will convince herself there's more between us when there's not.

At least not anymore.

"I was wondering where you disappeared to after dinner," Mom comments before turning to Fallon, offering her a warm smile. "I had to come tell you that dinner was outstanding. Theo was right to recommend you. I didn't think gluten-free beef Wellington could taste that good."

A faint blush spreads along Fallon's neck as she gives my mom a polite nod. "Thank you. I'm glad you liked it."

"You're incredibly talented," my mom praises. "Harrison is so lucky that you'll be his new chef. It's practically impossible to find someone who can make gluten-free dishes that he likes."

"Figures he's a tough critic who's hard to please," Fallon mutters under her breathe, glancing at the floor.

My mom moves closer. "What was that, sweetheart? Sorry, I couldn't hear you."

Fallon lifts her gaze to my mom. "Oh, I said it figures it would be difficult since not many chefs specialize in allergy-friendly dishes."

Mom lightly squeezes Fallon's arm. "You have a gift."

Judging by her expression, I'd think Fallon had unlocked the secrets of the universe. I have to shut this down before her excitement morphs into a grand scheme involving Fallon and me.

"Actually, Fallon isn't going to be my new chef," I interject.

My mom's expression shifts, tightening with disappointment. "Oh no, why not?"

"She's no longer available," I answer.

My mom looks at Fallon with a glimmer of hope in her eyes. "Is there anything we could do to convince you to reconsider?"

Fallon hesitates for a fraction of a second before shaking her head. "I'm afraid not," she replies.

A pang of disappointment hits me in the gut, which makes no sense. This woman played me, and I should be relieved I never have to see her again. Earlier, I told her I didn't want to work with her, so it's absurd to feel even the slightest bit conflicted.

I've got to get out of here.

"Mom, let's give Fallon some space to finish dessert." I place a hand on her back, gently nudging her out of the kitchen. "Lola couldn't stop talking about the painting she and Marlow made for Cash and Everly, so let's not make her wait to give it to them."

"Alright." She casts a final glance at Fallon. "Thanks again for the incredible meal. And if you reconsider working for Harrison, don't hesitate to call his assistant."

"Of course," Fallon says.

I can say with certainty she won't, and that's for the best. The sooner I can forget about her, the better.

CHAPTER 2

Fallon

As soon as the leasing agent turns the corner, I lean against the cold brick wall with a heavy sigh. It's barely two o'clock, and I'm ready to call it a day with some popcorn, a cold Diet Coke, and a new horror movie that's now streaming.

A dull throb pulses in my head, courtesy of the agent's endless chatter, and my toes are frozen from trudging through the snow to see overpriced apartments with peeling paint and drafty windows. I thought nothing could be more challenging than searching for a flat in London, but New York takes it to a whole new level.

When I arrived a few months ago, I was lucky enough to find a reasonably priced apartment in Manhattan. The lack of a lease should have been a giant red flag, but I didn't think much of it until my landlord announced that I was being evicted to make room for their cousin. The worst part? I only have two weeks to find a new place that doesn't come with a million-dollar price tag or a rat infestation. Which is why I spent the morning trailing a leasing agent, touring one dismal place after another.

The first listing we visited boasted "natural light," but the reality was a dim trickle of sunlight through a cracked window facing a brick wall. Meanwhile, the "affordable" studio was sandwiched between a karaoke bar and a 24-hour gym. The worst place came last—a so-called kitchen reduced to a sliver of countertop squeezed between the fridge and the bathroom door, with no room for a cutting board. The lack of kitchen space wouldn't be a problem if I weren't a private chef who tests recipes at home, and takes photos for the cookbook I'm hoping to publish someday.

I wouldn't be in this mess if I'd stayed in London instead of making the impulsive decision to move to New York. I've only been back to the States a few times for catering events since I lived in Florida for a few years after high school. Which is where I went to culinary school and met Theo. Once he opened his own restaurants in Europe, I went back to London to work for him.

Leaving behind a lucrative position with Theo Townstead, who's now a world-renowned chef, and incredible boss, along with a flat in the heart of the city, might seem foolish to some. But the drive to make it on my own outweighed everything else.

My dream is to open an allergy-friendly restaurant where people with food sensitivities can eat without fear of cross-contamination. My mom had a severe nut allergy, and I saw firsthand how frustrating it was for her to eat out and wonder if her meal would cause a reaction.

When I was ten, my parents brought me to New York, and I still remember my mom's voice when she told me this is the city where dreams come true. After my parents passed, I made a promise to myself that one day I'd return and turn my dream of opening a restaurant into reality, no matter what it took.

Right now, I'm questioning if it was all worth the risk.

My phone chimes, breaking the silence, and I smile when I see Lila's name appear on the screen. No matter what kind of day I'm having, she always knows how to cheer me up.

We first met when I catered a wedding a few years ago at Whispering Pines Inn, a popular venue in Vermont, where she works as an event planner. We clicked instantly, and despite living in different countries until recently, we've become best friends.

Lila: How's the apartment search going?

Fallon: Looks like my new place will either be a glorified broom closet with a view of a brick wall or I'll be cooking in the dark on the edge of the sink.

Lila: That bad huh?

Fallon: I'm one showing away from moving back to London. Remind me why I thought coming to New York was a good idea?

Lila: Because you wanted a new adventure!

Fallon: The next time I decide to spontaneously move to another country, please stage an intervention.

Fallon: As my best friend, it's your job to stop me from making impulsive decisions.

Lila: Duly noted. I'll get right on setting up a "Stay Put" hotline for when you start daydreaming about your next move. If that fails, I can always padlock your bedroom door.

Fallon: I appreciate the support.

Lila: I've got your back always. Even if it means becoming your full-time warden.

Fallon: Aww, you really do care.

Lila: Someone has to keep you out of trouble.

As I'm typing a reply, my phone rings with a call from an unknown number. Normally, I'd send it to voicemail, but I'm waiting to hear back on several private chef opportunities that I applied for.

"Hello, this is Fallon speaking," I answer.

"Ms. Hayes, this is Cabrina, Harrison Stafford's assistant. Do you have a moment to speak?"

What could she possibly want?

The last time we spoke was three months ago, the day before I flew to Aspen Grove as a favor to Theo. What I didn't anticipate was running into Harrison again, the man who still makes my blood boil. Ten years should have been enough to forget, but the memories still linger, sharp and bitter.

I tighten my grip on the phone, taking a slow breath to keep my annoyance in check.

"How can I help you?"

"Mr. Stafford wants to meet with you to further discuss the possibility of having you as his private chef, if you're still available, that is."

I clench my jaw, fighting the urge to argue. The nerve of that man is unbelievable. I made it clear when I was in Aspen Grove that I had no interest in working for him. He explicitly expressed that he felt the same way, so I can't figure out why he's suddenly treating this like an opportunity I'd jump at. And the gall of him to even think I'm still available? Absurd.

It doesn't matter that I am.

"I appreciate you reaching out, but Mr. Stafford and I agreed that I wasn't the right fit," I say, confused.

"He's hoping you'll reconsider," Cabrina says, followed by the soft rustle of papers in the background. "Your qualifications are unmatched, and we haven't found anyone else with your experience in gluten-free cuisine."

You've got to be kidding me.

How did she know that was the right thing to say? I figured when I moved to New York it would be easy to find clients, which at first it was, but I quickly learned that I'm not content working for those without dietary restrictions. It's much more rewarding spending my time helping those who benefit from my specialty.

"I understand Mr. Stafford isn't the easiest person to get along with," Cabrina admits with a half-hearted laugh when I don't respond. "That said, he pays incredibly well, and the hours are flexible, given his frequent travel schedule. It would mean a lot if you'd at least meet with him."

My resolve wavers as my gaze drifts to the apartment building I just toured. Finding anything decent within my current budget seems impossible. Cabrina said the pay is generous, so hearing Harrison out can't hurt—it's not like I'm going to accept the job.

I close my eyes, my grip tightening on the phone. "I'll come by to speak with Mr. Stafford, but I'm not making any promises."

"Thank you so much," she exclaims. "You won't regret this."

I already do.

I glance up at the imposing building, the glass-and-steel exterior gleaming under the afternoon sun. The modern design stands out against the surrounding historic architecture. Inside, the lobby boasts polished marble floors and high ceilings accented by contemporary art and geometric light fixtures. Floor-to-ceiling windows line the walls, flooding the space with natural light, and leather lounge chairs are arranged along the edges of the room for visitors.

As I approach the large reception desk near the bank of elevators, a security guard in a navy uniform looks up from his screen and gives me a courteous nod.

"Can I help you?" he asks.

"I have an appointment with Mr. Stafford," I say with a small smile.

"I'll need your name and identification for verification."

"Certainly. It's Fallon Hayes," I say, taking out my driver's license to hand it to him.

He glances down at his computer, typing on his keyboard before printing a temp badge and handing it to me, along with my ID.

"The last elevator on your right will take you directly to Mr. Stafford's reception area on the top floor," he directs.

I fasten the badge on my jacket. "Thanks." I stand a little taller as I move toward the elevator.

When I step inside, a soft chime rings, and the doors automatically close.

Cabrina sent a follow-up email after our call with instructions on how to get here, and I had just enough time to stop by my apartment and change into a black pencil skirt and ivory sweater.

I take a deep breath and glance at myself in the door's reflection, smoothing down the skirt, trying to ward off my nerves. I'm going to speak with Harrison and then leave. That's all there is to it. I can't let any amount of money change my mind about the position. I refuse to back down. I'm here to prove that he doesn't affect me anymore and that I'm not intimidated by him.

The problem is that the memories of our weekend together keep surfacing, unwelcome and persistent.

I check my watch again. Twenty minutes have passed, and still no sign of Harrison. The Huskies' event is long over, and I overheard another player mention the team was headed to a club. I can't help but wonder if Harrison stood me up to hang out with his buddies— or a puck bunny.

When the temp agency offered me a job waiting tables for a hockey team tonight, I almost turned it down. It doesn't matter that I need the money for culinary school.

My ex, Jeremy, plays for the Stormbreakers, the Huskies' biggest rivals. I followed him to the States after he signed a pro contract, but shortly after we arrived, he decided he wasn't ready for a committed relationship and broke up with me.

He left a bad taste in my mouth when it comes to hockey players in general. So, when I ran into Harrison tonight, I was already skeptical. Now I'm starting to think it was a mistake to agree to meet him. I'm halfway to the front door when I hear shouting behind me.

"Elizabeth, wait." The sound of my first name makes me flinch.

After my parents passed and I moved in with my grandmother, she insisted I use it. One day, I'm going to change it and never look back.

I turn around to find Harrison running toward me with a bouquet of white tulips in hand.

"Sorry I'm late. I spent the last thirty minutes trying to find a place nearby that sells flowers." He holds them out. "These are for you."

Butterflies flutter in my stomach, and I'm taken by surprise by the sweet gesture.

I take a bottle of Dom Pérignon out of my purse. "I got you something too."

He takes it, giving me the flowers in exchange. "This is amazing. Didn't think you had it in you to sneak a bottle," he chuckles.

"I didn't," I confess with a shrug. "The supervisor stashed a whole box in the closet for themselves, and I think he was worried I'd report him if he didn't let me have one."

"Either way, I'm impressed," Harrison says. "I hope you don't mind, but I grabbed takeout from a place nearby, including your

six-pack of Diet Coke. Thought we could eat at the park across the street. There's a game going on at the basketball court, so all the lights are still on. You must be starving."

The weather in Florida is perfect for May, so it's a great night to eat outside.

"That would be great." I smile, pushing a piece of hair behind my ear.

He holds open the door, ushering me outside. "Sounds good, after you."

I think I've severely misjudged this man, and I'm looking forward to getting to know him better. There's no telling where the night will take us, but I'm open to seeing where things go.

The elevator lurches, and I quickly steady myself.

That memory reminds me how much I hate the name Elizabeth. My grandmother claimed it was more proper, though I suspect it was only another way to spite my mother. For years after I moved out, I stuck with it since Jeremy only ever knew me as Elizabeth. But after my weekend with Harrison, I decided I was done letting others dictate my life. I legally changed my name to Fallon, reclaiming both my identity and my future.

I need to remember to stay guarded when I meet with Harrison and to ignore the traitorous thrum of my heart when we're in the same room.

As I step off the elevator, Cabrina is waiting. I recognize her from the video call a few months ago when I was first offered the job. Her hair is pulled back into a tight bun, her posture is impeccable, and the tailored suit accentuates her confident demeanor.

She offers me a polite smile. "Welcome, Ms. Hayes. It's so nice to finally meet you in person." She extends her hand.

"It's a pleasure to meet you in person as well," I say, returning her smile.

A marble reception desk is set up nearby with fresh flowers on either end, with a monitor and computer in the center. Soft ambient music plays in the background, but there's no designated waiting area, so I assume visitors are only called up when Harrison is ready for a meeting.

"We better not keep Mr. Stafford waiting," Cabrina says, motioning for me to follow as she heads down a hallway leading to a set of doors, her heels clicking against the wood floor.

"Right," I mumble, jogging after her.

My heart pounds with every step we take toward his office. I'm second-guessing my decision to even come here. Even though I have no intention of accepting Harrison's offer, part of me wants to give him a taste of his own medicine of what it's like to be led on. That thought is what drives me forward.

"Here we are," Cabrina announces cheerfully.

I lift my gaze to see her standing in front of a looming set of oak doors. She pushes one of them open, waving me inside.

"Good luck," she whispers before shutting the door behind her.

Guess I'm on my own now.

I swallow thickly as I look ahead at Harrison. He's at his desk, focused on his computer, his fingers flying across the keys. His hardened expression is a far cry from the cocky hockey player with an easy grin. The man before me appears carved from stone, nothing like the carefree athlete who could light up a room with his laughter.

He's somehow more attractive than before. His black hair is styled in a tapered fade, and he still has the physique of a hockey player—lean and athletic. He exudes confidence in his gray three-piece suit, his presence undeniably magnetic. I curse my libido for getting in the way of my mission to stay unaffected by him.

To distract myself, I take in the sprawling office, which makes the apartments I visited earlier seem impossibly tiny in comparison. Harrison's desk sits in the front of a wall lined with shelves, stacked with architectural models and real estate reports. Modern art pieces add color to the space, and there's a private lounge area complete with two chairs, a leather sofa, and a well-stocked bar cart. The space is bathed in natural light from the windows, offering a panoramic view of the city skyline. Its minimalist style makes a statement all on its own.

Harrison still hasn't acknowledged me, and his blatant disregard is grating on my nerves.

I clear my throat loudly, and he finally lifts his head from his computer, his frown deepening when his gaze lands on me. "How did you get in here?" he demands.

A flicker of irritation rises, but I hold my ground, lifting my chin to meet his glare head-on.

"Hello, Mr. Stafford, it's nice to see you too," I reply with a curt nod.

He sighs, leaning forward and resting his elbows on his desk. "I asked you a question. How did you get in?"

"Your assistant showed me to your office," I state the obvious.

"Why would she do that?"

He can't be serious.

I knew he was a jerk, but I didn't expect him to be this much of an asshole when he was the one who asked me to see him. How did I not see this coming—him luring me here under false pretenses and then pulling the rug out from under me just to make himself feel more powerful?

"This behavior is beneath even you, Harrison." I point at him. "Don't act like you weren't the one who had Cabrina ask me to come here so we could talk about me being your private chef."

He narrows his eyes, his jaw twitching as he rises from his leather chair, coming to stand in front of me. My palms grow clammy, but I force myself to stand tall, doing my best to steady my breathing as the anxiety tightens in my chest.

As the air between us thrums with the same invisible energy we shared ten years ago, my skin prickles with anticipation.

I square my shoulders and meet his gaze with an unwavering resolve, readying for whatever comes next.

"When we saw each other last, we agreed it would be best if you didn't work for me, did we not?" he asks sharply.

"That's correct."

He's not referring to Cash's wedding in Aspen Grove. A month ago, he showed up at a bar where I was catering an event on the upper level. He claimed it was a coincidence, but I don't buy it. He was keeping tabs on me, but I have no idea why. Our conversation was short and tense, ending with us both agreeing, again, that it was a good thing I didn't work for him.

"So, what makes you think I'd change my mind?" Harrison leans in, his voice low. "Better yet, why would you show up when you made it obvious that I was the last person you wanted to be around?"

I look awful in orange.

I absolutely cannot get arrested today.

Orange is not my color.

The mantra runs through my mind as I focus on keeping my expression neutral.

"Stop playing mind games and tell me why…" I pause at the soft click of the door, turning to see Harrison's mom enter his office. Her ocean-blue eyes sparkle, and her brown hair is styled in a shoulder-length bob, complementing her tailored blazer.

Harrison visibly stiffens, surprise flashing across his face as she strides past him and pulls me in for a hug. "Fallon, it's so good to see you, sweetheart." I'm momentarily stunned before reciprocating the gesture, puzzled by her warm greeting, given we've only met once.

"You too," I manage with a polite smile and glance between her and Harrison, trying to make sense of the situation. "Do you live in the city?"

I catered Cash and Everly's event at the Staffords' home in

Aspen Grove, but that doesn't mean they don't split their time between two places.

"No, she doesn't," Harrison interrupts. "She's here visiting, but I wasn't expecting her to stop by my office today."

Johanna moves to the lounge area, motioning for us to follow. "I had some urgent business to attend to," she says cryptically, her upbeat tone leaving me skeptical. "Take a seat, Fallon." She pats the cushion beside her and sets her purse on the armrest.

Harrison stops at the bar cart, pouring himself a drink. "Mom, do you want anything?" he asks with a resigned sigh.

Johanna shakes her head. "No, thank you." Harrison doesn't bother offering me one. "Is that necessary? It's barely past two p.m.," she adds.

"For this conversation. Absolutely," he replies, sitting across from us. His ankle is crossed over his knee, the picture of ease, but tapping his fingers against his thigh show's he's just as unnerved as I am.

I tug my lower lip between my teeth. This was meant to be a quick conversation where I told Harrison I'm not interested in being his private chef and to never contact me again. Yet here I am, caught in a tense silence between him and his mom over something I haven't figured out yet.

"Am I missing something?" I ask no one in particular.

Harrison runs a hand across his face. "I have a hunch my mom was the one who coordinated with Cabrina to get you here." He fixes his gaze on his mom as he takes a measured sip of his drink. "Isn't that right, Mom?"

Johanna lifts one shoulder in a casual shrug, her hands folded in her lap, appearing unbothered by the accusation. "I don't see what the issue is. You haven't been able to find a new personal chef who can handle specialty meals, and Fallon is as talented as they come." She pauses to flash me an approving smile. "I don't pretend to understand your initial reluctance, but I won't stand by and let you miss the opportunity to work with someone who not only understands your dietary restrictions but can provide gluten-free meals without the risk of contamination."

Harrison leans forward, placing his glass on the coffee table, making a point to use a coaster.

"Mom, I appreciate the concern, but I don't—"

She holds out her hand, fixing him with a pointed expression. "Need I remind you about last week, when the food service company you hired mixed up your meals, leaving you in the ER for hours, unable to stand because of the severity of the reaction?"

Despite my grievances with Harrison, I sympathize with him. My mom made several trips to the emergency room for her nut allergy when I was a kid, and a friend I lived with during culinary school had celiac disease. I've witnessed firsthand the toll food sensitivities can take on a person when they're experiencing a severe reaction.

Which might explain why I find Johanna's interference unexpectedly sweet. Most people brush off food allergies, particularly celiac disease, as a lifestyle trend, but Johanna is truly concerned. That doesn't mean I want to work for Harrison. He's still a brute, and no job is worth sacrificing my sanity, even if it offers the chance to specialize in gluten-free cooking like I wanted.

"Johanna, I really appreciate you thinking of me, but trust me, I'm not the best fit for the job," I say.

She waves me off. "Nonsense. Your cooking is exceptional, and you're one of the few who can make gluten-free beef Wellington taste good. That's a rare gift, sweetheart."

Why does she have to be so nice? Harrison could stand to learn a thing or two from her about how to treat people. And the worst part is, her sincerity makes it that much harder to turn her down.

I place my hand over my heart. "I appreciate the compliment, but I'm afraid I can't accept."

She purses her lips as she studies me. "Do you mind me asking why? Is it a scheduling conflict?"

This woman has persistence down to an art form.

Since I've been selective about my clientele, I only have a handful of part-time meal prep accounts. Occasionally, I work out of a client's home, and I have several upcoming gigs for the holidays, but no one I work with daily.

"Availability isn't the issue," I admit, stumbling over my words. "But I might have to move out of the city, and if that happens, I'll need to find new clients."

I sink further into the sofa with a resigned sigh, casting a sideways glance at Harrison. Sharing personal details about my life wasn't part of the plan, but it's definitely better than having to explain that her son's a Casanova who uses women and then leaves like a coward.

"Don't you like living in Manhattan?" Johanna asks.

"I love it here, but I'm currently in between places, and affordable housing is hard to come by in the city."

It's embarrassing to admit my options are quickly dwindling. I've spent four days searching for a new apartment, and I'm no closer to finding a new place.

I glance at the ground, avoiding Harrison's scrutinizing gaze. The last thing I need is for him to judge me without knowing all the facts. Not all of us can be billionaire ex-hockey players turned real estate moguls with limitless resources at our disposal.

"I have the perfect solution," Johanna says, clapping her hands together. "You can stay with Harrison. He has more than enough space, and it'll make the commute a breeze," she adds with a chuckle.

My mouth falls open. "What?" At the same time, Harrison responds with a sharp, "No."

I'm speechless, sure I must have misheard her. There's no way she just suggested that I *move in* with her son.

Harrison shakes his head, raking a hand through his hair. "Mom, it's nice of you to want to help Fallon, but she's not moving in with me," he states flatly.

While I agree with him, the coldness in his tone stings more than it should. He's the one who hurt me, yet he's acting as if I'm the one to blame. It stirs up old insecurities that I've buried deep, reminding me of the fear of being cast aside because I'm not good enough.

Thankfully, Johanna saves me from wallowing in self-pity when she asks Harrison, "Why not?"

"It's not a live-in position," he says.

She clicks her tongue in disapproval. "You're the boss, make it one," she challenges. "Your penthouse takes up an entire floor, so there's plenty of space for you both, and it's centrally located, so Fallon would be close to everything."

Harrison groans. "Mom, please drop it."

I bite back a laugh. Johanna is a force to be reckoned with, and its entertaining watching Harrison trying to hold his ground against her unyielding persistence. My money is on Johanna, which doesn't bode well for me either.

Maybe she'd ease up if she knew that Harrison and I have a past. It's obvious he didn't think I was important enough to mention. Granted, we only spent one weekend together, so I shouldn't be surprised.

I only wish I understood why she's so adamant that I accept the position. Private chefs in New York City are a dime a dozen, and there are at least a handful who make exceptional gluten-free meals. It's surprising that Harrison hasn't found a replacement yet. Then again, if he's as gruff with everyone else as he is with me, it's easy to see why others might hesitate to accept the position, even if the compensation is unmatched.

I hate to admit that if I wasn't paying rent, I'd be able to save more for my restaurant. Right now, I'll be lucky to start with a food truck or café, but I can always expand later.

"What do you say, Fallon?" Johanna asks. "You could move in as early as next week."

Harrison grabs his drink and downs the remainder in one gulp. "Don't you have plans with Presley this afternoon?" he asks Johanna, not giving me a chance to answer.

She glances down at her watch. "Not for another hour. That gives us plenty of time to sort this out." She leans over to pat me on the knee.

Harrison clenches his jaw as he watches. I flash him a smug smile, relishing in the fact that his mother's kindness toward me is clearly getting under his skin.

"What's it going to take for you to let this go?" he asks Johanna.

She grins as though she's already gotten her way. "For you to hire Fallon and have her stay in your penthouse," she says, not missing a beat.

Harrison scowls in my direction when I chuckle. "Care to share what you find so amusing?"

If I were to accept his offer—and I'm not saying I will—it would be for the generous salary and the accommodations. The chance to rattle him would just be an added bonus.

My shoulders tremble with nervous laughter. "Just picturing the two of us under the same roof and wondering if either of us would survive."

"Exactly," Harrison mutters. "Which is why it's a terrible idea."

"What? Afraid you couldn't handle the challenge?" I taunt.

What am I doing?

There isn't anything worse than spending more time with Harrison, much less living with him. It's bad enough that my pulse quickens and a swarm of butterflies erupts in my stomach whenever he glances my way. It's a shame my body hasn't gotten the memo that I can't stand him. Which begs the question, why am I encouraging him?

Think of the bigger picture.

If I want to achieve my goal of owning a restaurant, I'll have to save up far more than I have right now. Taking on a client like Harrison, even if it means letting go of my part-time ones, would help me accumulate what I need much faster. And if I didn't have to pay rent, I could focus all my energy on building my savings. No dream is achieved without sacrifice, and I can't let my emotions derail my future—even if it means putting up with someone I'd rather avoid entirely.

Harrison shifts in his seat, a challenge flashing in his gaze. "You underestimate me. The real question is, can you? Doesn't seem like you do well under pressure."

I bite my lower lip, swallowing the retort threatening to escape, mindful of Johanna's presence.

"There's only one way to find out," I challenge.

Things are about to get interesting.

CHAPTER 3

Harrison

MY MOM'S EXCITED OUTBURST RINGS OUT AS I ARCH A brow at Fallon, totally caught off guard by her reply. Which is probably exactly what she wants.

"Does this mean you'll take the job?" my mom presses.

"It does," Fallon says, locking eyes with me, daring me to disagree. "But I have conditions."

Of course, she does.

Every instinct tells me to put an end to this immediately, but I can't. My mom is determined to get her way, and frankly, I can't bring myself to shut her down. Add to that my refusal to let Fallon come out on top, and I'm inclined to go along with this charade.

"What conditions?" I ask.

Fallon hesitates briefly before she says, "I want an unlimited budget for ingredients. Quality should never be compromised, especially with gluten-free dishes."

I can work with that.

"Okay. What else?"

She leans back in her chair, a smirk playing at the corner of her lips. "An additional ten percent added to my salary than what was originally offered when I interviewed a few months ago. Call it a premium for navigating a demanding work environment."

Not only is she trying to get a rise out of me, but she's also trying to swindle me in the process. I can't decide if I'm impressed or annoyed. Fallon has a knack for forcing emotions to the surface I'd rather ignore. A battle rages inside me between putting her in her place or indulging the part of me that thrives on her challenging me.

I pinch the bridge of my nose, exhaling sharply. "Fine," I mutter. "Is that all?"

"I'd like to bring some of my things to make it feel more like home."

I bite back a groan. The idea of her moving into my space with all her things, sounds dreadful. But my mother's bright smile as she watches our interaction stops me from protesting. If I mess this up, she'll never let me hear the end of it. As long as Fallon keeps her things in her room and out of sight, I can live with that.

"If I agree, that's it. No more conditions. Understood?" I tell Fallon.

She nods. "Deal."

I extend my hand before my mom can interject. "But this is a trial run only. If things aren't going well within a couple of months, we're calling it off," I say.

Fallon gives a casual shrug. "I can work with that."

"This is so exciting, don't you think, Harrison?" my mom chimes in, clasping her hands together, watching me expectantly.

I grit my teeth. "Sure."

My days revolve around contracts, negotiations, and meetings. I'm skilled at making deals and getting the best outcome for myself and the company. Yet, when it comes to Fallon, I fold like a house of cards, especially when my mother is here leading the charge.

"We'll have Cabrina send you the contract to review and instructions for moving in," my mom says, patting Fallon on the arm.

"Great," she says, standing up to leave.

As she exits my office with a deliberate sway to her step, I'm left asking myself how she charmed my mom into taking her side. And to make matters worse, she looks fucking edible in her fitted pencil skirt that hugs her body like a glove.

I'm not happy with the turn of events, but there's no chance I'm backing down now. My pride won't allow me, and it's clear Fallon won't be the one to give in either. If she wants to play games, she's messing with the wrong man. I might have lost this battle, but I never lose the war.

"She's lovely," my mom remarks from her spot on the couch, a grin on her face as if she just won the lottery.

Unfortunately for me, my mom is right.

I glance over to find her staring at me with her lips curved into a knowing smile.

My palms grow clammy, and I adjust my cufflinks, clearing my throat. "You've got to stop interfering in my personal matters." I maneuver around her, going to my desk. "It's frustrating that you disregarded my decision not to work with Fallon."

I should have suspected she was up to something when she said she was stopping by my office. She comes to town once a month to visit my little sister, Presley, but I'm usually tied up in meetings, so she doesn't stop by here often.

Presley is a marketing associate at Sinclair Group, a large investment firm in New York City. She used to be the CEO's assistant, but after three years of sidestepping their mutual attraction, a disastrous work trip to Aspen Grove ended up with them pretending to date when they visited our family in Aspen Grove. They're now a couple and are hopelessly in love.

Cabrina's email earlier about my open schedule this afternoon should have tipped me off that something was up. My schedule is never open. I should have assumed my mother would have my calendar rearranged to serve her agenda. She doesn't like that I don't have plans to settle down and plays matchmaker at every opportunity, no matter how inconvenient it is for me.

During my brief stint as a pro hockey player, I had several fleeting encounters with puck bunnies wanting nothing more than a night of fun, with no strings attached. When I transitioned to working at Stafford Holdings, I had a revolving door of casual flings, mainly used as arm candy at events. It was exhausting juggling work commitments and hollow connections that offered little satisfaction.

When my dad retired, I took over as CEO at Stafford Holdings, a role I'd been preparing for my whole life, but it didn't make it any easier to accept my fate. I stopped making an effort to find dates for events or inviting women to spend the night with me. Running a multi-billion-dollar company leaves little room for a social life, let alone romance, and I've had no interest in pursuing one.

Admittedly, the only time I felt a connection strong enough to consider pursuing was with Fallon. Her quick wit and sharp tongue were a jolt to my system, and with a weekend free of obligations and a hotel suite at my disposal, I took the risk, unaware that a few days later, my world would be flipped upside down, and I'd never hear from Fallon again.

Until now.

My mom comes around my desk and stands next to where I'm drafting an email. "I'm your mother. Of course I'm going to worry about your well-being, and want to make sure you're taking care of yourself. Especially with your recent diagnosis. You have to be careful what you eat, and with the long hours you're putting in at the office, it's not realistic for you to manage that on your own.

I'm confident Fallon is the right person for the job, so excuse me for pushing back when you're being stubborn."

"I love you, Mom, and I know your heart is in the right place. But commandeering my assistant, setting up a plan to hire a private chef I don't want, and coercing me to let her move in is too much."

Mom places her hand on my shoulder, waiting until I look at her before speaking. "Sweetheart, I'm not going to apologize for wanting you to be happy and healthy. For that to happen, you've got to make changes, and this is one of them."

"I appreciate your concern, but shouldn't you leave soon if you're going to meet Presley?" I utter with a hint of annoyance.

My mom lifts a finger in warning, wearing a stern expression. "Harrison Ford Stafford, don't you dare try and change the subject." She's exceptionally pushy today. "How do you think I felt when Cabrina called to tell me that you'd been rushed to the hospital last week? It took me a couple of hours to get here from Aspen Grove and made me sick to my stomach that I wasn't closer."

I take her hand in mind. "Mom, I'm fine. I promise."

"For now, sure. But what if you experience another episode while you're alone at home, with no one around to call for help? Wouldn't you prefer to prevent it from happening again if you can?"

Her voice slightly trembles. "Would working with Fallon be so terrible even if it means giving me peace of mind?"

My god, she is good, I'll give her that.

I release her hand, fiddling with a stack of papers on my desk, even though they're already perfectly aligned. Mom watches me like a hawk, impatiently waiting for me to answer.

"Trust me, it would be an absolute disaster," I answer honestly.

She flicks her hand dismissively. "Oh, hush, you're being dramatic. The amazing food you'll get out of it will outweigh any negatives of having her stay with you. Besides, you're rarely home anyway."

That's beside the point. My apartment is my safe haven, the one place I have total control over how it looks. Everything has its place, and there's no clutter or chaos to disrupt my peace. That'll all change if I allow someone else into my space.

"Mom, I'm really—"

"Honestly, Harrison, will you stop being so difficult?" She sighs in exasperation. "Please do this for me." She mirrors my niece, Lola's classic puppy dog eyes.

"Good grief," I mutter.

If persistence were an Olympic sport, my mom would take home the gold. She has an uncanny ability to push until I give in to her every request. While she has good intentions, she has a tendency to take things too far. After thirty-seven years, I should have mastered the art of saying no, but she makes it impossible, even when it means upending my life to avoid disappointing her.

"Fine," I concede, throwing my hands up. "But if things go south, the trial period ends immediately."

My mom chuckles. "We'll see. Are you going to decorate the spare bedroom before she moves in?"

"No."

"Sweetheart, it's packed with your old hockey gear and stuff from college. Plus, the walls are bare, and there's no furniture."

"So? Isn't giving Fallon a place to stay good enough? She can move my stuff into the closet."

Why would I go out of my way for someone I don't want there in the first place?

"That's unacceptable," my mom scolds. "But don't worry. I'll take care of everything. Do you think Fallon would prefer cream or purple paint for the walls?" She pulls out a small notebook and pen from her purse and jots something down. "We'll go with cream, it's more neutral," she says, answering her own question.

I sigh. "Would you listen if I told you we're leaving the room as is?"

She pauses and reaches over to pat my cheek. "Not in the slightest."

"Just great," I mutter under my breath.

Once she's finished writing, she puts her notebook back in her bag and glances at her watch. "Oh, goodness." She picks up her purse and tosses it over her shoulder. "If I don't go now, I'll be late to meet with Presley." She bends down to give me a side hug and a kiss on the cheek.

"I'll work on the room tonight while you're at work. Have a great night, sweetheart." She beams as she waves goodbye.

"See you later, Mom."

I recline back in my chair, exhaling deeply. She thinks that because she's intervened with my siblings' love lives, and they've all found their better halves in part thanks to her, it means I'm free game. But this has gone too far. I might not have a choice of having Fallon move in, but that doesn't mean I have to make things easy on her. With any luck, she'll hate living with me and decide to leave on her own.

I glance over at the movers, who are carrying in another load of boxes into my apartment. "How many could there possibly be?" I ask, my patience wearing thin.

"This is the last of it," one of them calls over his shoulder.

"Thank god," I mutter under my breath.

It's been a week since I agreed to let Fallon move in, and I'm no less irritated by the predicament we're in, especially now that she's taking over my space. My once spotless living room is now unrecognizable, buried under a mountain of her things. When I was told she was having her stuff delivered, I didn't expect a moving crew to show up and unload for two hours.

My jaw twitches when I take in the dozens of plants and herbs lining the wall, the pile of blankets Fallon carelessly tossed on the couch earlier, and the sea of boxes labeled "living room". It's enough to make my blood pressure rise just by looking at the mess.

Is it a crime that after a chaotic day at work, I want to come home to peace and order, where I can decompress and focus without any distractions? There's a reason I asked the interior designer to avoid any unnecessary additions like plants, throw pillows, or extra furniture. Now, instead of a peaceful retreat, I'm surrounded by clutter, making my skin crawl.

When the movers finish, I give them a generous tip, sighing in relief when I shut the door behind them.

I'm ready to retreat to my home office when the sharp noise of cardboard tearing echoes from the kitchen. I go to investigate and find Fallon standing on a stepstool, digging through a box of spices on the counter.

At work, precision is non-negotiable. Every deal I close and the meetings I lead must be executed flawlessly. A single misstep or overlooked detail has serious consequences. I apply the same principle at home. A clean space leads to a focused mind. Disorder is a distraction, and I can't afford the chaos that follows. Unfortunately, Fallon doesn't seem to share my perspective, and her disregard for order has shattered the calm that I rely on to stay focused.

She's changed into a hoodie and form-fitting lounge shorts. I stumble slightly when I notice from this angle, I have a view of her backside, the shorts clinging to her curves, distracting me with her perfect ass.

This could be a problem.

Aren't chefs supposed to wear something more professional? The first one I hired wore slacks and a white shirt under their apron. Maybe I should impose a dress code for Fallon. The only problem is she lives here now, so it might prove difficult to demand she wear professional attire when she's not on the clock.

She's perched on a stool, pulling out a bottle of vanilla from the cabinet next to the stove and tossing it into the trash bin next to her, a sliver of creamy skin exposed where her hoodie lifts.

On second thought, why can't I enforce a dress code?

This is my house, which means my rules are non-negotiable. Biding my time, I observe as she unpacks the rest of the box, rearranging the cupboard to make room for all of her spices.

"Why did you throw that out?" I ask, my voice cutting through the silence. "I already have an organization system in place and didn't ask for you to replace anything."

My last chef arranged the kitchen and pantry, and it's what I'm used to. So, watching Fallon rearrange and throw things out without consulting me first is maddening.

"I'm updating your spice cupboard," she says as she drops a jar of crème de tartar into the trash.

"Why?"

"Because some of these spice blends could have traces of gluten, and I'd rather not accidentally poison you," she deadpans.

No, she'd rather do that on purpose.

"Do you really have to throw *all* of them out?"

"Yes." Fallon takes her arm and sweeps the remaining items from my cabinet into the trash bin and unpacks the rest of the box, placing the new spices in the cupboard.

A muscle tightens in my jaw as she moves to the next cupboard, her eyes scanning the shelves before she reaches for the juicer on the top shelf. When it proves too far out of reach, she braces a hand on the counter and hoists herself up, abandoning the stool.

"What the hell are you doing?" I exclaim in alarm. "You're going to hurt yourself."

I step toward her despite her waving me off. "I'm fine," she insists.

With determination, Fallon pushes her hair out of her face. "Come on, just a little higher," she mutters, reaching for the juicer. Her fingertips brush the edge, but it doesn't budge. She shifts her weight, stretching herself just a little higher—until her foot slips. She lets out a sharp gasp as she teeters, but I'm already there, gripping her waist to steady her and lowering her to the floor. Her feet hit the ground with a soft thud, and she stands there, breathless, her posture rigid.

My hands linger on her waist, my fingertips brushing against her bare skin where her hoodie has ridden up again. The contact sends a jolt of awareness through me, and I quickly pull my hands away, schooling my expression when Fallon spins around to face me.

"You need to be more careful," I say sharply. "And I hadn't considered a uniform addendum to the contract, but maybe I should have."

Fallon raises a brow as she steps toward me. "Excuse me?"

"You heard me. That outfit"—I motion to her hoodie and shorts—"isn't suitable for my private chef. Not to mention it's the middle of winter."

Am I being unreasonable? Possibly. Do I regret it? Not in the slightest. Fallon just arrived, and she's already pushing all of my buttons. It could have something to do with watching her nearly face-plant onto the floor, and the fact that I'm even worried about her well-being just pisses me off more.

She tosses her head back, letting out a dry laugh. "Nope. Not happening, Mr. Hotshot. My wardrobe isn't up for debate. I'm here to cook, not to conform to some archaic notion of what qualifies as professional attire, least of all when I'm off duty." She jabs a finger into my chest. "If your ego can't handle not being in control, that's your problem, not mine."

Ready to move on from this conversation, I say, "I have a conference call, I'll be in my office. That and my bedroom are off-limits, are we clear?"

When she first arrived at the apartment, I showed her around as we waited for the movers to arrive. I let her know which rooms were off-limits and pointed out the security cameras in the main living areas and my office.

"Crystal," she retorts sharply.

"Do me a favor and leave the space exactly how you found it. I refuse to live in a disaster zone."

"Got it, *boss*."

When I join the conference call, my brothers, Cash and Dylan, are already waiting.

Dylan is the chief financial officer for Stafford Holdings, and Cash is the chief operating officer. It's rare for all of us to be in the same room during meetings since Dylan works from home in Aspen Grove most days, and Cash is managing our European division from London.

"This is a first," Cash says with a smirk. "Usually, I'm the one running late."

He's the fun-loving, carefree brother and the life of any party. When we were kids, he was in an accident that left him with a jagged scar on the left side of his face, spanning from his ear to his chin. My mom was worried it would affect his confidence. Spoiler alert—it had the opposite effect.

"Hey, big brother." Dylan greets me with a nod. "I spoke with Mom earlier, and she said the big move was today. How did it go?" He attempts to hide his amusement but fails miserably, a grin spreading across his face.

"It's not funny," I deadpan. "She coerced me into letting

Fallon move in. I figured she'd show up with a duffle bag and a couple of suitcases at most. I was wrong. The movers were here for two hours."

Cash busts out laughing. "Oh, this is too good."

"Will you cut it out?"

"Not a chance. You were Mom's accomplice in scheming to get Everly and me together, so this is your well-earned karma."

After reconnecting in Vegas led to an impromptu wedding, I convinced Cash and Everly to stay married during the merger of Stafford Holdings and Townstead International, the company Everly's father owned. Their fake marriage quickly became real, and now they're happily married and living in London.

"Earth to Harrison." I snap my attention to the computer screen to find Dylan waving at the camera. Cash covers his mouth in an attempt to suppress a snicker.

"Enough," I scold them.

Dylan rolls his eyes. "You know, brother, I recall being this bothered with Marlow when I first met her, and look how that turned out."

She moved in next door to Dylan and stepped up to help care for his daughter, Lola, as her nanny. It didn't take Dylan long to fall for Marlow, and they recently got engaged.

"Just because you're both in relationships doesn't mean I want the same thing," I grumble.

That's not true.

There was a time when having a family of my own felt like the ultimate dream. My parents' love story was inspiring, and I grew up believing I'd find someone to share the same spark of magic they shared.

However, the knowledge that I would someday be the successor to a global empire has loomed over me since my dad dropped the bombshell when I was ten. Long before I fully comprehended what that meant, I carried the weight of our family's legacy on my shoulders that my siblings didn't have to.

Hockey became my way to escape the pressures of my future. After high school, I chased my dream of playing professionally, a rebellion against the life that had been laid out for me. But I was faced with a heavy dose of reality when I had to abruptly quit after my first and only season. I was forced to make a choice: work at Stafford Holdings, and prepare to one day take over as CEO when my dad retired, or make one of my brothers sacrifice their ambitions. The decision wasn't hard. I traded my freedom for theirs, and I'd do it again in a heartbeat.

"You have to admit it was clever of Mom to suggest Fallon stay with you," Dylan says with a twinkle in his hazel eyes.

"Sure, except it's not her house that's being invaded," I mutter.

"Oh, please, we both know Mom has other intentions in mind," Cash adds.

"God, I hope you're wrong."

"Don't hold your breath," Dylan says. "She won't rest until you're married with a kid on the way."

Cash reclines in his chair, propping his feet on his desk. "This is going to be entertaining. I'm going to need popcorn."

"If you're finished discussing my personal life, maybe we can get to the actual agenda for this meeting," I say tersely.

"Yes, boss," Cash taunts.

I glare at him, not impressed by his jab.

My brothers have been invaluable in helping to run the company, but with families of their own now, their priorities have shifted, leaving me to take on more of the day-to-day responsibilities so they can maintain a healthy balance between work and family. I'd rather carry this burden on my own than make anyone suffer alongside me.

For the most part, I enjoy my job, but it's not for the faint of heart. We're currently in the middle of a large expansion on the

West Coast and in Europe, so I've been managing endless meetings and negotiations and acquiring additional properties.

It has left me with little time for my responsibilities as the co-owner of the Mavericks, a local professional hockey team. Still, I make it work with lots of coffee and sheer determination because being a part of a hockey team again, even in an executive role, has allowed me to stay connected to the sport I love.

I pull up the presentation Dylan sent me this morning and share my screen so he and Cash can see it.

"Let's start by analyzing last month's financial report," I instruct. "Take it away, Dylan."

"Yeah, sure thing." He accepts the invite to take over as presenter.

I spend the rest of the meeting listening as Dylan walks Cash and me through updates while trying not to think about all the damage Fallon could be inflicting on my apartment right now.

The image of her in those damn shorts is all I can see—how they clung to her curves, the way the fabric stretched over her toned legs, and how they rode up when she moved.

I shake my head, mentally kicking myself.

What the hell am I thinking?

I need to get a grip. It's challenging enough having her in my space, but if my physical reaction to her earlier is any indication, I'd better establish clearer boundaries for myself—and fast.

CHAPTER 4

Fallon

WALTER, THE DOORMAN, NODS IN MY DIRECTION AS HE opens the door for me, leading into the lobby of the apartment building. The place screams old-money luxury with a grand crystal chandelier casting a soft glow on the gleaming marble floors. A reception desk is set off to the left and made of granite and glass with brass accents. Large pieces of artwork from local artists hang on the walls, bringing a personal touch to the space that feels more like stepping into a five-star hotel than a residential building.

"Good morning, Miss Hayes," Walter says, tipping his cap as I walk past him.

He's wearing his signature charcoal-gray suit with a nameplate pinned to his chest, paired with white gloves and freshly polished boots. His posture is impeccable, hinting at years of discipline.

"Good morning, Walter," I say with a smile. "And please, for the last time, call me Fallon. Miss Hayes is too formal."

Not to mention, it's my grandmother's preferred title, and being lumped in with her isn't a compliment. She's as cold and manipulative as they come. Her only redeeming quality is living in Hampstead, England. Which meant that once I moved to the States after I graduated high school, I didn't have to see her and flat-out refused to visit when I moved back to London to work with Theo. She might have raised me after my parents died, but that doesn't erase my disdain for her.

"Expecting another delivery?" Walter asks when I lean against the reception desk.

I nod with a smile. "A box of local produce from Eastside Harvest. It should be here any minute." I hold out a cup of coffee with extra cream and two sugars. "This is for you. I overheard you on a call with the building manager about the broken coffee machine in the breakroom, and with how busy things were when I left earlier, I couldn't let you go without this morning."

Walter offers a small bow as he accepts the cup. "You're too kind, Miss Fallon. I really appreciate the gesture."

I chuckle. "It's the least I can do since you've had to put up with all of my deliveries."

Cabrina sent over one of Harrison's credit cards and encouraged me to purchase whatever I needed. I compiled a long list of essentials, including new pots, pans, and baking sheets. When cooking for someone with celiac disease, it's critical to avoid cross-contamination. The smallest trace of gluten can trigger a flare-up or worse, cause serious harm, so I'm not taking any risks.

"It's never a bother," Walter says as he flips through a stack of incoming mail, sorting by apartment number. "You're a breath of fresh air. Most residents and their staff don't pay me any mind, let alone even consider bringing me a cup of coffee." He pauses his task to take a sip of his drink.

"Mr. Stafford included?" I ask, my curiosity piqued.

He shakes his head. "Mr. Stafford is the exception. He always waves when he comes and goes and gives me a generous holiday bonus every year. He's a good man."

I snort, a humorless laugh slipping out. "That's hard to believe."

When I moved in, he was rude, lecturing me about my wardrobe and shouting at my plants when he walked past. Since then, he's avoided me whenever he can, and our interactions have been minimal. I've been instructed to leave his meals on a warming plate in the dining room and not bother him while he's eating. In fact, I've spoken to Cabrina more in the past week than I have him.

Johanna wasn't kidding when she said the penthouse was huge. The primary bedroom and his office—both of which he's made clear are off-limits—are on the opposite side of the penthouse from my room, which is situated behind the kitchen and dining space.

Walter gives me a reassuring pat on the hand. "Don't worry, I'm sure Mr. Stafford will come around. He has a heavy load to carry, and trusting people doesn't come easy for him."

"He can keep his trust. I don't want it," I mutter.

Learned that lesson the hard way.

"I take it you two have history?" Walter questions.

I shrug. "You could say that."

Walter tips his head, a touch of concern in his eyes. "You might not want to hear this, but I'm sure there's a good reason for whatever Mr. Stafford did. He doesn't come across as the type to offend a beautiful woman without a valid explanation."

"What makes you think he did anything?" I ask.

"You were quick to shut down, like you were guarding yourself from something." Walter puts a comforting hand on my shoulder. "Give it time," he says gently.

That won't make a difference.

I would have respected Harrison more if he had been up front with me. Instead, he led me on, making me think he could have been interested in something more. There's no chance I will ever forgive him. Ever. All I feel toward him is bitterness and resentment, and I'm not sure any excuse or apology could change that now.

He's just my boss. I don't have to like him to do my job.

That's all this is.

A job.

"It's ancient history, now." I shrug, ready to switch topics. "He hired me to do a job, so I'm going to keep my head down and focus on my work." I hear a low rumble outside and look out the window to see Eastside Harvest's delivery truck pulling up out front. "There's my delivery. I better get going. Sorry, I talked your ear off," I apologize, giving Walter an appreciative smile.

He sets aside the stack of mail he was sorting. "Don't be sorry. I enjoy talking with you. Stop by whenever you'd like."

My shoulders relax, the tension easing away at his kindness. "I will, thank you."

His sincerity warms my heart. The small gesture means more than I can express. I don't have anyone in the city that I can confide in, so it's incredibly kind of him to offer a listening ear, despite having only met a few days ago. I'll have to find out what his favorite dessert is and make it for him as a way of showing my appreciation.

Fifteen minutes later, I'm in the penthouse's kitchen, putting the produce away. This place is every private chef's dream, complete with state-of-the-art appliances, custom cabinetry, and a sprawling marble counter with more space than I could ever possibly need.

The entire apartment is incredible. My bedroom is massive, with a king-size bed, a walk-in closet, and a soaking tub in the bathroom. The only complaint I have is how chilly the penthouse is. I've resorted to sleeping in sweats and a hoodie and wearing long-sleeved shirts and fuzzy socks during the day.

I've been wanting to ask Harrison about it, but he's never around long enough for me to bring it up. In fact, most of our communications so far have gone through Cabrina. My phone pings on the counter, and I check to find yet another email from her, noting Harrison's most recent requests and other instructions. She's emailed me several times a day, and I'm starting to wonder if I work for her, and not Harrison.

> To: Fallon Hayes <Hayescatering@email.com>
> From: Cabrina Clark <CClark@StaffordHoldings.com>
> Subject: Mr. Stafford's Meal Updates
>
> Ms. Hayes,
> I hope this email finds you well. Mr. Stafford asked me to inform you that he'd like dinner served at 9:30 p.m. tomorrow night since he has a meeting at the corporate office in Maine in the afternoon. I'll stop by at 7:00 a.m. in the morning to pick up this coming week's lunches to keep at the office.
>
> Warm wishes,
> Cabrina

It's Sunday, which means Harrison is working from his home office today, and yet he still had his assistant send me another email—on a weekend, no less. This is getting ridiculous. If he needs something, he can walk down the hall and ask. I'm done with this back-and-forth through Cabrina.

Enough is enough.

I pause what I'm doing when I hear footsteps in the dining room. Earlier, I prepared a plate of scrambled eggs with avocado and homemade gluten-free toast with almond butter and left it on a warming tray on the dining table for Harrison, along with a bowl of fresh fruit on the side.

After putting away a few cartons of berries in the fridge, I grab a bottle of water before shutting the fridge and march into the dining room where Harrison is at the table, raising a bite of eggs to his mouth.

He briefly glances over, a flash of annoyance crossing his face before going back to reading something on his phone.

"Did you need something, Fallon?" he asks, his tone bored.

"Yes, I do, actually." I slide into the chair beside him, resting my arms on the table as I wait for him to put down the phone permanently attached to his hand.

When I don't elaborate, he finally sets it down, giving me his undivided attention.

He lets out an exasperated sigh. "What is it?"

"If you need something from me, you don't have to go through Cabrina. I'm only a room away," I say, nodding toward the kitchen.

"Like I could forget," he retorts.

I lift an eyebrow in challenge. "What's that supposed to mean? You know what, never mind." I fold my hands in front of me, forcing myself to calm down. "I'm here to say that moving forward, I'd appreciate it if you came directly to me when you want something. There's no point in making your assistant be our go-between while I'm living here."

"Do you think it's wise to request changes to how we communicate right out of the gate? This is a trial period, remember?"

I straighten my spine and look him square in the eye. "Is this the part where I'm supposed to apologize for stating how I feel? Sorry, I must have missed the memo."

As we face off, the challenge clear in our eyes, I can't help but think of the night we met. When we were both young, carefree, full of trust, with the whole world ahead of us.

"Oh my god, this burger is amazing," I let out a satisfied hum.

"I'm glad you like it." Harrison grins. "I aim to please."

The streetlights cast a soft glow on the park bench, and the rhythmic bounce of a basketball and occasional cheers from players echo in the distance.

I take another bite, ketchup trickling down my chin. Before I can react, Harrison reaches out to gently wipe it away with his finger.

Heat blooms where his fingertips meet my skin, a simmering warmth that has nothing to do with the weather and everything to do with him.

"Thank you," I murmur.

"My pleasure, beautiful." He bends down to grab the bottle of Dom Pérignon off the ground and takes a sip. "Mind me asking what brought you to Florida?"

"It's complicated." I hedge. "I moved here with my boyfriend a year ago, but we recently broke up." I keep it vague.

I keep the fact that Jeremy dumped me to myself. My personal life is messy, especially my past. As much as I like Harrison, I'm not ready to open up about that yet. I'd rather keep our time together uncomplicated and lighthearted. Besides, I'm aware that Jeremy's team is rivals with the Huskies, and lost to them in the Stanley Cup. The last thing I want is for Harrison to think I chase hockey players.

"It's his loss," Harrison murmurs as he holds out the bottle of champagne. "It's not your diet soda, but it'll help take the edge off."

I tip my head back as he brings the bottle to my lips, his gaze fixed on mine while I drink.

"What do you think?" he asks.

"You're right. It's not my Diet Coke, but it might be growing on me," I tease, wrapping my hand around his and bringing the bottle to my mouth for another sip.

Flirting with Harrison comes naturally, and our conversation flows easily. I can be myself around him, something I could never do with Jeremy. With him, I was always on the edge, worried that I'd fall *short of his expectations and the person he wished I was. This feels like a breath of fresh air, and I'm not ready for it to end.*

"What about you?" I ask. "Do you live close to your family or girlfriend?"

I casually slip in the last part, hoping it's not too obvious. I'd like to think he wouldn't be on a date with me if he was seeing someone, but with hockey players, you can never be too careful.

He chuckles, setting the champagne on the ground. "I don't have a girlfriend, and I'm living in another state from my family, which my mother doesn't like. We're all really close, and as the oldest, it comes with lots of expectations that I'm unsure if I'm ready to handle. Which is one of the reasons I moved away in the first place."

I place my hand on his arm. "Don't sell yourself short. I might not know you well, but I can tell you're more than capable of dealing with whatever it is," I say.

"I appreciate it." His hand covers mine, his thumb softly tracing circles on my skin. "I hope this isn't too forward, but would you want to come back to my hotel? I'm here until Monday, and I'd like to spend more time with you."

I should say no. After Jeremy, I swore off hockey players and dating altogether. But right now, I'm second-guessing that decision. What would be the harm in spending more time with Harrison? Like he said, he leaves on Monday—meaning no strings or expectations.

Harrison watches me expectantly, and the vulnerability in his eyes cements my decision.

"Alright, I'm in," I agree.

He grins, wrapping his arm around me, drawing me closer. "Good choice. I was worried I might have to beg," he says playfully.

Maybe hockey players aren't so bad after all.

I glance over to where Harrison is still watching me. His gaze has softened, curiosity flickering in his eyes like he's trying to figure out what's on my mind.

I frown slightly, internally reprimanding myself for letting him affect me. It's hard to ignore his undeniable magnetism when he's close, especially with memories clawing to be set free and slipping out when I least expect them.

He clears his throat, his expression turning impassive as he picks up his phone, as if our exchange hadn't fazed him at all.

"What else do you need, Fallon?" he asks, his eyes glued to the screen. "I have a long day ahead, and would like to eat my breakfast in peace."

My temper flares, and I stand up, the chair scraping against the floor. "If you have certain times you'd like to eat or other requests related to your meals, you'll go through me. No more messages from Cabrina," I say as I head toward the kitchen, not giving him a chance to reply.

If we're stuck living together, we'll have to find a way to co-exist, at least somewhat peacefully.

CHAPTER 5

Harrison

'M AT MY OFFICE, BURIED IN A CONTRACT, WHEN MY PHONE chimes with a notification.

Stafford Siblings + Mom

<Cash has renamed the group chat "Parental Advisory">

Harrison: Cash, why did you change the name of the group chat?

Cash: Because "Stafford Siblings + Mom" was boring AF

Mom: Watch your language.

Presley: I'm impressed you're up on your lingo, Mom.

Harrison: The last thing I need is to be in a meeting and "Parental Advisory" pops up on my phone.

<Mom has renamed the group chat "Mom Want's More Grandkids">

Dylan: Way to be subtle, Mom.

Harrison: Can I leave the group now?

Mom: No. How is everything going with Fallon? Is she settling in okay?

Harrison: She's fine.

Mom: Have you asked her?

Harrison: Yes.

No.

But I'd rather not argue with my mom about it. Fallon is an adult. She can handle getting situated without me coddling her. Hell, she's certainly had no problem taking over my apartment without consulting me or vocalizing her grievances. Much to my dismay, it's safe to say she's acclimating just fine.

Dylan: I still can't believe you let her move in.

Presley: Right? He's always been protective about his personal space.

Harrison: Mom didn't exactly give me a choice.

Cash: Oh, please. You've never had trouble saying no in the past.

> Presley: Like when you refused to participate in the first group chat. You had no problem telling us you weren't interested.

She started a group chat for the whole family, but my dad didn't join because he never checks his phone. I left after one too many interruptions during my meetings, and Dylan followed shortly after he was teased about his nonexistent dating life before he and Marlow got together.

However, my reprieve was short-lived. Last month, Mom started this group chat that includes me and my siblings. She didn't give me a choice about joining this one, but thankfully, most of their energy goes into texting the main group with Everly, Marlow, and Jack, unless they're feeling particularly nosy about my life choices.

Harrison: I'm in this chat, aren't I?

> Presley: Only because Mom said you and Dylan would break her heart if you didn't join.

> Dylan: We're happy to be here, Mom.

> Harrison: Suck-up.

> Dylan: Says the guy who let a woman he doesn't like move in with him because Mom said so.

> Harrison: Says the guy who fell for his kid's nanny.

> Harrison: Remind me, Dylan. How's the dog training going?

> Dylan: Training is going well.

Harrison: Is Waffles still playing dead when you ask him to shake?

Mom: Harrison, be nice to your brother.

Cash: Yeah, Harrison, be nice.

Harrison: At least now we know why Cash is one of mom's favorites.

Mom: I don't have favorites.

Presley: Of course you do.

Dylan: You had a group chat that was literally called Mom's Favorites that only included Cash & Presley.

Mom: Presley wouldn't change the name.

Presley: I make no apologies. That's what Harrison and Dylan get for leaving the chat.

Mom: We're moving on to a new topic.

Mom: You're all coming to visit for the holidays, right?

Dylan is the only one who lives in Aspen Grove, preferring to give his daughter, Lola, a sense of normalcy. Cash and Everly live in London, and my sister, Presley, and her boyfriend, Jack, live in New York City.

While my primary residence is also in New York City, I also have an apartment in Maine, where the old Stafford Holdings headquarters used to be. I usually take a private helicopter when I travel there, although I mainly work out of the New York office, which we officially made headquarters earlier this year. I also own two hundred acres outside of Aspen Grove, where I've had a cabin built. It doesn't get much use since my parents always want me to stay with them when I visit. Still, it's a solid investment and a retreat in our hometown that I can call my own.

Dylan: Lola's looking forward to spending Christmas Day at your place. It's all she's been able to talk about the past week.

Presley: Jack & I wouldn't miss it.

Cash: Everly & I will be there.

Mom: Harrison, you're coming, right? You promised you'd spend the holidays in Aspen Grove.

Harrison: Yes, I'm coming.

Mom: Are you bringing Fallon?

Harrison: No.

Mom: Does she have plans?

Harrison: I haven't asked.

Mom: Why not?

Harrison: Because she's my employee, and I don't spend holidays with employees.

Mom: That's disappointing. Remember, no working while you're here.

Dylan: That's like telling him not to blink.

Dylan knows me well. I've already lined up multiple virtual meetings during the holidays and plan to handle business related to the upcoming mergers we have in the works. In corporate real estate, there's no slow season, and downtime doesn't exist in my world.

Cash: If Harrison doesn't have to work, I'm not either.

Harrison: You never work during the holidays, Cash.

Cash: Touché.

I'm exhausted when I finally get to my apartment that night. My first meeting was at seven this morning, and I didn't leave the office until nine, making me want nothing more than a good night's sleep and silence.

When I step inside, the savory aroma of garlic and tomato greet me, underscored by a rich, meaty warmth hinting at something simmering on the stove for hours. The scent alone is enough to make my stomach growl, reminding me I haven't eaten since Cabrina warmed up the salmon and sweet potato power bowl that Fallon prepared.

Sharing a space with Fallon might be unbearable, but even I can't argue her talent in the kitchen. Every dish is executed to perfection, from the seasoning to the garnish. If only her personality were as palatable as her meals.

When I get to the living room, I stop dead in my tracks, my gaze sweeping over the unrecognizable space. It makes me second-guess if I'm in the right apartment.

Potted plants of all sizes are arranged in every corner, from a towering tree by the floor-to-ceiling windows to a cluster of herbs on a vintage rolling cart. Several white ceramic pots hang from an iron stand in the corner, each holding a variety of succulents. It's like I've stepped into a jungle straight out of *Jumanji*, where the plants are taking over and fighting for every inch of space.

My leather sectional is now buried under a sea of mismatched throw pillows. A floral rug now covers a large portion of the room, and a coffee table has been placed in the middle, holding a large ceramic bowl overflowing with lemons. The once-empty walls now display London-inspired artwork and framed recipes, each scrawled in different handwriting.

Fallon was supposed to move all her stuff into the bedroom, not stage a hostile takeover of my living room.

This ends now.

The first place I look for her is the kitchen. Even when she's off the clock, she's usually there.

Sure enough, I find her perched on a barstool at the counter with her legs pulled up to her chest. She has her computer in front of her, and a photo editing app open with an image of a plated dish of hummus and vegetables on the screen.

A satisfied smirk tugs at my mouth when I notice she's wearing sweatpants and a long-sleeved sweater. Looks like my plan to crank down the heat is working better than expected.

The problem is, even in baggy clothes, I can't ignore how stunning she is. Over the years, she's only become more stunning, and it's annoying that I still have a visceral reaction whenever I look at her.

Fallon casually tips her head in my direction, her brow furrowed. "Harrison, is everything okay? Your dinner is on the warming tray in the dining room, like you wanted." She doesn't wait for a response before shifting focus back to her computer.

It's irritating that she's acting so comfortable in my space. My frustration is only fueled by the reminder that the living room has been overrun by an army of plants and throw pillows.

"Mind telling me why my living room has been turned into a botanical garden?"

With a sigh, Fallon saves her work and closes her computer. "I made it cozier," she explains without remorse. "The greenery brightens the room and helps with air quality too."

"If you want fresh air, go outside. I can't even see the television past that weird-looking plant."

"It's a fiddle-leaf fig tree," she corrects me.

"What the hell is that?"

"A difficult plant to keep alive. It requires just the right amount of sunlight and attention and is very temperamental in nature," she says with a pointed glare.

My fingers twitch at my sides as I release a sharp exhale. "Apologies, I thought I hired a chef, not an interior decorator. Oh wait, I did—when I moved in."

"Well, I hate to break it to you, but whatever you paid wasn't worth it. The apartment looked like a showroom—cold and impersonal. It's much better now that I've added a few personal touches," she says with a mischievous smile. "It feels more like a home instead of a mausoleum, don't you agree?"

I'm hyper-focused on the phrase *a few* changes. Our interpretation of the term doesn't align, and the thought of what she considers *a lot* makes me shudder.

"If you dislike this place so much, why don't we end this trial run right now?" The instant the words leave my mouth, I realize I've said the wrong thing.

Fallon stands up, the legs scraping loudly against the tile floor. "If you want me gone, just say so, and I'll pack my bags." She comes to stand in front of me. "However, if I stay, I won't tolerate you using that as leverage whenever we don't see eye to eye." Her chest heaves, and the faint tremble in her voice betrays the emotion she's trying to conceal.

I lower my gaze to the ground, conflicted. This is the

opportunity I've been waiting for. All I have to do is tell her to leave, and she'll be out of my life for good. It should be simple… so why isn't it?

It shouldn't be this difficult to cut ties, yet here I am, second-guessing myself. And now my conscience has decided to chime in uninvited, reminding me that I'm acting like a total ass for no concrete reason.

Just when I think I've fortified my walls around my emotions, I glance over to find her steely blue gaze holding its usual intensity, but beneath the surface, there's a trace of vulnerability.

Fallon has given up a lot to be here. She had to quit her part-time clients when she came to work for me full-time, and the catering gigs Cabrina mentioned that Fallon has lined up in the coming weeks won't be enough to support her while she searches for another job.

On top of everything, she doesn't have a place to stay. With New York's competitive market, it might take a while for her to find a new place to live. I can't shake the uneasy feeling when I picture her wandering the city, looking at sketchy apartments by herself.

I might be unyielding and hold my employees to high standards, but I take pride in looking out for them. Even those that grate on my nerves. Come to think of it, Fallon's the only person who's ever managed to get under my skin like this.

"Do any of your plants serve a purpose other than just taking up space?"

I wince at my botched attempt at acting civil.

Fallon nods. "I grow a lot of my own herbs to make sure there's no cross-contamination from processing facilities."

Fuck, I hadn't thought about that.

Guilt settles in as I run a hand through my hair. Here I am acting like a jerk, and she's going out of her way to make sure I don't get sick again.

"I appreciate all the effort you're putting in."

She folds her arms across her chest, arching a brow. "And?"

"Don't leave," I state firmly. "I shouldn't have been so angry about plants or hold the trial run over your head. I won't do it again, I'm sorry."

"Harrison Stafford apologizing?" Fallon feigns a gasp. "Is this real life?" She pinches her wrist, wincing.

"What the hell are you doing?"

"I had to make sure I wasn't dreaming. Didn't think you were capable of saying sorry for anything." She lets out a hum, giving me a side-eye. "What's the catch if I stay?"

"You'll have to deal with my charmingly stubborn nature, but you're no walk in the park either, so we'll call it even," I say, shooting her a side-eye of my own.

Fallon chuckles. "If I'm allowed to stay, does that mean the plants can, too?"

I sigh heavily. "Fine, but that's where I draw the line."

"We'll see." She smirks, sitting back down and opening her computer.

I'm way in over my head, and if I'm not careful, I might cross the line between indifference and actually giving a damn, forgetting why I've kept my distance from her in the first place.

CHAPTER 6

Harrison

'M ON THE ELEVATOR HEADED UP TO MY APARTMENT AFTER an early morning workout with the Mavericks hockey team. After pushing through a grueling leg workout and a three-mile run, sweat clings to my skin, and I can't wait to hop in the shower.

Aleksandr: Solid workout, old man, but I out-lifted you.

Harrison: Don't get cocky, I still own you at the mile.

Aleksandr: Enjoy it while it lasts.

Harrison: Tell you what. Beat me, and I'll teach you that faceoff trick you've been pestering me about.

Aleksandr: Game on.

He's the team captain, and he reminds me of myself when I was his age. Cocky, ambitious, and hungry for success, no matter the cost.

When I retired from playing professionally, I missed the thrill of competition and doing something I was passionate about. To offset the loss, I started practicing with the Mavericks, a pro team in New York, hoping to feel that competitive edge again. When the opportunity came up to invest as a part owner, I jumped at the chance. It meant more responsibilities, but I couldn't pass up being part of something important to me.

Despite my jam-packed schedule, I train with the team four days a week and workout in my apartment building's gym on the other days. I'm not as nimble as I used to be, and my time spent with the team pushes my limits. The majority are at least ten years younger, a fact they're quick to remind me of, but I welcome the challenge that comes with it.

Over the past two weeks, I've especially needed an outlet to release my frustrations. Work has been kicking my ass—between preparing end-of-year financials, dealing with unexpected zoning laws for a project we have in Houston, Texas, and managing day-to-day operations, I've had my hands full.

Not to mention the peace I once felt at home has been replaced with a simmering frustration.

There was a reason I was avoiding Fallon. Every interaction is a sparring match that leaves me equally frustrated and conflicted.

When I get to my apartment, I head straight for my room. I tug off my shirt and toss it in the clothes hamper in the corner. I'm halfway to the bathroom when I pause, spinning around to look at my bed.

My eyes widen when I register that the entire thing is covered in fuzzy pink and purple throw pillows. There must be at least fifty, and not a single inch of the mattress is visible under the pile of fluff.

Fallon.

In the past two weeks since she's been here, I've lost control of my own space. The house smells like vanilla and orange, plants have overtaken my living room, and now she's pulling stunts like staging a throw pillow blitz. In my bedroom no less, which I explicitly told her was off-limits.

If she were anyone else, I wouldn't think twice about firing her. Not after our conversation last night.

You brought this on yourself.

Apparently, my conscience has decided to make an appearance, conveniently forgetting why I'm distant with Fallon in the first place. It's not fair that she gets a free pass when she made the choice to move on without an apology or offering an explanation. Not that I want to hear her excuses anyway.

When I get to the kitchen to confront her, I come to a standstill when I find her hovering in front of the oven, taking out a loaf of bread. The lime-green tank top and boy shorts she's wearing leave little to the imagination, and I take in every inch of her as my gaze lingers on her curves.

Where are the rest of her clothes?

Come to think of it, why is it so warm in here?

Fallon tugs her lip between her teeth as she sets the pan on the stovetop and bends down to study it. Her hair is pulled into a messy bun, exposing the smooth slope of her collarbone, and an unwanted image flashes in my mind of me pinning her against the counter, wrapping my fingers around her delicate neck, my fingers digging into her soft skin as I kiss her soft lips.

Her voice snaps me out of my daydream. "The edges are too crispy," she mutters, still unaware of my presence. "I'll have to lower the oven temperature by ten degrees to avoid that next time."

I watch as she leans over the counter to write in a notebook, crossing out a line, then pauses, tapping the pen against her mouth in thought. Much to my annoyance, I can't help but notice how stunning she is. The light shining from the kitchen windows, illuminating her features, only adds to her beauty. After a beat, she scribbles something in the margin, her hand moving quickly as if racing against time.

"Plotting the perfect recipe for world domination?" I ask, breaking the silence.

Fallon jumps, letting out a startled shriek as she spins around to face me. "Don't sneak up on me like that," she huffs.

"I'll be sure to make a formal announcement next time," I reply flatly.

She rolls her eyes. "Funny, for someone who keeps on insisting on space, you sure seem to be in my kitchen a lot."

I scoff. "*Your* kitchen? Didn't realize I needed a permission slip to walk freely in my own apartment." I take a step toward her, lowering my voice. "Maybe you should worry more about staying out of my bedroom. Didn't I say it was off-limits?"

She taps her chin thoughtfully. "Hmm, now that you mentioned it, I guess you did. It must've slipped my mind." She shrugs.

Why this little troublemaker.

"And you thought it was a good idea to ignore my request?"

"To be fair, I was looking for the thermostat earlier because my hands were freezing. Luckily, I found it hidden behind the floral painting in the hallway," she explains with a sly smile. "I was browsing the settings when I found a 'usage' option. It turns out *someone* has been manually turning the heat down since the day after I arrived. Any idea how that happened?" There's an accusing note in her tone.

"No idea." I shrug, biting the inside of my cheek to refrain from smirking. "That still doesn't explain how all those frilly pillows ended up on my bed," I reply, steering the conversation away from her earlier question.

She closes the remaining distance between us, her chest flush with mine, her fierce gaze unrelenting. "While I was searching for the thermostat, I walked into your room since the door was open. I couldn't help but notice how bare it was, and in my cold haze, I remembered how much you loved the ones in the living room and must've gone overboard and ordered a bunch for your bed. Guess that's what happens when the temperature drops. Whoever messed with the thermostat should remember that next time they try to freeze me out."

"You enjoy testing my limits, don't you?" My voice drops.

"A harmless prank gets under your skin that easily, Harrison?" she taunts.

I suppress a chuckle. "If that's what you call a prank, you're in serious need of a crash course in execution."

"Think you can do better, hotshot?"

"I know I can."

"Do your worst." She grins.

Little does she know that my brothers and I were pranksters when we were teenagers. She's up against an expert, but who am I to spoil the surprise? Let her think she has the upper hand for now.

I'm feeling pretty smug until I realize Fallon is staring at my bare chest, her mouth slightly open. When I look down, I remember that I came in here wearing nothing but a pair of gray sweatpants.

I'm ready for Fallon to make a snarky comment when I see that her cheeks are flushed, and she's studying me with those brilliant blue eyes. I can't help but wonder if she's thinking about that night we spent together ten years ago when she ran her nails across my abs as I kissed her senseless.

My lips curve into a sardonic smile. Even with annoyance simmering beneath the surface, there's a thrill from knowing that she's enjoying the view.

"Taking a second look at what you missed out on?" I ask with a hint of amusement.

She turns her focus to my face, her eyes growing dark. "God, no. I was just thinking about how I dodged a bullet. You're not nearly as impressive as you think," she deadpans.

I take several steps forward so I'm standing next to her.

"You're right. I'm not *trying* to impress you. It just comes naturally." I smirk.

Riling her up is quickly becoming my favorite pastime. She's the one who walked into the lion's den without a hint of self-preservation.

Fallon shakes her head. "You're so full of yourself."

I lean in closer. "We both know I can back it up," I whisper, my breath brushing her ear.

Her breath catches as she watches me closely, as if trying to anticipate my next move.

Her reaction speaks volumes.

An intrusive thought flashes through my mind of what it might be like to kiss her again. I can almost taste her, the way her breath would mingle with mine, her velvet lips molded against mine as she melts into me, pressing herself closer.

As soon as I shut the door to my hotel room, my hands find Elizabeth's waist, tugging her against my chest.

"I've been counting down the minutes until we were alone," I murmur.

"What are you waiting for? Kiss me already," she demands with a wry smile.

"God, I love that sassy mouth of yours." I trail kisses along her jaw, my tongue teasing the seam of her mouth, edging her to surrender. The warmth of her mouth is intoxicating, and the soft moan that passes her lips has my heart racing with a heady mix of recklessness and desire.

I lift her into my arms, her legs instinctively wrapping around my waist and her arms around my neck. She's fucking intoxicating and I can't get enough. I grind my cock against her core, her heat searing through the fabric between us, and she leans into me in response. Our mingled moans fill the air as I greedily explore her mouth with fervor.

Damn, this woman is a temptation I'm unable to resist. I already know that one night with her isn't going to be enough, and I'm plotting how I can get her to agree to spend the entire weekend with me.

Goddammit.

I blink rapidly, turning away for a moment to adjust myself before clearing my throat.

"I'm leaving for the office soon. Make sure my breakfast is ready in ten. Oh, and, Fallon?"

"Yeah?"

"You better sleep with one eye open. You wanted a prank war and you're about to get one."

She smirks. "It's on."

I leave the room, massaging my temples. Despite my best efforts to keep Fallon at arm's length, it's proving to be difficult. If I don't get a grip on my mind, it'll lead me down the same path it did before. I let my guard down for her once, and it left me with nothing but unanswered questions and lingering bitterness. So why do I know her beautiful face will haunt me when I close my eyes tonight?

Once I'm back in my room, I fire off a text to Cash, asking for backup.

Harrison: I need your expertise, but you can't ask questions.

Cash: I'm intrigued. What's up, big brother?

Harrison: Got any solid prank ideas up your sleeves?

Cash: You've definitely come to the right guy.

Cash: I'll shoot over some ideas after my next meeting.

Harrison: Great, thanks.

Cash: Do I want to know what this is for?

Harrison: No questions, remember?

Although neither Fallon nor I seem to be happy about the living arrangement, I plan to make the most of it. I may not have total control over my thoughts where she's concerned, but I'm playing the long game —and I never lose.

CHAPTER 7

Fallon

I JOLT UPRIGHT AT THE SOUND OF MY ALARM, GROANING when I check my phone to see that it's only 5:30 a.m. As a chef, I'm used to getting up early, but it never gets easier. It doesn't help that I spent the past two nights tossing and turning, worried that I'd fall asleep and wake up to find a fake snake under my pillow, a creepy doll on the nightstand, or the wood floor coated in honey. It's hard to imagine Harrison, the guy who had a meltdown over plants and throw pillows, would risk his floors getting ruined for a prank. The other two, though? Definitely plausible.

I lean over to grab my phone off the nightstand, shocked to see I have a new text message this early.

Lila: Good morning!

Fallon: Why are you up so early?

Lila: Winston's in a committed relationship with the squeaky toy hedgehog my mom gave him, and apparently 5:00 a.m. is when the mood strikes.

Fallon: OMG, stop. At least one of us is getting some action.

Lila: Yes, my dog's love life is more exciting than mine. Perfect.

Lila is a hopeless romantic, longing for when she finds her Prince Charming. She's shared how difficult being a wedding planner can be, coordinating other couples' perfect day while she eagerly waits for her own happy ending. I may not share the same idealistic views as she does, but my greatest hope is for her to find someone who embraces her sense of adventure and encourages her to explore the world beyond Starlight Pines. She deserves nothing less.

Fallon: And mine, lol.

Lila: At least you have eye candy in a three-piece suit.

Fallon: Trust me, Harrison's grumpy demeanor cancels out any hotness happening.

Lila: Ah, still trouble in paradise, I see. You should consider asking him why he left after your weekend together. It might bring you closure.

Fallon: I'm not going to beg him for an apology. If he wants to fix things, he'll have to bring it up.

Lila: Remind me to never get on your bad side.

Still groggy, I rub my eyes and shuffle toward the bathroom, the soft light spilling from the hallway as my only guide. Halfway there, I freeze, my stomach lurching when I notice the swarm of shadows spilling from beneath the closed bedroom door. My pulse quickens as I make out the unmistakable shape of dozens of spiders. My hands tremble, and my phone clatters to the floor.

"This can't be happening," I squeak, my voice barely audible over the thundering of my heart.

My legs carry me backward, until I bump into the bed. I don't hesitate to leap onto the mattress, wrapping the comforter around me like a flimsy shield against the advancing army, growing more menacing by the second. It's like I'm stuck in one of the horror movies I'm obsessed with and that keeps me awake long after the credits roll, second-guessing every shadow. Only now they're real.

"Nope, nope, nope," I chant, covering my face with my hands and squeezing my eyes shut.

I could really use some backup right now, but I stay frozen, gripping the comforter like a lifeline as I exhale slowly, reminding myself this probably isn't the apocalypse, even if it feels like it.

When my breathing finally slows down, I risk peeking through my fingers. The spiders remain eerily still, and their glossy surfaces catch the light. A mix of relief and embarrassment crashes over me in equal measure. Sliding off the bed, I inch closer, kneeling down to pick one up. Plastic. Great.

Not caring to control my reaction, I throw the door open, stepping on several more spiders on my way out.

"Harrison," I shout, storming down the hall.

He's in the living room, reclined on the couch, reading the newspaper. Who the hell reads a physical newspaper anymore?

"Yes?" he asks calmly, adjusting the reading glasses perched on his nose.

Oh my god.

I'm briefly sidetracked from my mission at the sight of his five o'clock shadow and those infuriatingly sexy glasses.

"You wear glasses?" I cringe at how obvious the question sounds.

"They're for reading. Do they bother you?" he asks, tilting his head.

Not in the way he thinks.

"No, just curious." I shrug.

He leans back in his chair and directs his stern focus on me… mainly my attire.

"Is there a reason you're wearing a hockey shirt? And *only* a hockey shirt?"

I blink at him, snapping me out of my trance. "Huh?" I glance down at the oversized T-shirt falling to mid-thigh. My cheeks flush with embarrassment. At least I'm wearing panties underneath, but it's not like it makes a difference since he can't see them.

When I moved to the States, I lived with Jeremy before he broke up with me. He got a bunch of gear from the Stormbreakers when he signed on, including a bunch of T-shirts, and I snagged this one. It has no sentimental value whatsoever, but it's super comfortable, so I kept it.

After we broke up, I got a job as a server at an Italian restaurant. That's where I met my old boss, Theo. He was the sous chef, and when I took an interest in cooking, he showed me the ropes. To save up for culinary school, I picked up several gigs with catering companies. That's how I met Harrison, serving drinks at an event for the Huskies.

"I'd appreciate it if you don't wear that shirt again," Harrison says, his jaw tight.

"Why?"

"I have my reasons."

I fold my arms across my chest and square my shoulders.

"I'm not agreeing to anything until you explain why I woke up thinking my room was being infiltrated by an army of spiders."

He leans back into the sofa, lacing his hands behind his head. His nonchalance mocking the seriousness of my question.

"Spiders, huh?" he replies, a small grin playing at the corner of his mouth. "Sounds terrifying."

"This isn't funny," I hiss, clenching my fists. "I nearly had a panic attack when I saw the swarm at my door. They looked way too real."

"You've never been a fan of spiders," he states.

I squint at him. "What?"

"We watched *Arachnophobia* together, remember?"

How could I forget? During our weekend holed up in his hotel room, we spent Saturday bingeing horror movies. When I refused to go in the bathroom alone because of a mirror that looked like the one from *The Ring Two,* he suggested switching to a horror-comedy.

"If I remember right, we had to switch movies because you panicked when a woman appeared in the mirror. You nearly cracked my ribs squeezing me so tight," Harrison says.

"I was just trying to cop a feel," I counter, refusing to admit how scared I was.

"And when she yanked that guy's reflection into the glass? You nearly knocked over the popcorn scrambling into my lap."

"My attempt at rounding third base," I retort.

"We did more than just attempt." Harrison smirks.

The weight of unspoken tension hangs in the air, thick and undeniable. It's suffocating, wrapping around us like an invisible thread, pulling tighter with every shared moment.

On the surface, I'm keeping my cool, but inside, I'm reeling. He remembers more about that night than I expected. If it meant nothing to him like I assumed, why does he recall every little detail? Which makes me wonder what else he remembers about our weekend together.

I press my nails into my palms, grounding myself. It's important to remember that Harrison isn't my friend, and whatever past memories he has of us don't hold any weight after what he did.

"I better go change and get breakfast started," I say, shifting into work mode. "Consider this your fair warning that you might want to stay alert. I won't forget waking up thinking I was being attacked by an army of spiders," I warn, biting back a grin.

"Bring it on," Harrison replies, his mouth twitching with amusement.

Without another word, I rush out of the living room. The night we watched *Arachnophobia*, flashes through my mind like a worn-out film.

We're halfway through the movie, and already I'm regretting my decision to watch this one.

"Isn't this supposed to be a comedy?" I whisper.

Harrison chuckles. "It's a horror-comedy… don't worry, there should be a funny part coming up soon."

I give him a faint smile, appreciating his attempt to lighten the mood.

My focus shifts back to the screen when a giant spider scuttles across it, sending a chill down my spine. I clutch the blanket draped across my lap, trying to fight the panic rising in my chest.

I feel Harrison's hand gently slide over mine, lacing our fingers together, rubbing his thumb lightly over my knuckles.

"We don't have to finish the movie if you don't want to," he says, his voice low and steady.

"I don't think I'm a fan of spiders," I admit.

When I glance over at him, the tenderness in his eyes eases the tightness in my chest. We barely know each other yet he can read me better than Jeremy ever could.

"I think you need a distraction," he whispers, a sly grin tugging at his lips.

His hand cradles my cheek as he leans in, his mouth grazing mine, the movie fading to nothing in the background.

"I really like you, Elizabeth," Harrison says.

"I like you too, Mr. Hotshot," I murmur against his lips. "Now what are you going to do about it?"

He smiles mischievously, sending a flutter through my chest, and I squeal when he scoops me into his arms. I bury my face in his chest, laughing as he carries me to the bedroom. This weekend is quickly becoming one of the best I've ever had, and I don't want it to end.

There's no escaping the memories of our weekend together, etched in my mind—like the warmth of sunlight on a white duvet, and the feel of Harrison's scruff against my inner thighs. Even ten years later, our intense chemistry remains—a spark refusing to fade no matter how much time has passed, which only adds to my growing contempt for him. He still hasn't acknowledged what he did to me and has the audacity to act like he has the right to be upset with me. It makes me even more determined to turn the tables on him.

He wants to pull pranks? Fine, two can play this game.

The next morning, I'm in the kitchen whipping up a batch of orange rolls. I've spent a lot of time fine-tuning a gluten-free version, and I'm proud of the recipe I've created.

While I was waiting in the lobby for a grocery delivery, Walter told me that they're his favorite dessert, but he hasn't had them since his wife passed. He's been so kind to me since I moved in, and I want to find more ways to show my appreciation since it's not something I've experienced much in my life.

I had the unfortunate privilege of being raised by my

grandmother, Josephine Pembroke. She wasn't exactly the warm, nurturing type, and her version of love came in the form of silent disapproval and constantly trying to meet her impossible standards.

Born and raised by a wealthy family in England, her life was marked by strict traditions and the art of maintaining an impeccable reputation. When my father chose to attend university in the United States and fell in love with a waitress from New Jersey, she was mortified.

After her threats to cut him from his inheritance if he didn't come back to London failed, she severed all ties. That is, until twelve years later, when she received a call informing her that he and his wife had been in a car accident on their way home from dinner and didn't make it. She had no idea I existed before the officer informed her that my parents had left behind a daughter.

I had to move to London and spent my teenage years walking on pins and needles to avoid setting off my grandmother's disapproving gaze. There was no shared laughter or comforting embraces. Just a cold silence that settled over me like a heavy weight, a constant reminder that she resented me for being the spitting image of my mother. That's why, as soon as the opportunity presented itself, I moved to Florida with Jeremy. I've always considered the States my home since I grew up here with my parents.

The sweet scent of oranges fills the kitchen, and I close my eyes for a moment, imagining my mom beside me. I can almost hear her voice, reminding me to press the dough gently, her hands steady over mine, guiding me with the patience I miss so much.

My eyes flutter open when I hear Harrison's voice coming from the dining room.

"Fallon, get in here," he hollers.

I pause kneading the dough for the orange rolls, dust the gluten-free flour blend off my hands, and take my sweet time strolling into the room.

I stop next to the table where Harrison is scowling at his coffee. The plate of scrambled eggs, bacon, and gluten-free toast with homemade strawberry chia seed jam I made remains untouched.

He went for his coffee first, just as I predicted.

Good.

"You shouted?" I deadpan.

"What did you do to my coffee?" His tone is exasperated.

I bite the inside of my cheek, stifling a laugh. "You said you liked it black with one sugar. Isn't that right?"

"Yes." He eyes me warily, lifting the mug to his lips, and takes a sip. Immediately after, he spits it out, his face contorting in disgust.

His icy gaze locks on me with unrelenting intensity. "This isn't drinkable," he mutters, setting the cup down a little hard, causing it to slosh. "What did you put in it?"

"Maybe your taste buds are broken," I say, feigning innocence.

He watches me closely, a slight twitch at the corner of his mouth making me uneasy. "Would you mind giving it a try? Just to be sure?" He nudges the mug toward me, a subtle twitch at the corner of his mouth.

I shake my head. "I don't share beverages. Germs and all."

He arches a brow. "We've swapped more than our fair share of germs in the past. In fact, I recall sharing a bottle of champagne straight from the neck with you."

Heat rises to my cheeks, knowing that's far from the only thing we've shared.

Harrison pushes the drink closer when I don't respond. "Come on, take a sip," he commands.

He has me cornered, and he knows it. I stare down at the black liquid, debating my approach. One thing is for sure, there's no chance I'm putting a drop of it in my mouth.

I tap my chin thoughtfully. "Come to think of it, I might have accidentally swapped salt for sugar. They're in the same kind of container, and I got confused."

"Confused my ass," Harrison scoffs. "What about your coffee? Did you accidentally put salt in yours too, or was I the only victim of your *mistake?*"

"I don't drink coffee."

He pinches the bridge of his nose. "Please tell me you're still not a fan of Diet Coke."

I shrug. "It's my guilty pleasure."

"But having it this early in the morning?"

"At least my vice isn't bitter, burnt liquid and doesn't come with a side of crankiness," I quip, nodding toward his coffee.

"Oh, my vice is bitter, alright." He pinches the bridge of his nose. "Am I going to have to double-check everything I put in my mouth from now on?"

"Depends on what you're planning to put in it," I deadpan.

He heaves a sigh and picks up his phone from the table. "I'll have Cabrina pick up coffee on the way to the office. Looks like I can't trust my private chef with breakfast anymore." The small curve of his lip betrays his amusement.

"Don't be dramatic. A mistake with your drink order is one thing. My food will always be flawless," I say with confidence.

One thing he'll never have to worry about is me messing with his food. Cooking is my passion, and I'd never jeopardize my reputation as a skilled chef as a means to get back at Harrison. There are far more creative ways to mess with him without ruining my food.

"Great, so it's just my drinks that are at risk, got it," he says with a hint of teasing.

"Enjoy your meal, Mr. Stafford," I say before going back into the kitchen.

I drag a hand across my face, forcing a smile from breaking free. I'm unable to resist the urge of getting a rise out of Harrison, and our banter is always more entertaining than I care to admit.

The problem is, it's a challenge to stay indifferent when he looks like he belongs on the cover of a business magazine, creating fantasies in my head that I know I shouldn't entertain—even though a small part of me wishes they could.

Later that day, I'm riding the elevator to the lobby with a plate of freshly baked orange rolls in hand, heading down to visit Walter, when I get a text.

Harrison: I have to make a last-minute trip to Chicago.

Harrison: I'll be back in the morning. Have breakfast ready by 7am.

Fallon: Please.

Harrison: What?

Fallon: I think you meant to say will you please have breakfast ready by 7am.

Fallon: It's called good manners, but I guess you're not familiar with those.

Harrison: Maybe if you didn't push my buttons, I'd make an effort to ask nicely.

Fallon: Doubt it. You're too stubborn.

Harrison: You're one to talk.

Fallon: At least I'm not making excuses to avoid you.

Harrison: I'm not avoiding you. I have a business meeting, remember.

Fallon: And you couldn't go to Chicago, finish your meeting and be back by tonight?

Harrison: You're an expert on business trips now?

Fallon: Nope, just pointing out the obvious.

Harrison: Which is?

Fallon: You're avoiding me.

Fallon: It's okay. I get it. You can dish out a prank but can't take it when you know you have one coming your way.

Harrison: See you tomorrow, Fallon.

A smile crosses my face before I can stop it. I'm stunned Harrison actually took my request seriously. Communicating with me directly might not be his first choice, but I appreciate the effort. I refuse to read into the way my heart skipped a beat when his number appeared on my screen. It was just a reflex, that's all.

When the elevator chimes, I tuck my phone into my pocket and step into the lobby.

"Someone's in a good mood today," Walter says from his spot behind the reception desk. "Who's got you smiling like that?"

"Believe it or not, Harrison," I say, holding up my hand when he gives me a curious look. "It's only because he's out of town, and I'll have the apartment to myself tonight."

He chuckles softly, setting down the magazine he was reading. "Sure, that's it."

Okay, so I enjoy going toe-to-toe with Harrison more than I should. There's a rush in our verbal sparring matches, and the push and pull of our exchanges is exhilarating. But do I like him? Let's not get carried away. Just because his smirk sends a flurry of butterflies swirling in my stomach and the memories of the weekend he worshipped me like a goddess plague me at night doesn't mean I'm about to forgive him or, heaven forbid, make the same mistake twice.

The latter sends a traitorous shudder through me. It's exasperating how logic vanishes when it comes to Harrison, leaving me vulnerable to the possibility of him slipping through the defenses I've worked so hard to build.

I won't let that happen, right?

I redirect my focus on Walter, who's watching me with an inquisitive gaze.

"A courier just dropped off a package for you," he says, leaning over to grab a box and scoot it closer to me.

"Thank you."

I read the label to confirm that Theo sent it. He was in Japan recently and mentioned wanting to give me bluefin tuna as a housewarming gift. It's a delicacy that tastes incredible, though it can have a potent smell.

"I made these for you," I say with a smile, setting the orange rolls on Walter's desk.

He cocks his head, his gaze shifting to the pan. His hand hovers above it like it's a precious gift he's afraid to touch. "You remembered," he whispers.

I nod, passing him the napkins I brought. "You mentioned that today was your anniversary, and I wanted to give you something to remember the love you and your wife shared."

My chest tightens as he reaches out with a shaky hand, taking an orange roll from the pan. With his eyes closed, he takes a deliberate bite, chewing slowly, a nostalgic smile crossing his lips.

"It's like my Pearl is here with me," he says, his voice filled with reverence.

"I'm sorry she's not," I respond softly, resting my hand on his arm.

His eyes glisten as he looks at me. "You're a good soul, Miss Fallon. Don't ever change."

As we sit in a comfortable silence, I think about how Walter's love for Pearl runs deep. I didn't know them as a couple, but it's obvious their love was the kind people spend their whole lives searching for.

Until now, my perspective on the subject has been a different story. My grandmother divorced my grandfather when my dad was a kid, and after that, no man was good enough for her. And she made sure everyone knew it.

Over the past ten years, I've casually dated, but never for more than a few months at a time. Serious relationships require vulnerability, and the men I've been with in the past have taught me they can't be trusted—whether leading me on, ghosting me, or cheating. I've been through it all. So, the concept of finding someone who fits into my soul like a missing puzzle piece is a foreign concept.

But now that I've witnessed the aftermath of a lifetime of love, I can't help but wonder what it would be like to experience that myself. Great, now I sound like Lila, dreaming of a Prince Charming and my own happily ever after. Too bad I accepted a long time ago that love wasn't in the cards for me.

CHAPTER 8

Harrison

AFTER FLYING HOME FROM CHICAGO THIS MORNING, I stopped by the penthouse to shower and have breakfast. I considered working from home, but after running into Fallon in the hall, wearing another damn tank top and shorts, I opted to go into the office.

I don't want another reminder of how she felt in my arms or the way her body fit against mine. The past refuses to stay where it belongs, and being surrounded by Fallon's scent only makes it harder to forget, which is why I need to be as far away from her as possible.

A flicker of guilt twists in my chest for not thanking her before I left. It's her job to cook for me, but I can't shake the nagging feeling that I should show her more appreciation. Unable to shake my guilty conscience, I decide to check in.

Fallon: Why? Are you feeling okay?

Harrison: Are you worried about me?

Fallon: If you think you're having a reaction to gluten, then yes.

Fallon: Did you eat anything on the plane or at the office that could have been contaminated?

Harrison: I'm fine.

Fallon: You're not having an autoimmune response?

Harrison. No. I was just curious because whatever you put in the quiche tasted amazing.

Fallon: Oh.

Her concern for me means more than it should. I shouldn't care about what she thinks, period.

Yet, unfortunately, I do.

Harrison: You're really talented.

Fallon: Thank you.

Fallon: In case you're still wondering, caramelized onions and sharp cheddar cheese are my secret ingredients.

Harrison: Now you've got me craving it again.

Fallon: There are leftovers in the fridge.

Dammit. Why is it so easy to talk to Fallon through text? It would be easier if it wasn't. She has infiltrated every part of my life, and in moments like this, I forget the hurt she caused me—and that she hasn't acknowledged it once since coming back into my life. It's a reminder of the resentment I should feel because of it.

Ready for a distraction, I join the meeting I have scheduled with my brothers.

Dylan's already waiting.

"How was Chicago?" he asks.

I lean back in my office chair, looking into my laptop's camera. "Uneventful."

"How do you do it? I'm wiped after one business trip, but you've done seven this past month alone," Dylan says.

"It has to be done." I shrug. "Unlike you, I don't have to wrangle an energetic kid and four dogs when I get home. You've got your hands full," I add with a rueful smile.

Lately, my travel schedule has been brutal with recent acquisitions and the increasing number of offices we've added. My dad taught me the importance of regular in-person meetings with employees and partners to keep performance levels high. Although, back when he was CEO, we had a fraction of the staff we do now.

Dylan was wise to hire an additional senior analyst, giving him the freedom to be with Marlow and Lola more. Unfortunately, I don't have that luxury. Running the company means I'm the person everyone depends on for quick responses and urgent solutions, which means I have to be available at a moment's notice.

Just then, Cash's face pops up on the screen. "Hey, guys. Sorry

I'm late. I was wrapping up a call with the Townstead team," he says.

"Look at you being all professional," Dylan teases as he adjusts his glasses. "A few months ago, you would have skipped out entirely and pretended you forgot."

"What can I say? I'm a changed man now that I'm married." He flashes a grin as he rubs his thumb against his wedding ring.

"How are Everly, August, and Liam holding down the fort at Townstead?" I ask.

It's been a few months since Everly and her stepbrothers took the reins following Stafford Holdings' acquisition. It's been a welcome change, letting them handle things with minimal involvement from me or my team.

"Great. Everly loves her job." He pauses, a curious gleam in his eye. "But right now, I'm more interested in talking about you and Fallon. Did you end up using one of my prank ideas?"

I shoot him a sideways glance. "For starters, there is no me *and* Fallon. The woman's a menace, hence why I asked for your help," I grumble, still not over my apartment turning into a cluttered disaster zone since Fallon moved in.

It's a good thing I'm leaving for Aspen Grove tomorrow.

"Right." Cash nods, his lip twitching from holding back a laugh. "Is she by chance the reason your scowl is extra tense? I feel bad for anyone who has to cross your path today."

Dylan holds up a hand, eyes wide. "Whoa, hold up. Cash, you helped him prank Fallon?"

Cash shrugs. "He didn't say it was for her specifically, but I had a hunch."

"What did you do?" Dylan asks, his tone cautious.

I run my fingers through my hair, suddenly hesitant of my actions. "It wasn't a big deal. I just put a bunch of plastic spiders under her bedroom door while she was sleeping, so when she woke up, she thought a swarm of spiders had invaded her room."

I hadn't expected her to storm out in a T-shirt that show-cased her toned legs—legs that, to this day, I can vividly remember wrapped around my waist, her mouth on mine.

"What's wrong with you?" Dylan scolds, taking his glasses off and running a hand across his face.

I pick up a pen from my desk, spinning it between my fingers. "It's not a big deal," I say defensively.

"And you would know that how?" he asks.

"Because Fallon and I agreed to this prank war, and I always follow through on my commitments," I say with a smirk.

I'm not ready to open up about my history with her. Things ended abruptly after the weekend we spent together, and with everything my family had been dealing with, I never mentioned her to anyone. When things finally settled down, she wasn't someone I wanted to think about ever again.

Hell, if I told my brothers now, they'd probably tell Mom so they could watch the chaos unfold. She's already texting me daily for updates on Fallon, and if she even suspects a hint of a spark between us, her meddling will go into overdrive.

"You both better hope this feud never goes south," Dylan warns us. "If Everly finds out you helped, you'll be banished to the spare bedroom for a month," he says to Cash. "Worse yet, Mom would disown you, Harrison." He shudders dramatically, pausing before holding up his finger. "But if Fallon needs material, have her give me a call. I'm happy to share all your pet peeves and toss in a few embarrassing stories for good measure."

"Traitor," I mumble.

I glance at Cash, a slow grin spreading across his face as he listens to our exchange. "Let me guess, you're not going to help me with future pranks?" I observe.

"You heard Dylan," he says, not missing a beat. "I'm not going to chance getting on Everly's bad side, especially not during the holidays. Besides, chances are this is going to backfire, and I'm not going to risk getting on Mom's bad side either if you ruin this for her."

I press my lips together, idly clicking a pen. "What are you getting at?"

Cash covers his mouth, stifling a laugh as he looks at Dylan. "Should I tell him, or should you?"

Dylan shakes his head. "Let's give him a chance to figure it out on his own. I don't think it'll take long."

My gaze flickers between them on the screen. "Will someone please tell me what you're going on about?"

Dylan waves me off. "We'll tell you later. It's not important right now."

I glower at them, not liking that they've decided to gang up on me. "Yes, it is. Why are you—"

Dylan's office door swings open, and Lola rushes inside, out of breath. She's sporting a purple hockey jersey with a rainbow tutu, her hair is styled in fishtail braids with sparkly purple bows tied to the ends.

"Daddy, I missed you while I was at school," she exclaims, leaping into his arms.

"Ladybug, I'm on a work call with your uncles. Can it wait?" Dylan asks firmly.

"Hi, Uncle Harrison. Hi, Uncle Cash." She ignores him as she waves to the camera. "Uncle Harrison, do you like my jersey? It's just like yours," she says proudly.

When I was in Aspen Grove visiting, I took Lola to the ice rink. It was empty, so the attendant let me bring out my hockey stick and puck. Lola and I had a blast, and now she's all about hockey, telling everyone she's going to be a pro just like her uncle Harrison.

"It's perfect, ladybug. It looks amazing with your tutu and matches your hair bows."

She runs her hands down her hair, preening for the camera. "Thanks. Mom let me put the bows in by myself today."

I let out a low whistle. "You did a great job."

Lola throws her arms around Dylan's neck, tipping her head to look at him. "What do you think, Daddy? Do you like them?"

"They're beautiful, just like you." He beams, giving her a playful tap on the nose, causing her to burst into giggles.

It's great to see him so happy. When Marlow, his fiancée, came along, he was a grumpy cynic whose primary focus was raising Lola and growing Stafford Holdings. She has brought light into his life and taught him how to smile again.

"Ladybug, what can I help you with?" Dylan asks.

"Mom had to take a phone call and told me to play in my room until she was done. But Waffles and the puppies started playing tug-of-war with the pillows and ripped one open. Now there are feathers all over." She throws her hands up for emphasis.

That's when I notice a feather tucked in the waistband of her tutu, another caught in her hair. It could be worse. Last time she burst in during a call, she was covered in blue glitter, with the dogs trailing behind her in the same sparkly mess. Dylan said it took hours to clean up.

"Alright, ladybug, we'll take care of it." He presses a kiss to her head. "Sorry, guys, we're going to have to cut this short." He lifts Lola, setting her on the ground, and rises from his chair. "Marlow's probably on a call about her upcoming art exhibit, so I better take care of this before she's interrupted." He bends over so we can see his face on the screen.

"No problem. We can reschedule," I assure him.

"Thanks." Dylan drops off the conference call, leaving me alone with Cash, a smug expression on his face.

"Will you cut it out?" I ask.

He holds up his hands. "What? I'm not doing anything."

My phone pings on my desk. "Right," I say skeptically,

glancing down to read the incoming text before glancing back at Cash. "Listen, I have to call one of the board members. He wants to discuss a new land deal in Vegas," I say, grateful for the distraction.

Cash gives an exaggerated eye roll. "Uh-huh, you're just worried I'm going to keep pestering you about Fallon," he teases.

He's not wrong.

"Bye, Cash," I say, hanging up the call.

Something tells me the salt in my coffee was just the beginning of Fallon's retaliation for the spider prank. I'd be lying if I said I wasn't intrigued to see what she does next.

That night, I meet with my friend Dawson at the bar down the street.

I'm already seated with a drink in hand when he gets there, and he slides into the seat next to me. "Now a bad time to cash in my second favor?" he teases.

My brothers and I ran into some legal trouble when acquiring Townstead International, and I went to him for advice. After his team did some digging, they discovered that the former owner, Richard, had all but driven his business into the ground with embezzlement, tax evasion, kickbacks—the list goes on.

Dawson is a ruthless lawyer who doesn't shy away from controversy or difficult situations, and he agreed to help me deal with Richard with the caveat that aside from his exorbitant retainer, my brothers and I owed him a couple of favors.

"Now that your brothers have settled down, does that mean you're next?" he taunts.

I glance over, my expression flat. "I'm not in the mood for your antics today."

"You're gloomier than usual," he observes. "Want to talk about it, *friend*?"

"Nope."

Dawson used to be one moody son-of-a-bitch, but since he started dating his girlfriend, Reese, he's become far too chipper for my taste. I prefer brooding in silence and can't decide how I feel about his newfound cheerfulness. He nods at the bartender, who passes him two fingers of brandy. I'm about to ask for another drink, too, when my phone rings, and I groan when I see that it's Fallon.

What could she possibly want?

She's probably mad that I skipped dinner and didn't tell her. "Yes, Fallon?"

"Did you throw away the fish in the fridge?" she asks, her voice panicked.

"I might have," I hedge.

"You're unbelievable. That bluefin tuna was a housewarming gift from Theo, imported from Japan, and cost a hundred grand." I bite back a sigh, holding the phone at arm's length to avoid her raised voice. "If you want me to respect your request to stay out of your space, then stay out of mine."

"How was I supposed to know it was so damn expensive?" I ask defensively. "It smelled bad, so I tossed it out."

"You could have asked me before making an executive decision to throw it away," Fallon groans.

She has a point, but I'm not willing to admit I was wrong.

"Are you coming back to your apartment soon?" she asks. "Your food has gone cold, so I need to know if you want me to warm it up again."

"No, I'm out with a friend and won't be back until late." There's a long pause on the other end of the phone. "Are you still there?"

I toss the phone on the counter when the line goes dead.

"I can't believe she hung up on me," I mutter as I toss back the rest of my drink. "Fallon's upset because I threw out a bluefin tuna that supposedly was worth a hundred grand." I roll my eyes. "How the hell was I supposed to know something that smells so bad could cost as much as a sports car?"

Dawson glances at his watch. "Why is she at your place at ten at night? More importantly, why is she keeping her fish in your fridge? I thought you didn't like her."

I grit my teeth. "Because my mom can't help herself from meddling in my business and suggested Fallon be my live-in chef," I grunt, refusing to offer more details.

Dawson claps me on the back, chuckling. "Good luck, man; sounds like you'll need it."

I'm definitely going to need it now more than ever.

When I open the door to my apartment, it's dark inside, and I'm not expecting to hear the sound of guttural chanting followed by a terrified scream echoing down the hall.

What the fuck.

I flip on the light and check the entryway closet, grabbing the first thing that could be used as a weapon—my hockey stick.

My steps quicken toward the living room, my confusion mounting when the screaming intensifies into a demonic growl. Turning the corner, I find Fallon curled up with a bowl of popcorn in her lap, and a blanket pulled up to her chin. Her eyes are glued to the TV where a possessed girl thrashes violently on the bed. The girl's head snapping back at an unnatural angle as the priest chants while clutching his crucifix tightly as the girl snarls, her voice a horrifying mix of growls and screeches.

"Jesus, Fallon, what the hell are you watching?"

She shrieks, nearly leaping off the couch, and the popcorn

bowl flips from her lap, sending kernels scattering everywhere as her wide eyes lock on me.

"Oh my god," she exclaims, clutching her heart. "You scared me."

I raise an eyebrow, pointing at myself. "I scared *you*? How do you think I felt walking into my house, thinking someone was being murdered?"

She waves at the screen with a light chuckle. "They are. Spiritually speaking."

I set the hockey stick against the wall and bend down to pick up a few pieces of popcorn near my feet. "Do you think watching *The Exorcist* in the dark by yourself is a good idea?"

Fallon holds out the bowl for me to put the discarded popcorn in.

"I would have looked for a movie buddy, but I wasn't in the mood to become the plot twist in a true crime podcast." She shrugs.

She's drowned out by another spine-chilling scream coming from the TV.

"Will you turn that off?" I snap as I flip on the living room lights.

She grabs the remote from the coffee table and hits the power button, the screen going dark. "Happy now?"

"I'd be happier if you'd quit watching horror movies in the dark and didn't leave my couch buried in popcorn," I mutter, gesturing to the scattered kernels.

"First off, that's your fault for sneaking up on me," she counters. "Second, why do you care what I do when you're not home? Weren't you on a date?" She chews the inside of her cheek, avoiding my gaze. "I figured you wouldn't be back until later tonight—if at all."

"Why would you assume that?"

"Because you were out late and said you were with a *friend*," she says in air quotes. "Everyone knows that's code for a date."

I rest against the wall, folding my arms across my chest. "Are you jealous, trouble?"

Seems like a fitting nickname, considering she's always finding new ways to challenge me, whether she means to or not.

A blush tinges her cheeks as she leans down to pick up popcorn pieces from the couch and puts them in the bowl.

"What? No. It's rude to expect dinner at a specific time and then not show up. That's all."

"Uh-huh."

She's totally jealous.

I could set the record straight and admit I was with Dawson, but I bite my tongue. Let her believe I was with someone else. Maybe a little envy will make her rethink her decision of letting me go and remind her of what she missed out on.

Once Fallon has finished picking up popcorn from the couch, she places the bowl on the coffee table and turns to face me, putting her hands on her hips.

"Are you going to apologize?" she demands.

"For what?"

Her lips press into a thin line. "Tossing my hundred-thousand-dollar tuna."

"In my defense, it smelled like it had been dragged out of the dumpster, and I just assumed it was another way you were trying to get at me."

Her glare hardens. "That wasn't an apology."

"Wasn't meant to be."

She exhales deeply, fire flashing in her eyes. It's supposed to be intimidating, but I have to hold back a laugh at how ridiculously adorable she looks, trying to glare me into submission.

"I can't wait for the peace and quiet when you're gone," she mutters.

"I'm counting down the seconds," I shoot back, more annoyed by her indifference than anything else.

As we stand off against each other, I'm acutely aware of the sweet scent of vanilla and oranges that surrounds me, and it takes everything I have to resist the urge to lean in and inhale deeper. Her blue eyes flicker to meet mine, and for a second, I forget what we were talking about. There's been an unspoken shift in our dynamic. Lately, our sparring matches have started to feel more like a reason to stay within each other's space, both refusing to admit anything has changed.

I take a step back, running my hand along my neck. "I'm going to bed. I'll see you in the morning," I say.

Earlier, I told her I'm heading to Aspen Grove tomorrow for the holidays. It can't come soon enough—another day spent in close proximity, and I'd be closer to crossing a line I vowed I never would.

CHAPTER 9

Fallon

I GLANCE AT THE CLOCK ON THE MICROWAVE TO SEE THAT IT'S 5:45 a.m. Harrison should be heading out any minute to spend the holidays with his family in Aspen Grove. He'll be gone for two weeks and requested an early breakfast before he leaves for the airport.

My traitorous heart dips, an unwelcome pang of disappointment settling in my chest as I imagine how quiet the apartment will be without him. It must be the solitude I'm dreading, not his absence in particular.

At least that's what I'm telling myself.

I refuse to acknowledge that Harrison's comment about being out with someone last night got to me. But the memory of my nails grazing his chest and the heat of his lips pressed against my neck from that weekend we spent together played on a loop in my mind. The idea of him out with another woman and the possibility that he'd spend the night with her ignited a jealousy I couldn't shake.

As irritating as his arrogance is, and despite never missing a chance to argue with him, I've recently caught myself looking forward to seeing him. It's a troubling revelation, given our history. Did I learn nothing the first time? Apparently, I need constant reminders to keep my emotions at arm's length where Harrison is concerned.

The one bright side of his absence is that I'll get a reprieve from his pranks—at least, I hope so. The past few days have been nerve-wracking. The suspense of Harrison's next move has left me constantly on edge. No doubt this is all part of his plan, to leave me second-guessing and uneasy until he returns.

I'm hunched over the kitchen counter, typing out a new recipe for smoked salmon cucumber bites, daydreaming of the day I can serve these at my own restaurant.

I glance up from the computer screen when Harrison strolls into the room. He's in dark wash jeans and a white button-up with the sleeves rolled up to his elbows, the fabric straining over his forearms. When he runs a hand through his hair, the subtle flex of his muscles makes me lose my train of thought.

Oh my god.

Knowing he works out is one thing, but seeing the results firsthand is another. Even after all these years, he still looks like he's a star athlete.

In a three-piece suit, he's the epitome of power and devastatingly handsome. But in casual clothes, he's dangerously alluring in a different way. My throat tightens, schooling my expression, but resisting him feels like a losing game—even the devil is charming.

Against my better judgment, I steal another glance, lingering a second too long. When his gaze meets mine, my pulse spikes, and I quickly duck my head, praying the heat rising in my cheeks isn't too obvious.

He smirks. "Careful, stare too long, and you might go cross-eyed."

I shake my head. "Just wondering if you purposely buy shirts too tight or if you left yours in the dryer too long." I lick my lower lip, thinking about what that physique looks like sans clothes.

"Well, at least I'm not the one having trouble looking away," he says smugly.

"Right. Only when I'm in shorts and a hoodie. I remember," I remark with a sly grin.

He glances at the ground, and I catch a glimpse of what might be a smile, but I can't be sure. When he meets my eyes, he straightens his posture, his shoulders rigid.

"Do you have my breakfast ready? I was planning to eat it on the way to the airport."

I'm not the only one who gets frustrated by how easy it is to enjoy our banter when we're meant to be at odds. It's probably for the best that he's going out of town. A little space should help me think straight—unless it has the opposite effect. What's the saying? Distance makes the heart grow fonder?

I clear my throat, nodding. "Yeah, it's right here." I walk over to the oven, pull out the meal I prepared earlier, and place it in the bag on the counter. "I figured you'd eat on the go, so I made you a breakfast burrito along with a few other snacks I whipped up last night—homemade hummus with carrot sticks, a strawberry parfait, and a couple of gluten-free apple cinnamon muffins since airport food isn't conducive to your diet," I say, offering the bag to Harrison.

He looks at the bag with a slight furrow to his brow. "You made all this for me?"

"It's my job to look after you… uh, I mean your nutrition." I press the bag into his hands, his expression caught somewhere between shock and gratitude.

It's not a big deal. I just wanted to make sure he doesn't eat anything that could make him sick while traveling. The simplest way to do that is to send him with food. Doesn't change the fact that I'm just doing my job.

Harrison slips the food into his backpack. "Thanks. I'm going to head out, okay?"

"Yeah, have a good trip," I say, with a small wave.

He leaves the room, and soon after, I hear the front door click shut. An unexpected ache spreads through my chest, but I'm quick to dismiss it. It's only because the holidays make me nostalgic for my parents. It has nothing to do with Harrison leaving.

Right?

Ready for a distraction, I take a seat at the kitchen counter and open my laptop. I've just opened up the document for my cookbook when my phone pings.

Harrison: There's are a couple of vendors in the lobby with deliveries for you.

Fallon: It's supplies I ordered for an event I'm catering tomorrow at the New York Public Library.

Fallon: Should have asked if I could have everything sent here. Sorry.

Wow. Look at me trying to play nice.

Harrison: That's fine. Walter will let them up to the penthouse.

Fallon: Thanks.

Harrison: And Fallon…happy holidays.

I've just settled onto the couch to watch a murder mystery, armed with a bowl of popcorn mixed with Sour Patch Kids and a bottle of Diet Coke, when I hear a strange mewling sound.

What was that?

I shake it off, attributing it to my imagination running wild after a long day of preparing for the catering event I have scheduled for tomorrow.

My forehead creases when I hear the unmistakable sound of a cat meowing. I'm ready to dismiss it as my mind playing tricks until I hear it again.

I scramble off the couch, gripped with fear, as I follow the noise into the kitchen. My overactive imagination runs wild with potential headlines:

Woman Found Ambushed by Psychopathic Cat in Penthouse.

Penthouse Horror: Woman Attacked by a Ruthless Feline.

Cat Burglar Strikes Again: Woman Finds Feline Thief in Penthouse.

This is what I get for watching horror movies and listening to true crime podcasts—my mind running off the rails at the slightest noise.

When I round the corner, I come to an abrupt stop when I see a black-and-white cat on the kitchen counter, devouring the leftover salmon from dinner that I had set aside for a test recipe.

The cat is a pitiful sight, with a wiry coat, barely covering its bony frame. Its fur is matted with dirt and grime, and one of its ears is jagged and half-missing. A striking black patch of fur surrounds its left eye, lending the cat an edge of mystery. If you look past its disheveled appearance, it's kind of cute.

As I inch forward, the cat lifts its head mid-bite, fixing me with a glare and letting out a low hiss, warning me to keep my distance.

I hold up my hand in a show of peace. "I'm not going to hurt you," I vow. "Just curious how you got in here and when."

Great, now I'm talking to a cat. I really should get out more.

I rest my chin in my hand, unsure of what to do next. Then,

an idea hits me, and I dash into the living room to grab my phone and send a quick message before heading back to the kitchen.

Lila's tied up with a wedding today, so I text her to avoid interrupting her if she's busy.

Fallon: Help! There's a cat in Harrison's kitchen and I have no idea what to do.

Lila: Is that a kinky metaphor I'm not familiar with?

Fallon: Very funny. There's a literal cat eating my leftover salmon.

I snap a photo and send it to her.

Lila: He's a little straggly but still adorable. Why didn't you tell me Harrison had a cat sooner?

Fallon: Because he didn't tell me.

Lila: Are you sure it's even his? It looks like a stray.

Fallon: He lives in a penthouse, forty floors up. How would a stray cat get in here?

Unless...

Fallon: Oh my god, I think Harrison found a cat and left it here for me to deal with while he's in Aspen Grove for the holidays.

Lila: LOL

Lila: You've got to admit that's a good prank.

Fallon: Not helping.

Lila: What are you going to do?

I chew my bottom lip, glancing over at the cat, its greedy gaze flicking between me and the last bits of salmon. Has Harrison been hiding it in his office, or did he bring it in today? I'm tempted to call him and demand answers, not to mention to give him a piece of my mind, but that'll only give him the reaction he wants.

Fallon: I guess I'll take care of it until Harrison's back.

Lila: You sure? You've never taken care of an animal before.

Fallon: I'll have you know my plants are very much alive and thriving.

Lila: Ah, yes, very similar comparison.

Fallon: I'm glad we agree.

Lila: We need to work on your sarcasm detection, my friend.

Fallon: Remember when I said you could never be on my bad side?

Lila: You're going to do great.

Fallon: How do I tell if this cat is a boy or girl?

Lila: One second.

Lila: Just did a quick search, and it says to look at the area under the tail. Male cats have visible testicles; female cats don't.

Fallon: Lovely. Wish me luck.

Lila: You've got this!

I can do this, right?

After I slip my phone in my pocket, I slowly approach the cat and gently lift its tail, confirming he's a boy.

I sigh, stepping back. "You're a little demon, aren't you? Wish I knew your name." I notice he's missing a collar. "Hmm… what am I going to call you?"

The only response I get is a dismissive twitch of his unscathed ear.

"How about Cat?" I ask with a chuckle. "It'll do until Harrison gets back and tells me your real name."

Cat hisses at me, and a flick of his tail sends the empty bowl toppling to the floor with a loud clatter. I flinch at the sudden noise, but he remains unbothered. Instead, he gives me a slow, menacing glare before hopping off the counter and stalking into the living room like a king entering his domain.

I trail behind at a safe distance, my eyes widening in horror as Cat drags his claws across the bottom of the sofa, the sound of leather tearing making my stomach drop.

"Bad cat," I scold, wagging a finger in disapproval.

I'm careful not to get too close, afraid he'll attack me if provoked.

With one final swipe, he seems satisfied with his destruction and retracts his claws. He jumps onto the couch and settles in the middle of the blanket I left on the cushion, letting out a defiant hiss to defend his newfound territory.

I roll my eyes. "Fantastic. A demon cat with an attitude. Why am I not surprised you're as insufferable as your owner," I mutter, cautiously reaching for the remote, my bowl of popcorn, and my drink from the coffee table. I'm not about to sacrifice my snacks because a little tyrant has taken over the living room.

Making sure there's a substantial distance between us, I settle into the farthest corner of the couch, stealing glances at the unpredictable ball of fur. I'm clutching my treats against my chest like a shield against Cat's unpredictable mood. When he doesn't make a move to attack me, I turn on the TV, scrolling through the streaming services Harrison has until I find the horror film category.

"Now we're getting somewhere," I remark to the empty room.

It's ironic that Lila and I are best friends, considering her passion for all things Christmas and Hallmark movies. I'd rather spend my evening with haunted houses and vengeful spirits than cheerful townsfolk finding love in the snow.

That's the one upside to living with Harrison. He doesn't decorate for Christmas because he's always out of town. It's one less thing to remind me that aside from a few catering gigs, I'll be spending the supposed happiest time of the year alone.

"You better be okay with creepy twins asking you to play forever, or you might want to return to the kitchen," I warn Cat.

He shoots me another look of disdain before turning his attention to the TV.

"Okay, then," I say, hitting play on *The Shining*. Better to stick with something I've seen before if I want to avoid nightmares.

The next morning, I'm up before the sun rises, scouring the apartment for any supplies for Cat. After coming up empty-handed, I realize the only place I haven't checked is Harrison's office. Normally, I would ignore his request that it's off-limits, but I've already invaded the rest of his house. And aside from his spider stunt, he's left my personal space untouched.

It's the one line I'm not ready to cross…yet. But all bets are off if he pulls another stunt like leaving me alone with his cat without warning.

While I wait for the pet store to open, I whip up a fish and egg scramble for Cat, who's perched on the kitchen counter, eyeing me suspiciously.

"Do you have to judge me, too?" I ask, grabbing a spatula, folding the eggs with precision, making sure they're soft and fluffy. "I already have to deal with your owner's attitude, so I'd appreciate a little peace while I work."

Once I've finished prepping the dish and it's cooled, I place it in front of Cat. "Breakfast is served." He leans in, his nose twitching as he takes a tentative sniff, and recoils with a dramatic hiss.

I raise an eyebrow and shrug. "Suit yourself."

Not ready to give up, I leave the bowl in front of him and busy myself with cleaning up the aftermath of his breakfast. After wiping down the counters, I pull a loaf of banana bread from the oven that I made for Walter. I'll bring it to him once it cools and after my trip to the pet store.

I've just gotten the bread onto a cooling rack when the faintest sound of nibbling reaches my ears. I look over my shoulder to find Cat's already halfway through his breakfast, his face betraying a reluctant satisfaction. It appears he's not a fan of being watched while he eats—another thing he and Harrison have in common.

"I knew you'd like it," I say with a smug grin.

Satisfied that he's eating, I leave the room to get ready to leave the apartment. On my way out, I pull out my phone and send a text to Harrison.

Fallon: You do realize I'm going to prank you back, right?

Harrison: Not sure what you're referring to.

Fallon: Right, and I have no idea how salt got in your coffee.

Harrison: Are we speaking in riddles now?

The three dots dance across the screen and then vanish, making me wonder if he's ignoring me. Which leads me to picture what he and his family are up to. During the limited time I spent with them when I catered Cash and Everly's wedding reception, they appeared to be close-knit. Growing up, I wished I had siblings, and I can't help being a little envious of Harrison for the strong bond he shares with his brothers and sister.

After waiting for a response that doesn't come, I yank my scarf from the coat rack in the entryway and head out the door.

I refuse to let Harrison get to me any more than he already has.

The wind whips around me as I approach the apartment building, my arms weighed down with bags containing everything Cat could possibly need to be comfortable over the holidays—treats, a bag of catnip, and toys. The self-cleaning litter box I wanted was too heavy to carry in the subway, so I scheduled to have it delivered to the apartment.

The store attendant recommended a cat tree, but I opted not to order it. Serves Harrison right if Cat decides to shred the rest of his furniture. He's also not going to be pleased with the five grand hit on his card, but that's the price he pays for leaving me with Cat and no supplies to take care of him.

All this shopping for Cat has me a little giddy, and it's not just because I got to spend Harrison's money. I always wanted a pet as a kid. My parents promised I could get one on my thirteenth birthday, but by then, I was living with my grandmother, who hated animals and thought it was childish for me to want one. That woman has never had a problem tearing me down or reminding me that I was a disappointment.

She called me last week, but I let it go straight to voicemail. The only reason she'd be checking in is that she finally found out I quit working for Theo and wants to lecture me about my life choices.

Walter rushes to open the door when I get to the entrance.

"Thank you," I say, sighing in relief when I'm finally out of the cold.

"That's quite the haul," he observes, nodding to my armful of supplies. "Did you get a pet?"

I shake my head, adjusting the bags and brushing a strand of hair from my forehead. "No. Harrison left me with his cat while he's out of town." Walter steps forward to take a few bags from my hands, and I offer him a grateful smile. "Funny how I've lived with him for weeks and didn't know he had one. Did you?"

Walter scratches his chin thoughtfully. "That's curious. I've never seen him with a cat, but maybe he had all the supplies delivered in the past and had a vet come to his penthouse. There are other residents in the building who do that. Or maybe he recently got it."

I lower my shoulders. "That's what I figured since his fur is matted, and he smells like the sewer. Either way, Cat's a little demon, and I'm dreading our next standoff. He's already torn up the couch, so I can't imagine what he'll do when I try to give him a bath. I'd wait to make Harrison deal with it, but it can't wait."

Walter lets out a hearty laugh. "I love the name. Very original." He moves toward the elevator. "Come. I'll help you get everything up to Harrison's apartment."

"I appreciate it," I respond as I follow him. "There's a loaf of banana bread cooling with your name on it. I'll grab it for you to take once we get to the penthouse."

"I'd never turn down your food." Walter grins.

On our way up to the penthouse, I get another text from Harrison.

Harrison: Going through my credit card statement. I'm not sure whether to be impressed or horrified that you dropped $40,000 at Maison du Chef earlier this month.

Fallon: I replaced all the cooking supplies in your kitchen. I didn't want to risk anything being contaminated.

Harrison: Looks liked you bought out the whole damn store.

Fallon: You're lucky. I would have spent more, but they didn't have a tomato-red Dansk Enamelware pot.

Harrison: A what?

Fallon: It's nothing. There's just a particular pot my mom used when I was growing up, and it's been impossible to find one like it.

Fallon: Also, expect a charge on your card from Velvet Paw soon.

Harrison: Isn't that a pet store?

Fallon: Yup.

A smug smile plays on my lips as I put my phone back in my pocket. I'll let him stew about it.

I'll likely regret it, but I'm looking forward to Harrison's return. It's so much more fun giving him a hard time when he's here in person.

That's not the only reason you're looking forward to it.

A surge of irritation rushes through me, but I shut it down, pushing aside the nagging voice in my head. My interest in Harrison isn't personal—it's all about settling the score for the pain he caused and for the indifference he's shown me since coming back into my life. Yet, as I glance at my phone, his texts staring back at me, a flutter of old feelings stir beneath the surface, making me more concerned that it's more than just about getting even.

CHAPTER 10

Fallon

THE PAST WEEK HAS BEEN PURE CHAOS, JUGGLING catering events nearly every night for clients hosting holiday parties.

When I'm not cooking, planning menus, or restocking ingredients, I'm chasing Cat around the apartment, attempting to save Harrison's place from his reign of destruction. I was fine with a few claw marks to get a reaction out of Harrison, but Cat has declared an all-out rebellion against the furniture. At this rate, there might not be much of a penthouse for Harrison to come home to.

Cat is nothing short of a literal demon. The morning after I discovered him, I found the vase of flowers I had on the kitchen counter in fragments scattered across the floor, with water spread in every direction. The next day, he attacked the curtains in the dining room, scaling them like a jungle gym and tearing them to ribbons. And just yesterday, he wandered into the guest bathroom and treated the toilet paper like a ball of yarn, leaving a mess of shredded paper across the apartment.

I'm convinced he was either trained by an evil mastermind or is straight-up possessed. There's no other way to explain his behavior. The only time he isn't wreaking havoc is when he's curled up in my blanket, which he's since claimed as his own, watching horror movies with me on the couch. His favorite so far is *Poltergeist*. When I paused the movie to grab another Diet Coke, he wouldn't stop meowing until I hit play again. It's more proof that he's a hell spawn wrapped in fur.

It's two days before Christmas, and I'm catering a private art gallery in Chelsea. I'm prepping the ingredients and sauces for the dishes at the penthouse and will assemble everything in the kitchen at the venue.

My client requested crab cakes, so I'm making my signature lemon-dill yogurt sauce—always a crowd favorite. It's coming together nicely, but when I taste it, there's something missing. I set the spatula I'm using and grab a lemon from the fridge. When I turn back around, I find Cat sitting on the counter, next to the bowl, his green eyes fixed on the sauce.

"Don't you dare," I state sternly.

Before I can stop him, he bumps into the bowl, sending globes of sauce flying in every direction.

I blow out a slow breath, covering my face with my hands.

I've kept my temper in check, doing my best to stay patient whenever he creates another mess, but Harrison's so-called prank messing with my cooking is the final straw.

I don't bother trying to clean Cat's tail before marching out of the kitchen, my determined footsteps echoing all the way to Harrison's office, looking for the perfect payback.

"Off-limits, my ass," I mumble, pushing open the door with more force than necessary.

I peek my head inside, my eyes immediately landing on the

glass-top desk paired with an ergonomic chair. The desk itself is sparse, with only a monitor, notebook, and pen. On the wall behind his desk is a single photo of Stafford Holdings' Michigan headquarters, according to the nameplate below it.

At first glance, it's just another cold and impersonal space, matching the sterile vibes of the penthouse. It's apparent that Harrison doesn't like things that don't serve a purpose or that disrupt his desire for order.

That's why I'm perplexed when I glance over to the far side of the room where a custom display case has been built, designed to mimic a hockey rink's boards. It has built-in lighting, showcasing rows of sticks and several pairs of skates hanging from metal hooks.

Intrigued, my feet carry me farther into the room toward the display. On closer inspection, I notice several shelves filled with photos, signed pucks, and a collection of limited-edition hockey cards. The last thing I notice is a familiar jersey framed on the wall, triggering another memory of my weekend with Harrison.

I track his every move as he strides toward the bed, pausing to tug off his jeans and boxers. My throat goes dry as he crawls onto the bed next to me.

"God, you're so damn sexy," he murmurs reverently, his eyes raking over my naked body as I lie wanton on the bed.

My breath hitches as he teasingly traces his thumb around one of my nipples, his gaze never leaving mine.

I thread my fingers through his hair, tugging him closer. "I want your mouth on me. Now," I demand.

He smirks, bending to kiss the valley between my breasts, and I let out a low hiss when he flicks one of my nipples with his tongue. The small bud hardens at his touch, and he greedily wraps his mouth around it, biting down on the soft flesh.

"Don't stop," I cry out.

My nails sink into his scalp, my moans growing louder while he alternates between licking and biting my breasts, the fine line between pain and pleasure blurring as the sensations send me into a dizzying frenzy. I let out a pleading whine, trying to draw him back when he pulls away.

He chuckles, pressing a kiss to my forehead. "Relax, beautiful, we're not stopping until morning," he vows with conviction.

"I'm holding you to that," I tease.

A wave of heat spreads through me like wildfire as he sinks two fingers inside my tight heat.

"Fuck. You're so wet. I can't wait to be inside you."

"Not before you give me an orgasm with your fingers," I say with a smirk.

He slowly drags his tongue along the column of my neck as he adds a third finger, causing a strangled moan to pass my lips.

"Are you going to come on my hand like a good girl?" he whispers.

I nod, unable to speak.

My body coils tighter with each plunge of his fingers, and my back arching off the bed when he flicks my clit with this thumb, causing me to shatter around his hand. My head falls back on the pillow as I let out a cry of pleasure and plummet off the precipice.

I take a deep breath to steady my racing heart, a goofy smile spreading across my face.

Holy shit, this man is a god in bed. I don't think I've ever orgasmed so hard in my life.

"A god, huh?" Harrison grins, leaning down to tuck a stray piece of hair behind my ear.

I groan inwardly as I blink up at him, mortified. "Did I just say that out loud?"

Harrison's eyes crinkle with amusement. "Yeah, but no takebacks."

When my stomach rumbles he chuckles. "Let's order you something to eat—you'll need your energy for what I have planned," he adds.

Absentmindedly, I trace my fingers along his jawline, the stubble grazing my fingertips. "That's a good idea. After all, you promised we'd go all night."

"I always keep my promises," he whispers.

A sense of calm washes over me at hearing the sincerity in his voice. I believe him. Which makes me wonder if this could potentially be the start of something more than just a fun weekend together.

I place a chaste kiss on his mouth. "You better."

He climbs out of bed, stark naked and strides to the chair in the corner, grabbing the T-shirt and jeans he'd tossed there earlier, and puts them on. When he's finished, he rummages through his hockey bag and pulls out a jersey.

I sit up in bed when he walks toward me, clutching the sheet around my waist.

He holds out the jersey. "Put this on."

I raise an eyebrow. "Why?"

He leans in and gently cradles my face. "It'll make me so hard to see you in my clothes," he says, his voice low. "Now, arms up," he instructs.

Already caught up in the thrill of his possessive streak, I eagerly lift my arms as requested, letting the sheet fall into my lap. Harrison's gaze takes me in, his eyes dark as he studies me.

His gaze doesn't leave mine as he pulls the shirt over my head, guiding my arms through the sleeves in a slow, deliberate motion. His fingertips graze my skin as the fabric slides down my body, and once it's in place, he carefully tugs my hair free from the neckline, letting the strands loose down my back.

Harrison nods. "Perfect," he says, his approval ripples through me. "Tell me you'll spend the rest of the weekend with me," he adds, his eyes pleading.

"There's nothing I'd like more," I say with a sated smile.

A noise from down the hall has me snapping my head up, causing me to crash back to reality. It's probably Cat causing another disaster.

I glance at the framed jersey again, its silent presence a cruel reminder that I'm still bound to the past with no way to break free.

My vision blurs as a tear slips down my cheek, and I can't help but feel foolish. It might be naïve, but by the end of the weekend Harrison and I shared, I convinced myself he was different from the other guys I dated, including Jeremy.

Unlike my ex, who made me feel small and insignificant, Harrison had been eager and kind during our weekend together. Which is why his actions left me blindsided.

Even after the other waitresses gushed over rumors they'd heard that he'd been with several puck bunnies during the hockey season, I still believed that because we shared a meaningful connection, things would be different and that he'd actually give what we shared a real shot. Instead, I was just another tally on his stat sheet, a temporary indulgence to add to his collection.

I angrily swipe away another tear, scowling at the hockey sticks in front of me. The flood of painful memories, combined with having to deal with Cat's destructive behavior the past week, must have pushed me to the edge because I smirk when I spot a stick at the end with a white shaft and black blade. In my opinion, it's far too plain and could use a makeover. A wicked idea forms in my mind as a way to settle the score while having a little fun at Harrison's expense.

Hockey stick in hand, I head out of the office, glancing around to confirm no signs that point to Harrison being a cat owner. Which only adds to the mystery of Cat's sudden appearance. I'm still convinced Harrison picked him up before he left for his trip, thinking it would be funny to leave me to deal with a cat on a rampage. He'll regret it; I'll make sure of that.

Despite the mess he made in the kitchen, Cat doesn't deserve to bear the brunt of Harrison's bad decisions, and I have to admit he might be growing on me.

After running to the store to grab ingredients to remake my sauce, I went to the local art supply store to pick up blue and pink gems, rhinestones, glitter, and glue that now covers the dining room table. The hockey stick is laid out in front of me, its white surface now half-covered in sparkles.

With Harrison being out of town, I haven't had the chance to pull another prank on him, and there's something cathartic about getting back at him and reclaiming control. I'm buzzing with excitement, but there's a hint of nervous anticipation, too. He specifically told me not to mess with his hockey gear, and I push aside the smidge of guilt.

I recline in my chair, stretching my arms above my head, deciding a break is much needed. My project will be here waiting when I'm ready. Rising from the table, I go to the kitchen to grab a drink and check my phone that I left next to my laptop earlier.

Earlier, on my way to the craft store, I called Lila to check in.

Her brother's best friend is in town, and she's harbored a crush on him since she was in high school. I have a sneaking suspicion there's more going on between them than she's letting on. Unable to shake my curiosity, I type in Brooks' name on my computer, curious to put a face to the name.

Fallon: Girl! I just looked up Brooks Claus. He's hot AF!

Fallon: Is he as good of a kisser as you remember? He definitely looks like it.

Lila: OMG! I told you nothing happened. He's only staying with me because the inn is fully booked.

Fallon: You've had a crush on him since you were in middle school. This is your chance to act on it.

Lila: Oh, sure, because going after my brother's best friend sounds like a great plan.

Fallon: Life is short. What's worse, risking it or later regretting you never took the chance?

Lila: Don't you have a hockey stick to bedazzle?

Fallon: I couldn't decide between red rhinestones or silver glitter for the finishing touch.

Fallon: I think I'll use both.

Lila: Am I going to have to fly out there and intervene when Harrison gets back?

Fallon: I can handle him on my own, thank you very much.

Lila: You're not the one I'm worried about.

Fallon: Ha. Ha. Very funny.

Lila: I'm going to finish decorating for the wedding, but we'll chat later, okay?

Fallon: You can count on it.

I set my phone on the counter and go back to the dining room, admiring my work on the bedazzled hockey stick so far. It's turning out much better than I could have hoped for. Will Harrison be furious when he gets home? I'm counting on it. That's what he gets for saddling me with his cat from hell.

CHAPTER 11

Harrison

THE PAST WEEK IN ASPEN GROVE WITH MY FAMILY HAS been great. We don't often get the chance to all be together, so the holidays are extra special when we're under the same roof. The only problem is I haven't been able to get Fallon out of my head. Whether I'm caught up in family activities or working in my dad's home office, I find myself wondering what she's doing at that particular moment.

I've gone as far as texting her a couple of times. A few days ago, I asked for her gluten-free gingerbread recipe when my mom was looking for one, and yesterday, I asked for her advice on the best way to sear a steak—never mind that I've done it plenty of times before.

Now, after a long morning holed up in my dad's home office on back-to-back meetings, I'm unable to resist texting her again.

Harrison: Don't tell my mom, but your lasagna beats hers, hands down.

Fallon: Your secret is safe with me.

Fallon: How's your trip going?

Harrison: Good. My family goes all out for the holidays, so there's never a dull moment.

Fallon: Not working too hard, are you?

Harrison: Who, me? Never.

Harrison: Have any plans for Christmas?

Fallon: Catering a brunch in Brooklyn and a Christmas dinner on the Upper East Side.

My stomach churns. I shouldn't feel guilty, but the idea of Fallon being alone in my apartment for the holidays gnaws at me. I'm fortunate to have a close-knit family, and it makes this time of year that much more magical. No one should have to be alone for Christmas, not even Fallon.

Ready for a distraction, I head to my parents' kitchen to join in on our yearly cookie decorating tradition. There are bowls of icing on the table in every color, a variety of edible glitter per Lola's request, and candy cane pieces. I'm not a fan of glitter since it makes such a mess, but it's all about spending time as a family. And if Lola's happy, we all are.

My mom stands by the oven, taking out a fresh batch of cookies and slides them onto a cooling rack.

I notice a container of gluten-free ones she's set aside for me. Since I was diagnosed with celiac disease, she's gone out of her way to make sure all of my meals are cooked with separate utensils and cookware, careful to avoid any traces of gluten. She also has a cabinet dedicated to gluten-free foods, labeling everything clearly to avoid any mix-ups. It makes it so much easier to visit, not having to second-guess whether the food is safe to eat.

I step closer, pressing a quick kiss to her cheek. "It smells good in here. What can I do?"

She glances at me with a smile. "Go help your siblings with decorating. We've got twelve dozen cookies to decorate and less than two hours before we have to start delivering them."

I nod. "Sure thing."

It's her way of making sure we spend every possible moment together when we're all in town.

Mom pulls the oven mitts from her hands and sets them on the counter. "We're aiming for Pinterest-worthy cookies. I can't hand out ones that look like they were iced with a blindfold on," she calls out, making sure everyone at the table hears.

"If that's the standard expected, Marlow and Everly are the only ones qualified to decorate," Presley answers with a chuckle.

She's seated next to Jack, who's glued to her side. Their chairs are pulled close together, with his arm draped around her shoulder.

"You're doing great," Jack praises her. "The design on your snowflake cookie may be abstract, but it's bold and artistic."

"Aww, that's sweet of you, babe." Presley flashes Jack a grin, nodding to the uneven lines of icing and clumps of sprinkles. "But that's stretching the truth. It looks more like flies tangled in a sticky web than a snowflake."

"It's perfect because you made it, little vixen." Jack plants a tender kiss on her forehead.

"Love you," Presley murmurs, stars in her eyes as she gazes at him. She's totally smitten, and he's just as captivated by her.

"Don't worry, you can thank me for my supportive comments later," Jack smirks.

They fell in love two years ago during Christmas. When they got to Aspen Grove, Mom insisted they stay in Presley's childhood room with only one bed since they told her they were a couple.

She knew who Jack was the whole time, which is why I'm skeptical of anything she does.

"If you two get any cheesier, I'm going to have to bill you for emotional damages," Cash complains, mimicking a gag.

"You're one to talk," Presley quips, gesturing to Everly, who's perched on Cash's lap, his hand resting possessively on her hip.

Cash shrugs, giving a lopsided grin. "There weren't enough chairs for everyone, so we improvised."

Presley rolls her eyes, then turns her attention back to her cookie, frowning when she notices the icing dripping off the edges.

I take the only empty seat next to Cash and Everly. His gaze is fixed on her as she's immersed in decorating a Christmas tree, meticulously piping on green icing.

She glances at Cash, raising an eyebrow. "Afraid to get your hands dirty?" she teases.

He shakes his head, reaching out and swiping a speck of frosting from her cheek. "Nope. Just enjoying the view." He winks, licking the frosting off his finger.

"Maybe you two should take this somewhere private," I taunt, trying to keep a straight face. "Are you forgetting there's a kid present?" I nod toward Lola, who's drowning her snowman cookie in white frosting, her tongue sticking out in concentration.

Cash scoffs. "Oh, right. Like Dylan and Marlow are any better at keeping their PDA under control."

"We're literally just holding hands," Dylan says, lifting up their intertwined fingers. "That's tame compared to sitting on top of each other," he says, nodding at Cash. "Or exchanging those ridiculous googly eyes every five seconds," he adds, eyeing Presley.

"Yes, and even that makes it very difficult to decorate," Marlow teases as she puts the finishing touches on her gingerbread man's perfect smile with her other hand.

"Look how silly Waffles, Muffin, Jellybean, and Cheez-It look running around in the snow," Lola interrupts with a giggle.

Everyone turns toward the windows, looking out into the backyard to see Waffles bounding through the snow with three tiny furballs with floppy ears trotting closely behind him, yipping with excitement. My dad installed a doggy door leading from the heated garage to the outside, and even in the cold, they prefer it.

"It's going to be a pain to clean them all up when they come inside," Dylan grumbles, his voice softening as he glances at Marlow with affection. "Please tell me we're not adopting another dog anytime soon."

"Not as of now," she says vaguely. "But I make no promises if any others come to the shelter that fit with our family."

"That's what I thought," Dylan mumbles.

Marlow swats him on the chest. "You love our dogs, and if another came into the mix, you'd feel the same."

"You're right, sunshine." He assures her with a smile.

"Let's hope you have better luck training any future dogs than you did with Waffles and the puppies," Cash taunts with a playful smirk.

"Hilarious," Dylan responds dryly.

"I thought so." Cash grins triumphantly, squaring his shoulders.

"Leave your brother alone," Mom scolds as she brings over another tray to the kitchen table.

While everyone is caught up in conversation, my dad tries to sneak a fresh cookie, only for my mom to swat his hand away as she walks over with more cookies.

"What was that for?" He scowls.

"You've eaten three cookies and haven't decorated a single one. At this rate, there won't be enough to give to the neighbors."

He wipes his mouth with the back of his hand. "Someone has to make sure every batch is safe for consumption. It's a tough job, but I'm willing to make the sacrifice."

Mom sighs, shaking her head. "What am I going to do with you?"

Dad winds his arm around her waist, guiding her head down for a kiss. They might tease each other, but their love is undeniable. When Dad was still running Stafford Holdings and had a hectic work schedule, he always found ways to show Mom how much he cared—bouquets of flowers from the local farmers' market, weekly Saturday date nights, and love notes tucked under her pillow.

He stayed at Stafford Holdings longer than he wanted to, but he was concerned about leaving me to shoulder all the responsibility. Since retiring, he and my mom have been able to travel, attend cooking classes, and spend time working in the garden, filling their days making new memories and making up for lost moments. It's made all the late nights and sacrifices worth it to see them finally enjoy the freedom they've earned.

"Eww," Lola shouts, wrinkling her nose. "Kissing is gross."

Laughter erupts around the room. "Couldn't have said it better myself, ladybug." I wink.

"Careful, Harrison," Cash interjects. "You might change your tune when you meet the right person and can't keep your hands off her."

Fallon's face flashes in my mind, uninvited. Her blonde hair tangled in a messy bun, her lips curving into a half-smile when she's giving me sass, and her bright eyes lighting up when she's making one of her favorite dishes.

Though I've sent her a few texts, I've purposely avoided checking the cameras in my apartment. I turned off the notifications before I left, not wanting to give in to the temptation to watch her while she works in the kitchen.

The guilt persists, weighing on me as I can't stop thinking of her alone for the holidays. Even though she's busy catering events in the city, she'll be home at night. It strikes me that there are no decorations or a Christmas tree at the penthouse. I never bother since I'm usually in Aspen Grove and prefer a clutter-free space. I hadn't considered that Fallon might want a more festive atmosphere.

Before I can change my mind, I send an email to Cabrina, instructing her to have a tree delivered to my penthouse and to hire someone to decorate it. Mom would probably disown me if she found out I skipped putting up a tree, so this is the practical solution. It's not about wanting Fallon to be happy or making her feel at home for the holidays. That's the excuse I'm running with anyway.

CHAPTER 12

Fallon

I STIFLE A YAWN AS I APPROACH THE APARTMENT BUILDING. The event at the gallery ran late, but my client gave me a generous tip, bringing me one step closer to opening my restaurant. I've got a long road ahead, but at least I'm moving in the right direction, and eventually, all the early mornings and late nights will be worth it.

To my surprise, Walter is at the entrance, holding open the door with a cheerful smile.

"What are you doing here so late?" I ask.

"I'm covering for Dan so he could take his wife out to celebrate their anniversary," Walter replies as he ushers me inside.

I nod in thanks. "That's very kind of you."

"I'm happy to help him out."

"Are you still going to your friend's for Christmas?" I ask.

Walter and Pearl never had children, and he doesn't have family nearby. But that hasn't stopped him from becoming a beloved fixture in the community. He spends his weekends playing chess in the park and volunteering at the homeless shelter, and I'm fortunate to be among his friends.

"Yes, in the afternoon. I'll probably stop by the shelter in the morning to help out beforehand." He follows me into the lobby. "How about you and Cat? Any big plans? You could always be my plus-one."

I'm touched by his offer. The holidays are a difficult time of year, reminding me of all that I've lost. And I usually don't celebrate.

My grandmother hated Christmas, calling it a commercialized sham where people feigned affection. I was scolded whenever I got swept up in the holiday spirit, and at sixteen, she even made me throw away the small tree I had bought to put on my dresser. Her reluctance to celebrate stemmed from her obsessive need for control. And losing my dad, despite their estrangement, left her so bitter that she avoided anything that could evoke emotion or connection—including me.

She tried calling again this morning, but I let it go to voicemail. True to form, she didn't leave a message—probably annoyed that I won't pick up.

"I appreciate the offer," I say to Walter with a smile. "I'm actually catering a brunch in Brooklyn and a Christmas dinner on the Upper East Side, so it'll be a busy day. There's no predicting how Cat will meet his daily destruction quota. I have a hunch he doesn't take holidays off."

Walter chuckles. "Don't work yourself too hard."

"What's the point of work if not to provide a little distraction," I joke, though there is a hint of truth to my words.

I have one foot in the elevator when Walter calls my name.

"Yeah?" I hold my hand out to keep the door from closing.

"A delivery came for you earlier. It's in the penthouse," he says with a grin. "I think it'll do the trick in getting you in the holiday spirit."

"What is it?"

"Why don't you go up and find out?"

I laugh. "Alright, I will. Happy holidays, Walter."

"You too, Miss Fallon."

On the way to the apartment, I can't help but wonder what awaits me and if Harrison had anything to do with it.

When I walk into the penthouse, the first thing I notice is the smell of pine and cinnamon. As I move past the hallway, I see that the living room has been transformed into a winter wonderland. It's bathed in a soft glow from the twinkling lights on the Christmas tree in the corner. Strands of popcorn drape across the branches, nestled among red and white ornaments, with garland hanging above the fireplace. The room looks like it's straight out of a holiday catalog.

Upon closer inspection, I chuckle when I notice several custom ornaments—a bottle of Diet Coke, a cup of coffee, a spider, and a chef's hat with my name engraved at the bottom.

I'm struck speechless, my breath caught in my throat. I prepared myself to accept the quiet of the holidays without celebrating, convinced it's what I wanted. But now, seeing the tree, I realize that I needed this more than I could have imagined.

In stark contrast to my grandmother, my parents loved the holidays. The season was always filled with music, lights, and the comforting smell of cinnamon and pine filling the house. As a kid, my mom made it a tradition to let me decorate the tree. She never corrected my ornament placement or tried to rearrange things. She let it be my masterpiece, no matter how uneven or chaotic it turned out.

Those happy memories made the transition to living with my grandmother all that much harder. As an adult, I've always preferred to stay busy during this time of year, avoiding the reminder of how things used to be.

A printed note with my name in elegant script peeks out from one of the branches of the tree, catching my eye. My curiosity piqued, I pick it up to read it.

> Fallon,
> You can't have Christmas without a tree. I apologize for leaving without decorating the apartment first. I hope this makes up for it. The glitter and ornaments might not be my thing, but if it makes you feel more at home, that's all that matters.
> Merry Christmas.
> Harrison
> P.S. I hope you like the gift.
> P.S.S. Check the fridge for a peace offering.

Curiosity gets the best of me, and I head to the kitchen to check what's in the fridge. Inside, I find bluefin tuna in an insulated box, its deep crimson color visible through a layer of clear plastic wrap. A smile tugs at my lips as I run through the recipe for tuna poke bowls in my mind. I didn't expect Harrison would actually replace the tuna, and I admit I'm touched.

That's when I remember the mention of a present in Harrison's note. When I go back into the living room, I find a present under the tree, wrapped in shiny gold paper and tied with a big satin ribbon. It's a miracle Cat hasn't gotten to it yet.

I kneel down to open it, observing how heavy it is. As I

unwrap it and remove the lid from the box, my fingers tremble as I pull out the tomato-red Dansk Enamelware pot. It's identical to the one that my mom would use for all our family dinners. When my parents passed, I was only able to take a small box of photos and mementos with me when I moved to London. I always regretted not grabbing that pot when I had the chance. Now that I have one exactly like it, it's like a piece of my mom is here with me.

Harrison may not understand the significance of the gesture, but the fact that he paid attention speaks volumes.

Fallon: Thank you for the tree and the gift. You're more generous than I give you credit for.

Harrison: My sister's Christmas spirit must be rubbing off on me.

Fallon: How so?

Harrison: She has a holiday checklist, and this year, she enlisted the whole family to participate.

Fallon: What kind of activities are we talking about?

Harrison: Yesterday, she roped us into a Christmas scavenger hunt, and we had to trek around town in the snow.

Fallon: That doesn't sound so bad.

Harrison: Try getting stuck in a snowdrift with a bunch of kids and lugging a giant candy cane so large it could be a walking stick for giants.

Fallon: Those poor kids.

Harrison: I'll have you know I'm a pro with them. My niece Lola adores me.

Fallon: Do you bribe her?

Harrison: Sometimes.

Harrison: Did you check the fridge?

Fallon: Yeah. Thanks for replacing the tuna.

Harrison: It was the least I could do.

Harrison: What about the pot?

Fallon: It was very thoughtful.

Harrison: Is it what you had in mind?

Fallon: It's perfect.

Fallon: Why'd you do all this for me?

Harrison: Everyone deserves a little holiday magic.

My body shivers at his unexpected kindness, leaving me breathless.

Damn him for being so unpredictable. One minute he's being a jerk, and the next he's playing Santa, going out of his way to make sure I have a good Christmas. It's downright frustrating. Before, the line between us was clear, and staying mad at him was easy. Now that he's playing the nice guy, I'm thrown off balance, at risk of the defenses I've carefully built to start crumbling.

Fallon: This doesn't mean I forgive you.

Harrison: Likewise.

I should get rid of the tree and be done with it. I'm only staying with Harrison until I've saved enough to cover a few months' rent for a small storefront where I can open my first restaurant. My past with Harrison should be nothing more than a reminder never to trust a hockey player.

But I can't bring myself to toss the tree. The smell of pine transports me to Christmas morning as a kid. My parents would let me open one gift before breakfast, and then we'd make my mom's famous eggnog pancakes together, paired with her homemade cinnamon syrup. She would patiently help me pour the milk into the bowl and fold in the flour, making sure I didn't overmix the batter. Her hands would gently cover mine, guiding my every move, leaving me with a memory that stays close to my heart.

I brush away a tear as Cat enters the living room. My body stiffens when he notices the tree, but instead of reacting, he hops onto the couch and settles into the blanket in the corner, meowing loudly as he looks at the TV.

"Seriously?" I ask with a raised brow. "You can't comfort me like a normal pet?"

He meows louder, clawing the blanket, giving the TV another purposeful glance, clearly wanting me to turn it on.

"Fine, but don't think I don't see through your innocent act. You're plotting an attack on the tree, and I'm not letting that happen." After we watch a movie, I'll move it into my room to avoid it getting destroyed. "You might be sorely disappointed," I warn Cat. "Tonight, we're watching *Elf.*"

Caught in the Christmas spirit, I decide once I turn the movie on for Cat, I'm going to whip up a batch of my mom's pancakes for dinner. I've avoided her recipes in the past because it's been a painful reminder that she's not here with me. However, tonight feels like the right time to give myself permission to enjoy the holiday spirit that I've been missing since my parents died.

And, though much as I hate to admit it, I have Harrison to thank for that.

CHAPTER 13

Harrison

It's the day after Christmas, and I'm supposed to be reviewing year-end financial reports, but I can't focus. My thoughts kept drifting to Fallon and her message thanking me for the Christmas tree and gifts.

When Cabrina confirmed the delivery to my penthouse two days before Christmas, I anxiously paced my dad's office, waiting for Fallon to text me. There was no guarantee she would, but I couldn't help wondering what she thought of everything.

Until now, I've resisted the urge to check the security cameras. It's become harder by the day to ignore the pull to see Fallon's face. Ten days without giving in, and suddenly my restraint is ready to fold like a tower of cards all because of a silly thank-you text.

Checking on her is harmless, right?

She won't even know I did it if I don't tell her.

Against my better judgment, I open the security app for my apartment on my personal computer and pull up the feed to the living room first. I frown when I notice the Christmas tree and decorations are gone. There's no way she'd discard them that fast. Would she?

I check my office next. I made it clear it was off-limits. But I have a sneaking suspicion she might not have listened. When the live feed loads, nothing seems out of place—my desk is undisturbed, and the chair is exactly where I left it. But when I zoom in on the hockey wall, I spot a glint of something shiny that definitely wasn't there before.

I squint, rubbing the back of my neck. "What the hell is that?"

One of the hockey sticks I have on display is now covered with bright blue and pink rhinestones.

Fallon.

My hunch is confirmed as I scroll through the alerts and find movement recorded a few days ago. I click on the timestamp and watch her peek inside, her gaze scanning the room before landing on my hockey gear. She tiptoes closer to get a better look.

A sense of unease settles in my stomach when she stops in front of my jersey, staring at it as though she's seen a ghost. Her shoulders fall forward, and the light in her expression dims, replaced with a haunted sadness. Which leads to me remembering the last time I saw her and that jersey together in the same room, a moment I've tried to bury deep in my psyche.

I wake up to the faint scent of vanilla and oranges.

The first rays of sunlight filter through the window, signaling that morning has arrived.

Elizabeth and I are entangled in a mess of limbs—she's draped across my chest, her legs intertwined with mine, and her head nestled in the crook of my neck.

Last night, we curled up in bed with a bucket of popcorn mixed with Sour Patch Kids and ice-cold Diet Coke to watch A Nightmare on Elm Street.

She has a love-hate relationship with horror movies—loving the adrenaline rush but curses at every jump scare. Which explains why she sleeps with the bathroom light on.

My phone buzzes on the nightstand. I ignore it at first, but when it keeps going, a sense of unease settles in.

I disentangle myself from Elizabeth, easing her arm from my hip so I can get up. I pause when she stirs, letting out a soft moan, but within seconds, her breathing evens out.

Once I'm out of bed, I grab my phone and go into the bathroom, shutting the door behind me.

"Hello?" I whisper.

"Harrison." Mom's strained voice comes through the line. "Thank god you answered."

"What's wrong?"

"Your dad had a heart attack. He was getting out of bed to get ready for work when he grabbed his chest and collapsed." Her voice trembles as she struggles to get the words out. "It's not good. We're at Regional Mountain Hospital, and they were pumping on his chest the whole way here and…I'm scared, Harrison."

The room spins, and I'm gasping for air. My dad has always been a pillar of strength, someone I believed was untouchable. He taught me how to ride a bike and made it to every sports event I had growing up. Every Friday night, he brought home pizza to celebrate the end of the week with me and my siblings.

"Your father has been pushing himself too hard lately, working around the clock. I should have done more to make him slow down."

My mother crying has me moving at lightning speed.

I toss my toothbrush, toothpaste, and comb into the toiletry bag I had stored on the shelf under the sink. "Since when has Dad ever listened? You did everything you could, so there's no point in blaming yourself." I pause, grabbing my shampoo and conditioner from the shower, and toss those in too. "Listen, I'm leaving my hotel now to head to the airport."

"Okay." She sniffles. "Cash booked you a charter flight. It should be waiting for you when you get there. Please hurry, Harrison. In case your father doesn't…"

"It's going to be okay, Mom. I'll be there soon," I promise. "Where is everyone else?"

"Presley is pacing the hallway, and Cash is on the phone with Dylan."

"Okay, I'm going to hang up so I can finish packing. If you need anything else, call me back."

"I will, love you, Harrison," she says.

"Love you too, Mom."

Elizabeth is still sleeping soundly, and as much as I want to wake her up, I can't. Right now, my focus is on Dad.

I throw on a pair of pants and a T-shirt, and toss my toiletry bag and the clothes I wore last night into my duffle. My hand lingers over my jersey tossed on a nearby chair. Elizabeth wore it while we had dinner last night, but the second we were finished, she slipped it off, along with her shorts. With a crook of her finger, she led me to the bed, where I spent the rest of the night ravishing her body.

I put the jersey in my bag, and once I'm packed, I rush into the other room and grab a pen and the hotel stationery, scribbling down a note.

> Good morning, beautiful,
>
> My dad was hospitalized, so I have to go home to be with my family. Please don't be mad at me for not waking you up. You looked far too peaceful to disturb. This weekend was perfect, and I want to see you again…and soon. Order room service when you wake up and call me while you're waiting for your food.
>
> Yours,
> Mr. Hotshot

I scribble my number at the bottom of the note before leaving it on the nightstand and lean down to kiss Elizabeth on the forehead.

God, she's mesmerizing. It may sound like a cliché, but I've never met anyone who makes me feel so at peace. She's the calm in the storm, quieting the chaotic noise in my mind. Regardless of the uncertainties in my life, if Elizabeth is willing to take a chance, I'd like to see where this goes between us. I'll do whatever I can to make it work somehow, if she feels the same. I'd rather take the risk than be haunted by what could have been.

"See you soon, beautiful," I whisper as I leave the room.

Fallon never called. I felt silly, staring at my phone, willing it to ring. She never shared her last name, so I couldn't look her up. When I reached out to the catering company, they told me they couldn't give out private information and that the waitstaff from the hockey event were only contracted for one night and were paid cash. After weeks of obsessing over what could have been, I finally had to face reality. She was never going to call.

Shortly after I'd come to terms with it, I stumbled across a photo on the Stormbreakers' social media page. It showed several players posing with their families at a charity event. I was shocked when I recognized Fallon with her arm around Jeremy, one of the team's left wings.

She played me for a fool.

Of all the people Fallon could have moved on with, she chose someone from my rival team? I shouldn't have felt betrayed since we barely knew each other, but I couldn't shake the feeling that what we had would have been far more than just a weekend if she'd given us a chance. It hurt more than I cared to admit that she hadn't shared the same sentiment. I tried to ignore the resentment, but it kept twisting at what was left of my pride until I eventually gave in.

I pull myself from my thoughts, switching to the live feed in my kitchen, guessing Fallon is probably cooking breakfast. As I dial her number, I see her at the counter, kneading dough. A tablet is propped up in front of her, and when I zoom in, the screen flashes a title: *Cold Case Chronicles: The Silent Killer.* She has the podcast on speaker, the narrator recounting a baffling case of a silent killer who left no trace, haunting a small town for years. Her phone's sharp ring makes her jump.

"Shit," Fallon grumbles, yanking her hands from the dough and rushing to rinse them off.

She lets out an exasperated breath as the phone continues its shrill insistence. "I'm coming," she shouts to an empty room.

After quickly drying her hands off on a paper towel and turning off the podcast, she retrieves her phone from the pocket of her apron.

"Hello," she answers.

"Look at you branching out from horror movies," I tease. "Have they revealed who the killer is yet?"

"No, not yet. The narrator always builds up the suspense before—" She stops short, glancing toward the camera in the corner. "Wait a minute… are you spying on me?"

"Spying? No. Watching? Maybe." I lean back in my chair, propping my feet on the desk. "I've got to keep a lookout for trespassers who forgot boundaries, like ignoring instructions to stay out of my office." Her jaw drops as she glares at me through the camera. "Now would be a great time for you to explain why my hockey stick looks like my niece decorated it in one of her craft classes," I say, my tone heavy with accusation.

Fallon folds her arms, tapping her foot impatiently. "I warned you. If you hadn't left your demon—"

Out of nowhere, a cat I've never seen before scurries past Fallon and leaps onto the counter, stepping in the dough Fallon was kneading earlier before casually plopping in the middle of it, unfazed by her gasp.

"Must you always make a mess when I'm in the middle of

cooking?" she mutters before spinning around to face the camera. "This is all *your* fault." She jabs a finger in my direction. "How could you think leaving me with your demon cat for ten days would be funny? It's a low blow, even for you, since you had to know he was a menace. This isn't a prank—it's just plain cruel."

I furrow my brow as I process her words. I've never had a pet, let alone a cat. They're messy, unpredictable, and require constant care. I don't have time for that. Which begs the question, how the hell did a strange cat end up in my penthouse apartment? Based on Fallon's frantic response, it's clear she doesn't have the answer either. One thing I do know is that I'm certain it didn't wander into my penthouse on its own.

"How bad could it possibly be?" I ask, feigning innocence. "He's just a cat."

It's too entertaining watching Fallon get worked up over thinking the cat is mine to spoil it by revealing the truth. After all, I owe her a prank for bedazzling my hockey stick. Since she already thinks I left the thing behind as my own practical joke, I might as well go along with it and let her deal with the demon cat a little while longer.

She barks out a humorless laugh, fixing the camera with a sharp look. "Right. *Just* a cat. I must be overacting," she replies, her voice sweet and laced with sarcasm. "Like when I had to give Cat a bath, and he scratched me like a feral beast. Or when he at-tacked my plants, simply because they were in his way." She throws her hands in the air.

Seems like those plants are our shared nemesis.

"Wait. Back up. You named the thing Cat?" I cover my mouth with my hand, stifling a laugh.

I should probably be more concerned about the mess that's waiting for me when I get back to my apartment, but I can't help finding humor in how Fallon not only assumed the stray was mine but that she also went ahead and named it. She might be more rattled by this than any other prank I could have pulled, but I admit she has a heart of gold for taking care of what appears to be a psychotic cat.

She gives an exasperated sigh. "Why does everyone keep asking that? What was I supposed to call him? John Doe?"

"Who's everyone?" I demand.

She better not have had another man in my apartment.

"Walter, the doorman." She clarifies. "He was nice enough to help me carry up the bags from the pet store when I got everything Cat needed since *someone* conveniently left us with nothing," she mutters at the end.

Had it been any other man who helped her, or if Walter were thirty years younger, we'd have an issue. The idea that I'm even jealous of the idea of her with someone else leaves a bitter taste in my mouth.

"What makes you so sure it's a boy?" I ask.

"He's got the necessary parts," she explains as she shoots him a glare. "Though, I could have lost an eye when I was checking. He has a habit of hissing and swatting at anything that gets too close."

"Sounds like a real charmer," I chuckle.

I should come clean and admit he isn't mine, but I decide to hold off. Might as well let her think it was a practical joke for a little while longer. Serves her right for bedazzling my hockey stick.

"Thanks again for the Christmas tree and the gifts," she says begrudgingly, almost like it's painful to thank me for anything.

"If you liked the tree, why isn't it in the living room anymore?" I ask, curiosity getting the better of me.

"Still sticking to the story that you weren't spying on me?" she teases. "Cat would've used the tree as his personal jungle gym, so I moved it to my room."

"I see. And what about the other gifts?"

Fallon meets my gaze through the camera and smiles. "I appreciate you replacing the tuna." She tugs her lower lip between her teeth as she tucks a piece of hair behind her ear. "And the pot… I've been looking for that one forever. It was very thoughtful."

A dozen questions press at the back of my mind, but for once, I keep quiet. We're getting along for once, and I'm not willing to risk this rare moment of peace.

"You're welcome, I'm glad you—"

I pause when I notice Cat in the background swiping at an open bottle of Diet Coke on the counter. Before I can warn Fallon, he knocks the soda over, sending it crashing to the floor in a burst of fizz.

Fallon spins around, throwing her hands in the air when she sees the mess. "Cat, not again," she exclaims. "Harrison, I have to go." She hangs up and rushes toward the mess, wagging her finger at the cat.

I chuckle as I log out of the security system. I've just set my phone on the desk when my mom walks into my dad's office, a steaming cup of coffee in hand. "You were up early this morning, so I figured you could use this," she says, handing it to me.

She and Presley are obsessed with holiday creamers, so my coffee is never without one when I'm here.

My mom doesn't budge, studying me with an unreadable expression. I should have expected she had an ulterior motive to bring me coffee. With everyone visiting for the holidays, she hasn't had a chance to corner me, but it was only a matter of time.

I sit up in my chair, taking my legs off the desk. "Thanks for the coffee, Mom," I say, giving her a skeptical glance.

"How's Fallon? Did she have a nice Christmas? I hate thinking that she was all alone in your penthouse. Did her catering events go well?" She fires off questions, each one more frantic than the last. "That was her on the phone, right?"

I set my coffee on the desk and rub my temples. Of course, she was eavesdropping. That's what I get for not closing the door.

"Yes, Mom, it was. How much did you hear?"

She shrugs. "Not much. Who's Cat?"

Clearly, she heard more than she'd like to let on.

"A stray that somehow got into the penthouse."

Mom covers her mouth with her hand to stifle a chuckle. "And Fallon named it Cat? I like her sense of humor."

That makes two of us.

"That's one way to look at it."

"Are you keeping Cat?"

"No."

Which is why I've decided to cut my trip short. I was supposed to stay in Aspen Grove until after the New Year, but I have to get back to the city and deal with this cat fiasco before Fallon decides to keep it as part of her personal vendetta.

I'd be lying if I said I wasn't looking forward to seeing Fallon. It's been strange not seeing her every day after having shared my apartment with her for weeks. It must be the delicious food that I miss. My mom is a great cook, but Fallon has made it into an art. She has a gift of elevating gluten-free dishes, which are often mediocre, transforming them into flavorful masterpieces that leave me craving more, long after the meal is over.

"Do you mind if I go back to the city tonight?" I ask my mom. "I have some things to take care of that can't wait until after the New Year."

She nods with a wide smile. "It's no trouble. Should I call to see if I can arrange the private jet here in a few hours?"

My eyes narrow, noting the sudden enthusiasm is a sharp contrast from when yesterday she begged me to extend my trip.

I clasp her hand in mine, making sure I have her full attention. "Mom, Fallon and I are never getting together." It's best to set expectations now rather than give her false hope later.

"Oh, don't be ridiculous," she scoffs with a dismissive laugh. "I'm only being supportive. Why are you so convinced I'm playing matchmaker?"

Because she has a track record a mile long.

"I should go check on the breakfast casserole I have in the oven," she says, pausing at the door.

"Harrison, your father and I are incredibly proud of you. All we want is for you to be happy."

She steps out, and I'm left alone, thinking about the one woman I shouldn't want but can't get out of my mind. The truth is the weekend Fallon and I spent together ten years ago was one of the best damn memories I've ever had, and my reasons for being resentful are fading, piece by piece.

CHAPTER 14

Fallon

"Cat, get down from there," I snap with my hands on my hips. "I'm trying to make meatloaf for Walter, and the last thing he wants is your fur in his dinner."

He yawns, lazily stretching out on the counter, unimpressed with my scolding.

"Would you rather be out in the cold?" I ask, gesturing toward the snow falling outside. "Because you're making it hard to resist sending you on a little winter vacation."

Cat gives me a bored meow, refusing to budge. He's had plenty of time to size me up, coming to the conclusion that I'm not going to actually follow through on my threats, no matter how much I wish I could.

With a defeated sigh, I head to the fridge to pull out the chicken and rice I made earlier. Buying store-bought cat food didn't sit right with me after reviewing the questionable ingredients of some of the most popular brands. So, I'm sticking to homemade meals, even though Cat hasn't exactly shown his gratitude.

The second the container lid comes off, I glance over to see Cat lift his head, his eyes trained on the food in my hand. Aside from our shared affinity for horror films, meals are the only other area where we've found common ground. It's also my secret weapon to getting the little rascal to cooperate.

I take a small glass dish from the cupboard, scoop some chicken and rice in it, and take it to the other side of the kitchen, away from where I'll be cooking. After setting the bowl on the ground, I go about my business, putting the leftovers in the fridge.

Sure enough, Cat jumps off the counter and races to his dinner, not even bothering to acknowledge me.

I roll my eyes. *Unbelievable.*

I take out my phone, shooting a message to Lila.

Fallon: It's not fair.

Lila: What's not?

Fallon: You have a cute, cuddly dog who adores you, and I'm saddled with a demon cat who is hell-bent on making my life miserable.

Lila: I take it Cat is still giving you trouble?

Fallon: He hasn't stopped since he arrived.

Fallon: Just this morning, he dragged all of my shoes from the closet and chewed on the laces.

Lila: When is Harrison supposed to get back?

Fallon: Next week, I think. I should have asked him when he called earlier.

Lila: Wait. He called you?! Why?

Fallon: He checked the cameras in his office and saw that I tampered with his hockey stick.

I really hope he didn't see the footage of me when I saw his jersey. The last thing I want is for him to think I'm still hung up on what happened all those years ago.

Lila: What did he think of your bedazzling job?

Fallon: Judging by the volume of his complaints, I'd say he wasn't a fan.

Lila: The nerve of him.

Fallon: I know, right!? It took me hours, and he can't even show a little appreciation?

Fallon: He and Cat have that in common.

Fallon: Are you and Winston excited to move to California?

Lila: A little nervous, but Brooks promised we'll love it.

Fallon: Is now a good time to say I told you so?

Lila: For once, I'm glad you were right.

Fallon: I'm really happy for you and Brooks.

Lila: Thanks, Fallon.

I grab a disinfectant wipe and clean the counter where Cat had been. Once my workspace is spotless, I discard the used wipe in the trash and finish collecting the ingredients for the meatloaf. I carry them over to my workstation, along with a mixing bowl and baking pans.

When I'm in the kitchen, I lose track of the world around me. The rhythm of chopping vegetables, the sizzle of oil in a pan, and the fragrant smells that fill the room when a dish is cooking is almost meditative. These moments are my sanctuary, and I wouldn't trade them for anything. Normally, I don't cook with music on, but being in the apartment alone for the past ten days has made me crave some kind of distraction other than scary movies and true crime podcasts.

I connect my phone to the built-in speakers and hit play on my favorite soundtrack.

Now that my workspace is free of uninvited furballs, I begin prepping the meatloaf as I hum along to Def Leppard's "Pour Some Sugar on Me." I sway my hips, moving to the rhythm, stirring the ingredients along to the beat.

My hands move on their own accord, combining the ingredients with ease. After years of practice, my instincts are precise, and smell, taste, and muscle memory have replaced any recipe or measurements for my tried-and-true dishes.

Once I've stirred everything, I take the pans I've prepared and scoop a handful of the mixture into the bottom of each one.

As the chorus hits on the song, I can't resist singing along. My voice is a little off-key but full of enthusiasm, throwing my arms into the air like I'm on stage.

The thud of footsteps breaks my concentration, far too heavy and deliberate to belong to Cat. When I glance over my shoulder, Harrison is standing in the doorway, his gaze fixed on me and his expression unreadable. My traitorous heart skips a beat, and a blush creeps up my neck as I clutch my chest.

"Oh my god, you scared me," I say, trying to sound unaffected.

"Sorry, it wasn't intentional," he replies.

I nod, going back to molding the meatloaf into the pans and transferring the loaves into the waiting oven, pretending that I'm not affected by Harrison's unexpected presence.

As I wash my hands at the sink, the rustle of fabric and movement in my peripheral vision weaken my resolve. I glance over to find Harrison slipping off his jacket and draping it over a barstool. I'm unable to take my eyes off him as he rolls up his sleeves, revealing those damn forearms of his again—strong, veiny, utterly distracting. I swear they should be illegal.

My pulse betrays me, kicking into overdrive, and I bite the inside of my cheek, cursing how he always manages to rattle me with so little effort.

"Careful, or you might turn the kitchen into a swimming pool," Harrison says with an amused tone.

My brows knit together, realizing my hands are still under the faucet. "Oh." With a small shake of my head, I turn off the water and grab a towel to dry them.

"Weren't you supposed to be in Aspen Grove until after the New Year?" I ask.

He smirks. "Missed me that much?"

"Don't flatter yourself," I reply with a forced laugh, busying myself with straightening the dish towel.

After everything, I should be immune to him by now, but instead, I'm acting like a teenager with a silly crush. I should be fortifying my defenses, not letting my emotions get the better of me, and opening doors I swore I'd sealed shut.

CHAPTER 15

Harrison

DAMMIT.

I was convinced my fixation with Fallon was a result of our time apart, a fleeting illusion that would fade once I got back to New York.

I was wrong.

The sight of her knocks the air from my lungs—her hair falls in loose waves, framing her face, while her ocean-blue eyes and the tilt of her chin exude confidence.

When I walked into the kitchen, I was mesmerized when I saw her singing her heart out. I couldn't break the spell. Not when I had a front-row seat to the way she moved, carefree and lost in the moment. Her shorts molded to her ass, the fabric hugging every inch of her as she swayed her hips along to the music.

I shouldn't have stayed away for so long. The reasons I found her unbearable don't seem to matter so much anymore. Before

I left, I was ready for space, but now all I can think about is kissing her again.

"Now who's the one zoning out?" Fallon says with playful sarcasm. "Good thing you weren't the one using the sink, or the entire apartment would be underwater by now." She's leaning casually against the counter, a smug smile spread across her face.

"You had to have thought about me at least once while I was gone."

"Oh, I did. Every time I made it through a horror movie without interruptions or strolled through the apartment in nothing but my underwear." She smirks.

An image of her doing just that flits through my mind, and now I'm wishing I had peeked at the cameras at least a few more times while I was gone to see if there was any truth to her statement.

"Very funny," I say.

"I'd like to think so," Fallon says, moving toward me. "Don't forget, you were the one texting me while you were in Aspen Grove." My cock stirs as she takes hold of my tie and wraps it around her fist. "Multiple times, if I remember correctly." She tugs on it, pulling me in.

"You texted back," I counter, my hand slipping to the small of her back, bridging the space between us.

We're close enough to share a breath, but neither of us moves away. It's like the banter, and unspoken tension has finally spilled over, and we're locked in a silent battle of wills.

Our gazes clash, neither of us willing to surrender as the weight of our unspoken desire lingers between us.

"What are we doing?" she whispers.

"I'm not sure," I admit.

But I like it.

My finger follows the curve of her collarbone, while my other hand rests on her back. I'm tempted to lift her onto the counter and drag her sleep shorts off to see what sweet noises I can coax from her—still haunted by ones she made during our weekend together all those years ago.

Fallon's breaths come out in quick, uneven bursts, her eyes fixed on mine, mirroring the same confusion as me.

We aren't supposed to get along or whatever this is between us. Hell, if she could read my mind, she wouldn't hesitate to slap me for my wandering thoughts. Why does that make me so damn hard? My primal instincts don't care if I like her or not. They're consumed with thoughts of her full lips, her long legs secured around me, and my hands gripping her hips with unrestrained possessiveness.

My rational side is quick to remind me that she's my private chef—the one I'm supposed to despise—and getting too close is a dangerous game, no matter how tempting she may be. There's also the fact that she's taken over my apartment, and made it hers. Although, I admit the plants are growing on me since she's using the herbs in her food, making everything taste even better.

Then I'm reminded of the hurt Fallon caused and how I thought I mattered to her, only for her to prove that wasn't the case.

I stumble back, visibly shaken, and Fallon releases her hold on my tie.

That was a close call… too close.

A brief flicker of disappointment crosses her face before schooling her expression.

Fallon smooths out her apron, clearing her throat. "How was your trip to Aspen Grove?" she asks.

"Great. It's always a good time when my family is all in the same place."

"I'm surprised your parents let you leave early. Sounds like they take the holidays very seriously," she observes as she grabs a bottled water from the fridge, twists off the cap, and takes a drink.

My mom practically shoved me out the door, but I'll keep that part to myself—otherwise Fallon will ask why.

"They have the rest of my siblings to fuss over until the New Year. How about you? Did you and Cat have a nice time together?"

I'm asking for trouble by bringing up the topic, but I ignore the guilt rising in my chest in favor of my desperation for a confrontation to snap me out of this ridiculous attraction and reignite my irritation.

Fallon sets the bottle on the counter, narrowing her eyes at me. "Oh, you mean *your* feral cat who hisses whenever I get close?"

"That's the one," I answer, biting back a dry laugh.

He's not mine, but I can't resist playing along for a little while longer.

"Cat's living his best life, destroying everything in his path," Fallon answers smugly, motioning around the kitchen.

I take in my surroundings, including the claw marks on the wooden floor, the shredded curtains hanging in tatters, and one of the barstool cushions that has been reduced to tufts of stuffing littering the floor. I'm shocked I hadn't noticed sooner, but my focus was entirely on Fallon when I got here.

"Are you going to tell me when you got Cat and explain why you kept him a secret? Please say you didn't get him solely to mess with me," Fallon says, folding her arms as she levels me with a suspicious glare. "And did you really have to hide all of his supplies? Not that I minded the shopping spree," she adds with a smirk.

That explains the five-thousand-dollar charge at Velvet Paw.

"I didn't get him," I say, bracing myself for her reaction.

Fallon tilts her head, frowning. "Come again?"

"Cat isn't—"

I'm interrupted by something running across my shoes. I recoil, my eyes widening when I glance down to find the cat in question racing past us, hopping up onto the counter next to the stove to investigate a batch of muffins Fallon must have baked earlier.

"Cat, stop," Fallon shouts as she quickly moves to shoo him away.

He ignores her, sniffing the baked goods, nudging a muffin with his nose before tipping it over the edge of the counter onto the floor.

Fallon shoots Cat a sharp look, pointing an accusing finger at him. "You're even more of a menace than your owner, you little devil." She spins around to face me. "Do you see what I've had to deal with while you've been gone? He's the reason I bedazzled your hockey stick." I can't help but laugh, earning a glare from Fallon. "What is so funny?" she bites out.

"I'm sorry, but it's one thing seeing him misbehave on camera and another in person." I manage to stifle another laugh as Fallon's glare deepens.

She shoos Cat off the counter, earning an indignant huff before he hops down and sulks to the other side of the room.

"Why are you surprised? Obviously, you've seen him misbehave before. He's your cat."

I rub my neck. "That's what I was trying to tell you earlier. Cat isn't mine."

Fallon blinks rapidly, her expression hardening when she registers what I said. "Excuse me?"

"I've never seen that cat before." I nod toward the scruffy creature, noticing that part of his left ear is missing, only seeming to emphasize his rebellious streak. "And I sure didn't leave him with you while I was away to mess with you. You think the guy who lost his mind over some plants and throw pillows would be willing to trash his own apartment just to prank you?"

The chaos Cat has caused is almost enough to push me to the brink. But I remind myself that once he's gone, replacing the furniture and curtains and fixing the floors will be simple enough.

That's not the mindset I would have had two weeks ago. I'd have been in full-blown panic mode, angry at the state of the penthouse. However, despite Fallon's frustrations with Cat, I can tell she's fond of him. He's a handful, but I'm glad she had someone to keep her company over the holidays, even if he's a mischief-maker.

Fallon's eyes widen as she swats my arm. "Are you serious? Why wouldn't you tell me when we spoke on the phone?"

I shrug. "I figured I should handle it in person, and seeing your reaction is definitely priceless."

She rolls her eyes, throwing her hands in the air. "Oh my god, you're insufferable. Don't you dare ask for an apology about your hockey stick. You're not getting one after this stunt."

I cross my arms. "Wouldn't expect one anyway."

In the past, I'd be furious with her, and make sure she knew it. However, I've got more pressing issues to deal with, like Cat wreaking havoc on my apartment. It's just a hockey stick and I'll be the first to admit it was a damn good prank.

"I'll have Cabrina call animal control first thing in the morning. For now, we'll keep the cat in the bathroom before he can cause any more trouble." I move past Fallon, mentally mapping out how to corner the thing without losing a hand.

She grabs my arm, stopping me. "Wait! You can't call animal control." Her voice is panicked.

"Why not? In case it escaped your notice, there's a stray cat lounging in my penthouse." I gesture to the furry intruder who's now sprawled out on a cushion in the corner as if it's his personal throne, indifferent to the mess he left behind.

I press a hand against my face and inhale sharply. "Fallon, please don't tell me you're thinking about keeping the cat. We have no idea where he came from."

I'm still convinced there's no way he could have strolled into the penthouse alone. That means someone had to let him in, or he must've followed one of the delivery people through the lobby and into the elevator without being noticed. Which is hard to believe.

Fallon plucks a nonexistent piece of lint from her apron before lifting her gaze to meet mine. "What if I do want to keep him?" She casts a glance at Cat with sympathy in her eyes. "He's definitely a stray with no other place to go."

"Too bad. I have a strict no-pets rule." I move around Fallon to grab a paper towel and scoop up the muffin Cat left behind, tossing it into the trash. "Especially not one who thinks it's okay to tear up furniture and treat the kitchen like his playground."

Fallon squares her shoulders, moving toward me. "Cat is staying," she declares.

"What if I say no?" I counter, closing the remaining space between us.

She doesn't flinch or waver. If anything, her resolve only strengthens as she stands her ground. "Cat stays, or we both leave." She's so damn passionate. It's both exhilarating and exasperating.

I've wanted Fallon gone from the start, so why am I hesitating to let her walk out the door and take the cat with her? The obvious answer is her cooking. It's out of this world, and after not having it for so long, I admit I missed it.

Yeah, that's definitely the only reason I don't want her to go. It has nothing to do with my inability to stop thinking about her. Or how badly I want to trace my hand along her jawline and feel the pulse in her neck against my thumb.

I rake a hand through my hair, exhaling sharply. "Fine. Cat can stay for now," I mutter, my patience wearing thin. "But you need to take him to the vet to make sure he's up to date on his shots and doesn't have fleas. We also have to figure out how to stop him from causing damage. If he ruins any more furniture or messes with my meals, he has to go."

"Oh, thank you, Harrison.," Fallon exclaims. "You have no idea how much this means to me."

I freeze when she throws her arms around me.

Her appreciation sends a ripple of warmth through my chest,

leaving me feeling unexpectedly content. Unable to stop myself, I wrap my arms around her and lean into her hug.

"You're welcome."

It's strange, but with Fallon in my arms, everything else falls into the background. I stop worrying about the flood of emails in my inbox, the financial reports waiting for me, and even Cat's destruction. All I can focus on is the warmth of her body and the soothing rhythm of her heartbeat against mine.

She goes rigid when she realizes we're in each other's arms and slowly removes her hands from my shoulders. I'm forced to let her go when she steps back.

"Sorry, I got carried away," she says, glancing at the ground.

"It's fine." I do my best to sound unaffected as I dismiss it with a shrug.

Fallon turns to glance at the clock above the stove. "Dinner should be ready in an hour. I'm making meatloaf, and I'll whip up a salad and potatoes to go with it once I've prepared something for Cat."

I pinch the bridge of my nose. "You've been feeding the little terror gourmet meals?"

She nods. "I wouldn't skimp on his food or he'll revolt. Mealtime and horror movies are the only things we've managed to bond over."

I hold out my hand. "What do you mean you've bonded over scary movies?"

"Cat loves them. He meows uncontrollably when I have to press pause or when they end," Fallon says, like she's talking about a friend, not a mischievous creature with fur.

"I'm going to regret letting him stay, aren't I?"

Fallon grins, patting my chest. "Probably."

CHAPTER 16

Fallon

THE NEXT MORNING, I'M BACK IN THE KITCHEN, AND I realize how much I missed it. I catered a few events while Harrison was away, but it's far more satisfying cooking meals for clients every day and having a steady routine. For breakfast, I'm making a gluten-free quiche with caramelized onions, mushrooms, spinach, shredded cheddar cheese, eggs, and cream.

Harrison mentioned that he liked it, and figured it would be a nice gesture to make it for him as a thank-you for letting Cat stay. An unexpected warmth fills my chest at the fact that he agreed. Part of me figured he might grab the little guy by the scruff and boot him to the curb in retaliation for me bedazzling his hockey stick. But instead, he handled it with more patience than I expected.

Maybe the carefree and thoughtful man I met all those years ago is still under that hard exterior.

I put Cat in the bathroom with his bed and toys, wary of letting him roam free. Not only would he try to sabotage breakfast, but he'd probably create another mess, and I'd prefer to keep the peace between Harrison and me. I'll make it up to Cat with a turkey and green bean medley when Harrison leaves for work. Plus, the bathroom is nearly as big as my bedroom, so he has plenty of space to explore, and undoubtedly, cause more chaos.

All bets are off if Cat goes on a rampage and ruins anything else in the penthouse, like another piece of furniture or scuffing Harrison's shoes. So, I'll do my best to prevent any other mishaps.

Once I've plated the breakfast bowl, fresh fruit, and coffee, I carry the tray into the dining room, stopping short when I find Harrison at the table, reading the newspaper with his reading glasses on. The sight of him wearing them will be permanently etched in my mind, and it's totally unfair how good he can make something look that's so ordinary.

I avert my gaze, checking the clock to confirm I'm not late. "Were you waiting on me?"

Harrison folds the newspaper and sets it aside. "No, I just wanted to get a jump on the day after being out of town for so long."

I nod, setting the tray in front of him.

He stares at the quiche as if it might bite him first. "Why did you make this today?"

I frown, shuffling from side to side. "Because you said you liked it."

Harrison furrows his brow. "That's the only reason?"

I guess we've pulled one too many pranks if he's this skeptical of me being nice. Then again, given how we've butted heads since I arrived, I suppose I can't fault him.

"Yes. I swear." I cross my heart with my finger. "I was hoping we might call a truce, at least for now."

Harrison leans forward in his seat, eyeing me warily. "Why? Afraid I'm plotting payback for my bedazzled hockey stick?"

I shake my head. "No."

Okay, maybe a little.

Harrison digs into the quiche, briefly closing his eyes as he savors the first bite. "This is even better than I remember," he remarks.

"I'm glad you like it," I say. Wanting to let him eat in peace, I slowly move toward the kitchen. "Have a good day, Harrison."

"You too, trouble."

I turn away from him, concealing the small smirk on my lips, secretly enjoying the fact that he gave me a nickname.

Harrison: I won't be home until late, so don't worry about dinner.

The tightness in my stomach eases. I agreed to cater an event tonight under the assumption that Harrison would still be out of town. The topic slipped my mind during our exchange, and I was worried he might not be okay with it.

The pay for this event was too tempting to turn down though. The Mavericks, the local pro hockey team, is sparing no expense to ensure their players are well-fed before and after the game. I wonder if Harrison ever attends their games or uses their training facility. Some mornings, he leaves with his hockey gear, so he's obviously practicing somewhere.

I've always been curious about why he left hockey. As a rookie, he was already one of the league's best players with a promising future.

The season following our weekend together, a friend invited me to a hockey game. The Huskies happened to be in town to play, and despite my resentment toward Harrison, curiosity won out. I hoped that seeing him would bring closure to the mystery of his disappearance that left me with so many unanswered questions. But when I arrived, I was shocked to learn that Harrison wasn't on the team anymore. No explanation given. I'd always assumed he was traded to a new team or something, but now I know that wasn't the case.

Fallon: Okay. I'll leave a couple of turkey sandwiches in the fridge in case you're hungry when you get back.

Harrison: Thanks.

Harrison: Are you going out tonight?

Fallon: Why do you ask?

Harrison: Don't want you roaming the city alone or meeting up with some weirdo.

Fallon: Weird how?

Harrison: Like someone you matched with online.

Fallon: Since when do you care who I date?

Harrison: I don't.

Fallon: Sure.

Harrison: I can't have anything happen to you. No one else can make a quiche like you can.

Fallon: Admit it. You're worried about me.

Harrison: I'm late for a meeting.

Fallon: Can't wait to tell you all about my date later.

Harrison: So, it is a date?

Fallon: Don't you have a meeting to get to?

Harrison: If I say yes, are you going to ignore my question?

Fallon: You know me well.

A smug smile tugs at my lips as I slip my phone into my pocket. There is no date, but Harrison doesn't need to know that. Let him stew about it. I'd be lying if I said I didn't enjoy the idea of him being jealous. Not that it means anything. Except the flutter in my chest suggests otherwise.

After making the sandwiches for Harrison and giving Cat an early dinner of leftover turkey and green bean medley, I head out.

The team eats three hours before their game, so I have to be ready in advance. Fortunately, I was at the arena yesterday to handle the deliveries and prep the ingredients. All that's left now is to assemble everything when I arrive.

The apartment lobby is quiet when I head downstairs, and Walter is thumbing through a sports magazine at his desk. The moment he notices me, he stands up.

"Good afternoon, Miss Fallon. Heading out?"

I nod. "On my way to a catering event." I hold out a box of gluten-free chocolate chip cookies. "These are for you. I wanted to make you dinner, but I ran out of time after prepping."

He waves me off. "Nothing beats your homemade sweets. Thank you."

"Always." I smile as I adjust my bag on my shoulder. It's

heavier than normal since I brought some of my own kitchen supplies with me.

"Where is your event?" Walter asks.

"The Ironblade Arena, for the Mavericks game. If Harrison gets back before I do, tell him I'm on a date, will you?" That'll get a rise out of him.

He arches a brow. "Do you know where Mr. Stafford is tonight?"

I shake my head. "No."

"Does he know you're catering?"

I let out a short laugh. "No, but I doubt he'd care."

Walter laughs, quick to cover his mouth. "I'm not so sure about that."

I furrow my brow. "Why do you say that?"

He waves his hand to dismiss me. "Oh, it's nothing."

My gaze sharpens. He's hiding something, but I'm not sure what.

He glances at his watch and ushers me out the door. "You better go, or you'll be late," he says, deflecting.

My suspicions that he's hiding something from me are long forgotten as I pull out my phone to check. "Shoot, you're right. Looks like it'll take forty minutes to get there with traffic. Thankfully, the food is already prepped so I don't have to worry about hauling everything across town."

He opens the front door for me. "Have fun." He waves as I dash down the street.

"Thanks, Walter. Wish me luck."

"You'll do great." He winks. "And who knows? The night might hold a surprise or two."

CHAPTER 17

Harrison

AFTER A LONG DAY AT THE OFFICE, I HEAD TO THE Mavericks game. I've missed the past few while I was away, and tonight seems as good as any to check in with the guys. Being part owner of the team means I enjoy the perks of their success without dealing with the majority of the responsibilities that come with managing the players and staff. I get VIP access to all games, private events, and post-game parties, though I rarely attend anything other than the games themselves unless it's a fundraiser.

I have an office at the arena and stop by at least one night a week to review financials, meet with management, and review upcoming events. It's helped me reclaim a piece of what I lost when my hockey career was cut short. While I don't regret stepping away to work for my dad, it made me realize how deeply the game shaped who I am and how much I still needed hockey in my life, even if in a different capacity.

I yank my tie loose around my neck and recline in the back seat of the car service that's taking me to the game.

Irritation prickles under my skin at the thought of Fallon on a date. How dare she mention it casually like it wasn't a big deal. My jaw tightens as I run a hand through my hair. On second thought, it would be better if she was dating. Maybe then I could stop fixating on that smug smile of hers or the desire to draw her close and brush my nose along her neck as she watches me with lust in her eyes. But damn, just picturing another man with his hands on her makes my blood boil, jealousy burning hot through my veins.

Before I can spiral further, my phone buzzes.

Mom Want's More Grandkids

Mom: Harrison, are you okay? You haven't checked in.

Mom: We miss you.

Presley: I'm changing my vote to Harrison for Mom's favorite kid.

Cash: Me too. What the heck, Mom? He's the one who left early.

Harrison: For the record, she practically shoved me out the door on my way out.

Mom: Yes, you all abandoned me and your father tonight to play games at Dylan's.

Dylan: We asked you to come.

Mom: Who schedules game night for 8pm? That's too late.

Cash: Hey I shoveled the driveway this

morning. That should earn me a 'Get out of Jail Free' card.

Mom: That was very kind of you. You're forgiven.

Cash hearts message

Presley: And just like that Cash is the favorite again.

Dylan: How come no one ever thinks I'm the favorite?

Cash: Two words. Middle child. It's a tough gig.

Dylan: Like you would know. Mom treats you and Presley like the babies of the family.

Mom: For the last time. I. Don't. Have. Favorites.

Presley: I think we broke Mom.

<Cash has renamed the group chat "Mom Doesn't Have Favorites">

Harrison: Are you all texting in the same room?

Dylan: Yes. I better go. Marlow's giving me the side eye.

Mom: Don't stay up too late. Love you all very much.

Harrison: Love you too, Mom.

I tuck my phone into my pocket as the town car pulls up to the arena, and I breathe a sigh of relief. This place has become like a second home, a refuge from the constant demands of running Stafford Holdings.

When I returned to Aspen Grove after my dad's heart attack, I immediately stepped in as his intern. With Mom keeping him sidelined, I stayed by his side, learning everything about the business. It wasn't long before I realized just how much he had on his plate, so I made the difficult choice to step away from playing professional hockey and go all in at Stafford Holdings. It was a responsibility I'd been putting off, but it was time to accept the role I'd always known was mine, whether I was ready or not.

Before I became CEO three years ago, I held various other roles across the company, gaining firsthand experience in every department. My dad made sure I earned the title of CEO and was capable of handling its demands when the time came. Early on, I took on as many responsibilities as I could to ease his burden and reduce his stress. After everything he's done for my siblings and me, it was the least I could do.

There was no chance I was going to let one of my siblings take over when they all had their own dreams. Dylan would have stepped in if he'd been asked, but he'd never shied away from wanting a family. When Lola came along, she became his priority.

My toxic trait is putting everyone else's happiness first, even if it means sacrificing my own. Not that I would change it. My family is my world, and I'd do anything for them. Hockey has always been my personal escape, and I'm fortunate to still be able to have it in my life in some form.

When I get to the players' lounge, Ryan greets me with a clap on the back. "Hey, man, I didn't think you could make it tonight."

Ryan Hicks is the head coach for the Mavericks, and someone I consider a good friend of mine. We both played for the Huskies, and he went on to have an incredible career as an elite goalie, posting record-breaking save percentages, and led his team to three championship trophies. After retiring from pro hockey, he went on to coach in the American Hockey League before being brought on to coach for the Mavericks.

"I had a change of plans and came home early," I say.

He crosses his arms across his chest. "Your mom let you do that? I thought she had you on a tight leash." Ryan has met her several times, so he understands how intense she can be.

"She's convinced that my private chef is about to become my new wife, so she was quick to rush me home," I mumble.

He chuckles. "Speaking of private chefs, I had the guys' pre-game meal catered tonight. With everyone taking some time off for the holidays, I want to make sure they returned ready to hit the ground running and perform their best."

I nod. "Good idea. Did you go with Central Park Catering again?" The last time they mixed up all the dietary requests, and a few of the guys weren't thrilled they had to go without their usual meals.

Ryan shakes his head. "Nah, I went to a holiday party last week at a friend's house, and they hired a private chef. She made *the* best mini crab cakes, and I was shocked to learn later on they were gluten-free. So, I figured if we hired her, you could eat something."

The team is aware that I have celiac disease and they go out of their way when they know I'll be at an event to make sure the food is safe for me to eat.

There's a low buzzing in my ears when I register what Ryan said.

Holiday party. Gluten-free. Her.

There's got to be other private chefs in the city who are women, catered holiday parties last week, and specialize in allergy-friendly food, right? There's no way he's talking about Fallon.

As my eyes drift across the room, a jolt of recognition sends my heart racing when I spot her near the table of food, replenishing a bowl of fruit. Her movements are smooth and controlled, her ponytail bouncing with each motion. She carries herself with a quiet confidence, shoulders straight, proving that she's comfortable in her own skin, even surrounded by a rowdy bunch of hungry athletes.

My frown deepens when Aleksandr, the team captain, comes to stand next to Fallon. He offers her an easy smile as he fills his bowl with what appears to be a second helping of pasta. He's only twenty-seven, but I'm certain he wouldn't be fazed by Fallon being five years older. She's strikingly beautiful, commanding attention without lifting a finger.

A red haze clouds my vision, and my jaw twitches when he leans in to whisper in her ear, and she laughs. I rarely hear the musical sound, and it's like a drug, drawing me closer.

"I'll talk to you later," I tell Ryan, not bothering to elaborate.

I move across the room with determination, oblivious to the players and staff who give me a wide berth as I pass. When I get closer, I can hear Fallon talking. "Everything to your liking?"

"Amazing. This pasta and turkey meatballs are diabolical." Aleksandr grins, taking another bite. "I never thought I'd be a fan of gluten-free food, but I'm pretty sure you're a magician because this food is damn good."

Fallon's cheeks flush, and my gaze moves to her shirt… no, not her shirt, a jersey. She's wearing Aleksandr's damn jersey.

Why the hell is she wearing that? Better question: Why does she look happy about it? Could they be dating? Puck bunnies flock to Aleksandr in droves, swooning over his thick beard, chiseled jaw, wavy blond hair that falls past the nape of his neck, and broad shoulders, which hint at a powerful presence on and off the ice.

Damn, I like the kid, and we have a solid rivalry during

workouts. But now I'm starting to think of ways to get him booted off the team if he's with Fallon.

"Thanks for the compliment," she says, flashing him a smile. "It's rare to hear someone appreciate my cooking."

What does that mean?

I compliment her cooking all the time… don't I? Now that I think about it, we're usually bickering when we're in the same room, but she has to know I like it. After all, I did text her about how much I liked her quiche. And I've kept her around even after she redecorated the apartment, bedazzled my hockey stick, and insisted we keep a feral cat that's out to get us. That counts for something.

"Your cooking is as irresistible as you are," Aleksandr says, his green eyes gleaming with a playful edge. "Can I see you after the game?"

"To get your jersey back?" Fallon asks. "Thanks again for letting me use it. I'm never this clumsy on the job, but I guess there's a first time for everything." She lets out a nervous laugh.

"It's no problem," he says, resting his hand on her arm. "Glad I had it in my bag. You can keep the jersey if you want. I'd actually like to take you—"

Hell no.

"Aleksandr, don't you have to get to the locker room to change into your uniform? Warmups are starting soon," I cut in, my tone cold.

Fallon's eyes widen with recognition at the sound of my voice, and her gaze shifts in my direction.

"Harrison?" she says with confusion.

Aleksandr glances between us, taking a step back when he senses the heated tension between us. "I better go get changed. It was nice meeting you, Fallon, hopefully I'll see you after the game," he says with a smug grin.

Not if I can help it.

"Yeah, of course. Thanks again for this." She tugs at the jersey, causing me to grind my molars.

"My pleasure," he answers. "Enjoy the game, old man," he says, shooting me a cocky grin as he passes, earning him a glare.

As soon as we're alone, I turn to Fallon. "I thought you had a date tonight," I whisper-shout.

Fallon fixes me with a dagger-like stare. "What are you doing here?" she asks, sidestepping my question.

"I'm part owner of the Mavericks."

Her lips part in a silent, "Oh."

"And no, I wasn't involved in hiring you for the event. The head coach was at a party you catered last week and was impressed."

I don't know why I felt it was important to clarify, but the look of relief on her face tells me it means more to her than she'd admit.

"Is there a particular reason you're wearing Aleksandr's jersey?" I question.

I'm not about to admit I overheard most of her conversation earlier.

Fallon smooths a hand over the jersey with an exaggerated flourish. "Oh, this? I spilled sauce on my shirt, and he graciously offered to let me borrow it. He's such a gentleman, right?"

I shouldn't have overplayed my hand and let her see how much it bothers me. Naturally, she's milking this for all it's worth.

"Are you still wearing your shirt underneath?" I motion to her, keeping my tone even.

She nods slowly, suspicion flickering in her eyes.

"Good. Take it off."

Fallon lets out a bitter laugh. "I don't know…" she muses, toying with me. "I think it looks great, and I do love the number ten."

"The only jersey you'll be wearing in the future is mine," I state, moving closer. "Don't make me ask again, trouble. Take. Off. His. Jersey."

Thankfully, the room has cleared out, aside from a few staff members to witness my unhinged reaction, but I couldn't care less what they think. My sole focus is getting that damn jersey off Fallon, even if I have to take it off myself.

Fallon's gaze sharpens, sizing me up. Whatever she reads in my expression must convince her I'm not playing around because she sighs in annoyance and yanks off her apron, dropping it on the table. However, she takes her sweet time with the jersey, slowly taking it off to reveal a tight white T-shirt that does little to hide the curves of her body.

She holds out the jersey for me. "Happy?" she deadpans.

My mouth falls open as I take her in, but I quickly snap it shut and say, "On second thought, you should put it back on."

Fallon shakes her head. "After the fuss you just made? No, you should take it, I insist." She pushes the jersey against my chest, and I begrudgingly accept it, unable to pull my gaze from her lithe body.

I wonder if Aleksandr would be pissed if I set his jersey on fire. At the very least, it's getting washed twice before he gets it back. No way is he putting it on with Fallon's scent clinging to the fabric.

The sight of her in another man's clothing is grating on my nerves, and all I can think about is the night she wore mine. I remember the way it hung low on her frame, the fabric reaching mid-thigh. She was effortlessly sexy, her long slender legs on display, like she was ready to walk down a runway.

It occurs to me that I'm acting like an overprotective boyfriend, which is ironic considering Fallon and I can barely tolerate each other. Or at least, that used to be the case. But standing here, staring into her piercing blue eyes, I can't deny that something has shifted for me.

When I glance at Fallon again, I frown, not wanting her to walk around in that fitted T-shirt with a red stain on the front. I take out a black button-up from my backpack. It's not my jersey, but it'll do for tonight. I'll just have to find an excuse for her to wear my one of my jersey's another time.

I like the sound of that.

"Here. Wear this." I put the shirt in her hands. "I don't want you in any other man's clothes tonight."

Fallon rolls her eyes. "Yes, sir," she retorts sarcastically.

"That's more like it," I say smugly.

She tugs on the shirt, buttoning it up, and tucks it into her jeans, adjusting the collar to give it a more fitted look. It's still unmistakably a man's shirt, and I like the idea of people seeing her in it.

I glance at my watch, trying to divert my gaze. "I better get going. I have to meet with some VIPs." I turn on my heel and head through the doorway before I do something drastic like throw her over my shoulder like a caveman.

"Thanks for the shirt," Fallon calls out after me. "But don't think this means we won't have a conversation about your brutish behavior later."

"Looking forward to it," I answer over my shoulder.

When I get to the hall, I take a quick look to make sure there's no one around before tossing Aleksandr's jersey in the trash. I'll gladly foot the bill to replace it, but this one has to go.

CHAPTER 18

Fallon

THIS IS THE FIRST HOCKEY GAME I'VE BEEN TO IN ALMOST ten years, and I'm having a great time. I was given a ticket for a lower bowl seat and decided to watch for a while since most of the prep for the post-game meal is done. I just have a few final touches to add before serving it.

I'm on the edge of my seat as the final seconds of this nail-biter tick away. The players move so quickly that it's hard to keep up, and the energy of the crowd is infectious, drawing me into the moment.

The other team has the puck when Aleksandr suddenly veers in the opposite direction, his movements sharp and purposeful. An opposing player is ready to break free, but Aleksandr cuts him off, intercepting the puck. The energy in the rink is electric as he sends it sailing toward number four, who's already moving toward the net, outmaneuvering the goalie and scoring the winning shot.

The crowd erupts into chaotic celebration, and I stand to cheer right alongside them.

My eyes drift to Harrison, standing in one of the private suites. From my seat in the stands, I have an unobstructed view and have been stealing glances at him all night. Thankfully, his focus has been on the action on the ice, his intensity matching that of the players.

Only this time, his gaze locks on mine, and I swear a smirk tugs at the corners of his lips. I narrow my eyes in response, irritation flaring at his earlier antics, demanding I remove Aleksandr's jersey in front of an audience. There's no chance I'm admitting that it was hot as hell… but damn his possessive behavior made my skin flush and a shiver run down my spine.

Now, here I am, wearing his shirt, the tension between us burning even hotter. His smirk widens, like he enjoys seeing me in it a little too much—and I hate how much I like it.

I avert my gaze and roll up my shirt-sleeves as I stand, and head to the kitchen to finish prep for the smoothie bowls and chicken wraps for the team. They'll have to shower and change first, so no doubt they'll be starving when they're ready to eat.

An hour later, I'm just finishing getting the food set up when the team files into the room. Aleksandr's at the front of the line, grabbing a chicken wrap, and coming around to stand by me so he's out of the way. He lets out a low groan after his first bite.

"I was right. You really are a magician. How do you make a simple wrap taste this ridiculously good?"

"It's the sauce," I answer politely, but I'm barely paying attention as my eyes drift around the room, searching for Harrison.

Despite my annoyance at his earlier behavior, a twisted part of me wants him to see me talking with Aleksandr again. My lips press into a thin line when I don't see him.

What's wrong with me?

"I see you ditched my jersey," Aleksandr remarks.

I blink, realizing he's talking to me. "What was that?"

He chuckles.

"Oh, right." I glance down at Harrison's button-up. "I'm actually not sure what happened to it," I admit sheepishly.

"Don't sweat it." Aleksandr pauses to take another bite of his wrap. "One of the guys mentioned Harrison made you take it off. I'm pretty sure I won't be seeing that jersey again."

My cheeks grow warm as I shift uncomfortably. "I'm sorry. I don't know what's gotten into him."

He smirks, waving me off. "I think I do, and the last thing I want is to be on his bad side."

Aleksandr might be a bit full of himself, but there's an undeniable sweetness about him. If I weren't living with a certain moody billionaire who happens to own the team, I might consider agreeing to go out with him. Then again, I don't feel a spark with Aleksandr and wouldn't want to lead him on. Unfortunately, I've always been drawn to the brooding, tall-dark-and-handsome type. Even though I wish I wasn't.

"You shouldn't be intimidated by Harrison," I say.

"I take it you haven't seen him on the ice. He's a powerhouse, and I'm not just saying that because he has influence over my career," Aleksandr replies.

It's not hard to imagine that Harrison is every bit as intense on the ice as he is in person. The idea of watching him in action, sweat glistening, muscles straining—my breath catches just thinking about it. Good thing I haven't had to watch him play, or I might be in more trouble than I already am.

I laugh softly. "He has control over my career too. I'm his private chef."

Aleksandr lets out a low whistle. "That explains so much."

I tilt my head, frowning. "Meaning?"

"Oh, it's nothing. I just wouldn't accept another man's clothes in the future if you don't want to ruffle his feathers again," he chuckles.

I nod, pretending to understand why Harrison cares so much if I wear someone else's jersey.

"Duly noted."

Harrison never shows up, making me even more vexed. He doesn't get to storm in and make demands, then hide out when he knows damn well I want to speak to him.

It's late by the time I'm finished cleaning up, and most of the hockey team and staff have went home for the night.

I adjust my bag on my shoulder, the strap digging into my sore muscles. A scalding hot bath is practically calling my name, and all I can think about is getting back to the apartment. Yet, as I walk down the hallway, the faint glow of the arena lights catches my eye, and the sound of skates carving through the ice drifts down the corridor.

Too tired to think it through but too curious not to investigate, I change directions, veering off toward the open double doors at the far end of the hallway where a Zamboni is parked off to the side.

As I get closer to the rink, the chill of the air hits me. I peek out to see a lone figure gliding effortlessly on the ice. When he looks to the side, his face comes into view, and my breath hitches when I see that it's Harrison. There's something mesmerizing about the way he controls the puck, his stickwork fluid and instinctive, a testament to years of practice.

I watch in awe as he shifts his weight, carving arcs across the smooth surface, his skates barely make a sound as they cut into the ice. With one swift motion, he lines up and shoots, sending the puck straight into the net with a clean shot.

It strikes me that I've never seen this side of him before—carefree, unburdened, content. This must be his escape, where the outside world fades away, and he's free to pretend he's still the rookie for the Huskies, chasing his dreams.

I'm contemplating what to do next when I notice a shelf stacked with skates in the corner. Before I can talk myself out of it, I grab a pair that look about my size and sit on the ground to put them on. They're a half-size too big, but I force the laces tight, hoping that'll hold them in place.

I slowly rise to my feet, pushing past the nerves, and ignoring the fact that I've only skated a handful of times. I'm not missing the chance to talk to Harrison without disruption.

Like a newborn calf learning to stand, I inch toward the edge of the rink, my knees trembling with each step. When I finally plant one skate on the ice, I cling to the boards, afraid of losing my balance.

"Fallon?" Harrison shouts across the rink. "What are you doing out here? Can you even skate?"

"I'll manage," I call out.

I stand tall as if I've done this a thousand times, even though my legs feel like jelly.

He glides toward me like it's the easiest thing in the world. "What were you thinking, coming out here by yourself? You could get hurt."

"I'm fine. I just need a chance to get used to it." I exhale sharply, holding out both my hands to try and stay balanced. "We need to talk, and this is as good a place as any."

He comes to a stop in front of me, setting his hockey stick against the boards so his hands are free. "And it couldn't wait until we were both on solid ground?"

Before I can answer, I start to teeter. Harrison encircles my waist with one hand, anchoring me in place.

"I can't think with you this close," I murmur.

He tightens his grip, laughter rumbling in his chest. "This better?" he taunts.

I huff. "You're insufferable, you know that?"

The air is icy, but the warmth from his body leaves me flushed, and my skin tingles, torn between desire and defiance.

Fueled by frustration, I push off him, convinced that if I create space between us, I can regain control of the situation before I'm consumed by the attraction I'm trying so hard to ignore.

Harrison's childish behavior makes it easier to stay composed, but it doesn't stop my heart from practically pounding out of my chest.

I turn and pick up speed to create more distance, and just when I think I'm finally getting the hang of this whole skating thing, the tip of my skate snags on the ice, sending me flailing, arms windmilling to try and stay balanced.

"Fallon," Harrison shouts behind me.

My eyes are wide with panic as I fall backward, Harrison catching me in his arms as we are sent sprawling onto the unforgiving ice. The impact knocks the wind out of us both, and Harrison lets out a low grunt.

"Oh no," I exclaim, my body crashing into his as I land on top of him with a hard thump.

"Fallon, are you alright?"

Genuine concern is evident in his voice as he shifts me in his arms to face him and props himself on an elbow. His touch is frantic as he gives me a once-over, his face etched with fear as he scans for any signs of injury.

"Does anything hurt?"

"I'm fine," I say softly. "I had you to break the fall."

He chuckles as he brushes my hair from my face. "Leave it to you to still make a jab after I saved your life."

I arch a brow in challenge. "That's a bit of a stretch, don't you think?"

"Can't be too careful where you're concerned."

"Why is that?" I ask, curiosity getting the best of me.

"Because for reasons unknown, the idea of you getting hurt sends a sharp pain through my chest," he admits, drawing me closer. His breathing is rapid.

Our faces are mere inches apart, and I'm drawn in by his chiseled jaw and the way he looks at me as if I'm the only thing that matters. A shiver travels down my spine when he traces his finger along the curve of my chin, and I'm mesmerized as he gently grazes my mouth with the pad of his thumb.

Harrison shouldn't have this profound effect on me, but the conflict warring within me since the day he came back into my life has only grown louder, refusing to be silenced.

"Mind explaining why you had a problem with me in Aleksandr's jersey?" I ask softly.

"Because it was his."

I lift a brow. "And that bothers you?"

"Yes."

"But you had me wear your shirt instead. It might not have your name on it, but it's still making a statement."

Harrison nods. "Exactly. It's not just anyone's shirt. It's *mine*."

His bold statement has our gazes colliding, holding each other in place.

"You're staring," I whisper.

"I can't help it when you're still wearing my shirt."

My skin tingles when he leans in closer, running his hand along my cheek. My heart races as his usual cold expression has been replaced with a tenderness that I've only seen a handful of times since our weekend together all those years ago.

"I really want to kiss you, trouble," he admits softly. "Now is your chance to tell me no."

Every cell in my body is screaming at me to speak out. This is a dangerous path to go down, and there's no guarantee we'll recover if we do. I'm supposed to despise this man, so why is the idea of his mouth on mine again so tantalizing.

One kiss can't hurt, right?

I place my palm over his hand, keeping it pressed against my cheek.

"I don't want to say no," I murmur.

The words are barely out of my mouth before Harrison crushes his mouth to mine, claiming me with a searing kiss. He lets out a low groan as he weaves his fingers in my hair, drawing me in. I run my hands along his chest, curling my fingers into his shirt. The steady rhythm of his heartbeat is a silent reassurance, anchoring me in the moment.

He tilts my head, deepening the kiss. I nip his bottom lip in response, moaning as I delve my tongue inside his mouth. God, I forgot how intense kissing him was—a heady blend of longing and fire, leaving no space for restraint.

Harrison rocks his hips against me, his bulge rubbing against my stomach. I look at him and am met with his eyes, dark with desire, as though he's ready to devour me whole. I'm not much better—my mouth still tingles from his scruff, my chest rising and falling like I've just sprinted a mile.

This feels too familiar.

A reminder of another time I was lost in his pleasure, only to be left with bitterness and regret.

I let out a stifled groan as I stretch out my arms and legs, my body deliciously sore.

We stayed up well into the night, having mind-blowing sex. He treated me like a queen, showering me with words of affection and praise, and I couldn't get enough. Agreeing to go to dinner with him on Friday was one of the best decisions I've made.

Although now that the weekend is over, I'm not sure where that leaves us. I guess I'll go back to my apartment, and he'll fly back to Pennsylvania, where the Huskies are based. But that doesn't mean I'm ready for this to end. Last night, Harrison alluded to the fact that he wanted to see me again, but it's hard to tell if he meant it or if he was caught up in the moment. The only way I'll know is if I ask him.

I reach over to the other side of the bed, confused when I find it empty and the mattress cold to the touch. Harrison must be in the bathroom or the living room having breakfast.

"Harrison," I call out, hoping he can hear me, and can coax him back to bed for another round.

There's no answer.

"Harrison," I say a little louder, frowning when there's still no response.

I climb out of bed, wrapping the comforter around me to keep warm.

I check inside the bathroom to find it dark and empty. After turning on the light, I take a quick peek in the mirror, mortified to find mascara streaks under my eyes, and my hair shooting out in all directions. I take a minute to wash my face, removing the residual makeup.

When I reach over to grab a towel to dry off, I pause midway when I notice Harrison's toothbrush and comb are missing from the counter.

That's odd.

I look down on the shelf below the sink, the nagging voice in my head growing louder when I notice his toiletry bag is also gone.

"Harrison, are you here?" I say with a shaky voice as I rush out to the living room, coming to a halt when I find it empty.

My heartbeat thunders in my ears as I rush back into the bedroom, confirming what I already knew when I find his hockey bag is gone. All that's left in the place is my purse and shoes.

I scan both nightstands, hoping he left a note, but find nothing. I sink onto the bed, burying my face in my hands, running through our weekend together, trying to think if I could have misinterpreted something he said to make me think it meant more than a fleeting connection.

How could I have been so foolish? I barely know Harrison, yet I spent the whole weekend wrapped up in him, believing what we shared meant more.

I was wrong.

God, I can't believe I fell for his charm. I was right to begin with. All hockey players are the same—charming, reckless, and only care about themselves.

Lesson learned.

It's like a bucket of ice water hits me when I remember how things ended last time.

God, what was thinking?

I wasn't. That's the problem. I let Harrison's good looks, his kernels of kindness, and possessiveness cloud my judgment.

When he left without a goodbye all those years ago, I was left to pick up the pieces, not only from my recent breakup but from the possibility that Harrison could have been a shining light in my otherwise lonely existence. Instead, he taught me that I can't rely on men and that I'm better standing on my own.

I've got to put an end to this.

I quickly climb out of Harrison's lap and scramble to the side of the rink, struggling to get to my feet.

"Fallon, where are you going?" Harrison calls out after me.

I ignore him, concentrating on keeping my balance as I shuffle toward the exit.

"Fallon, wait."

My heart races, the weight of what just happened sinking in. Harrison's probably going to kick Cat and me to the curb, and honestly, I'd rather move out myself than have to face him ever again.

"Fallon…"

Lost in my thoughts, I don't notice my skate slipping on the smooth ice again until it's too late. I shut my eyes, bracing for impact, when suddenly Harrison's strong hands land on my waist, pulling me safely into his chest.

CHAPTER 19

Harrison

ONE SECOND I'M FED UP WITH FALLON'S ANTICS, PREPARED to let her storm off, the next, the sound of her skate catching on the ice has me reacting without thinking. Thankfully, I'm already on my feet when she stumbles and my body reacts faster than my mind, closing the distance between us. My hands wind around her waist, and I pull her flush against me before she can fall.

Her hands cling to my shoulders, the steady rise and fall of her breath presses against my chest. I brush her hair back from her face, my fingertips skimming her skin, and she trembles beneath my touch. Every nerve hums with awareness of how her body seems to fit perfectly against mine, and the space between us practically buzzes, charged with a magnetic pull, drawing us closer.

Fallon's eyes darken with apprehension. "You can let go now. I've got this handled."

"Right, I can tell by the flawless way you almost face-planted," I retort.

She places her hands on my chest to create distance, and tilts her head. "I'd rather take my chances with the ice," she grumbles.

"You might think so now, but you wouldn't be saying that if you were nursing bruises or a concussion."

I lift her into my arms, carrying her to the safety of solid ground.

"Harrison, put me down," she protests as she clings to me, holding on for dear life as I skate across the ice.

I grunt in annoyance. "Dammit, woman, will you let me take care of you for once?"

"This is ridiculous. I'm not a helpless damsel in distress," she huffs, her grip tightening around my neck.

Her words are curt and dismissive, but her body tells a different story. The way she steals a glance at me every few seconds, thinking I don't notice. Her fingers curl tightly at the nape of my neck, and her breath hitches when I adjust my hold. For a fleeting moment, I revel in being so close to her—the warmth of her presses against me, the thrum of her pulse, keeping in time with my own.

Over the past month, we've put all of our energy into sparring, each argument a fight for dominance. Yet, as I hold her in my arms, that familiar spark I once felt has become a blazing fire. It makes me wonder if things could be different if I let go of the resentment I've been holding on to for the past ten years. Is it really worth letting it simmer until we're both consumed with nothing but bitterness? Or is it time to confront the past and break free of the chains that have kept me in an endless cycle of anger and frustration even before Fallon came back into my life?

As an athlete and CEO, risk assessment, tough decisions, and taking chances are second nature. So why have I avoided a real conversation with Fallon? It's not like me to shy away from difficult conversations. The difference is, for once, the stakes are personal, and the wrong step could cost me more than I'm prepared to lose—no matter how I've tried to convince myself otherwise.

When we reach the home team's bench, I carefully set her down and retrieve the blade guards I left there earlier. I slip them on before kneeling in front of Fallon to take off her skates.

She scoots back, her eyes as big as saucers.

"What are you doing?" she demands, her tone high-pitched.

"Taking your skates off so you don't break your damn neck when you decide to storm off again," I say sharply. "I promise you can go back to yelling at me in a minute, just let me take off your skates so you don't get hurt first."

Fallon sighs, crossing her arms in defiance as I kneel down to untie the laces. Her eyes burn into me as I trail my fingers down her jean-covered thighs. Even with the fabric of her pants between us, I notice the goose bumps rise on her arms, and her lip tucked between her teeth, fighting her reaction.

"You can't keep me here," she growls.

"You wanted to talk, so let's talk." I stay right where I am, sliding my hands around the right boot, pulling gently to lift it off her foot. "Why the outburst on the ice?"

"Kissing you was a mistake." She shrugs. "End of story."

"Bullshit." I take off her other skate and set it down next to the other one. "Ever since the day we saw each other at Cash and Everly's wedding celebration, you've been distant and harsh."

Fallon raises her hands in exasperation. "I can say the same thing about you, except you've been cold and calculated."

"Because I had every right to be."

Fallon blinks, her expression shifting from confusion to irritation. Before I can react, she pushes me back, sending me off-balance. She turns on her heel, leaving me there, stunned.

I rise to my feet, prepared to follow her, but she stops and spins around to face me.

Her eyes burn with accusation. "How dare you."

"Whoa, slow down," I say, holding up my hands. "I'm not sure what you're talking about."

"I knew you were a jerk, but this is a new low, even for you," she accuses as she steps toward me. "How do you think it felt waking up after one of the best weekends of my life, only to realize that you were gone," she spits out, her hands balling into fists. "You humiliated me beyond belief, but that wasn't enough for you, was it? You had to dig up old wounds and treat me like dirt because your ego couldn't handle that I wasn't still pining for you all these years later. I was just another one of your puck bunnies. Good for a weekend, only to be discarded." She exhales deeply, her lips trembling.

I furrow my brow, resting my hand on her arm. "Fallon, that's not what happened," I reply softly, hoping my calm tone will keep the situation from escalating.

She yanks her arm away from me and takes two steps back. "Don't you dare patronize me. I remember every detail like it was yesterday." She briefly closes her eyes, trying to hold in the emotion threatening to spill over. "I woke up to an empty bed, your side cold and empty without an explanation. I get that it was a no-strings-attached situation, but you could have said goodbye or at the very least, left a note."

I drag my hand across my face, the truth settling in—both of us have been clinging to distorted versions of events, and neither is accurate.

"Fallon, I did leave a note," I say, the words rough against my tongue.

She lets out a humorless laugh. "Are you serious? That's what you're going with? Why lie about this?"

I close the distance between us and take her hands in mine, waiting until she looks at me to speak. "I'm telling the truth. My mom called to tell me my dad had a heart attack. He was going into surgery, and there was a plane waiting. It all happened so fast." I swallow against the tightness in my throat. "You were still asleep, so I left a note with my number. I told you to call me while you had breakfast."

Her gaze drops to our joined hands as she bites on her lower lip and shakes her head in disbelief. "I checked both nightstands. There was no note," she whispers.

"I swear to you, Fallon, I never would've left after that weekend without saying goodbye. Hell, I even signed it *Mr. Hotshot.*"

A faint smile tugs at her mouth but quickly falls, her eyes lowering to the ground as she processes the new information. "I'm just…I don't understand. All this time, I thought you left without a word, and now you're telling me there was a note…" She trails off, her voice barely a whisper. "What did it say?" she adds after a brief pause.

Could it have been more than a weekend fling if things had turned out differently?

The unspoken question lingers in the air. Despite the ache forming in my chest, I know I have to tell her the truth, even if it's the most painful answer either of us wants to hear.

"I said the weekend was perfect and that I wanted to see you again."

Fallon's gaze lowers to the floor, and her hands go limp in mine. "What did you think happened when I didn't call you?" she asks, her voice so soft I have to lean in closer.

"I figured something came up, and you would call me when you could. I even reached out to the catering company, hoping to track you down, but they said they couldn't give out private information." I rub the back of my neck, dreading to admit the next part. "I figured you ghosted me, and a few weeks later, I saw a photo of you on the Stormbreakers' social media. You had your arm around Jeremy, their star left wing, and I assumed you were together."

"I moved to Florida with him after he signed with the team,

but he broke up with me after his first season. He wanted the freedom to date other people and didn't want to be tied down. That was a year before I met you. The team must have posted an old photo to their page." She chews on her lower lip, glancing at the ground. "I'm assuming you resented me because you thought I ghosted you?"

I slowly nod.

I'm not proud of assuming she used me for a good time before moving on, but there's no point in bringing it up now. I'd rather not reopen any more old wounds.

The silence between us is almost suffocating. We've both spent ten years deceived by our own assumptions, and our stubborn refusal to address the topic until now has only fueled the misguided distance between us. There's no time machine that can undo the damage we've done in the past month. Now we're left with the remnants of the resentment and hostility that we've allowed to fester between us, and I'm unsure how we move past it.

"I'm not sure where we go from here," Fallon admits, avoiding my gaze.

I tip her chin, guiding her eyes to meet mine. "Simple. We take it one day at a time and figure it out... together."

She lets out a dry laugh. "Simple? That's a stretch, don't you think? What if we can't get past this?"

There's the Fallon I know—stubborn, fierce, and unwilling to bend, even when it's for her own good. It's one of the many reasons I respect her, and why I'm done holding back.

"The best things in life are worth fighting for, you most of all."

I won't sugarcoat it—I royally screwed up. When I saw her at my parents', I should've swallowed my pride and taken the high road. Instead, I let my ego take over and cloud my judgment. There were plenty of moments in the past month where I could have put the past behind us, but I didn't. Every opportunity I had to bury the hatchet, I took another jab at her, convincing myself she deserved payback for what I thought was her ghosting me. Now I see I was wrong in more ways than one. Which begs the question, what happens next?

Now that I know the truth, I'm certain of one thing—I'm not ready to let her go. We've sealed our fate with another kiss, and I don't want it to be the last one. Everything has shifted, and I only hope it'll lead us toward something better.

CHAPTER 20

Fallon

WHEN WE GOT HOME LAST NIGHT, I WENT STRAIGHT TO my room, unable to quiet my thoughts—my weekend with Harrison kept replaying in my mind, every moment together still as vivid as ever. I always knew our bond was rare, and now I find out that he felt the same way. Still, it's difficult to escape the resentment I've carried for so long, assuming he ghosted me, and now I'm left trying to reconcile my perception of the past and what actually happened.

Harrison had a family emergency.

He left a note.

He wanted to see me again.

It's hard to wrap my head around the idea that a note existed all along, and I never knew it. The what-ifs mock me like a cruel joke.

After a restless night, I leave my cocoon of blankets, ready to ease my mind with the one thing that always calms me: cooking.

I'm in the kitchen testing a new recipe for gluten-free bagels when my phone chimes with a text.

Harrison: I'll be home by 6pm.

Fallon: Is everything okay?

Harrison: Yes. Just decided to leave work early tonight.

Harrison: Will you join me for dinner?

I don't respond right away.

He's never asked me to eat with him. In fact, he's complained whenever I've interrupted him while he's at the dining room table.

That was before he decided his main reason for disliking you wasn't warranted.

I'm not blameless in this situation, but it doesn't soften the blow. It's not as simple as flipping a switch when he's made me feel unwelcome since the day I moved in. A part of me wishes things could have stayed the same. It was simpler when I had a justified reason to despise him. Now I'm left facing the possibility that he was never the villain I made him out to be.

If I'm not careful, the lines could blur, and the looming fear of getting hurt again could quickly become all too real. A single kiss has already left me second-guessing every wall I've built to protect myself. The way his hands felt secured around my waist, and his lips molded to mine, a perfect fit. My phone chimes with another text.

Harrison: It's okay if you'd rather not.

Harrison: Why don't I eat out tonight so you can have some space?

I groan. How am I supposed to resist him when he's being so considerate? If he had been this thoughtful when we saw each other in Aspen Grove, I would have been done for, despite thinking he had left me high and dry after our weekend together.

> Fallon: No.

> Harrison: To which part?

> Fallon: Don't eat out.

> Fallon: I'll have dinner with you.

> Harrison: Perfect. I'm looking forward to it.

Determined not to overthink my decision, I set my phone to the side and wash my hands. Once I'm finished, I sprinkle a gluten-free flour blend on the counter and ease the dough I prepped earlier onto the surface. My palm presses into it, stretching and folding, the steady rhythm grounding me. Cooking is my safe space, where the outside world fades away. I especially enjoy trying new recipes—never knowing how they'll turn out but trusting the process anyway.

I'm startled when my phone rings.

My hands are now covered in dough, so I use my pinky to answer the call, then lean down, managing to wedge the phone between my shoulder and chin. I slowly straighten up, pressing the phone closer to my ear.

"Hey, Lila. Is everything okay?" My tone is tinged with worry. "It's still early there."

After a whirlwind Christmas romance with Brooks, her brother's best friend, she and Winston

moved to California. She says it's a trial run to see if they'll like it, but there's no question she'll stay. Brooks is head over heels for her, and she's equally as smitten with him. I'm so happy for them both.

I'm quick to squash the tinge of jealousy, reminding myself until very recently that a relationship was the last thing on my mind. Still, it's hard not to envy how Lila and Brooks fit together so effortlessly, making me long for that kind of bond.

"At the first hint of daylight, Winston insisted we wake up so I could let him outside," Lila says, the sound of a car starting in the distance carries through the phone. "The only downside to apartment living is the long trek to take him outside."

I press my hands into the soft dough, sprinkling a dusting of almond flour across the top when it starts sticking to my fingers.

"How is everything else?" I ask Lila. "Are you and Brooks still in the honeymoon stage?"

I hear a dog barking in the background followed by Lila's scolding voice. "Sorry, Winston's having a meltdown over some squirrels."

"No worries," I say, kneading the dough with more pressure to incorporate the almond flour. "Now, back to my question," I tease.

"I'd say so. Yesterday, Brooks took me to a lingerie shop and we lost track of time in the dressing room."

I pause what I'm doing, nearly dropping the phone in the dough. "Oh my god. That's so hot."

"Why does your reaction not surprise me?" Lila laughs. "Now, enough about me. Are we going to talk about *the* kiss?"

"There's nothing more to talk about," I hedge.

On my way home from the hockey game, I caved and texted Lila. It was a weight lifted off my shoulders to tell her. My emotions are in a tangled mess. There's no easy way to process the fact that my version of events of the day Harrison left me at the hotel was wrong. If he's telling the truth—and I believe he is based on the genuine confusion in his eyes—he left me a note, and I missed it.

It doesn't erase the hostility and disdain we've harbored, and there's no way to hit rewind. All we can do is navigate a fragile truce, where we decide if our shattered trust and unresolved feelings can be mended or if the walls between us are too insurmountable to climb.

Silence stretches on the other end of the line. "Are you still there?" I ask.

"Yup. Just waiting until you cave and give me more than that."

I leave the dough to wash off my hands before adjusting the phone next to my ear.

"The kiss was electric. That's not the problem."

"You don't have to decide anything right now," Lila reminds me. "There's nothing wrong with taking it day by day to see where it leads."

I lean against the counter. "He just asked me to have dinner with him, and I said yes."

"Fallon, that's great," Lila exclaims. "Just warn him that if he dares to hurt you again, I'm flying out there to kick his ass."

"At least that would be highly entertaining. Although there's no way Brooks is letting you get that close to another man."

"Good point. He doesn't even like when I hug his brother," she complains.

My mind drifts to how possessive Harrison was last night before the game. Initially, I was furious at his attempt to tell me what to do, but I can't deny that there was something undeniably sexy about the way he reacted to me wearing another man's jersey. It proves that he cares, making me all the more conflicted.

I hear more barking in the background. "Winston is chasing another squirrel, so better go, but keep me updated, okay?"

"Will do."

I set my phone on the counter and look over at Cat, who's lounging on his bed in the corner.

"Harrison and I are having dinner, so you know what that means? You're spending another night in my bathroom because

I'm not letting you make an already precarious situation worse. Don't worry, I'll make you some salmon delight. Your favorite."

As I finish pouring the wine, I hear the front door open. I found a bottle of Dom Pérignon at the store and couldn't resist picking it up as an ode to the night Harrison and I met. I take a final glance at the spread I've prepared—seared duck with pomegranate glaze, Brussel sprouts, and a grilled pear and blue cheese salad. Heat rises to my cheeks as I take in the lavish spread, realizing I might have gone overboard. I don't want Harrison to misinterpret my efforts. It doesn't mean anything… at least, that's what I'm trying to convince myself of.

The sound of Harrison's footsteps coming toward the dining room has me yanking off my apron and shoving it into the cabinet in the corner. I turn around just in time to see him walk into the room. He looks irresistibly charming in charcoal-gray slacks, a white button-up shirt, and a cobalt-blue tie. His hair is tousled, like he's run his hands through it all day, and he shoots me a smile.

That's new. I like it.

"Something smells delicious," he says, glancing at the food. "These are for you."

He comes to stand next to me with a vase of white tulips and a six-pack of Diet Coke.

He bought me flowers and my favorite drink?

"Thank you. What's the occasion?" I take the vase with shaky hands and set it in the middle of the table.

Harrison's fingers twitch at his side, his eyes darting around the room. "Dylan's fiancée, Marlow, is a famous artist, and flowers are kind of her thing. She once told me that white tulips symbolize forgiveness and peace, so I figured they'd be a good icebreaker for tonight."

"They're beautiful. Why the soda?"

"Because it's your favorite, and I noticed you were running low this morning when I grabbed a water from the fridge."

His thoughtful gestures catch me off guard. I'm more accustomed to practical jokes and indifference from him than acts of appreciation or kindness.

"Let's eat before everything gets cold," I suggest.

Harrison nods. "Good idea. You really outdid yourself tonight."

"No more than usual," I shrug, not wanting to admit I spent an extra two hours to make it perfect.

When I move to sit, he unexpectedly pulls my chair out, making me look at him with a raised brow. "Thank you, but since when are you a gentleman?" I tease.

He takes the seat next to me. "Never claimed to be one. Just trying to be on my best behavior."

"I was half expecting a whoopie cushion on my chair or for you to cancel altogether," I admit.

"I'll always show up for you, trouble." He leans in, a playful glint in his eye. "And if you want something to sit on, I'm happy to oblige."

My stomach does a flip, a slow burn spreading through me. Wanting to shake off the rush of nerves, I reach for the spoon to serve the food.

Harrison places a hand on my wrist. "Allow me."

I settle in my seat, watching as he serving me like he's the one working for me, and not the other way around. The gesture may be small, but it speaks volumes, showing me that he's trying to rebuild our trust, one meal at a time.

We sit in silence for a few moments while we eat.

I attempt to sort through the thoughts crowding my mind, mulling over what to say.

Luckily, Harrison takes the lead.

"I should've asked this sooner, but what made you come to New York?" he asks, swirling his wine before taking a sip. "Cash mentioned, as Theo's protégé, you could have had your pick of running any one of his restaurants. What made you leave that all behind?"

I concentrate on my plate, slicing the duck as I take a moment to gather my thoughts. "It sounds silly to hear it out loud. Who would turn down such an incredible opportunity to work as a private chef in a city they've only been to once, and no clients up before they arrived?" I plop a piece of duck into my mouth, savoring the tender texture as it melts on my tongue.

Harrison sets down his glass of wine, frowning. "Wait. Why wouldn't Theo help you find new clientele? He must have connections in New York."

"Oh, he has plenty, but I refused to let him use them."

I bite my bottom lip to stifle a smile, remembering the baffled expression on Theo's face when I turned down his offer to help. He was perplexed as to why I wouldn't accept his help. He even went as far as to offer me a year's salary to get started, but I couldn't accept it.

Theo started as a dish-washer in a diner and now owns twenty-seven restaurants, has written four bestselling cookbooks, and has hosted numerous successful TV shows. Although I'm lucky to have him as a mentor and often ask him for advice, I want to make a name for myself in the culinary world on my own terms, not because I relied on his success to get there.

I glance over to find Harrison staring at me. "What?"

"I'm curious—what inspired you to specialize in allergy-friendly food?"

"My mom had a severe nut allergy, and I watched her struggle for years with limited options for what she could eat. She had to double-check every menu, and item, making the simplest outings stressful." I pause to take a drink of my wine. "I also had a friend in culinary school who frequently went to the emergency room with crippling stomach pain. I took her several times and it was terrifying to watch her writhe in agony only to be sent home without any answers. When she was finally diagnosed with celiac disease, she was relieved that it wasn't something more serious, but also overwhelmed by what she could no longer eat and how few restaurants accommodated for it. With food allergies and celiac disease, especially, many people still believe it's a fad or a minor inconvenience and not worth taking seriously."

Harrison nods. "You're right. It was challenging in the beginning. When I was first diagnosed, I pretended it wasn't a big deal. I was embarrassed, thinking that everyone would brush it off. But after dealing with fatigue, excruciating stomach cramps, and multiple hospital visits, my mom flew into town and tossed everything with gluten out of my kitchen."

"I'm glad she did. You're lucky that she cares so much."

"Yeah, there are pros and cons to her meddling," he laughs.

"I might not know her well, but it's clear she wants what's best for you."

Harrison's mom is a stark contrast to my grandmother, who only cares about her image. The only thing I was good for was maintaining the illusion that she was a saint for taking me in, a fact she never let me forget. When I told her I wanted to be a chef, she was mortified, her disapproval unmistakable, as if my career choice would tarnish her carefully crafted reputation in England's elite circles.

It's been a long time since I've experienced the kind of love only a family can offer, and I hope Harrison realizes how fortunate he is to still have his mom around and advocating for him even when he might not appreciate it.

I'm grateful when Harrison speaks, pulling me out of my pity party.

"Hiring a chef made things easier, but he retired after a year.

Lucky for me, that brought you back into my life." He casually reaches over for my Diet Coke and takes a sip.

A hint of amusement plays on my face. "This is you on your best behavior? I thought you hated Diet Coke?"

Harrison tilts his head, a slow smile forming. "Turns out I was too quick to judge. In fact, I think I'm now hooked," he adds, taking another sip.

I don't think we're talking about soda anymore.

We resume eating, both sneaking glances after each bite. The shift between us is subtle but unmistakable. We've stepped into uncharted territory, and now that the truth is out, nothing will ever be the same. The question remains—is it for better or for worse?

"Is being a private chef the end goal, or do you have other plans for the future?" Harrison asks, breaking the silence. "I hope you don't mind me asking."

"I want to open my own restaurant, actually," I say, skewering a Brussel sprout with my fork. It's savory and delicious, and I swallow before continuing. "One that's completely allergy-friendly. It's hard to find places with safe options, and oftentimes, they're cross-contaminated. My dream is to create a safe space where people with allergies can dine without questioning what's in their food or worrying about getting sick."

"That's impressive." He takes my hand, his expression tender as his eyes meet mine. "Would you open it here or somewhere else?"

"New York City has won me over, and based on the research I've done for Theo's restaurants, there's a demand for this kind of place. I'm also writing a cookbook. It's still a work in progress, but the goal is to help people navigate cooking with food allergies at home too."

He leans in, closing the gap so our faces are almost touching. "I knew you were up to something in that kitchen besides cooking and plotting my demise with pranks."

"What about you?" I ask, tapping his chest lightly. "As I recall, you weren't exactly innocent, doing your best to get under my skin, hoping I'd hit my breaking point and leave. Don't think I didn't notice."

"That's what the spiders were for," he says with a rueful smile. "I'm really glad you didn't leave."

"Me too," I say softly.

I lean back in my chair, letting the comfortable silence settle in around us. Harrison carries the weight of the world on his shoulders. He's usually drafting emails, constantly on the phone, or rushing out the door. It's a welcome change to see him so at ease, and to be on the receiving end of his undivided attention, and I can't help but crave more of it.

CHAPTER 21

Fallon

After dinner, Harrison steps into his office for a work call, so I check on Cat. He's in the middle of tearing apart one of my towels, giving me a disinterested glance when I enter the bathroom. The bowl I left in the corner earlier has been licked clean, not a trace of salmon delight in sight. If I hadn't left him with an extra portion, the towel might not have been his only casualty.

When he notices the door ajar, he saunters toward it, meowing loudly, begging for freedom.

I widen my stance, blocking his exit. "I'll let you out if you promise not to cause any mayhem tonight. Harrison is in a good mood, and the last thing we need is to mess that up." When I step aside, Cat darts out of the bathroom, tail flicking as if taunting me to chase him.

"You better behave," I call out after him.

Not that there's much I can do if he doesn't. That cat has me wrapped around his finger, whether I like it or not.

I follow close behind, keeping an eye on him in case he tries anything mischievous. He makes a beeline for the living room, hopping on the couch, and curls up in the blanket he's now claimed as his. Once he lays his head down, signaling that he's not going anywhere, I take it as my cue to leave.

I head into the dining area to collect the dirty dishes from dinner and carry them to the kitchen. I set them in the sink and turn on the faucet for hot water. I'm just about to start washing them when Harrison strolls in, sporting gray sweats low on his hips and a dark green T-shirt stretching across his chest. He must have changed out of his suit after his call. Thank god he has no idea that seeing him in casual clothes is my kryptonite—otherwise, he'd probably wear them around the apartment just to torment me. Now I'm convinced that's why he has a problem with me wearing shorts and tank tops.

Damn our mutual attraction.

I've learned the hard way that taking risks with men—Harrison included—only leads to pain. It's difficult to imagine a situation where it could turn out for the better. If things go south, not only would I lose my place to live, but also the generous salary I'm using to save up for my restaurant.

Harrison steps behind me and nudges my shoulder. "Scoot over," he instructs.

I stay rooted in place, still dazed by how good he looks in sweats. "Why?"

"You made dinner, so it's only fair that I help with the dishes." He edges closer, his leg brushing against mine. "Why don't you rinse, and I'll load the dishwasher," he suggests.

I absentmindedly nod, and my senses becoming hyperaware of the subtle pressure as his proximity fills the space. A simple touch shouldn't hold this kind of power, yet here I am, fighting the urge to lean in.

To stay busy, I grab the dishcloth hanging from the faucet and swipe one of the plates clean. I hand it off to Harrison, careful that our hands don't touch, not wanting to risk inciting a spark I won't be able to extinguish.

Harrison moves with practiced precision, his motions steady and efficient. I scrub a dish, barely noticing the water running over my hand, too caught up in watching the way his thumb strokes the edge of a plate before setting it into the dishwasher. He exhales softly, a slow, controlled breath sending a shiver down my spine.

"I didn't peg you for a dishwasher pro," I tease. "I'm impressed."

He rolls his eyes. "My family may be wealthy, but my parents taught us the importance of humility and hard work, regardless of the balance of our bank account. That's why they raised us in Aspen Grove—to prioritize giving us a loving, supportive environment where we could stay grounded."

I swallow back the lump in my throat. His words trigger memories of living with my parents in a row house with peeling linoleum floors, where the heat rarely worked. My dad worked construction, and my mom waited tables at the diner down the street.

Every day after school, my mom waited for me at home, pulling me into a warm embrace when I stepped through the door. She always let me help her with dinner, and we'd gather around the kitchen table as a family. We didn't have much, but love was in endless supply. Now it feels like a relic of another life—a rare treasure, no longer within reach. I miss my parents so much. Their absence is a hollow space in my heart I'll never be able to fill, no matter how much time passes.

Harrison gives me a concerned look, wiping his hand on a

towel before resting his hand on my arm. "Fallon, where did you go just now?"

I stare at him, tempted to lie, but the truth weighs heavy tonight. "Listening to you talk about your family makes me miss my parents," I admit.

"Do they live in London?" he asks with genuine curiosity.

My heart clenches in my chest as I shake my head. "They passed when I was twelve," I whisper.

During our weekend together, I didn't open up about my past. I prefer to keep it private unless I'm close with someone—I've never been one to invite pity from strangers or acquaintances.

"I'm sorry, I had no idea," Harrison says, his expression softening. "That must have been really hard losing them so young, I can't even imagine." He gives my arm a gentle squeeze, letting the silence hang between us. "They must have been amazing people to have raised someone like you. If you ever want to talk about them, I'd love to listen."

I tilt my head, giving him a faint smile. "Thank you, I really appreciate it."

A few days ago, I never would have confided in him, worried that he'd make light of my situation. However, now I know the truth. He cares more than I give him credit for, and he's not judging me or making me feel less than. Instead, he's simply here, acknowledging the invisible scars I carry, and it means more than I care to admit.

Harrison's hand drifts down my arm as I speak. "I was just a kid when I lost them," I continue. "One minute we were having breakfast together. The next, the police were at our doorstep that night, telling me my parents had been in an accident on their way home from a concert." I glance down at the bubbles swirling in the sink, fighting back tears, the emotions I've kept buried for so long bubbling to the surface. "My mom had a passion for cooking, and because of her experience with her nut allergy, she often talked about opening a restaurant that catered to those with food allergies. But she never got the chance." The last part comes out in a whisper. "She was my inspiration to become a chef, and when I open my own place someday, it will be in her honor."

"That's a beautiful sentiment. I know there's nothing I can say to ease the pain of losing her, but I hope you know she'd be so proud of you," Harrison says gently.

"It means a lot for you to say that. I want to name it Catherine's Table, after her."

"I love that. It's the perfect name for a restaurant that will undoubtedly be a successful venture," he states. "You're a talented chef who has a gift for turning simple ingredients into a culinary masterpiece. Not to mention you're driven, determined, and have unwavering focus—traits every successful entrepreneur needs."

"If you say so." I laugh lightly. "My aspirations pale in comparison to building a billion-dollar empire."

One thing about Harrison is his unrelenting work ethic. He's like the Energizer Bunny, always on the move, fueled by ambition and impossible standards.

Harrison laughs dryly. "My grandpa and dad were the ones who built Stafford Holdings from the ground up. All I had to do was step in and take the reins." He briefly pauses to load several utensils into the dishwasher. "What you're doing is far more impressive. There aren't many people willing to put in the work and create a business from the ground up."

I offer him a shy grin, my cheeks flushing slightly. "It's definitely scary, but without risk, there's no reward."

I'm not used to his praise, so it takes me a moment to fully appreciate it, especially coming from someone as successful as him.

The quiet hum of the running water is a welcome distraction. It's impossible not to keep stealing glances at Harrison. His hair is tousled, giving him a roguish look compared to the polished man he usually is, while the scent of pine needles and fresh mint surrounds me, wrapping around me like a subtle invitation.

"You might break that if you scrub any harder," Harrison warns, nodding toward the bowl I'm washing.

"Oops," I say, heat rising to my cheeks.

Our hands brush when I give it to him, and my breath catches as the warmth of his skin sends a shiver up my arm.

Harrison has a way of making me react before I can think twice, and the fact that we're in uncharted territory only amplifies the charge in the air.

"There are only a few dishes left. Go take a break. I know you've been on your feet a lot the last few days," Harrison says, expecting me to obey without argument.

"I think this might be the one time I actually like it when you're bossy," I quip, nudging his shoulder playfully.

Harrison raises an eyebrow, his lips curving into a sly smile. "If you want to see me bossy, that can be arranged."

He moves behind me, his chest pressing against my back, effectively pinning me to the sink. The hard lines of his body against mine sets my pulse racing.

"It's difficult to think straight when you're this close," I say softly, tilting my head to look at him.

Harrison leans in to switch the faucet off, his breath whispering across my neck. "I could say the same thing about you."

I arch a brow. "Just a few months ago you were adamant against me moving in."

"That was before you won me over with your interior decorating skills."

"Cute. Are you always this charming?" I ask sarcastically.

"Only when it comes to things I care too much about to lose," he murmurs.

I shift to the side, trying to put distance between us, all too aware of how close he is.

"Twenty-four hours ago, you couldn't stand me and were probably plotting your next prank," I speak slowly, willing my voice to remain steady.

He doesn't move, forcing me to tilt my head to look at him.

"Who says I've stopped?" He leans in, his mouth grazing my ear, sending a ripple of heat across my skin. "Just because our kiss is all I can think about, doesn't mean my usual antics are on hold." His tone playful.

"Good to know I'm still keeping you on your toes." There's a hunger in his gaze, as if he's devouring every inch of me with his eyes. "Why are you looking at me like that?" I whisper.

"Like what?" He trails his hand down my cheek, his touch lingering as he twirls a strand of my hair around his fingertip.

"Like you're starving, and I'm the only thing on the menu."

"I'm curious if our next kiss will be as intense as the last one," he admits without shame, his eyes locking on my mouth.

I shake my head. "There won't be a next time."

"Oh really? And why is that?"

"Have you forgotten the past month? Obviously, we're not compatible."

"That's where you're wrong, trouble," Harrison tells me. "We might have misjudged each other, but if memory serves me right, we had one hell of a connection ten years ago, and let's not forget how great the sex was," he adds with a wistful smile.

My gaze falls to his mouth as his tongue glides along his lower lip, annoyance creeping in since I can't seem to control my reaction to him. "Physical attraction only goes so far. We can't even go five minutes without arguing."

"That means the makeup sex will be explosive," he says with a smug grin. "Like they say, all is fair in love and war, baby."

The term of endearment is nearly my undoing, but I force my lips into a neutral line, swallowing the warmth rising in my chest. The last thing I want right now is to feed his ego into thinking

I'm falling for his charms. But damn, his smile makes it hard to pretend.

"I'm not your baby."

Harrison runs a finger along my arm, an electric thrill shooting through me, leaving my skin covered in goose bumps.

"Not yet," he says it like it's a promise of what's to come.

There are countless reasons why I should walk out of this room, but the main one is that he has the ability to shatter me completely if I let him—body and soul. Yet, as he stands mere inches from me, I can't help but wish he'd draw me against him and kiss me with everything he's got.

My hand betrays me, settling over Harrison's, which is now resting on my hip. I exhale deeply as I move my hand to the hem of his sweats, my thumb tracing under his shirt to the heated skin above his V-line. A deep growl rumbles from him, his eyes igniting with raw intensity.

I wet my lips, tilting my chin to meet his piercing gaze. He lowers his head, his mouth inches from mine, when the sound of shattering glass from the living room interrupts us. Harrison draws me into his arms, shielding me from whatever caused the noise.

"What the hell was that?" he asks.

I sigh deeply into his chest. "Probably Cat knocking the flowers off the table."

That's what I get for letting him out of my bathroom.

I go to move, but Harrison tugs me closer.

"I'll handle it."

"You will?" I ask, surprised. "Why?"

He shakes his head. "I'm going to clean up the glass, so neither of you gets hurt. Don't think I haven't noticed your aversion to shoes." He gestures to my fuzzy socks.

Without giving me a chance to respond, he releases me and grabs a roll of paper towels off the counter and a broom from the pantry. He heads into the dining room to assess the damage.

My head is spinning, struggling to grasp how quickly things have shifted. Just yesterday, Harrison and I were at odds, constantly butting heads, and now that tension has shifted into something much more intense—pure, undeniable lust.

During our weekend together, he was practically a stranger, and still, I felt a strong connection with him. However, this time, if things go further, there's a real chance I'll have to confront the feelings I've left buried for the past ten years, and that terrifies me beyond belief. Now that he's showing his thoughtful and caring side again, it's a reminder that I don't actually hate him and why I was intrigued by him from the start.

Cat protested Harrison's efforts to clean up the mess in the dining room. However, after bribing the troublemaker with a dish of chicken and rice, the deviant feline retreated to his bed in the kitchen, making it possible for Harrison to work without disruption. Apparently, wreaking havoc really takes it out of Cat because he never causes a disturbance at night.

Harrison's presence is all-consuming, his gentle touches and unexpected chivalry leaving me flustered, leaving me hot and bothered. When I finally retreat to my bedroom, I'm eager for a release.

I'm ready for a long shower, and after closing my bedroom door, I strip down to my bra and panties, tossing my shirt and jeans in the hamper. I stop at my nightstand to retrieve my trusty black rabbit vibrator. I haven't used it since I moved in, which explains why I'm so desperate for a release. I'm wound like a spring and just need to relieve the tension so I can sleep.

With Harrison on the other side of the apartment, he won't ever know. Not if I'm in the shower, the water drowning out any sound.

I'm stunned speechless when I pull my vibrator out to find the handle has been bedazzled in the same pink and blue gemstones that I used for the hockey stick.

Harrison.

Oh my god.

He touched my vibrator, and I hate that I'm more turned on by it than anything. Still, he has some explaining to do.

All rational thought goes out the window, and I storm out of my bedroom, vibrator in hand, and march down the hall to find Harrison.

I storm past the empty living room and Harrison's office, entering the primary bedroom without knocking, and coming to a sudden halt when I see him standing near the bed. The only thing he's wearing is a towel wrapped around his waist, and his hair is damp like he just got out of the shower.

Seems like we had the same idea.

"Ever heard of knocking?" He scowls, using a second towel to dry his hair before tossing it over the closet door to dry.

"Why should I respect your boundaries when you haven't done the same for me?" I challenge, holding out my bedazzled vibrator.

He steps closer, scrutinizing it like it's an object he's never seen before. "That looks like a vibrator, but personally I've never used one, so I could be wrong," he says, his tone smug.

I raise a brow. "Are you implying it bedazzled itself?"

"Could be." He shrugs. "Or maybe you have a habit of leaving your nightstand drawer open, and someone spotted it while looking around for prank inspiration."

I blow out a breath, attempting to keep my attention on his face, but his bare chest makes it nearly impossible. Several droplets of water cling to his chest, running along his abs, past his V-line.

"My eyes are up here," Harrison taunts, tilting my chin to meet his gaze.

"I'm just wondering where the rest of your clothes are," I retort.

He snorts. "I could ask you the same question, trouble."

I purse my lips, glancing down at myself. My eyes widen when it dawns on me that I'm standing here in just my bra and underwear. I was in such a hurry to confront him that I forgot to put my clothes back on.

I fold my arms across my chest and square my shoulders. "If you're not ashamed of walking around practically naked, why should I be?"

His eyes trace over me, from head to toe, before settling on my face, his voice low and deliberate when he says, "You shouldn't be. You're beautiful."

I squint my eyes. "Has that line worked for you in the past?"

"You tell me. You're the only one I've ever tried it on."

"I find that hard to believe." The slight tremor in my voice betrays me.

"I'm many things, but a liar isn't one of them. So, I mean it when I say, you're fucking gorgeous." My nipples harden at his words and smoldering stare. "Looks like only the handle has been bedazzled, so I imagine it's still usable," Harrison adds, motioning to the device I'm gripping like a lifeline. "Unlike my hockey stick that's covered from butt end to blade in sparkles."

"This is *not* usable," I say, holding out my vibrator.

Harrison cocks a brow. "May I?"

He holds out his hand, and I hesitantly give him the device, the warmth of his touch making my breath hitch.

I watch with bated breath as he tinkers with the settings, pushing several buttons until the device starts to vibrate. He looks at me with a grin spreading across his face, and I duck my head to hide the heat rising in my cheeks.

"Hmm. Seems to work just fine. Why don't you give it a test drive while I supervise?"

I lift my head, eyes wide. "What?" I'm convinced I heard him wrong.

"Stop overthinking, and let me make you feel good, trouble," he says softly. "Get on the bed, and you'll see what I mean."

The stillness hangs in the air as Harrison turns off the vibrator and gives it to me, the silence thick with anticipation. His eyes, dark with desire, leave no doubt that this is my decision to make. I could walk away if I wanted to, but why would I? Not when he's offering me the release, I've wanted all night.

I inhale deeply, and with my vibrator in hand, I crawl to the middle of the bed and lie on my back, the mattress molding to my body. I glance over to find Harrison's heated gaze on me as I take off my bra, flinging it to the ground, then shimmy out of my underwear, tossing them in his direction. He easily catches the panties, a frantic beat pulsing through me when he lifts them to his nose and inhales deeply.

Oh my god.

"Take the vibrator and slip the tip into your pussy," he orders, my lacy underwear still gripped in his hand. "Unless you're not up to the challenge," he taunts.

I shoot him a glare. Part of me wants to protest out of principle, but a bigger part craves the pleasure I know he's capable of offering, thrilled by the thought of him watching me.

Anticipation crackles in the air as I push the vibrator inside me, groaning at the welcome intrusion. I'm already soaked from fantasizing about Harrison's thick cock behind that towel. The sensation feels incredible, given my heightened state.

"Don't put it in any farther," Harrison warns, chuckling when a groan passes my lips.

"Is this another way to torment me?" I mutter.

I wouldn't put it past him to try and deprive me of an orgasm.

He leans over the bed, pressing a chaste kiss to my mouth.

"Turn the vibrator on, and you'll find out," he says with a small smirk. "But only use shallow strokes, and don't go near your clit."

I narrow my eyes as he pulls back, making it clear it's my move.

There's no chance I'm giving him the upper hand, especially not when an orgasm is on the line.

I exhale sharply, shoving all doubts to the back of my mind, and focus solely on the gratification he's promised. A soft hum buzzes through the air when I turn the device on. The pulse courses through me, and I moan softly as the vibrations tease my entrance.

"With your free hand, tease your nipples," Harrison orders.

A jolt of pleasure shoots through me at his command, and I don't hesitate to grab my left breast, cupping it tightly before flicking the nipple like he ordered. His heated gaze is locked on me, watching my every move from his spot by the bed.

"Pinch your nipple hard," he demands.

I squeeze it firmly between my fingers, my mouth parting open in a surprised gasp.

"Now push the vibrator in and out deeper, but go slow."

I move the device in a steady motion, my mind wandering to an image of Harrison using his skilled tongue, licking me as he coaxes pleasure from my body. His fingers pressed into the tender flesh of my thighs. I pick up my pace, desperate for more friction, letting out a groan.

"Slower," Harrison scolds gently.

I tilt my head toward him, frowning. "I hate you."

He chuckles. "Doesn't sound like you hate me."

My eyes widen when he drops his towel, revealing his thick cock, pre-cum already leaking from the tip.

Maybe I should be self-conscious that I'm spread eagle on the bed with a vibrator shoved in my pussy while my boss, and the man who's been the bane of my existence, looks on like he can't get enough.

I'm emboldened, aware that while Harrison may be calling the shots, I have all the power in this situation. Especially when I look over to find him wrapping the lace panties around his shaft and stroking it in slow, steady pumps. He lets out a sharp hiss as he rubs the lace against his skin, sending a shock of arousal through my veins as I watch.

"Okay, so hate might be a strong word," I say on a gasp. "But you are infuriating."

"Likewise," he taunts. "Now move the vibrator to your clit."

Thank god.

I pull the device from my entrance and press it against my clit, my muscles taut with the prospect of a climax.

"You'll look at me when you come," Harrison states, and my gaze instinctively meets his. "Imagine I'm kneeling before you, my hands gripping your thighs." The pace of my breathing picks up when I turn up the speed of the vibrator. "I'm licking your pussy with my tongue as I play with those pretty little nipples of yours, squeezing them so damn hard." He tightens his grip on his cock as he watches me rub the device over my clit in frantic strokes. "I'd make you writhe beneath me, begging until your voice was hoarse, and only then would I allow you to fall over the edge."

"Oh god, Harrison," I cry out.

"That's it, baby," he croons, his chocolate-brown eyes ablaze with heat. "Come for me."

I put more pressure on my clit, and with my other hand, I pinch my nipple hard. My back arches off the bed as I chase my release.

"Fuck Fallon, those noises you make are my undoing," Harrison pants.

He finds his own frenzied release with my panties wrapped

around his cock, pumping it roughly. Watching him sends me over the edge, our mingled moans filling the room.

My body is simmering with a lustful haze, and I feel like I'm floating, suspended on a cloud of pleasure. The lingering aftershocks bring a smile to my face as my head falls back on the pillow to catch my breath.

I look over to find Harrison wiping his cock with my panties, tossing them into the hamper in the corner. He crawls onto the bed, lying down next to me, and slides his arm down my hip, pulling me into his side. "That was fucking incredible, trouble."

I tilt my head, running my finger along his lips. "It was nice." I shrug.

Fucking incredible actually.

He arches a brow. "Based on the wet spot on my comforter, I'd say that was more than *nice*."

Heat rises to my cheeks as I glance down at the evidence, not ready to admit it out loud.

After we lay a clean blanket on the bed, I relax into his protective arms as they tighten around me, overcome by a sense of belonging, like this is where I was always meant to be. Cared for and worshipped by a man who makes me feel cherished in ways I've never experienced before.

As Harrison runs his fingers through my hair, I'm reminded of just how long I've gone without affection. Being on my own has never been easy, and right now, I just want to believe even for a moment that this could be real.

But that's also when the fear creeps in, remembering what happened the last time I let my guard down. The threat of getting hurt again has me retreating behind my walls, desperate to shield myself from the vulnerability I'm not ready to face. A knot of panic coils in my stomach, its tendrils spreading until my hands tremble. I clench my fists, refusing to let Harrison catch a glimpse of the chaos swirling inside me.

Reluctantly, I slide out of Harrison's arms, easing off the bed.

He sits up, watching me. "Where are you going?" His voice carries a hint of confusion.

"It's late. I better get back to my room since I have to be up earlier to prep breakfast in the morning." I grab the vibrator and bend down to get my discarded bra off the floor and bolt for the door. "Thanks for the orgasm, Harrison," I call over my shoulder as I exit the room, shutting the door behind me before he can ask me any more questions.

I slump against the wall, breathing in deep. The walls I've built around my heart are now so fragile, and I'm afraid even the smallest crack could shatter them completely.

Then again, is that really such a bad thing?

CHAPTER 22

Harrison

THE PAST FEW DAYS HAVE BEEN CHAOTIC. BETWEEN year-end reports and new project proposals, I've been buried in paperwork. Fallon has also been busy with several catering events through the New Year. When she has been at the apartment, she's gone back to tiptoeing around me and stays in the kitchen, leaving my meals in the dining room like she used to.

I miss her.

The truth of the matter is I've believed a lie for the past ten years, and it shakes me to my core. Fallon never ghosted me like I thought, and when she came back into my life, I allowed my anger to control the narrative and distort how I perceived her. My biggest regret isn't addressing the problem sooner.

Now that my eyes have been opened, I see Fallon for who she truly is: fierce, loyal, and generous, with dreams as bold as her spirit. She won't stand down to anyone, not even me. I've admired that about her from the day we met.

Living under the same roof is becoming more complicated by the day. It took every ounce of restraint to let her leave after witnessing her come undone under my direction, and every night since, I've gotten myself off to the image of her writhing on my bed with her lips parted and hand between her legs. While I want to respect her boundaries and not rush her into anything, that doesn't mean I'm willing to stand idly by while she continues to put distance between us.

I carry the dishes from my breakfast into the kitchen, where Fallon is stirring something on the stove.

She glances over as I approach. "I could have gotten those."

"It's no trouble," I say, setting the dishes in the sink before moving next to her and placing a hand on her hip. "What are you making?"

She briefly stiffens but doesn't pull away. "Butternut squash risotto." She leans over to grab salt and pepper and sprinkles a pinch of each into the pot.

"Is that for me?"

"I'm testing a new recipe for my cookbook," she says, her gaze shifting back to the stove.

Fallon's drive is extraordinary. She's carving out her own path and chasing dreams most wouldn't dare pursue. Now that I know about her desire to own her own restaurant, I'll do whatever I can to help without undermining her need for independence.

"Mind if I try a bite?" I ask with a hint of mischief.

She nods, lowering the spoon into the pot, and scoops out some risotto, cupping her hand beneath it. My gaze lingers on her lips as she blows on the food to cool it.

"Here," she says, offering me the spoon.

Instead of taking it, I gently grip her wrist and lean in, tasting the risotto straight from the spoon. I savor the creamy bite, dragging my tongue along the surface to get every last morsel.

"Delicious," I murmur.

Fallon's piercing gaze is glued to mine, and I catch the faint tremble in her hand as she watches my every move.

"I'm glad you like it," she whispers, lowering her head in a futile attempt to hide the blush spreading across her cheeks.

Being near her sharpens everything, like a lens finally coming into focus.

I've made my decision—I'll do whatever it takes to get another shot with her. The problem is that she's caught in an internal struggle, and I don't fault her for it. I didn't exactly roll out the welcome mat when she arrived, and until recently, I've done everything to make her life more difficult.

Not anymore.

"I'm playing in a charity hockey game tonight, and I want you there," I blurt out.

Real smooth, Harrison.

A flicker of disappointment crosses Fallon's face before it's gone. "What time does it start?" she asks, busying herself with getting out a clean spoon. "I usually have more time to prepare, so my menu options will be limited. I hope that's alright." She avoids my gaze as she goes back to stirring the risotto.

My hand moves to her jaw, tilting her face to meet my gaze. "You misunderstand. I don't want you to come as a private chef—I'm asking you to be my date." I cringe inwardly. That sounded far smoother in my head, and there's a good chance my poor delivery could send her running. Damn, I'm definitely out of practice—back in the day, I would have executed that line perfectly.

Fallon scrunches her nose. "Your date?"

I caress her cheek with the pad of my thumb. "No

pressure—I wasn't implying anything. I'd really like to have you there, but if you'd rather not go, I understand."

"Who else did you invite?" she asks.

"My sister, Presley, and her boyfriend, Jack."

I rarely play hockey anymore, but they don't miss a game when I do. I'm relieved my parents weren't able to come out for this one. My mom doesn't know how to hold back, and if she saw Fallon and me spending time together outside of a professional capacity, she'd probably start grilling us about our current nonexistent relationship. Now that would definitely scare Fallon off.

Fallon turns down the heat on the stove and sets the spoon on a small saucer. "Oh, it sounds like a family thing. I wouldn't want to intrude," she says hesitantly.

She's usually a force to be reckoned with, so seeing her uncertain doesn't sit well with me.

"Consider this your chance to get dirt on me without being interrupted. Presley's got plenty of stories and loves spilling my secrets," I tease with an exaggerated side eye.

"Will I have to interact with any of the puck bunnies?"

My eyes widen, taken aback by the unexpected question. "Absolutely not. They sit in the stands, too focused on the players to notice anyone else."

She quirks a brow. "Even you?"

Damn, I can't help but love seeing the spark of jealousy in her eyes.

"I'm not interested in the puck bunnies. Sure, I went out with a few at the beginning of my season with the Huskies, but that was ten years ago. Not to mention that I quickly realized they were more interested in bragging rights for being with a hockey player than getting to know me. And they always said whatever they thought would keep me interested." A strand of hair falls across Fallon's face, and without thinking, I tuck it behind her ear. "When we met, you didn't hold back your opinion of me, and your honesty was refreshing."

Fallon taps her chin, like she's contemplating her answer. "Considering you're playing, I better go. Wouldn't want to give any of the puck bunnies any ideas that they might have a shot with you tonight. Plus, I can't pass up the chance to get the inside scoop from Presley," she adds, her eyes twinkling with mischief.

"I do have one request."

She tilts her head, squinting at me. "Which is?"

"I'll be right back," I say, not answering her question outright before exiting the room.

I stride past the living room where Cat is busy clawing the base of the couch. He doesn't even look my way, immune to my disapproving glare. I'll have to research how to curb his appetite for ruining my furniture or risk my sanity trying to coexist with a four-legged menace.

When I get to my office, I take down the jersey hanging on the wall and pull it from the frame. Fallon was the last one to wear it, so it's fitting that she has it on tonight.

As soon as I step inside the kitchen, her gaze lands on the jersey in my hand, and she backs away like she's seen a ghost.

"What are you doing with that?" She gestures to the jersey.

"I want you to wear it."

Her eyes flicker with uncertainty. "Why?"

So everyone knows you belong with me.

"A hockey game isn't the same if you're not wearing a jersey," I murmur, moving in closer. "And the only one you'll wear from now on is mine."

She eyes it suspiciously. "How many other girls have worn it?"

"Only you."

And if I can help it, she'll be the last.

The Mavericks host a monthly charity hockey game, bringing together players, coaches, and donors on the ice for a good cause. I look forward to it every time, and there's nothing like hitting the ice with a crowd cheering me on from the stands.

Tonight feels extra special because Fallon is here.

My skates carve into the ice as I speed down the left side of the rink, eyes locked on the puck in the neutral zone as Zach, one of my teammates, sends it toward the boards. I power through, leaning into the turn, my muscles burning with the effort. The noise in the arena fades into the background as my focus sharpens.

The opposing defenseman isn't giving me much space, closing in fast on my line. But I spot a split-second opening for a pass to Aleksandr, who's playing center. With a quick flick of my stick, I tap the puck through a tight gap between the defender's skates. His head snaps toward the pass, leaving him scrambling to recover.

I don't hang around to see if it lands, already charging toward the net. When the puck hits Aleksandr's stick, I catch the tilt of his head, his trademark signal. He fakes the goalie out, pulling him to one side, and like I expected, he passes me the puck. I don't waste a second taking my shot, sending the puck flying through the air, landing at the back of the net.

Aleksandr cheers, pumping his fist. "Hell yes."

I slam the boards with my stick, the roar of the fans echoing in my ears. Usually when I play, I feed off the crowd's energy. However, tonight, my attention goes straight to Fallon, standing in the owner's suite, cheering with my sister.

She must sense me watching, because her gaze meets mine; she flashes me a broad smile that lights up her face. Possessiveness hits me like a wave. Nothing beats the sight of her in my jersey. She might not know it yet, but she'll be wearing it at every game from now on.

Aleksandr slaps me on the shoulder, catching my attention. "We have a game to win, old man. You can make googly eyes at your woman later."

I like the sound of someone else calling her mine.

Now if only I could make it a reality.

I let out a low laugh, drawing a puzzled glance from Aleksandr. He's used to my gruff demeanor, not this lighter side. But between the rush of the game, and the sight of Fallon in my jersey, adrenaline surges through me. I'm more than ready to finish this game so I can go to her.

CHAPTER 23

Fallon

"I'M GLAD YOU'RE HERE," PRESLEY SAYS WITH A SMILE.

"Me too," I say.

We're seated in the suite of the arena, waiting for the second period to start. She and Jack arrived a few minutes late, and judging from their attire, they must have come straight from the office.

Jack commands attention in a three-piece suit. Beside him, Presley is his perfect match in a black pencil skirt, a white turtleneck, and a tailored blazer. Her pumps and brown hair pulled into a high ponytail complete the polished ensemble.

Seated side by side with Jack's hand possessively resting on Presley's thigh, they make a striking pair, like they belong on the cover of a business magazine, powerful and perfectly in sync. I don't miss the way he looks at her as if she's the greatest prize, more valuable than any deal or business empire.

It leaves me to wonder how it would feel to be the object

of such fierce and unwavering admiration. I look over to where Harrison is seated on the bench next to the other players, taking a drink from his water bottle.

I may have my reservations, fearful that this could end badly, but there's no denying I'm hooked on this man. When it comes to the battle between my heart and body, the latter is winning, leaving little room for resistance.

I'm not ashamed of what we did—in fact, I'm tempted to do it again—but this time with his hands roaming my body, and his cock buried inside me. However, that would mean our already precarious relationship would become even more complex, if that's even possible.

Harrison is like a match, and if I stand too close, we'll both end up in flames—but I'm unable to resist striking one more spark.

To distract my rogue thoughts, I dig into my bag and pull out a container of snickerdoodles. I made a batch for Walter beforehand and brought a few with me, knowing sweet treats have a way of winning people over. I wanted an easy way to break the ice with Jack and Presley.

I hold out the cookies to them. "Would you like one?"

"Absolutely. Those look so good," Presley exclaims, taking two and passing one to Jack.

He nods in my direction. "Thanks."

"You're welcome."

Presley takes a bite, her eyes lighting up as she chews. "This is hands down the best cookie I've ever tasted," she declares between mouthfuls.

"I'm glad you like it," I grin.

Jack's phone goes off and he fishes it out of his pocket, glancing at the screen.

"Sorry, little vixen, I have to take this." He presses a kiss to

Presley's head before stepping out into the hallway behind us, separating the two spaces.

As soon as he's gone, Presley leans over, casually resting her elbow on the arm of my chair. "I hear my mom had a part in you moving in with Harrison. I'm sorry if she overstepped. She means well, but as you might've noticed, she tends to get carried away." She glances back at Jack with a knowing grin.

"Her persistence is the reason I moved in and agreed to become Harrison's private chef. It's been an amazing opportunity, though I'm sure Harrison has regretted it on multiple occasions," I say with a small smile.

"I heard about the spider prank he pulled." Presley shakes her head. "I would have retaliated against Harrison if I had been in your shoes. He and my other brothers did something similar to me when I was a teenager, conveniently when my parents were out of town for the weekend. I was terrified, but when I realized it was a trick, I couldn't let them get away with it." She takes another cookie from the container in my lap.

"What did you do?"

She smirks. "I served them mashed potatoes with chocolate syrup and told them it was ice cream. Their shocked expressions were well worth it."

I let out a low whistle. "Damn, that's impressive."

"Thanks. How about you? Please tell me you made Harrison pay." She takes a bite of her cookie while she waits for my reply.

"I put salt in his coffee," I admit.

Presley laughs as she wipes a crumb from her face. "That's a good one."

"He didn't think so," I remark smugly.

"I hope I'm not crossing a boundary, but I have to tell you that aside from our family, Harrison has never invited anyone to watch him play in a charity game before. And he most certainly hasn't left a trip in Aspen Grove early for anything other than work." Presley takes a sip of water and quickly glances at the rink where the Zamboni finishes its final pass. "Beneath his broody exterior is a fiercely loyal man, ready to weather any storm for those he cares about. For example, he loves hockey more than anything, but after our dad's heart attack, he gave it up."

I frown, tilting my head. "What do you mean?"

Harrison explained that he had to leave the hotel when he got a call about his dad being hospitalized. Now that I know how much his family means to him, I can only imagine how distressed he must have been when he got the news. It's only now that I grasp how much of an impact that must have had on Harrison and his future.

"Dad couldn't work at full capacity for months, so Harrison stepped in as his full-time intern, learning the ropes. It was obvious hockey was his dream, but he's carried the weight of running Stafford Holdings since he was a kid," she explains. "There's nothing he wouldn't do for our family, and I only wish we could ease some of that burden. He's spent so long taking care of everyone else, he's forgotten how to put himself first."

"Doesn't taking a vacation or dating qualify?"

I might have tossed in the latter for purely selfish reasons. While I can't change the past, that doesn't mean I'm not curious about Harrison's dating history.

Presley lets out a dry laugh. "Harrison taking a vacation? That's funny. I don't think he's taken a single day off in the past ten years. Even during the holidays, he sneaks in a few hours of work when he can. As far as girlfriends go, he's never had one. Sure, he's taken women to events and gone on dates to appease my mother, but never anything serious." She taps her chin thoughtfully. "Come to think of it, he's never brought anyone to Aspen Grove to meet the family. If he ever does, she'll be special."

It sounds like Harrison and I have more in common than I

thought. We've both been wary of relationships in the past and don't trust easily. Only dating casually, never getting attached.

Harrison especially likes his space, and the only reason he let me move in was because of his mother. It wasn't that long ago when he would have been relieved to have me leave. Now that the truth has come to light, everything between us has shifted.

I can pretend our connection isn't real, but that's a lie. The truth is, there's an undeniable pull between us, and we've reached a crossroads. The real question is whether I have the courage to take a leap of faith and see where this leads, consequences be damned.

"Harrison is fortunate to have someone like you in his corner," I say to Presley. "From what I've heard, it sounds like you've got your hands full trying to keep your brothers in line."

She laughs warmly. "You can say that again. I can see why Harrison likes you. You're a riot, and your food is the bomb. I'm going to have to come visit more often if you're cooking," she gushes before plopping the last bite of cookie in her mouth.

Her sincere compliment means so much.

"You're welcome anytime. I'm always testing new recipes for a cookbook I'm working on and would love to have another taste tester."

"Oh my god, I'd love that." Presley reaches into her purse to take out her phone. "Put your number in. I want to know when your cookbook is released because I have to buy a dozen copies."

I take it, entering my number before handing it back.

"That's really sweet of you, but you don't have to do that."

She waves me off. "Of course, I do. That's what friends are for."

Her kindness leaves me speechless. There's something about the Stafford siblings—they have a way of drawing you in and making you never want to leave. What I wouldn't give to be a part of a family who cheers each other on through thick and thin like that.

Presley points to the ice where the players are skating into position. "It looks like the second period is going to start soon."

I put the rest of the cookies in my bag and check my phone, finding a message from Theo.

Theo: How's my favorite chef? Could go for one of your gluten-free apple strudel muffins right about now.

Fallon: That's only because you taught me how to make them, and you're a big fan of your own cooking.

Theo: I'll take a little credit, but you make the gluten-free version better than I ever could.

Fallon: I did learn from the best.

He wouldn't compliment me if he didn't mean it. It isn't lost on me that he refers to me as his favorite chef, even though he's a world-renowned chef with a reservation waiting list six months out at all of his restaurants. It gives me hope that someday I might actually be able to make a name for myself in the industry like he did.

Fallon: You'll never believe it. I'm at a charity hockey game.

Theo: I'm shocked. You're not exactly a sports enthusiast.

Fallon: I only hate running, and that's your fault.

Theo: It was supposed to be a team bonding activity.

Fallon: Yeah, if the plan was for us all to bond in the back of an ambulance.

> Fallon: You're lucky no one sued you for that debacle. I think it was those hefty bonus checks you gave us.

A few years ago, he had the brilliant idea to have all his employees go on a scavenger hunt across London. The catch? We had to run in the heat during summer, and after a mile, half of us were hobbling along with blistered feet and the beginning of dehydration setting in.

Aside from his bad choices in team-building activities, he was an incredible boss. He always made sure everyone's voice was heard and gave us all a chance to shine.

I think because he caught a break early on in his career, he wants to provide others with the same opportunity. After he graduated culinary school, a celebrity chef dropped by the restaurant he worked at and was so impressed she requested to meet the chef. They had a long conversation, and she gave Theo her card before she left. Within two years, he'd opened his first restaurant.

Theo: We miss your attitude around here.

> Fallon: As you should.

Theo: How's everything going? Dare I say I'm shocked that you're staying with Harrison.

> Fallon: Don't worry. I'm giving him a run for his money.

Theo: I have no doubt.

Theo: Just know that you have a job waiting if you want it.

> Fallon: You're the best, Theo.

It's wild to think that just a few months ago I was living in

London and still working for Theo. So much has changed since then, and something tells me this is only the start.

After the game, Harrison texts me, asking me to meet him in his office at the arena. He had an urgent work call with a potential client and needed somewhere quiet to take it. I didn't even know he had an office here. It seems like he's constantly working no matter where he is, leaving me to determine that he never actually has any downtime to relax.

Presley and Jack went home, citing an early morning tomorrow. I suspect they wanted some alone time, and I don't blame them. The entire walk to find Harrison, my thoughts kept circling back to what happened in his bedroom the other night. I feel my cheeks flush when I think back to the look in his eyes when he watched me come.

When I get to Harrison's office, the door is open. The space has exposed steel beams, polished concrete floors, and dark wood accents. I step inside to find Harrison at a walnut desk near an expansive window overlooking the arena.

"Just how many offices do you have?" I joke.

He glances up from his phone, smiling when he sees me. "I work more often than I don't, and this is one of my favorite places to be. It's even better when there's a game or practice, and I can watch all the action from here." He motions to the rink.

I stride across the room and perch on his desk, leaning back on my arms with my ankles crossed. "Isn't it exhausting to work all the time?"

I take his phone from him and setting it to the side.

Harrison shrugs. "That's the downside of running a company. I'm always on the clock." He looks up at me quizzically.

"I'm glad you're back to your usual self. I was missing your sass the last few days."

"I appreciate you giving me some time to think things through."

With a raised brow, he cocks his head. "Do you need more time?"

I shake my head. "I'm right where I want to be."

There's no telling where this might lead, but I'm done pretending I don't want Harrison. Even if it's temporary, I'd rather embrace our physical attraction than act like it doesn't exist.

With a low growl, he tugs the hem of the jersey, drawing me closer. "Fuck, Fallon, you look damn good in my jersey."

"I do," I answer smugly, tapping my chin. "Although I think I might look even better in Aleksandr's. Black and gold are my colors," I tease. "You wouldn't happen to still have it, would you? I'd love to try it on again."

It's clear I've struck a chord when Harrison moves forward in his chair, pulling me to the edge of the desk, his hands resting firmly on my waist.

"What did I say about wearing another man's jersey?"

I tilt my head, pursing my lips, pretending to mull it over. "I can't seem to recall."

"Then let me refresh your memory. The only jersey you'll be wearing is mine." His mouth grazes my neck, his warm breath making my skin prickle. "Tell me, when you're lying in bed at night, whose face do you imagine is between your thighs, making you come?"

I inhale sharply, squeezing my thighs as he tilts my chin, peppering kisses along my jawline. He gets to my mouth, and I moan softly when he traces his tongue along the edge. Unable to resist, I tug his lower lip between my teeth, and what starts as gentle exploration erupts into wild, frenzied passion. I'm aware of the faint, metallic taste of blood from biting down hard.

"Fuck," Harrison groans. "I want you."

"How much?" I murmur, gripping his hair and giving it a tug.

His brown eyes glow with intensity, sending heat down my spine. "So damn much, it hurts."

My pulse quickens, a flicker of challenge lighting up my eyes. "Beg."

I'm not sure what drives my brazen command, but his raw need makes me want to push him further. He's been acting like he's been in charge since I moved in, but now it's time to turn the tables.

Part of moving forward is learning to let go of the negative emotions tied to his resentment toward me. I'm done pretending that his presence doesn't make me ache for him, longing to be held in his arms.

That doesn't mean I can't make him work for it.

"Beg," I repeat firmly.

He leans in closer until our noses brush. "I want you. From the moment I crashed into you and that tray of champagne, I've wanted you—every damn inch. Please, trouble."

I grip the collar of his shirt, flicking my tongue along the seam of his mouth.

"Please what?" I ask with a raised brow.

"Let me lick that sweet cunt of yours until you come," he begs, his eyes searching mine for an answer.

I gaze at him with a sly smile. "You're welcome to try, but I'm not sure you're up for it. Directing me is one thing, but doing the work yourself is another."

We both know that's bullshit. He has an incredibly skilled tongue. It's something I remember vividly from our weekend together.

"You're playing with fire," he warns, kissing along my collarbone. "Don't worry. I'm more than ready to get burned if it means pleasing you."

I gasp when he drops to his knees, pushing the chair aside. He gently lifts my right foot, and I place my hands on his shoulders for balance. His lips graze the inside of my leg; his slow, deliberate movements heighten the anticipation as he removes my shoe and sock. He repeats the same with my left foot, the cool air against my exposed skin sending a wave of goose bumps across my skin.

"I rather like you on your knees," I say with a smug grin.

"Careful, baby. You may be calling the shots, but don't forget I'm about to have total control over your pleasure."

Harrison taps my hips and I lift up so he can tug down my pants and underwear, carefully sliding them down my legs and discarding them on the chair.

He hikes my leg over his shoulder again, giving him an unobstructed view of my pussy. I wait with bated breath as he plants a kiss on my knee. His stubble rubs against my skin as he moves up my thigh, my legs quaking with anticipation when he reaches my apex.

My breath hitches when he leans forward to press his nose against my core, inhaling deeply.

"God, your sweet scent is intoxicating."

Harrison slowly licks along the seam of my pussy. Teasing me. I dig my fingers into the desk as tremors ripple through my body. After several tortuous strokes, he thrusts his tongue inside my opening, and I buck my hips, grinding against his face. He eagerly explores, alternating between licking my core and sucking my clit.

I'm already writhing beneath him when he adds his finger, the pressure building inside me, a shiver coursing through my veins. I weave my fingers through his hair, tugging just enough to make him groan.

"Damn, is this all for me?"

I whimper, unable to find my voice, when he inserts another finger. The fact that we're in his office, where anyone could walk in, turns me on even more.

I lift my hooded gaze to meet his heated stare, gripping his hair tighter as he moves his fingers in and out of me at a rapid pace as his tongue teases my clit in short strokes.

I'm distracted by a low hum, my gaze shifting out the window overlooking the rink, where someone from the maintenance crew maneuvers the Zamboni across the ice. Several other staff members move through the stands, collecting trash left by fans.

"Does it turn you on knowing that anyone could look up to watch as I worship your perfect pussy?" Harrison croons.

"God, yes," I moan.

I noticed earlier that the windows are made of one-sided glass, but it's intoxicating to think someone could look in to find Harrison on his knees before me with his face buried between my legs.

The crude sound of my arousal fills the room as he alternates between torturing me with his warm mouth, the tip of his tongue pressing inside my entrance, and three thick fingers, both keeping me teetering on the edge. I'm desperate to lose all control as he draws out my impending orgasm, toying with my mind.

"You're so fucking wet." Harrison's voice rumbles with satisfaction. "You taste even better than I remember."

He latches his mouth on my clit again, swirling his tongue in languid circles as my body coils tighter with each thrust of his fingers.

"Don't you dare stop," I pant.

He groans around my core, gently biting down on my clit, and I shatter around his hand, tossing my head back with a strangled cry.

My eyes widen when he brings his fingers to his mouth to suck them clean, and shoots me a wicked grin.

The aftershock of pleasure ripples through me, my breath quick and shallow as I glance at him. He hasn't undressed, yet his presence is electric, filled with a desire to match mine.

I nod toward his tented pants, the outline of his erect cock pressing against the fabric. "What about you?"

"Tonight was about *you*." He strokes my jaw before picking up my discarded underwear and pants, handing them over so I can get dressed.

I blink at him, finally coming back to reality. "Thank you," I whisper.

"Watching you come is my new favorite pastime."

I blush at his words, not sure how to respond.

"I'm not ready for anything beyond that right now," I confess. "I have no qualms admitting that you have a skilled tongue, and that as much as I try to fight it, I'm still attracted to you."

"So, that means multiple orgasms with my roommate every day? Count me in," Harrison replies.

A swarm of butterflies takes flight in my stomach. I appreciate him meeting me where I am, and not pushing for more than I'm ready to give. The physical attraction we share is easy—it's the depth of our emotional connection and the possibility of what this could become that terrifies me.

My entire adult life has been about carving out my own path, chasing the dream of running my own restaurant and making a name for myself in the culinary world. Getting involved with a client, especially one that I have a past with, was never part of the blueprint.

Harrison shuts his laptop, putting it in the briefcase he had under his desk. He grabs his hockey bag in the corner, slinging it over his shoulder.

"Ready to head home?" Harrison questions. "I'm sure Cat is anxious to get out of the bathroom."

"Yeah."

When he gets to me, he leans down to kiss me.

I bring my fingers to my lips. "What was that for?"

"A reminder of how much you mean to me." He takes my

hand in his, giving it a light squeeze. "Now that I've had another taste, I'm never going back."

It's evident that he is ready to take the next step, yet he respects my need for time to process it all. With anyone else, what just happened would have been enough. But with Harrison, my body is still humming with need, already craving his touch again.

I may not be ready to rush into a relationship, but I'm more than willing to take things one day at a time and indulge in the perks of having a dangerously attractive roommate who can't keep his hands off me.

CHAPTER 24

Fallon

SEEING HARRISON IN HIS ELEMENT LAST NIGHT, SKATING across the ice, intensified the draw I felt toward him. Once we were alone in his office, and he dropped to his knees with his face buried between my legs, I was a goner. It was *the* hottest sexual experience I've had thus far, with our weekend together coming in a close second.

What happened was like striking a match in a tinderbox, instantly burning away any pretense that our sexual chemistry didn't exist. The notion that a thin glass wall was the only thing that separated us from the cleaning crew or anyone else left in the building made last night even hotter. Leave it to Harrison to bring out my inner exhibitionist. Just thinking about it is enough to make my pulse race.

It doesn't help matters that I haven't stopped thinking about kissing him again since the night on the rink. And once his mouth was on mine again, I couldn't resist letting him go further. Images of him gazing at me with those chocolate-brown eyes as he traces my jawline torment me. His scent lingers on his jersey that I wore that night—a reminder of what we shared.

It's Saturday morning, and I should be preparing breakfast, but Harrison suggested I sleep in today. I'm about to throw the covers over my head and pretend that I don't have any responsibilities when I hear the sound of a drill whining, followed by a loud clunk.

What is going on?

I scramble out of bed, tug a hoodie over my head, and go to investigate.

When I get to the living room, I'm shocked to find Harrison surrounded by wooden planks, a mess of screws and a manual tossed to the side. Walter kneels beside him, shaking his head.

"Why are there so many pieces?" Harrison grumbles.

"You're doing it wrong," Walter points out. "You've got the base upside down. Did you read the instructions?"

Harrison frowns at the half-assembled cat tower that looks more like an abstract piece of art. "I don't need them."

"Are you hearing this, Cat?" Walter asks, gesturing toward the mess. "He's putting the climbing post where the perch is supposed to go, unbelievable."

Cat glares from his spot on the couch, clearly offended by the disruption.

"Does it matter?" Harrison mutters.

Walter arches a brow. "Only if you want Cat to survive his first climb."

Harrison's eyes light up with mischief. "Well, in that case—"

"You better end that sentence with 'we better get it right,'" I interject as I step into the room.

The little demon has wormed his way into my heart, and I can't help but feel protective of him.

"Good morning, Miss Fallon." Walter grins.

"Good morning," I say with a smile. "What are you doing?" I ask Harrison.

"I did some research, and based on what I found, I ordered a climbing tree to give Cat a dedicated scraping post. It was supposed to come assembled, but they mixed up the orders and it arrived like this." He gestures to the jumbled mess. "Assembling furniture isn't my forte," he begrudgingly admits.

"I can tell," I tease. "Please tell me you didn't force Walter to come up and help you."

"He didn't," Walter chimes in. "Another delivery came shortly after this one, and when I brought it to the penthouse, I saw Mr. Stafford struggling." He covers his mouth to stifle a laugh. "I'm training a new doorman who'll be working the night shift, so I was available to stay and assist, but *someone* is being stubborn and not following the instructions."

Harrison sighs, tossing Walter a playful glare before reluctantly sliding the unrecognizable cat tree his way.

"Let's see you have a go of it," he challenges.

"Certainly," Walter says, not hesitating to take over assembling.

"I'm going to the kitchen to whip up some breakfast," I tell them. "I'll make something for you to take with you when you're finished, Walter. We really appreciate your help."

He nods, keeping his focus on the task at hand. "Always, Miss Fallon."

I turn away, not wanting Harrison or Walter to be alarmed at the tears in my eyes. It's hard to hold back the emotion when someone shows me kindness, especially after years of learning to fend for myself. Even something simple like setting up a climbing tree for a mischievous cat I've grown to care for, even though he causes more trouble than anything, means a lot to me.

My circle has always been small, and I'm closest to Theo and Lila. But with one living far away and the other being my boss until recently, I've had to learn to handle things like assembling furniture on my own.

Getting a glimpse of what it means to have a reliable support system is making me emotional, and the fear that it could all be gone tomorrow has me fleeing to the kitchen to pull myself together.

After preparing breakfast, I'm whipping up a batch of red velvet cookies to thank Walter. He left a few minutes ago, but I plan to bring them down to him later.

I glance down to find Cat rubbing against my legs, meowing. *That's new.*

It's the first time he's shown me any affection since he got here, and I'm not going to lie, I'm thrilled. It's a welcome change from being hissed at or given the cold shoulder.

"Hungry?" I coo. "Must have been exhausting supervising this morning."

"Seriously?" Harrison says from the doorway. "I put blood, sweat, and tears into building his climbing tree, and he rewards you instead?"

I maneuver around Cat to get a container of homemade salmon delight from the fridge and scoop some into a bowl.

"If you want to be his favorite, you'll have to learn to make his favorite meals." I set the food in the corner where Cat prefers to eat. "I'm sure Cat will appreciate his climbing post when he tries it though. It was a nice gesture."

Harrison follows me over to the counter. "I didn't do it for him." Heat rushes my cheeks, as he closes the distance between us. "I did it for you."

"Why?"

"Cat means a lot to you, so he's staying. Which means he and

I have to find a way to coexist, and part of that is keeping him away from the new couch we're getting. I've instructed Cabrina to send you options on Monday."

"This is your apartment. You should choose."

Harrison reaches out to stroke my cheek. "You live here too, so your opinion matters just as much as mine. I want this place to feel like your home."

I'm caught off guard by his sentiment. "The first month I was here, you were hell-bent on resisting any changes I made to the place."

It's a complete shift from how he's now going out of his way to make me comfortable. I could be bitter about the change, but the truth is his effort hasn't gone unnoticed.

"Have you forgotten that during that time, you transformed my living room into a jungle and buried my bed under a mountain of pillows?"

"Yep, and you wouldn't have it any other way," I say playfully.

"You're right about that," he remarks with a smile.

I scoop a generous dollop of frosting with a spoon and bring it to my mouth. I close my eyes and slowly swirl my tongue around the sweet cream, a soft groan passing my lips.

"Wow, that's good," I note quietly.

I experimented with a new recipe, adding a touch of lemon juice to brighten the flavor without overpowering it. This addition is a keeper.

I open my eyes to find Harrison's heated gaze on my mouth.

"Want to try some?"

He nods obediently.

I swipe another dab of frosting with my finger and hold it out to him.

Harrison takes hold of my wrist, leaning forward to suck my finger into his mouth, his gaze never leaving mine. Heat rushes through me when I feel the warmth of his mouth, and his affectionate words send a shiver down my spine. Damn, this man has me at his mercy, and it's hard to find a reason not to give in. Especially when I know he'll worship me in bed and give me countless orgasms.

Which might explain why I don't pull away when he gently grips the base of my neck and moves forward to brush his nose against mine. His touch is soft, almost reverent, as if he's imprinting this moment in his memory.

"This is so damn sweet, but I've tasted sweeter," he murmurs.

A whimper escapes me when he tilts my head to nip at my bottom lip, trailing his tongue along the seam before sealing his mouth to mine. The kiss triggers an inferno within me, and I grip his shoulder with one hand, and my other trails down his chest, landing against his sweats. A guttural groan passes his lips when I move my fingers in a circular motion, tracing the outline of his cock in teasing strokes. My teeth graze my lower lip as I look up at Harrison, my eyes wide.

"I forgot just how big you are," I say, my tone sultry.

"If you keep saying things like that, I'm half liable to throw you over my shoulder and remind you what I can do with it."

"I'm not so sure, hotshot. You're constantly working, so you might be a little rusty."

He flashes me a cheeky smile before bending down, and before I can react, he lifts me over his shoulder, striding toward my bedroom.

"What's gotten into you?"

"It's about damn time I make you mine."

CHAPTER 25

Harrison

NO MORE WAITING.

Fuck, the things I want to do to Fallon. A primal desire to make her mine claws at my chest.

I shut the door behind us, not wanting to risk Cat interrupting. He has no concept of personal space and will explore any open room.

I set Fallon on the bed with ease and take a step back. Her breath is shallow as she watches me with a playful gleam in her eyes.

My gaze is glued to hers as she gets up, her hips swaying as she approaches me. My throat tightens when she drops to her kneels in front of me.

"What are you doing?" My voice is strained.

"It's my turn to taste you properly," she murmurs.

My jaw is set tight as Fallon tugs down my sweats. I step out of them, kicking them off to the side. She licks her lips, her eyes trained on my cock straining behind my boxers. She moves her hand between us to rest against me, grazing the outline of my dick in teasing strokes.

I inhale deeply, fighting to remain composed. The last thing I want is to lose control before she's even put her mouth on me. She'd never let me live it down. But it's so damn hard to maintain control when her skilled fingers are intent on torturing me with every stroke.

Fallon slowly drags my boxers down my legs, and I step out of them. She looks up at me and touches my abs beneath my T-shirt.

"Off," she commands. I quickly obey, ripping off my shirt and tossing it in the pile with my other clothes.

I watch with rapture as she curls her fingers around my dick and I let out a hiss when she gives it a gentle squeeze. She moves her hand up and down my shaft in unhurried, steady strokes. Pre-cum leaks from the tip, and she leans forward to lap it up with her tongue.

"Fuck," I groan.

Fallon lifts her hooded eyes to meet my lust-filled gaze as she leans forward. She wraps her warm mouth around me, her lips closing around the aching head.

Damn, this must be what heaven feels like.

I wind my fingers through her hair, my head rolling back as my eyes fall shut while she sucks the crown like it's her favorite dessert.

I tighten my grip. "That's right, take me deeper."

She hollows her cheeks until my head is at the back of her throat, and I let her set the pace while she adjusts, not wanting to hurt her.

Fallon is the embodiment of desire—gorgeous, clever, and undeniably confident. She's strong-willed and determined, and for all the power I wield, she has the uncanny ability to leave me utterly defenseless.

I'm so enraptured by the pleasure I'm feeling that I'm stunned when she abruptly stops, taking my dick out of her mouth.

"Do you like it when I suck your dick, Harrison?" She traces my shaft with her fingertip as it bobs inches from her mouth.

A low hum rumbles in my chest, reveling in her bravado, my restraint slipping with every second that passes.

"You know I do."

She clicks her tongue in disappointment. "We've been through this. That's not how you beg."

Fallon runs her tongue along my shaft and applies pressure on the vein, sending shock waves through my body. She laps and sucks, fulfilling every erotic thought I've had about her and multiplying them by a thousand. I let out a guttural groan when she swirls her tongue around the crown and back down my shaft, her taunting gaze never leaving mine.

It looks like I've created a monster. God, she's in total control right now, and I fucking love every second of this push and pull between us.

I tilt her head back to look at me. "You're so damn pretty on your knees."

She shakes her head. "I'm disappointed. Aren't you supposed to be a master negotiator? If you want to come, you'll have to do better than that."

I let out a ragged breath when she licks the tip of my cock. "Holy shit, please let me come," I beg, not giving a damn that I'm at her mercy.

"That's more like it," she croons.

Fallon grips my cock, putting it back in her warm mouth. This time she cups my balls, squeezing gently as she sucks me off. Unable to resist asserting my own control, I wrap my hand around her neck, her pulse fluttering under my thumbs. My hips move faster as I fuck her mouth with abandon, growling in approval as her swollen lips bob up and down around my shaft.

"Jesus Christ," I groan as my muscles tighten, my orgasm shooting through me.

My cock jerks under her hand as cum fills her mouth.

"Swallow for me, baby," I order, relaxing my grip around her neck.

I can't look away as she laps up every drop, licking me clean. When she's finished, my cock springs free from her mouth with a loud *pop*. I reach out to wipe away a bead of cum dripping down her chin, holding it out to her. She takes my wrist, drawing it closer, her tongue darts out to clean it off.

I take her hand to help her off the floor.

"Let's get you out of those clothes, beautiful."

"You've got two hands. Better put them to good use," she taunts.

"You better watch that mouth of yours, considering I'm in charge now," I caution her with a sly grin. "Now, be *my* good girl and lift your arms."

She slightly narrows her eyes, but complies.

I tug her shirt over her head and drop it to the floor. My hands are back on her within seconds, unclasping her bra. I have to suppress a groan when her pert breasts come into view. They're begging for my attention, but I restrain myself for now. There will be plenty of time to worship her perfect tits later.

I pull her shorts down until they pool at her ankles. She lets out a sharp exhale when I trace lazy circles on her thighs. My fingers reach her panties, observing that they're damp, accompanied by the smell of her arousal. I slowly drag them down her legs, and Fallon grabs hold of my shoulders to keep her balance, as she lifts one leg at a time.

She stands before me, her shoulders squared, gloriously naked. I'm captivated by her sinful curves, her ocean-blue eyes that seem to sparkle when she smiles, and her swollen lips that are slightly parted.

Fucking hell. She's a wet dream come to life.

I take her hands in mine, bringing them to my mouth for a kiss. "God, you're perfect like this. I just wanted to take a moment to look at you," I say, pressing a kiss to her forehead.

Fallon blinks, offering me a soft smile, turning to her nightstand, and pulling out a condom. She stares at it in her hand, glancing up at me.

"Honestly, I'd rather not use this. I have an IUD."

My heart is hammering in my chest as I tuck a piece of hair behind her ear. "Are you sure? I'm clean, and I've never gone without a condom before. But if you're not ready…" I trail off, my hand twitching slightly.

I've never gone bareback, but it's something I want to experience with Fallon. It requires trust that I know we're still building, so if she's not ready, I'd never pressure her.

Fallon cups my jaw, tilting my head to face her. "I want you without anything between us, and that's final," she adds with a grin.

Her words bring warmth to my chest.

I lose my train of thought when I spot something sticking out of the open nightstand drawer. When I look closer, I see her bedazzled vibrator.

This is a pleasant surprise.

Yes, I've watched her take care of herself while using it, but I'd be lying if I said I hadn't fantasized about getting her off with it.

"This is familiar," I say coyly, retrieving the device and holding it out. "I think the sparkles give it a nice touch, don't you think?"

Fallon smirks, climbing onto the bed and crawling to the middle.

"It'd be even better if it were in use, don't you think?" She spreading open her legs, giving me an obscene view of her pussy.

"You read my mind." The mattress dips as I join her, hovering above her.

I lean down and wrap my mouth around one of her nipples, gliding my tongue across the areola.

"Harrison," she breathes, my name falling from her lips like a prayer. She inhales sharply as I alternate between flicking her nipple with my tongue and tugging it taut with my teeth. "Oh, shit," she cries out.

There's nothing better than having her at my mercy while I worship her. I grin as I continue to ravish her tits with my mouth, my hand trailing down her chest until I get to her stomach, drawing patterns with the pad of my finger. When I reach her legs, they fall open, eager to accept me.

I groan when I find her dripping for me. I pick up the vibrator, gripping it firmly in my hand and slowly push it inside her tight cunt. It's not nearly as big as my cock, but she moans at the welcome intrusion, regardless. A soft hum buzzes through the air when I turn the device on, her body jolting slightly.

God, I'm mesmerized by the way Fallon's body moves beneath mine. The way she responds so greedily to my every touch makes me want to draw out every ounce of passion from her and awaken her deepest desires. Like she's done to me.

Before her, I was on autopilot—emotionally detached and lost in my routine. She taught me how to have fun again, and now, I live for the moments I share with her.

I pull the vibrator out, increasing the setting, and move it to Fallon's clit, eliciting a loud moan. She quivers as I bite down on her breast while teasing her with the device. She's hanging on by sheer determination, sweat dripping from her brow, and it's euphoric, knowing it's caused by my hand. When I turn the vibrator onto the max setting, my name falls from Fallon's lips.

My cock is as solid as granite, aching to be inside her as I watch her fly higher with each passing second. When her eyes fall shut, signaling she's close to an orgasm, I toss the vibrator on the bed. I take hold of my shaft, guiding the tip into her perfect pussy, hissing as she clenches around me.

"Don't worry, baby, you can take me," I say, leaning down, to kiss her forehead.

Once I'm fully seated, I grip her waist as I move in a steady rhythm, and she eagerly meets me, thrust for thrust.

God, I was an idiot allowing assumptions to get in the way of being with Fallon. There's no denying that I'm powerless against this woman, and I'm basking in the gratification of claiming her.

I look down to where our bodies join. "Damn, Fallon, you feel so good. You were made for my cock, weren't you?"

"Less talking, more fucking," she scolds, her nails digging into the comforter.

There's nothing sexier than when she tries to call the shots. The push and pull is its own form of foreplay, a constant tug-of-war that fuels the fire between us until surrender is inevitable.

My tongue dances along the seam of her lips, groaning when she opens her mouth to let me in. I seal my mouth over hers in a possessive kiss, the taste of us on my tongue. She moans against my lips when I pick up my pace, driving into her hard.

"You almost there, beautiful?" I ask as she clings to me.

"God, yes," she mewls.

I reach down and roll her clit with my thumb and forefinger, and soon we're both barreling toward release. I roar as uninhibited pleasure surges through me at the beautiful sight of Fallon unraveling.

I hold her tight as we ride out our orgasms together and nuzzle my nose into her neck, inhaling the scent of frosting as I ease out of her, not wanting to cause her any pain. I stifle another groan as I watch our mixed cum drip onto her thigh.

"I'll be right back," I say with a kiss to her temple.

After grabbing a washcloth from the bathroom, I come back to clean Fallon up before wiping myself off. I toss the towel into the dirty laundry and climb back into bed, drawing her into my embrace. She rests her head against my chest, and I gently push her hair back, wanting to see her face. She has a soft smile on her lips, revealing her dimples, while her half-lidded eyes drift closed as she nestles closer.

Silence lingers between us as we lie wrapped in each other's arms, and Fallon might not know it yet but she's mine now, and I'm never letting her go.

CHAPTER 26

Harrison

I WAKE TO THE SUNLIGHT STREAMING THROUGH THE WINDOWS, and a quick look at the clock shows it's past seven, much later than my usual 5:00 a.m. wake-up time. It must be due to barely getting any sleep last night. Pampering Fallon in the shower by washing her hair and body led to another round of sex. Afterward, I carried her back to her bedroom and fucked her doggy-style on the already crumpled sheets. My hand gripped firmly in her hair, the curve of her back on display as I drove into her, leaving imprints of my teeth on her neck and shoulder. She's insatiable— and thankfully, so am I. We've missed out on too much already, and I refuse to waste another minute.

When we finally collapsed from exhaustion, I held her in my arms and watched as she drifted off to sleep. Nothing feels more right than holding her close, and it reminds me why I was capti- vated with her from the start. She quiets the storm in my head, making everything else fade into the background.

As much as I want to pursue a relationship with Fallon, there's a real possibility she doesn't want the same thing. For all I know, she could consider this a temporary fling, or something to pass the time until her next big adventure.

I push aside my restless thoughts and concentrate on the present. When I roll over to her side of the bed, I panic when I find it empty.

What the hell?

My mind races as I climb out of bed, panic clawing at my chest when I find the bathroom empty. I'm brought back to ten years ago when I thought she had ghosted me, and the hollow ache I felt when I never heard from her. A reminder of the past decade that I had to live without her.

It makes me think how hurt Fallon must have been when she woke up and discovered I was gone, with no explanation. At least today, I know she couldn't have gone far—or so I hope.

My anxiety builds with every step, and when I get to the kitchen, only to find it empty. My irrational fears suffocate me, making me think about what it might mean to lose Fallon, and how everything could come crashing down in an instant.

Where could she have gone?

"Looking for me?" I spin around when I hear her melodic voice.

She's in my T-shirt from last night and looks fucking edible. Where I once found her choice of clothing bothersome, it now only adds to her allure, especially when she's in my clothes.

I stride toward her and wind my arms around her waist, tugging her close. "Good morning, beautiful. You were supposed to be in bed when I woke up," I grumble.

"Guess you were eager to find me since you're running around shirtless," she says, gesturing to my bare chest.

I cup her face, brushing my thumb along her jaw, and give her a heated kiss. "You took my shirt, so I didn't have much of a choice."

"I could get used to watching you walk around in nothing but your boxers," she murmurs against my lips.

My mouth curves into a satisfied smile as my hands roam down her back. "If you would have stayed in bed, you would have gotten a far better view."

"I'll have to keep that in mind for next time," she replies coyly. *I like the sound of that.*

"How come you're up so early?"

"I made us breakfast. Come eat before it gets cold."

She steps out of my embrace and goes over to the oven to pull out two plates with avocado and egg toast, drizzled with olive oil. As I take my seat, she carries the food over to the counter and places them down next to a cup of coffee and a bottle of Diet Coke.

"It looks delicious, but you don't have to cook every morning if you don't want to."

The line between our professional and personal lives has been obliterated, and I don't want her to feel obligated because she's worried about her job.

"I actually cook for myself. I enjoy it immensely. You just happen to reap the benefits of my passion," Fallon says smugly, pulling out the chair next to her and patting the cushion.

I slide into my seat and watch as she twists the cap off her Diet Coke, taking a long sip.

"I'll never understand your obsession with that stuff."

She creases her brow. "Just the other day, you said you were hooked," she reminds me.

"I wasn't talking about the Diet Coke."

Hell, I can't even recall what it tasted like. All I could focus on was Fallon, and the undeniable fact that I was completely gone for her.

She gives me a knowing smile. "I'd get an IV of it if I could, and I don't want a lecture about how unhealthy that would be." She slides the bottle in my direction. "I think you need another taste."

I stare at it suspiciously before taking a cautious sip, only to spit it out. "How the hell do you drink that shit? It's like drinking a cleaning product."

"Better than drinking sludge," she teases, nodding toward my untouched coffee.

"Touché." I grab the fork next to my plate and get to work on my breakfast.

After a few minutes, Fallon breaks the silence. "When we were at the game, Presley told me more about what happened after you quit hockey when your dad had his heart attack, and how you stepped in to help him at the company."

I chew slowly, giving myself a chance to think. Naturally, Presley would choose the most sensitive topics to talk about with Fallon. It's not that I want to hide the truth from her, but it's not something I like to revisit often.

"Yeah, it was either me or one of my brothers, but neither of them was in a position to take it on. My dad was going back to work, whether anyone liked it or not, and I wasn't going to let him risk another heart attack from all the stress."

Fallon's eyes soften. "That must have been a difficult decision since you love hockey so much."

"It was," I confess. "My siblings moved forward, following their passions, while I left mine behind and took on a career and responsibilities I never wanted." I set my fork down, turning to face her. "Don't get me wrong, I've grown to enjoy it for the most part. Being CEO of Stafford Holdings has its perks, and I'm proud of the accomplishments I've made, but it comes at a cost."

"Like not smiling much?" Fallon teases.

I chuckle. "Among other things."

For starters, working around the clock and not allowing myself personal time outside of co-owning the hockey team. It's never been a priority since all my goals revolved around the business. However, for the first time in forever, I have a reason to want balance and to make room for Fallon. Now I just have to find a way to make that possible.

"Would you change things if you could?" she asks, her voice edged with a touch of uncertainty.

I shake my head. "No. It might not have been my first choice, but taking on the role of CEO has brought me closer to my brothers. And my dad's pride in the company's recent growth has made it all worth it. If I'd kept playing hockey, my career would have long been over by now. Luckily, as part owner of the Mavericks, it allows me to stay connected to the sport I love and participate in the monthly charity events."

I hadn't intended to share so much. Normally, I keep my feelings to myself, but if I want a real chance at winning Fallon's heart, I need to be willing to open up to her. Fortunately, she makes it easy with her genuine kindness and the way she appreciates what I've done for my family.

Which only adds to the regret of how I treated her before. Even when we bickered, she was easy to talk to, but I was too stubborn to see past my pride and admit it.

I glance at her, my expression softening. "Fallon," I say softly, covering her hand with mine. "I owe you an apology for how I left the hotel after our weekend together. I shouldn't have gone without an explanation. I'm deeply sorry."

She smiles, giving my hand a reassuring squeeze. "There's nothing to forgive." Her tone is earnest. "I'd have done the same thing if I were as close to my family as you are." She glances down at her plate, nibbling on her lower lip. "If I had found your note, there's no telling what would have happened. In the months after, you were helping your dad at the company, and I started culinary school. As much as it hurts to accept, I think everything turned out like it was supposed to." She glances over at me as she brushes a strand of hair behind her ear.

I hate to admit it, but she's right. Even with good intentions, there's no guarantee we would have seen each other again or survived the strain of a long-distance relationship. Not when the past ten years of my life revolved around Stafford Holdings. Work still dominates my time, but it doesn't seem as important, compared to the beautiful woman next to me and the possibility of a future together I'm willing to fight for.

"What about now?" I ask Fallon. "Are things falling into place how you want them to?"

We've avoided discussing what comes next, but we can't put it off forever. I've already lost her once, and I won't let it happen again. I'd rather deal with her doubts now than deal with them later when it might be too late.

Fallon nibbles her bottom lip, glancing at her plate. "I'm enjoying our time together very much. But I took a huge leap of faith moving to New York to start a new venture, and I don't want to risk being distracted from making my dreams a reality."

My chest tightens as her shoulders slump. I may not be able to predict the future, but I can give her the reassurance I couldn't before.

I lean in, cupping her jaw, guiding her eyes to mine. "I've lost you once, and I won't let it happen again. Even if it takes a lifetime, I'll wait for you because you're my end game."

Fallon's breath hitches, and I wonder if I've gone too far. But I've never been one to stand on the sidelines and hope for the best. This time around, I'm not leaving any room for doubt about what I want.

"You mean it?" Fallon asks.

"Every damn word." I press a kiss to the back of her hand, causing her cheeks to turn red. "I have somewhere I want to take you."

We've barely ventured outside the apartment together. I want to show her that I'm serious about us, which means taking her somewhere that holds a special place in my heart and inevitably bringing her around my family. But first, I want to savor some alone time before introducing her to that chaos.

Fallon wipes her face with a napkin, pausing when she notices me staring at her. "What is it?"

I flash her a mischievous grin. "We're going away for the rest of the weekend."

A flush creeps up her neck as she stares at me slack-jawed. "To where?" she asks.

"Aspen Grove."

"What about Cat?" She motions to the feline who's just sauntered into the kitchen, casting a disdainful glare my way. It's obvious who his favorite human is, and it's not me.

"He will manage on his own for the most part. He only retaliates when we try to intervene." Hell, he still hisses whenever I try to approach him. "We'll have Walter check on him throughout the day and put him in your bathroom at night. It's only for a couple of days."

Fallon sighs, running a hand through her hair. "You can't ask your doorman to watch our cat."

A smirk tugs at my lip, hearing her call Cat *ours*. I'm still apprehensive about having a pet, but it's obvious he's here to stay.

"Walter's more than just the doorman, he's a friend," I say.

Fallon's expression softens, so I know I've said the right thing. She and Walter have become close since she moved in, and I'm grateful he looked out for her when I was too busy being an asshole. From what she's shared, she hasn't had much of a support system since her parents died, but that ends now.

Between me, Walter, and the whole Stafford crew in her corner, she'll never face anything alone again.

"We can ask him, but I don't want to pressure him to say yes."

I take her hand, guiding her from her seat to my lap, my palm resting on her lower back. "I spoke to him last night—he's more than happy to look after Cat while we're gone."

Her tongue darts out before a slow smile spreads across her lips. "Okay, but only if he's fine with it. I don't want him to feel pressured."

"He's not" I assure her.

"Are we going to see your family while we're there?" she asks.

"Only if you want to. I have a place outside of town so we can avoid them if you'd rather not spend time with them yet."

Even when just a few of us are together, things can get intense, and I don't want to overwhelm her during our first visit together.

She raises a brow. "Do you think your mom would let us skip out on stopping by if she found out we were in Aspen Grove?"

I laugh. "Good point. We'll just have to keep it a secret." Which could be challenging since she knows most everyone in town. "She'd probably call a search party if I don't stop by for my niece's birthday tomorrow. Lola is obsessed with hockey as of late and wanted me to teach her and her friends how to play. But I can always stop alone for a couple of hours, if you'd prefer to stay at my cabin."

"I'd love to celebrate with Lola at her birthday party," Fallon smiles.

"Great, it's settled then," I say enthusiastically, kissing her before taking our plates to the sink. "We'll leave this afternoon, but I'd prefer to wait until tomorrow to let my parents know we're in town. I have something special planned."

Fallon tilts her head, her gaze locked on mine. "What is it?"

"It's a surprise." I come around to her side of the counter and kiss her on the forehead.

"I'm not a big fan of surprises," she mumbles.

"Says the queen of pranks."

"Correction. I don't like surprises when it comes to *me*."

"Don't worry, you'll like this one," I promise.

CHAPTER 27

Fallon

I CROUCH BESIDE CAT, SURPRISED WHEN HE LETS ME SCRATCH behind his good ear. "I'm going to miss you, little troublemaker."

"We'll only be gone for two days. He'll be fine," Harrison says, rolling our suitcases to the front door.

I shoot him a playful scowl. "You're just jealous Cat still won't let you touch him."

Cat's finally warming up to me, but still gives Harrison the cold shoulder. The best part is Harrison pretends he doesn't care, even though I've caught him sneaking treats to win Cat over—with zero success so far.

"Right, because gaining the approval of a moody feline is the pinnacle of my life's achievements," Harrison mumbles.

"Cat's not moody, he just has standards." I pat Harrison's shoulder with a grin. "Don't worry, keep bribing him and he'll come around eventually." I grab my coat from the closet and put it on.

"I don't know what you're talking about." His tone is defensive.

"The variety of gourmet snacks stashed in the pantry say otherwise," I counter.

The deliveries of fancy cat treats haven't gone unnoticed, but none of them have won Cat over. It's clear he prefers my home-cooked meals to those expensive snacks.

Before Harrison can answer, Walter comes out of the kitchen with a bowl of tuna and zucchini mash. "Don't worry, Miss Fallon, I'll take good care of Cat while you're away." His eyes crinkle with warmth.

He has the day off and was kind enough to stop by before we left to get instructions on taking care of Cat while we're away.

Harrison's jaw drops when Cat trots over to Walter, rubbing against his leg, and meows insistently until he places the bowl down.

"Seriously?" Harrison mutters.

"It's not a reflection on you, Mr. Stafford," Walter explains. "The staff at the animal shelter call me the cat whisperer. Even the most stubborn ones warm up to me quickly." He scratches Cat behind the ear before pushing himself to his feet.

"You never told me you volunteered at the shelter," I say.

Given how open he's been about his personal life and hobbies, it's odd that he didn't mention it sooner—especially after I told him Cat was a stray.

Walter tugs on his shirt cuffs and clears his throat. "It must have slipped my mind." He glances at his watch, then looks over at Harrison and me. "You two better get going. You don't want to miss your flight."

"You're right. Thank you again for helping with Cat. We really appreciate you," Harrison says. "Come on, Fallon."

On the way out the door my phone buzzes in my pocket, and I check to find a new text.

Theo: I have something to run by you when you're free to chat.

Fallon: Okay. I'm heading out of town but will be back in a couple of days.

Fallon: Don't work too hard.

Theo: I won't. Please tell me you're going somewhere fun and not for a catering gig.

Fallon: I'm going to Aspen Grove.

Theo: With Harrison?

Fallon: Yeah.

Theo: Good for you.

Theo: He better treat you right, or he'll have to go through me.

Fallon: Thanks for having my back.

Theo: Always.

Theo: Enjoy your weekend. I'm filming this coming week, but I'll call you when I can.

Fallon: Perfect.

"You coming?" Harrison calls out.

I glance up to find him standing by the elevator with our luggage, holding his hand out to keep the doors from closing.

"Yeah, be right there." I slip my phone back into my pocket and hurry to catch up.

Thankfully, the plane ride to Aspen Grove is quick, and I savored every minute curled up beside Harrison. Although I don't think I'll get used to traveling in a private plane. It may be the norm for him but it's a luxury I can't quite wrap my head around. If I'm being honest, this entire situation is surreal, and I'm waiting for someone to pinch me to wake me up from this dream.

You're my end-game.

Despite the lingering questions about what comes next, Harrison's admission has played on a loop since our conversation this morning. It gives me a sense of peace to know that what we share is genuine and not a passing distraction for him. That doesn't mean I'm ready to dive into a serious relationship just yet, not until we've had more time to have a conversation about it. As predicted, I've gotten attached and my heart is now on the line, which means I have to make sure this is worth the risk before I go all in.

Right now, I'm going to focus on making new memories with him.

When we arrive at the airfield, Harrison exits the plane first, our hands intertwined as he leads me down the stairs. As we walk across the tarmac, he inhales deeply, the tension melting from his shoulders, a stark contrast from his usually tense posture.

"You seem more relaxed," I observe.

Harrison glances over at me. "I am. Aspen Grove will always be home. Having you here makes it even better," he adds with a smile.

My stomach flips, and I rise on my toes to kiss him. "Thank you for bringing. When I came for the wedding, I didn't have time to explore, so I'm excited to see Aspen Grove with you."

"I'm honored to be the one giving you the official tour," he says with a playful wink. As we approach a white SUV, Harrison steps ahead to open the passenger door for me and holds out his hand to help me inside.

"Thank you."

He shuts the door, jogging around to the driver's side, and gets in.

"You ready?" he asks.

"What about our luggage?"

"It's in the trunk. The crew unloaded it before we got off the plane."

I nod, the whole thing still feeling unreal. "Where are we headed? How far is your parents' house from here?"

"A couple of miles, but we're not going there tonight. I made other arrangements, and had Cabrina call ahead and make sure everything's ready when we arrive. I'd rather stay under the radar like we talked about. If my mom finds out that we're here, she'll insist we come over and I'd like to have you to myself tonight."

"I like the sound of that, but I am looking forward to spending time with your family too."

"Don't worry, we'll have plenty of opportunities, I promise."

I relax in my seat as Harrison starts the engine. "I can't wait."

He pulls out of the airfield gates, his tall frame at ease as he takes my hand in his, resting it on his lap, a small smile on his face.

I look out the window at the snow-covered landscape before closing my eyes. Harrison's family dynamic is everything mine wasn't—full of affection and love, while mine with my grandmother was cold and distant.

For the first time since my parents died, there's a spark of hope that I could experience those feelings of warmth and connection again, and it makes me even more excited to spend more time with the Staffords.

"Fallon, are you okay?"

Harrison's voice has my eyes fluttering open. When I look over, he's watching me with a concerned expression.

"I was just thinking about my grandmother." I decide that now is a good time to open up more. "When my parents died, I went to live with my her in London. She disowned my dad when he came to the States and married my mom, and my grandmother couldn't stand that I was the spitting image of my mom." I glance out the window at the snow falling. "She made sure I got a good education, but there was no love or kindness to soften the edges. Everything was a transaction with little thought for emotional support."

I take a deep breath before continuing.

"She had a large social circle but kept me hidden, like a dirty little secret she was ashamed of. I don't know if it was me or the fact that she didn't want to admit her estranged son had married a poor girl from New Jersey, and had a kid." My eyes drop to my lap. "The hardest part was not being able to talk about my parents after they died. They were gone, and all I had left were my memories."

Harrison tightens his hand around mine, running his thumb along my skin in soothing strokes.

"I'm here to listen always. I'd love to hear more about them." His offer has me nodding as I look up at him. "Do you have any other family? What about your mom's parents?" he asks, briefly glancing over at me before turning his attention back to the road.

"Neither of my parents had siblings, and my mom lost both her parents the year she graduated high school. I used to dream of being part of a big family who would spend summer vacations together, have game nights filled with laugher and playful bickering, and be a safe space when I felt lost."

Harrison brings my hand to his mouth, pressing a kiss to my wrist. "You have that now. Whether we become an official couple or not, you'll always have the Staffords in your corner. My mom and Presley are already smitten with you, and the rest of my family will love you too. Whatever you need, we'll be there." Tears blur my vision as they roll down my cheeks, and I use my free hand to wipe them away. "Fallon, what's the matter? Should I pull over?" Harrison's voice is edged with unease.

I wave him off. "I'm okay."

"You sure?"

I give him a reassuring smile. "I couldn't be better."

When I glance out the window, I notice a movie theater at the corner of Main Street with a red brick exterior and a marquee flickering with golden lights. A sign reads *Tonight's Feature: Private Screening.* The letters are slightly crooked, like they were arranged by hand.

We pull up in front and Harrison leans over to look at the marquee.

"Are we going to the movies?"

"Yes."

"But it says it's a…" I turn to him, giving him an incredulous stare. "Harrison, please tell me you didn't rent an entire theater."

He chuckles. "Okay, I won't." He drives around back to an empty parking lot. "I wanted us to have our privacy; plus, I'm pretty sure *Arachnophobia* would clear out any other moviegoers faster than a blizzard warning."

This man is going above and beyond to make me feel special, and I'm soaking in every minute. From the beginning, he's paid attention to the little things—like my favorite drink and the first movie we watched together—and it makes me feel seen in a way I never have before.

Harrison shuts the engine off, taking the keys out of the ignition, and gets out of the car, coming around to open my door. He takes my hand and guides me to the back of the theater, ushering me inside.

Fairy lights hang along the ceiling, and the walls feature black-and-white photographs with moviegoers in hats and overcoats. I notice there isn't a single worker in sight, but follow Harrison who walks over to the concession stand where a bottled water, Diet Coke, bucket of popcorn and a mini charcuterie board covered in plastic wrap is set out with a selection of cheeses, meats, nuts, olives, chocolates, and crusty bread.

"I gave the manager a heads-up when we were five minutes out, and they pulled all of this out of the fridge for us so it was still cold." He gathers the charcuterie board and popcorn in his arms, nodding for me to get the drinks.

I grab his arm. "Wait. Are you sure this is all gluten-free?" Concern edges my voice.

Gluten-free foods are often mislabeled or contaminated, but I shouldn't worry so much considering Harrison eats foods prepared by others when he's out of town and is diligent about his celiac disease.

He gives me a grateful smile. "Don't worry. Cabrina had it special ordered just to be safe."

I shoot him a pointed look. "Worrying about what you eat is literally in my job description."

"Damn, I thought it was because you liked me." He winks.

I grab the drinks off the counter. "Like is a strong word," I tease.

"Come on, trouble," Harrison says, moving toward the screening room. "The manager is going to start the movie soon so we better take our seats."

The theater may be small, but it does have reclining leather seats, albeit a little worn.

Harrison leads me to the back row, making me feel like we're in high school looking for a secret place to make out. We settle into our seats just as the lights dim, and I find myself laughing at the idea that he rented an entire theater to watch a low-budget indie film from thirty-five years ago.

He catches me giggling and gives me a quizzical look. "What's so funny? The movie hasn't even started yet."

I bite my bottom lip, fighting back a smile. "Just thinking about us making out," I answer wryly.

"Thinking about it is fun, but doing so is much better." He pats the open space in his recliner, and I slide in beside him. I'm halfway in his lap with my legs draped over him, but he seems to like it.

"Comfortable?" he asks, wrapping an arm around my shoulder.

I nod with a grin. "Very."

We're so close our lips are almost touching, and I lift my chin to kiss him. His tongue darts out and sweeps against mine as a soft moan passes my lips. I pull away when the movie starts, resting my head against Harrison's chest. He leans his arm over and grabs a tray of snacks, setting it on the empty seat next to us as we enjoy the film and cuddle.

Since we landed in Aspen Grove, he's been noticeably more relaxed, free from the usual weight of deadlines and business meetings. It's refreshing to see him in his element and giving himself the chance to slow down and have a break from his usual work-driven mindset. It makes me wonder how I can help him find a better balance, because it makes me happy to see him carefree and at ease.

Toward the end of the movie, however, I notice Harrison's body is tense, clutching his stomach.

At first, I think he's reacting to the movie, but when I look over, he's grimacing in pain.

A pit of dread forms in my stomach. "Are you alright?" I whisper.

"I'm fine," he says with a forced smile. "The movie is almost over, so let's finish it."

I notice the beads of sweat on his forehead, and his breathing is shallow, each inhale coming faster than the last.

Something is wrong.

"You don't look okay," I say, my concern growing. I gently touch his face and watch closely as he tries to hide his discomfort.

"Don't worry about—" He stops short and bends forward, groaning.

"That's it, we're going to the hospital. I think you're having a reaction to gluten."

I glance at the charcuterie board, trying to figure out what caused it. My suspicion falls on the crackers. Harrison had a couple handfuls, and if they had gluten, that would explain his reaction.

I'm sure Cabrina ordered our food from a reputable place, and this isn't on her in any way. Dealing with celiac disease means that even "gluten-free" food, when ordered from a restaurant or prepared in a shared kitchen, can still have traces of gluten, often without them even realizing it. I'll just make sure to bring our own food next time to stay on the safe side.

I stand up, offering my arm to Harrison, doing my best to keep him steady as he struggles to stand. "Lean on me. I've got you."

"This isn't how I wanted our night to go," he mutters as we slowly make our way to the exit.

"I know, hotshot, but we'll get through this together," I promise.

The hospital in Aspen Grove is a modest building, nestled on the edge of town. Its exterior is well-maintained, and thankfully the waiting area was nearly empty when we arrived, and they were able to take Harrison back to a treatment room right away.

The doctor that confirmed Harrison was having a severe reaction to gluten. He's been given an IV to administer fluids and a dose of medicine to ease his stomach pain. I'm seated at his bedside, running my fingers through his hair while we wait for him to start feeling better.

Seeing him like this brings a startling clarity about how much he means to me. The pranks, the anger and lingering resentment seem so trivial now, especially with Harrison sick, and the thought of how much worse it could have been.

"Harrison?" Johanna's frantic voice echoes down the hall.

He cracks open an eye and glances at me. "Dammit, who the hell called my mom."

"The nurse mentioned earlier that your mom was listed as your emergency contact."

"Of course she is," he grumbles. "She must have had it changed from Dylan to her."

From what I've observed, it doesn't seem like it would be too difficult for her to get added. The doctor said he lives just down the street from the Staffords and shares a beer with Mike at the local bar every week. One of the nurses mentioned that Johanna volunteers at the hospital twice a week and is well-liked by the staff.

Before I have a chance to move from the bed, the curtain is pulled back and Johanna rushes into the room, her eyes frantic.

"There you are. I was worried sick. Why didn't you tell us you were in town? I nearly had a panic—" She pauses when she notices me sitting on the bed next to her son.

I remove my hand from his head, folding my hands in my lap.

"Fallon, darling, I'm so glad you're here." She comes over to my side of the bed and wraps me in a hug. "I would've loved to have you over for dinner tonight."

"Dear, give the girl some room to breathe," Mike says when he steps inside the room.

She laughs softly and reluctantly pulls back. "Sorry, I'm just so excited you're here."

"We can tell," Harrison mutters.

"Don't worry, sweetheart, you're next." She rushes over to his side of the bed and draws him into a bear hug. "I was so worried when I got the call that you were here. You were supposed to be at a movie. What happened?"

Harrison runs a hand across his face. "How did you know we were in Aspen Grove?"

She shrugs. "I'm your mother, it's my job to know where my children are."

He glances over at his dad. "Make her stop."

Mike chuckles. "We both know there's only one way to make that happen."

"I'm working on it," Harrison answers cryptically.

I swallow a lump in my throat, wishing we were alone so I could ask him what he means.

"Mom, you could have just called. It was only a mild reaction I'm fine," Harrison insists. "There's no need to blow it out of proportion."

I arch a brow, folding my arms across my chest. "She's not overreacting. You had a severe reaction, and it could have been a lot worse if we hadn't gotten here when we did."

Johanna gives a theatrical sigh. "She's a keeper," she declares to Harrison.

He wraps his hand around mine, kissing the knuckles. "I know."

I lift our joined hands to my cheek, and when Johanna sees, she looks like she's about to faint. "Once you're discharged, you're coming home with us."

Harrison shakes his head. "No."

She gapes at him. "Harrison Ford Stafford, you're not staying in a hotel in your condition. You'll come home where I can take care of you."

"First of all, I have Fallon to look after me," he says, shooting me a smirk. "Second, we're not staying in a hotel; we'll go to my place. That was the plan before the unexpected detour."

She scrunches her nose. "Where is this place of yours?"

"A few years ago, I bought property outside of town and built a cabin there."

Johanna gapes at him. "How did I not know about this?"

Harrison rubs the back of his neck, giving his mom a sheepish look. "It's under an alias."

She purses her lips, narrowing her eyes at Mike. "You knew about this, didn't you?"

He holds out his hands. "I plead the fifth."

Harrison rests his hand on his mom's arm. "I've only stayed there a few times. I just wanted my own space, especially since it gets so crowded at your place, and eventually, there won't be room for everyone when we're all in town to visit."

She exhales sharply, her gaze darting between Harrison and Mike. "I'm not happy that you both kept this from me. There better not be any more secrets from here on out, got it?"

"Yes," they say in unison.

"You're still coming to Lola's birthday party tomorrow, right?" Johanna asks Harrison. "She's been telling all her friends her uncle was a hockey player and can't wait to show you off."

God, that's the cutest thing ever, making me look forward to being there even more.

"We wouldn't miss it," Harrison says.

Johanna's eyes widen. "*We?*"

He gives my hand a gentle squeeze. "Yeah. Fallon and I will be there." He confirms.

A tear glistens in Johanna's eye, but she quickly blinks it away. "That's wonderful news, we can't wait."

Neither can I. But my priority tonight is getting Harrison discharged and back to his cabin so he can rest. I can't think of anything I'd rather do than be the one to take care of him.

CHAPTER 28

Harrison

EVEN AFTER A LATE NIGHT AT THE HOSPITAL, I WOKE UP early to watch the sunrise from the back deck. Much to my disappointment, I'm stuck drinking water instead of coffee—doctor's orders to avoid acidic drinks and to stick to a bland diet for a few days.

Fallon was still asleep when I got out of bed. Last night was supposed to be romantic, but it ended with me in a hospital bed, with severe stomach cramps, sweating like a pig, and making for a less-than-glamorous date night. Yet, she took it in stride, and there's no one else I would rather have had at my bedside.

As I stare out at the lake, I breathe in the fresh air and take in the calm.

When this property came on the market a few years ago, I made a generous offer within hours of it being listed. Like I told Fallon, Aspen Grove will always be home—it's where my family is, and laying down roots here felt right. I bought the full two hundred acres, and while I knew I wanted to build a cabin, I didn't have concrete plans for the rest. Lately, I've caught myself picturing it as a place where my nieces and nephews, and hopefully my own kids, can explore the property, build forts, share stories by bonfires, and maybe even build their own cabins here one day.

I'm surprised when I catch myself smiling. I'm not the type to get lost in thoughts about my future. Success has always been about tangible achievements and hitting milestones. Yet, being in Aspen Grove with Fallon is proof that sometimes the best things in life are ones you didn't plan for.

After I finish my bland water, I head inside where Fallon is in the kitchen wearing a tank top and shorts, moving around with ease. When I designed the cabin, I spared no expense for the kitchen with exposed wooden beams, quartz countertops, and high-end stainless-steel appliances. There was no particular reason other than wanting a space where family and friends could gather when we're not able to go to my parents' house.

My imagination runs wild, thinking of how we could find a way to spend half our time here and half in New York. Which would give her a quiet place to finish her cookbook and make plans for her restaurant.

She glances over at me. "Good morning. How are you feeling?" Her voice is sweet and husky.

"Much better." I come up behind her and wrap my arms around her waist, peppering kisses along her neck. "What are you making?"

There are a dozen strawberries and a bottle of canola oil on the counter.

"Chocolate-dipped strawberries and homemade chocolate bars. I wanted to make something special for Lola's birthday." The microwave beeps and Fallon moves over to take out a bowl of melted milk chocolate. She stirs it with a spoon before bringing it over to the counter. "Last night, your mom showed me how to place an online order at Main Street Market, and it was delivered this morning. Didn't think that would be an option in a small town."

"I'm glad you were able to get what you need. I really appreciate you taking care of me last night. I wanted it to be a romantic night out, and it turned out to be anything but."

She turns to me, running a hand along my five o'clock shadow, and kisses me. "I'm just glad I got to spend it with you."

"If I didn't know better, I'd think you liked me, trouble," I tease and she squeals when I lift her up, setting her on the countertop.

"We can't have that, now, can we?" she taunts.

My cock stirs when she wraps her legs around my waist and tugs me flush with her body. I lean in, grazing my teeth along her earlobe, enjoying the way she melts into my touch, as she lets out a shaky breath. I glance down at her full breasts peeking out of her tank top, and my mouth salivates for something sweet.

An idea comes to mind as I reach for the bowl of chocolate and strawberries.

"I've been thinking. You're a chef, but we haven't taken full advantage of that fact," I drawl.

Fallon eyes me suspiciously as I take a strawberry from the bowl and slowly dip it in the melted chocolate, twisting it around to cover the whole thing. I lift it to her mouth, holding my hand underneath to keep it from dripping.

"Have a taste, baby."

She parts her lips, and takes a bite. Her eyes flutter closed as she savors the sweetness.

"See, I have this roommate who's hot as fuck when she struts around the kitchen in her shorts and tank top, and I can't get enough of watching her hips sway as she cooks."

Fallon opens her eyes as I gently wipe a smudge of chocolate from her bottom lip, bringing my finger to my mouth to suck it off.

"Delicious," I say, my gaze locked on Fallon. "I have this fantasy involving strawberries, chocolate and you naked."

The corners of her mouth twitch, her blue eyes glinting with amusement. "Show me."

Damn, she's so fucking sexy.

"Take off your shirt," I instruct, my voice low.

I set the strawberry on the counter next to her, waiting to see what she'll do next. I'm half expecting her to mess with me, so I'm captivated when Fallon shoots me a mischievous grin as she slowly pulls her tank top off, teasing me with a glimpse of her purple lace bra. When she reaches behind her, I place my hand on her shoulder to stop her.

"Let me help," I state, leaving no room for discussion.

I lean forward to kiss the swells of her breasts, and she shivers, a trail of goose bumps scattering across her arms at my touch. With ease, I unclasp her bra, letting it fall to the ground. Her plump breasts are sexy as fuck, and I bend down to greedily take one of her rosy nipples in my mouth, grazing it with my teeth and pinching the other nipple between my fingers.

"Oh, god," Fallon moans, sending a jolt of pleasure to my dick.

Foreplay is one of my favorite parts about sex with her. She's so damn responsive and likes a little pain with her pleasure. She lifts her hips when I tap on her thigh, and I keep my gaze pinned on her as I drag down her shorts and blue panties, tossing them to the side.

"You're so pretty," I say reverently.

"You have too many clothes on," she pouts.

"Well, in that case." I tug off my T-shirt and toss it on the ground.

When I look over at Fallon, her eyes are wide, and she's licking her lips. "You're very pretty too."

She drags her finger along my abs, following the curve of my waistband. She nibbles on her lower lip as she watches me pull down and step out of my pants and boxers, revealing my cock proudly jutting out, pre-cum leaking from the tip. A testament to the chokehold Fallon has on me.

She isn't the only one affected by this little game.

"Do you trust me?" I ask.

There's a beat of silence before she runs a hand along my arm, giving me a warm smile. "Yes, I do."

I sigh in relief, returning her smile. After all we've been through, earning her trust is a privilege I'll never take for granted. She's claimed me—and I'd do anything for her. I lean over and grab a clean kitchen towel out of the drawer and gently brush away a few stray hairs from Fallon's face.

"I'm going to blindfold you. Alright?"

"But then I don't get to see you," she frowns, glancing at my abs.

I bring her hands to my chest. "For a few minutes, I want you to focus on what you *feel*, and if that's my abs, I won't complain," I say, my lips curving upward.

She runs her fingers slowly down my stomach, mapping the contours of each muscle. "You should be grateful I'm so easily distracted." She laughs softly.

I fold the towel and wrap it around her head, tying a knot at the back. Her breathing is shallow and I take her hand in mine, kissing her fingertips. There's something intoxicating about having this woman's irrevocable trust and at my mercy, leaving me feeling both powerful and humbled.

I gaze at Fallon with an insatiable hunger I can't contain. "This might be warm," I warn.

She nods slightly as I grab the strawberry I set aside earlier and dip it into the melted chocolate again. Thankfully, there's another bag of chocolate on the kitchen table that she can use for Lola's desserts, since I've claimed this batch for a more pressing need.

Fallon gasps when the tip of the strawberry connects with her supple breast, shivering underneath my touch. I glide it in swirling motions, covering her nipple in melted chocolate and stroking back and forth in a teasing fashion, watching it grow taut under my ministrations.

I lower the strawberry back in the chocolate and draw wavy lines on her other breast, slowly dragging the piece of fruit along the sides. I furrow my brow in concentration as I move across her chest, creating a trail of chocolate to her lips.

I press the fruit to her mouth. "Suck," I demand, groaning when she does as I ask, and strawberry juice trickles down her chin.

Unable to control my temptation, I lean forward and lick it off, eliciting a moan from Fallon. I continue my exploration as I trail my tongue down her chest and across her left breast, cleaning the chocolate from her skin.

"You taste so damn good, baby," I murmur.

She has one hand propped on the counter, while her other hand is draped around my neck.

My tongue continues to lavish her breast as I place one hand on her hip, and with the other I tease her pussy, noting how wet she is after playing. Slowly I sink one and then two fingers inside her pussy, the crude sound of her arousal is music to my ears as she shamelessly grinds against my palm. "Oh, fuck, Harrison."

"Damn, you're fucking drenched." I lower my mouth to her ear. "You have no idea how much pleasuring you turns me on. I live for those little whimpers out of that sweet mouth and the way your hips buck every time I curl my tongue around your clit. When you squeeze your knees around my head, I know you're close to coming, and it's the sexiest thing I've ever seen or felt in my life."

She whimpers, unable to find her voice.

I pump my fingers in and out in a steady rhythm while massaging her clit in languid circles.

"You're such a greedy little thing," I goad her. "When you come, it'll be around my dick."

I remove Fallon's blindfold, and she blinks up at me. Her eyes glistening.

"Are you alright, trouble?"

"Yeah. I'm looking forward to seeing what creative things you can do with other fruits," she says, a satisfied smile on her lips.

"My little chef likes food play. We're not done until I've fucked that perfect pussy of yours." I take hold of my cock, sliding it around her entrance, coating myself in her arousal.

She inhales deeply when I line myself up at her entrance, impaling her in a single thrust. I stroke my hand through her hair, giving her a moment to adjust. When I gaze down at us joined together, my breathing picks up, loving the fact that she's stuffed full of my dick.

Fallon molds her mouth to mine, and I caress her cheek, deepening our kiss. Something spurs me on as if we're in a race against the clock as I pick up my pace, letting go of my last ounce of self-control. With every thrust, I feel her clench around me, only intensifying how fucking good she feels.

My senses become heightened, and I'm acutely aware of her sweet groans as she ascends further into her bliss. Her fingernails sink into my skin, clinging to me as if I'm the only thing keeping her grounded.

"I'm so close," she pants.

I slant my mouth across hers, kissing her fervently as I buck my hips, picking up my pace. All rational thinking is gone as the primal sound of flesh slapping against flesh resonates in the air. Fallon's eyes glaze over as she flies higher into oblivion, digging her fingernails into the nape of my neck, and I relish the flash of pain.

We kiss roughly and I'm aware of the faint, metallic taste of blood when she bites down hard on my lip. It sends my release barreling forward like a freight train, and I reach between us, moving my thumb in circles against her clit until she's writhing beneath me, chasing her release.

"Scream for me, baby," I encourage her. "There's no one here but us."

She lets out a throaty cry as her eyes meet mine, connecting with a charged silence.

Fallon is like a drug, and I'm always craving another fix. From the moment she waltzed into my life with a sassy smile and a bottle of champagne, to lingering in my mind for ten years, she's now the only future I see. No intervention will ever break this addiction—and I don't want one.

I'm falling in love with Fallon Hayes, and it feels like it was always meant to be.

"Come for me." My command is irrefutable, and after a few more strokes of her clit, she detonates like a bomb. She tremors as her orgasm rips through her, and I follow right behind as my climax shudders through me.

I rest my head against her forehead, trying to catch my breath. When I glance down, I see the chocolate smeared over our skin.

"Damn, you made a mess, trouble," I say, leaning forward to plant a kiss on her forehead.

"I'd like to see you get creative with a cherry and whipped cream the next time we play." She winks as she hops off the counter, her gorgeous backside swaying.

I smile, admiring the view. "I see you're already plotting our next round. You might regret giving me ideas."

Fallon stops in the doorway and grins. "I think I'll manage. Now, are you joining me in the shower, or do I have to wash all this off myself?" She motions to the chocolate on her chest.

I push off the counter. "Joining you. Definitely joining you."

As I follow her into the bathroom, I welcome the sense of calm washing over me. I want every day with Fallon to be like this—where the ordinary turns extraordinary because we're together. And I can only hope this is the start of our forever.

CHAPTER 29

Fallon

"Uncle Harrison, you're finally here," Lola exclaims when we enter the indoor skating rink.

She's decked out in glittery pink leggings, a rainbow tutu, and a blue hockey jersey with her name written across the front.

"Happy birthday, ladybug," Harrison says.

He scoops her in his arms, and spins her around, her laughter filling the air.

Lola cups his face with her tiny hands, making sure she has his full attention. "Are you going to play hockey with me and my friends?"

"You bet. I came all the way from New York just to make sure you have the best birthday ever."

"Really?" She beams.

"I couldn't let my favorite girl down, now, could I?" he says ruffling her hair.

She vigorously shakes her head. "Uncle Harrison, is that your girlfriend?" Lola asks loudly, pointing at me.

The rink falls silent as heads turn toward us. I duck my head, hoping no one notices the heat rising in my cheeks. I'm not embarrassed by her question, but Harrison and I haven't had *the talk* yet, and I'd prefer to have that conversation in private when we do.

"This is Fallon." Harrison motions toward me. "She brought you a gift." I should have guessed Harrison would be a master deflector.

Lola's face lights up as he sets her down, and she rushes toward me the second her feet touch the ground.

"Hi, Fallon, I'm Lola, what did you get me?" she asks, dancing on the balls of her feet.

God, she's adorable.

A woman's voice grabs my attention. "Lolabug, remember, it's not polite to ask for gifts. We should be glad Fallon came whether she brought you something or not, isn't that right?"

I recognize Marlow from her videos on social media. She posts the coolest tutorials for her art, and they're fun to watch. We also met when I catered Cash and Everly's wedding celebration, but I didn't have a chance to talk to her that night.

She's wearing floral overalls paired with a red long-sleeve shirt and silver sneakers. Her golden-blonde hair falls in waves to her waist, framing her distinct, mismatched eyes—one blue, the other green.

Lola scrunches her nose and sighs. "Thanks for coming to my party, Fallon."

She tugs on my pant leg and crooks her finger. I crouch down so I'm on her level.

She leans in and whispers, "You did bring me a present right?"

Marlow looks at me, mouthing, "I'm sorry."

I give her a subtle shake of my head, reassuring her that Lola's question doesn't bother me. It's refreshing to be around someone who isn't afraid to speak their mind, especially when there's a present at stake.

Lola's gaze follows my movements as I take a small rainbow gift bag from my purse. "This is for you," I say, handing it to her.

"Mom, can I open it now, pretty please?" She flashes her best puppy dog eyes.

"Sure, Lolabug, but just this one gift. Then it's time to skate, okay?"

"Yay." Lola grins, eagerly yanking out the tissue paper to reveal the charm bracelet I picked out for her at the local toy shop, complete with a hockey stick, a dog, a rainbow, and a unicorn. "It's so pretty," she says, holding out her arm. "Can you put it on me please?"

"Of course, sweetie," I reply, fastening it around her wrist. "And there's one more gift in there." I motion to the bag. "Harrison told me you were a fan of candy."

Her eyes light up as she takes out the last of the tissue paper, squealing when she spots the chocolate bars wrapped in unicorn parchment paper. "These are for me too?" she asks, clutching them to her chest.

I nod. "I made them just for you, but you might want to hold off on eating one until you get home. I'm afraid there isn't enough to share with all your friends."

She's quick to stuff them back into the bag. "I don't want to share with anyone."

Marlow laughs. "Your dad might have something to say about that when he finds out they're homemade."

"If you promise not to tell, I'll share with you." Lola smirks, sounding like a seasoned negotiator.

Marlow does her best to suppress a grin. "We'll talk about it later. Your friends are waiting for you." She motions to the bench area, where a group of kids around Lola's age are putting their skates on, excited chatter filling the air.

"One second," Lola says, turning back to me and throwing her arms around my neck. "Thanks for the bracelet and chocolate, Fallon. I think Harrison should keep you."

My heart fills with warmth as I hug her back.

I steal a glance at Harrison, our eyes meeting with a silent recognition passing between us. After seeing him sick and in the hospital, it puts things in perspective. And now, watching how he interacts with his family makes my heart swell. It's made me realize how much I want a future with him.

I want to be his person.

His confidant.

His lover.

His.

What we share has been years in the making, and while it might be frightening as hell, I want to take that leap of faith and see where this leads.

Lola pulls back and runs over to where Harrison is standing.

"Let's go, Uncle Harrison." She practically drags him toward her friends.

"Sure thing, ladybug." He glances over at me. "Will you be okay here?"

"Fallon can hang out with me. I could use some help setting up the snack table," Marlow says, flashing me a smile. "Have fun, you two." She waves as Harrison and Lola head to the benches.

I follow her over to a corner where several tables and chairs have been set up. She brings several boxes over and unpacks tablecloths, paper plates, cups, and other party essentials.

I brought along a few gluten-free snacks that I prepared for Harrison so he could eat with everyone else. Fortunately, all the kitchenware at the cabin is brand new, so I didn't have to worry about cross-contamination.

"Please don't judge me when you see what food I brought," Marlow warns, taking out a box of Cheez-Its, a bowl of fruit skewers, and a tray full of cupcakes. "Cooking isn't my forte and Lola was adamant we serve her favorite snacks."

"I would never," I assure her, taking one of the tablecloths and draping it over a table. "I may be a private chef, but I survive on Diet Coke, popcorn, and leftovers. And who doesn't love Cheez-Its? They're elite."

Marlow sets a pack next to each plate she's set out. "I know, right? They're my favorite. Lola's too."

"Has she always been a fan of hockey?"

"Dylan and I took her to a Mavericks game a couple of months ago. Harrison had her out on the ice afterward showing her how to skate, and she's been obsessed ever since," Marlow says as she sets out juice boxes. "He's such a good teacher, and when he's out on the ice, it's obvious that he loves the game."

"Yeah, he does," I agree. "I got to watch him play in a charity game and he's incredible."

I glance over at the rink to find the kids clustered around Harrison. They hang on every word as he speaks. He demonstrates how to hold their sticks properly and uses an encouraging tone, giving every kid a thumbs up when they get it right. He waves them forward as he moves across the ice and they follow him like ducklings, some teetering on their skates as they get used to them.

He's an incredible uncle to Lola, and an image pops into my head of him with his own kids, holding his hand as he teaches them to skate. I've never thought about starting a family in the past. Since graduating from culinary school, my life has centered around my career. Now, the idea of a mini- Harrison running around has me thinking about what it might be like to have a family of my own.

"So, are you two officially an item?" Marlow questions with a curious smile.

I want to be.

But that's something I want to discuss with Harrison first, before anyone else.

When I don't answer, Marlow adds, "Sorry if I'm being nosy. The Staffords have no boundaries, and I think it's rubbed off on me."

"You're not, I promise." I take the fruit skewers and put one on each plate that Marlow has set out on all the tables. "Do you spend a lot of time with Johanna and Mike?"

She nods. "We go over several times a week, and Johanna watches Lola often. Some might find it overwhelming, but I'm so grateful for it. As an only child who's not close to my parents, being part of a family that supports each other is something I never imagined I'd ever have the chance to experience."

We share a similar background, though my parents couldn't be here, whereas hers chose not to be. That must be a heavy burden to carry. She's lucky to have the Staffords, and from what I know about Johanna, I'm sure she's embraced Marlow as one of her own.

"I can relate. My parents passed away when I was twelve, and I had to live with my grandmother. To say there's no love lost between us is an understatement," I explain.

She covers her mouth with her hand. "Oh, Fallon, I'm so sorry for your loss."

"I appreciate it," I say. "It's nice to chat with someone who can relate."

"Same." She puts her hands on her hips, scanning the setup to make sure we didn't miss anything before setting the boxes off to the side. "Whatever happens between you and Harrison, consider me a friend. For what it's worth, it's obvious Harrison is smitten with you." She lets out a nervous laugh. "There I go again overstepping."

"No, it's okay. I'd like to know why you say that."

Marlow nods to where Harrison is standing on the ice,

helping Lola hit the puck with her hockey stick. "For starters, he can't go ten seconds without looking this way."

Sure enough, a few seconds later, he glances in our direction, and when our eyes meet, he waves. I give him a broad smile in return.

My focus shifts to the main entrance where Johanna and Mike are walking in, carrying a stack of presents wrapped in rainbow paper.

"Hello, sweetheart," she says, pulling Marlow in for a hug. "Sorry we're late. We didn't have any birthday wrapping paper left, so we had to stop by Brush & Palette on the way here. Quinn was so sweet and let me wrap Lola's gifts in the back."

"I'm glad she was able to help," Marlow says.

Johanna turns her attention to me. "I'm so happy you made it." She comes over to give me a hug too. "How is Harrison feeling today?" There's a tinge of worry in her voice. "He never called me this morning like I asked him to."

I bite the inside of my cheek to keep from grinning, not wanting to draw attention to it. Harrison was a tad preoccupied with me on the kitchen counter to check in with anyone.

"He's doing much better," I say, keeping light on the details.

"Oh, good, I'm so glad he had you to look after him." She grins before turning to Marlow. "Sweetheart, I have one last gift in the car for Lola. Would you mind helping me get it?"

"Of course."

As they head out the front door, Mike comes to stand next to me, his hands shoved in his pockets. "My wife tends to come on strong, but she has a heart of gold, and there's nothing she loves more than her kids." He watches Lola squealing as she makes a goal, Harrison and Dylan cheering her on. "Harrison has been taking care of his family since he was a kid. When Dylan was twelve, he broke Johanna's favorite glass vase, and Harrison took the blame, knowing that Dylan had plans with his friends that night and didn't want him to miss out." Mike pushes his glasses up higher on his nose. "When I had a heart attack, during his only season as a pro hockey player, he retired so he could help me run the company."

"He's a good man," I whisper.

"Damn right he is," Mike states with conviction. "Unlike my wife, I prefer not to get involved in my kids' love lives. I just wanted to tell you something about my son." He glances toward the entrance before glancing back at me. "He's a workaholic because of me. As the oldest, he has a sense of responsibility to his siblings, and I should have done more to make him feel like he had more options when it came to taking over the family business."

A lump catches in my throat, making it difficult to swallow. Now that I understand Harrison better, it's clear why he'd do everything in his power to protect his siblings, even if it meant shouldering the burden alone. It must have been difficult giving up the sport he loved and throwing himself into the family business instead. From what he's told me, he spent years learning the ins and outs of the company, preparing for when he took over when his dad retired.

Harrison has turned Stafford Holdings into a billion-dollar empire and somehow makes it look easy. Even with all the stress he carries, it's clear that he takes pride in his work, and that level of commitment only comes when you care deeply about what you do.

"You're too hard on yourself, Mr. Stafford. Harrison is the man he is today because of you, and I know he enjoys the work he's doing."

"I can see why he cares about you." Mike observes.

"I care about him too," I admit, looking out at the rink to catch a glimpse of the man in question.

Until now, I've been careful to vocalize my feelings, but this seems like a safe space to admit that what Harrison and I have is real and far more than just a fling.

Mike chuckles. "Funny. I had a similar reaction when I met my wife. Now, here we are, with four wonderful kids, an energetic granddaughter with hopefully more on the way soon, and a lifetime of happiness." He pauses, putting his hands in his pockets. "The only complaint I have is the heart-healthy diet Johanna has me sticking to. No more bacon for breakfast—just oatmeal and fruit. It's the worst," he grumbles.

I cover my mouth to keep from giggling. "Sounds like you and Harrison are both dealing with diet restrictions, which isn't always easy."

"We're lucky to have women who know what's best for us."

"I couldn't have said it better myself," I agree.

"Going back to my earlier point about a lifetime of happiness? Do you see that in your future?" he presses gently.

"Now you're starting to sound like your wife," I tease.

"She's a wise woman."

He's right about that. Johanna saw what was between Harrison and me while we were still too consumed by resentment and anger to recognize our mutual attraction. But somehow, Johanna did, and I'll always be thankful that she helped us find our way back to each other when we were too stubborn to see what we could have.

Spending time with the Staffords makes me feel like part of a real family. They genuinely want to get to know me and offer a sense of belonging I've been missing. I can't help but think my parents played a part in leading me to this moment and guiding me to where I'm meant to be.

CHAPTER 30

Fallon

THE PAST FIVE DAYS SINCE RETURNING FROM ASPEN Grove have been nothing short of perfect. Harrison and I have made the most of every moment outside of work. We cuddle in bed each morning and share breakfast before he heads to the office. He's even been coming home earlier and putting his phone away when we're together.

Our evenings are spent making dinner, which means me cooking and him trying to distract me with kisses and the promise of sex. Most nights, we've ended up on the couch, with Cat on the other end, watching an episode of *American Horror Story*.

This penthouse has become my safe haven, and Harrison has made it clear it's my home too, and I don't want to risk losing that… or him. We've avoided a serious conversation about defining things between us so far. And while I've made up my mind that I want a future with him, I haven't found the right time to tell him. For now, I'm content staying in our little bubble—where we have lots of sex and enjoy each other's company.

Tonight, I planned to make gluten-free spaghetti and meatballs, but when I noticed I was out of tomato sauce and fennel, I went to the nearest grocery store rather than waiting on a delivery.

When I get back to the apartment, Walter opens the front door for me.

"Good afternoon, Walter," I answer cheerfully, confused when he doesn't reciprocate my smile.

"Hello, Miss Fallon," he says.

I study him closer, noticing there's a crease in his forehead and his lips are pressed into a thin line.

I rest my hand on his arm. "Are you alright?"

"You have a visitor waiting for you," he explains.

I furrow my brow, unsure who it could be. Aside from the Staffords, Theo, and Lila, no one else knows that I live here.

"A visitor? Who would—"

"Elizabeth, there you are." Grandmother's voice cuts through the lobby, and I glance over as she gets out of her chair and heads toward me. "It's rude to keep your elders waiting," she scolds as she approaches me. "And your doorman is dreadful—wouldn't let me wait upstairs and doesn't even address you properly. What a disgrace."

Walter stays silent beside me, his tight smile, the only hint of his irritation. He takes prides in his work and is, no doubt, insulted by my grandmother's rude comment.

I cross my arms, narrowing my eyes at my grandmother. "What are you doing here?"

She ignores me in favor of addressing Walter. "Why are you standing here?" she snaps. "Don't you have a job to do?"

"He's my friend," I interject defensively.

Walter waves me off. "It's alright, Miss Fallon. I have a few things to take care of, so I'll be at my desk if you need me." He gives me a backward glance as he walks away.

Grandmother sighs. "I thought the insufferable man would never leave."

"How did you find me, and more importantly, what do you want?"

She taps my shin with the end of her cane. "Don't talk to your grandmother that way."

I grit my teeth, struggling to process that she is actually here. The last time I saw her was over a year ago at one of Theo's restaurants. She had been on a date with a retired stockbroker, and when I politely introduced myself, she acted like we'd never met and thanked me for the meal. We haven't talked since, which leads me to question how she knew I was here.

As I release a deep breath, I adjust the grocery bag on my shoulder. "Grandmother, I have plans, so can you please get on with why you're here?"

"It's shameful that you ignored my calls, but you've always been disrespectful," she huffs. "I had to reach out to Theo's assistant to check in and imagine my surprise when she told me that you quit your job to become a private chef and moved to the States. Thankfully, she was kind enough to track down your whereabouts." She fusses with her gold-and-silver scarf, resembling tinfoil more than couture. Grandmother might have money, but she's never had style.

I let out an exasperated sigh. "You came all this way to comment about my new job?"

"Just when I thought you couldn't be more of a disappointment, you make another disastrous decision."

I almost believed I overexaggerated how bad things were between us, but then she shows up and proves me wrong.

"If I'm such a failure, why bother visiting?"

She rolls her eyes. "I'm in New York for the weekend

visiting a friend and decided to stop by since you wouldn't return my calls. You're worse off than I thought. What a shame. At least you're working for someone wealthy. Are you making as much as you did working with Theo? With him, there was a chance you'd manage your own restaurant someday. Now you're just a personal chef, cooking like a glorified housekeeper. Hardly the career you envisioned for yourself, right?"

Grandmother has a way of dragging up old insecurities I've spent years pretending didn't exist. She knows just how to twist the knife for maximum damage, smiling all the while.

The irony is, even when I worked with Theo, she disapproved. To her, being a chef was an embarrassment, and it didn't align with the prestige she wanted me to project.

I think the real issue is that my mother wanted to be a chef, and the fact that I chose to follow in her footsteps bothers Grandmother more than anything.

"I appreciate your concern, but I'm doing just fine on my own," I say, deflecting her question.

She scoffs. "I don't buy it, Elizabeth. You used to go on and on about owning your own restaurant someday, and look at you, resigned to slumming it as a cook. It could be worse. At least you're not a waitress like your mother." I bristle at her insult. "You're just like her—dreaming big, but never going anywhere."

I lift my chin, my fingers curling into the grocery bag still on my shoulder. "My mother was hardworking and taught me more about strength and resilience than you'll ever understand. I'd be lucky to be half the woman she was."

Why is it that I can easily go toe-to-toe with a CEO of a multi-billion-dollar company, but my grandmother throws me off-balance? She has an uncanny ability to make me feel small and insignificant, even as an adult.

This time is different.

She crossed a line when she insulted my mother, and there's no chance I was going to let her get away with that.

Grandmother sighs. "It's a shame you're as much of a disappointment as she—"

"You need to leave." Harrison's voice startles me, and I glance over to where he's standing near the entrance, his gaze narrowing in on my grandmother. "It's time for you to go," he repeats.

"How dare you speak to me like that." Grandmother shakes her cane at him. "I'm the second cousin of the prime minster of England, and I demand respect."

Harrison glares at her, causing her to recoil. His gaze meets mine, silently confirming that I'm okay. "Lady, I wouldn't give a shit if you were royalty. You won't come into my place of residence and speak to my woman like that."

His woman? I like the sound of that.

He comes to stand beside me, taking my hand in his and giving it a gentle squeeze. He's a physical anchor, holding me steady when I need it most. I like this protective side of him. Like he'd burn the world down to protect me, even from a bitter old woman with a cane.

"I'm merely trying to have a conversation with my granddaughter," grandmother says, her tone dripping with disdain.

"Doesn't look that way to me," Harrison growls. "You think you can walk in here and belittle her achievements without repercussions? You're wrong. This woman is a culinary genius, and when she's a household name, I'll make sure you're blacklisted from every one of her restaurants and Theo's too."

My eyes widen at his sheer boldness, completely unfazed by who she is.

"You have no right to threaten me. I'm Elizabeth's only family."

"Her name is Fallon," Harrison retorts. "And you're wrong.

You may share blood, but that doesn't mean shit. She deserves to be surrounded by people who will build her up, not tear her down. She has that in me, and with my family, and we'll stand by her no matter what." His posture stiffens, his tone growing more frigid with each word. "I'm going to tell you one more time before I call the police and report you for trespassing. "Leave and never come back. You're not welcome here."

"You'll regret this." Grandmother jabs a finger at us. "You both will." She storms out of the building, and my shoulders relax in relief.

I'm grateful Harrison got here when he did. For the most part, I prefer to do things on my own, including standing up to my insufferable grandmother, but in this instance, it's such a turn-on that Harrison was willing to stand up for me.

He lifts the bag from shoulder. "Let me take that for you."

I throw my arms around his neck. "Thank you."

Harrison presses a kiss to my forehead. "Always, beautiful."

I glance at the clock on the wall to see that it's only 3:30 p.m. "How come you're home so early?"

"Walter called me when your grandmother got here and mentioned you had stepped out for an errand and would be back shortly. I wish I could've been here sooner to intercept her."

I offer him a feeble smile. "It's alright. I appreciate you getting here when you did."

"Do you want to talk about what happened?"

"Not right now."

"Okay, well, I'm here when you're ready and don't let a damn thing she says get to you."

I force a smile to mask the insecurities creeping in. What if my grandmother is right and my dreams are meaningless? What if I end up as a washed-up chef with nothing to show for it, all because I wanted to carve my own path?

The next afternoon, I'm in the kitchen making dinner when my phone pings.

Lila: Are you alive? Do I need to call 911 or have a Diet Coke IV delivered?

Fallon: The latter. Stat.

Lila: I'll get Brooks right on that. The man's a walking Rolodex.

Fallon: Fully leaning into the girlfriend perks, I see.

Fallon: My grandmother stopped by uninvited yesterday.

Lila: Shit. I wish I could have been there to give her a piece of my mind.

Fallon: Harrison beat you to it.

Lila: I'm glad. Does this mean you two are official?

Fallon: Is it too late to invoke my right to remain silent?

Lila: Yup.

Fallon: Harrison took me to Aspen Grove this past weekend.

Lila: Omg really? I'm so jealous. I've always wanted to go.

Fallon: We'll have to plan a trip. Winston and Cat have to meet soon.

Fallon: They'll either love each other or start a feud. Both scenarios will be entertaining.

Lila: You didn't answer my question. Are you and Harrison official yet?

Fallon: Not exactly.

Lila: What does that mean?

Fallon: We're having hot sex and enjoying each other's company.

Lila: It's never that simple.

I wish I could argue, but she's right. Every day that Harrison and I spend together, the more intertwined our lives become, and although it's not easy to accept, I don't see a future without him. The person who used to be a thorn in my side has become as essential to my happiness as the air I breathe. It's a startling revelation that I haven't fully come to terms with yet.

Fallon: I'd like to live in my bubble for a little while longer, thank you very much.

Lila: Falling in love isn't something to be ashamed of.

Lila: Not when you find someone who treats you right.

I can't shake the memory of Harrison defending me in the lobby yesterday. He didn't benefit from it, but he still left work early and stood up for me when my own flesh and blood put me down. If I wasn't already falling hard for this man, that would have been enough to seal the deal.

I'm distracted by an incoming call, smiling when I see who it is.

"Took you long enough to call," I answer.

"Sorry," Theo says. "I haven't had a second to myself this past week."

I pull the mixture I made earlier for shepherd's pie out of the fridge as I speak. "You've always been impossible to reach, acting like you were too important," I remark playfully.

"I was your boss," he retorts smugly, a detail he never fails to remind me of.

"Maybe on paper, but we both know who everyone listened to."

Theo was frequently out of town, so I oversaw the culinary operations at one of his restaurants in London.

I hear someone shout, "Camera B, get a tight shot on the garnish," in the background, followed by another voice yelling, "We need a drizzle in the shot next." A chorus of voices agreeing follows.

"Where are you?" I ask.

"I'm at the studio in LA. Hold on just a second." The voices fade and a door slams shut. "Are you still there?"

"Yeah." I wedge my phone between my shoulder and ear as I scoop out the shepherd's pie into the glass dishes I prepared earlier.

"Sorry about the noise. We're filming season two of *The Great Cook-Off Challenge,* and the crew is trying to get some still shots between takes," Theo explains.

"It's no problem. I know you only have a few minutes, so why don't you tell me what you wanted to talk about."

He clears his throat. "During the last meeting with my market research team, they suggested that we open an allergy-friendly restaurant in London. Based on the data, there's a big demand. I told them I had to talk to you before I made a decision."

"Wow," I say, shocked, setting the bowl down on the counter.

"It's a lot to take in," Theo agrees. "I know your dream is to create a safe place for people with allergies, and I want to help you make that a reality. London might not be New York, but there's always the possibility of us expanding down the road. Just know that I'm only doing this if you're involved." My heart races, and I pull the phone from my ear, staring at it in disbelief.

The news is unexpected. I hadn't thought about moving back to London since arriving in New York. Now, just the idea of leaving has knots forming in my stomach. Harrison and I haven't discussed next steps yet, but we've been down this road before. I know what it's like being apart from him and that was before I was falling in love with him.

I bring the phone back to ear. "Can you repeat the last part?" I want to make sure I didn't misunderstand what Theo said.

"If you're not interested, I won't move forward. You've wanted this for so long and I'd never take that away from you," Theo states.

"What kind of autonomy would I have?"

"You'd have the final say over the menu, and would work with my team on the design elements, and hiring the staff. And of course you'd have a state-of-the art kitchen."

"You're serious, aren't you?"

"Very. If you're on board, the investors want to get started right away."

"When would I need to—" The shrill sound of the timer for a batch of snickerdoodles I have in the oven catches my attention. "One second, Theo."

My head is spinning as I take the cookies out and set them on the stovetop to cool.

This is a once-in-a-lifetime opportunity. There aren't many companies willing to invest in specialty restaurants and this could be the chance to create something truly special. The problem is that it's not mine. I wouldn't have full ownership, so most decisions would go through Theo and his team before being approved.

On the other hand, my practical side understands this could

be as close as I'm going to get—unless I settle for a food truck or run a pop-up kitchen at local events. Even the considerable savings I've built up since working for Harrison won't make a dent in what I'd need for a lease on a storefront in New York City. And opening a restaurant without a seasoned team would prove to be challenging.

Theo's offer might not be everything I envisioned, but it comes close. The question is, can I compromise on my dream?

"Fallon? Are you still there?" he asks.

"Yeah, I was just thinking about what you said."

"Take all the time that you need. This is a big decision and I want to make sure you do what's best for you. I'd never want you to put your own career or dreams on the back burner if this isn't what you want. Whatever you decide, I'm here to support you."

"I really appreciate it, Theo."

"That's what friends are for," he replies warmly. "I've got to run, but we'll chat when you've had time to think about this, okay?"

"Sounds good, thank you."

When he hangs up, I stare at the phone, still trying to wrap my head around our conversation.

Maybe I should have turned Theo's offer down outright, but my grandmother's remarks about me not being good enough play on a loop in my mind. What if this is my only shot at getting remotely close to honoring my mother's legacy and making a positive impact for those with food allergies?

My mind is racing, realizing that I have to tell Harrison about the offer. Which means I can no longer avoid the talk about where we stand, and what our future looks like. And if we even have one together.

Now the question is how to bring it up?

CHAPTER 31

Harrison

IT'S BEEN A LONG DAY AT THE OFFICE, AND I'M COUNTING THE hours until I can get home to Fallon. Thankfully, my mom and siblings have kept me entertained through our group chat.

Mom Doesn't Have Favorites

<Cash has renamed the group chat "Harrison & Fallon Sitting in a Tree">

Harrison: What the hell Cash?

Mom: Watch your language, Harrison Ford Stafford.

Dylan: Oh snap. Mom used your full name. That's not a good sign.

Cash: Someone is in trouble.

Harrison: Should be you for changing the name of the chat again.

Presley: This is going to be good.

Mom: Please tell me you've made things official with Fallon.

Mom: We loved spending time with her at Lola's party.

Dylan: Speaking of Lola, she won't take off the bracelet Fallon gave her.

Cash: I never thought I'd see the day when our big brother settled down.

Mom: Stop teasing your brother.

Presley: OMG. This is the best news. I love Fallon and her cookies.

Presley: The holidays are going to be so fun with her around to help bake.

Harrison: You all realize I haven't confirmed or denied anything, right?

Cash: Better be careful, brother. Sounds like Fallon is taking your place in the family if you mess this up.

Mom: Do I need to have your father talk some sense into you, Harrison?

Harrison: What do you mean?

I glance up when I hear Cabrina's voice outside my office door, which is slightly open.

"You can go right in, sir," she says brightly. "I'm sure he'll welcome the interruption. It's been a long day."

"Thank you, Cabrina." I would recognize my dad's voice anywhere.

What is he doing here?

Guess I should have taken my mom's warning literally.

"Hey, son, it's good to see you," Dad says as he walks inside my office.

My brow creases as I rise from my seat to greet him. "You should have told me you were coming into town. I would have picked you up from the airport."

"I took a taxi. You have more important things to do than driving your old man around." He holds out a cup of coffee. "I picked this up at the place you like down the street."

"Thanks." I grab the to-go cup and take a sip. The flavor of toasted marshmallow reminds me of the holidays in Aspen Grove. "Couldn't resist adding a specialty creamer, huh?" I ask with a grin.

"What can I say? Your mom's influence has rubbed off on me." He goes over to the bar cart to pour himself two fingers of whiskey.

"You didn't get yourself a coffee?"

He shakes his head as he sits in the chair across from my desk. "I wanted something stronger. Your mother banned alcohol at home. She says I need to cut back on drinking and has me eating healthier too," he grumbles, clearly not thrilled about it.

"Mom just wants you to be around as long as possible. We all do," I say with a smile.

My dad relaxes in his chair and drinks his whiskey, studying me. "I've missed this version of you."

I tilt my head, squinting at him. "I'm not sure what you're referring to."

We have a good relationship, but it's a lot different than with my siblings. He and Cash love cars and spend time in the garage working on his Jeep. With Dylan, they have Lola to talk about, and

Presley gets to enjoy his doting side as the youngest and only girl. Me, on the other hand, our conversations have always centered around Stafford Holdings and business matters, with him occasionally asking how the hockey team is doing. I'm taken aback by his impromptu visit and unusual line of conversation.

"Dad, what are you really doing here?"

"You're smiling," he notes, disregarding my question. "That's not like you."

"I smile all the time," I argue with a frown, unwilling to admit he's right.

My dad leans forward, setting his drink on the desk. "Bullshit. You've a signature scowl—just like you're wearing now," he says, gesturing to my face. "This is the first time since you took over as CEO three years ago that I've walked into this office and actually gotten your full attention."

"That's not true."

"You usually look straight through me, glued to your phone or computer, busy handling another acquisition or poring over contracts."

"That's my job," I deadpan.

"Yes, but it's essential to maintain a healthy balance between personal and business. I know from experience. You've heard your mother's side of how we met, but I think it's time I told you my version." He leans back in his chair, wrapping his fingers around his glass.

"When I met her, it was love at first sight. God, she was the most beautiful woman I'd ever seen. I lived in Maine and was learning the ropes at Stafford Holdings. Like you, I wasn't sure it was what I wanted, but I felt obligated to my father and grandfather. One summer, I went to California to meet with an associate at a law firm we did business with regarding our properties on the West Coast. Your mother worked as a part-time assistant at the firm, and when I asked her to have dinner, she said yes. She was unapologetically bold, and when she walked into the restaurant wearing a robin blue slip dress with a pair of combat boots, I was officially a goner." He glances at the floor, removing his glasses to rub his eyes, a deep crease forming on his forehead.

"Are you okay?"

"I'm not proud of what I did next," he admits, taking a deep breath before continuing. "We had an incredible time, and I was smitten. From then on, I flew out to the law firm in California every three months. I took your mother out during every visit, but I never contacted her when I was back in Maine."

"Why not?"

While I've heard the story from my mom, I'm glad I can hear it from his perspective to better understand why he hesitated to take things further. My dad is like me. We have a reason for everything we do.

He slides his glasses back on and meets my gaze. "Stafford Holdings came first, and getting seriously involved with a woman would only be a distraction. My father made it clear that I would be his successor, and I couldn't see how a family would fit with the demands piling on my shoulders. This went on for a couple of years, and a month before your mother graduated college, I was back in town for a business trip. I even brought her flowers, but she declined my invitation to dinner. She told me she was going on a date with someone else that night and refused to let me string her along any longer."

I let out a low whistle. "Damn, Dad. You messed up big-time."

He chuckles. "I did, and I nearly let your mother slip away. But as I sat alone in my hotel room that night, I realized no amount of money or prestige could make up for losing her. In that instant, I knew I had to get her back, because without her, nothing else mattered. I went to the restaurant she said they were going to, ready to fight for her, and found her sitting alone in a corner booth, drinking a glass of wine. When she saw me coming, she smirked and said, 'It's about time you showed up.'"

Given her talent for matchmaking, it's fitting that she played a key role in her own love story—carefully laying the groundwork for her happily ever after.

I let out a low whistle. "Mom never leaves anything to chance, does she?"

Dad shakes his head. "No, and I love her all the more for it."

I understand why he made the choices he did. He was devoted to my mom but felt bound by duty to his family's business, struggling to find a way to have both. In the end, love won out, but not without sacrifice and confronting his own fears.

Dad is watching me with a downcast gaze. "I've failed you, son."

I frown, leaning forward in my seat. "Why do you say that?"

Despite his heavy workload at Stafford Holdings, he always made time for his family. Even though the headquarters was an hour from Aspen Grove, he took a helicopter home every night, unlike other executives who would only go home on the weekends or raise their families in the city.

He fidgets with one of the pens on my desk. "I did to you what I despised my father for. Instead of offering you a choice, I set the expectation that you would run the business someday. Even when I saw the signs that it might not be what you wanted, I brushed them off, failing to see that I was taking away the very thing your mother and I wanted most for you—to be happy."

"Dad, you didn't make me do anything. If I had told you I didn't want to work at Stafford Holdings, you would have respected my decision." My words are measured and resolute. "It was my choice to follow in your footsteps, and any resentment I experienced was my own doing. I'm honored to have had the chance to carry on your legacy. Not only has it shaped the man I am today, but it's also given Dylan and Cash the freedom to shape their careers in the company without sacrificing time with their families."

When Presley and Jack started dating, I was protective of her but also relieved she found someone who treated her right. With Dylan and Marlow, I was grateful that he found a splash of color in a world of black and white and that Lola gained a maternal figure who loved her unconditionally. I even played a part in getting Cash and Everly together. But once it occurred to me that I was the only one still single, it was hard not to feel left behind, even if it was my own doing.

"That's my point, son," Dad says. "You've always been so concerned about how things will affect your family but never yourself." He spins the pen in between his fingers absentmindedly. "Like I told Fallon at the skating rink, I'm not one to get involved in my children's personal lives, but this is the one instance where I couldn't stay silent."

That's unexpected. Fallon never mentioned speaking with him. He tends to keep to himself at parties and events, so I'm glad he felt at ease with her. Still, I can't help but wonder what they talked about.

"You deserve a life filled with joy, and if Fallon is part of that, all the better," my dad offers with a smile. "Life is too short to let your career or fears of the unknown make you miss out on what could be the chance of a lifetime."

I sit up straight, dragging my fingers through my hair. "I misjudged Fallon in the beginning, and I've hurt her in ways I'm not proud of. I'm afraid she doesn't think I'm committed or in this for the long haul."

The more I think about it, I realize I have to *show* her that I'm here to stay. I've got an idea in mind of how to do just that, and I only hope that it'll be enough to make her see that if she gives me a chance, I'll give her the world. She's become my one and only, and I'm determined to show her every day.

My dad sets the pen down and leans forward, making sure

I'm looking at him. "It's simple, son. Tell her how you feel. You might be surprised by the outcome."

I glance out at the floor-to-ceiling windows.

That's easier said than done. Once I lay it all out, there's a real chance Fallon might turn me down, and I'm not prepared for that.

Until now, we've been focused on our explosive sexual chemistry, and she's been reluctant to define our relationship. I can understand why. She's been hurt in the past—by her ex, her grandmother, and even me, and is always waiting for the other shoe to drop.

In spite of that, she's become a pillar of strength, learning to navigate life on her own. Now that true happiness is within her reach, I think she's scared that it could all disappear in an instant. I thought avoiding the conversation to give her space to figure out what she wanted was the right call. But in the process, I've failed to communicate my intentions, which I believe has contributed to her doubts about our future.

My dad stands up, setting his empty glass on my desk. "Looks like you have a lot to think about," he says, heading for the door. "I'm going to head out. Your mom is expecting me home tonight, but if you need anything, call me."

"Hey, Dad?"

"Yeah?"

"Did Mom send you to New York to talk to me?"

I wouldn't put it past her to have him fly out just to talk some sense into me. She was over the moon when she found out Fallon was in Aspen Grove with me this past weekend—odds are, she's planning our wedding as we speak.

The idea of making Fallon mine in every way is appealing, but there's no rush. After everything we've been through, I want to cherish every moment with her, and when the time is right, I'll make it official.

Dad shrugs. "Where did you get that idea? My schedule was free, so I decided to pay my son a visit. There's nothing more to it." A smirk tugs at his lips. "And if there were a piece of truth to that, you should consider yourself lucky to have a mother who will go to any lengths to ensure your happiness."

"I love you, Dad. I'm glad you stopped by."

"Love you too, son," he says before leaving my office, closing the door behind him.

I glance at my watch to see that it's only 4:00 p.m. It's still early, but there's no use pretending I'll be able to concentrate on work now. Not with Fallon waiting for me at home. My dad was right. I have to tell her exactly what I want—I just hope she wants it too.

When I get home, Fallon is seated at the counter in the kitchen, editing a photo of grilled salmon and asparagus on her laptop. Cat lies at her feet, eyeing me warily. Fallon's his favorite person in this house, and it's a relief to know that if a burglar ever got into the penthouse, Cat would take them out before they even reached the hallway.

Fallon glances over, smiling at me. Her hair falls in waves to her shoulders, and her eyes sparkle with warmth. She's breathtaking.

I stride over, sliding my arm around her, drawing her in for a kiss. "I missed you today."

"I missed you too. You're home early."

"Am I interrupting?" I nod toward her laptop. "I can always go back to the office," I tease.

She tugs me down for another kiss. "Not a chance. You're stuck with Cat and me the rest of the night."

There's nowhere else I'd rather be.

"You should have told me you'd be back sooner. I put a casserole in the oven, but it won't be ready for another thirty minutes."

"Guess we'll just have to find a way to pass the time." I tug on my tie, loosening it from my neck.

"I can think of something we could do." Fallon closes her laptop and gets out of her chair, carefully stepping around Cat as she heads toward her bedroom.

"Where are you going?"

She stops, glancing back at me. "Going somewhere to *pass the time*. Come on, hotshot."

Her confidence is magnetic, and I'm hooked on her as much as she is on me.

I was planning to talk about our future, but that can wait until tomorrow. Right now, I want to lose myself in her—one night to worship her and to show her just how much she means to me. I'm prepared to do whatever it takes to earn another chance with her because she has my heart, and I'm ready to give her the love she's always deserved.

Fallon stands by the bed, her gaze unwavering as she slides off her shorts, kicking them off to the side. Next to go are her panties. She shimmies them past her hips, far enough for me to see her pussy. As she pulls them off, I approach her, wrapping my hand around hers. I take the panties, stuffing them inside my pant pocket.

"You have an unhealthy obsession with my underwear, don't you?"

"No, trouble. I have an obsession with *you*."

I tug off her hoodie, noticing that she's bare underneath, her full breasts on display. "Damn, these are perfect," I murmur, bending down to eagerly suck a nipple into my mouth, biting down on the soft flesh just the way I know she likes.

"Oh, god," Fallon cries out as I lavish her breasts with attention. "Harrison, I want you inside me. Now."

I lean forward, pressing a kiss to her forehead. "Lie down on the mattress."

She does as I ask, her chest heaving as she glances over, waiting for me to join her. I take a moment to appreciate what's in front of me, committing every detail to memory—the way her blonde hair spreads around her head like a halo, her dimples deepen as she smiles, and the soft curve of her waist. The universe must be on my side bringing Fallon back into my life.

Unable to stay away a second longer, I take off my suit and tie in record speed. When I get to my boxers, I pull them down, and my rigid cock springs free. Fallon keeps her eyes glued to mine as I get on the bed and crawl up her body, settling between her thighs.

I glance down at her heaving chest, tracing her nipple with my finger. She whimpers when I move to her other breast, this time lightly pinching the nipple, watching it pebble under my touch.

"I love your hands on me," she pants.

"I'll never get enough of you."

Her gaze holds me captive, as though she's unraveling every hidden part of me, seeing me in a way no one else can. I cup her cheek, gently tipping her face up with my thumb. Our mingling breathing is the only sound in the room as I brush my lips over hers, earning a soft groan. My touch is slow and tentative, a promise of what's to come. I pour my unspoken words into every kiss, saying more than I could ever articulate.

I trail my hand down her chest until I get to her stomach, mapping patterns with the pad of my finger. Drawing lower, her breath hitches when I reach the apex of her thighs.

"Harrison," she moans, begging for more.

I lock eyes with her as I line up my cock with her entrance. Slowly, I work my hand up and down my shaft as I push in slowly. The feel of her clenching around me has me letting out a low groan.

She gasps when I pull out, then push back in deeper.

I press a kiss on her nose. "Relax for me, beautiful. I'm not all the way in yet." I claim her mouth with mine, relishing in her soft sighs as I ease the rest of the way in.

Once fully seated, I intertwine our fingers, and stretch her arms above her head. A sense of calm washes over me, paired with a fierce need to claim her as mine and *show* her the effect she has on me. My energy is focused on moving slowly, wanting to savor every second inside her.

I lean down, brushing my tongue against her lips before slipping it inside her mouth, coaxing out a breathy sigh. Fallon's fingernails dig into my palms, the sensation sending a spark of electricity through me.

"I need more," she pants out, writhing beneath me.

"I know, baby, but I need to take it slow this time."

She looks up at me with those big blue eyes as I angle my hips in short, deep thrusts. Her desire is magnetic, pleading for release. God, she's so wet and warm, making me wish I could stay here forever.

Unable to deny her any longer, my free hand moves to her clit, exploring different strokes until her body goes taut. She arches off the bed, squeezing my hand that's still holding hers above the bed. I match her grip, silently telling her I'm caught up in this moment as much as she is.

I watch in awe as she cries out, tumbling into a free fall. She's never been more beautiful than in this moment, sending me barreling toward my own release. I capture her mouth with mine, craving to be connected in every possible way.

I lean down, resting my forehead against hers, trying to catch my breath. When I glance at her, the tension is wrung from her body, a thin sheen of sweat covering her breasts. My heart is still racing after what just felt like an out-of-body experience.

Fallon gives me a sated smile as I lower myself beside her, wrapping an arm around her waist. She instinctively curls into me, resting her head on my chest, and I kiss into her damp hair. She tips her head, bringing her soft lips to mine.

"I need you in my bed tonight," I murmur.

"There's nowhere else I'd rather be."

CHAPTER 32

Fallon

I'M GRIPPED WITH ANXIETY THE MOMENT I WAKE UP. I HAD every intention of talking to Harrison about Theo's offer last night, but that plan vanished when he walked through the door. Nothing seemed more important than being held in his arms, and what we shared last night was confirmation that I want this to last forever.

My worry is that if we make things official, I'll get too comfortable and lose sight of my ambitions. What if I wake up years from now realizing that I never chased the goals I set for myself and worked so hard to achieve? And then there's the challenge of balancing work and personal life. I don't want my role as Harrison's private chef to define us. What we have is rare, and I want him to know that I'm in this for the right reasons.

Harrison is on a conference call in his home office when I get out of bed.

After I check on Cat, who's perched in his climbing post, I

head down to the lobby to chat with Walter. It's early enough to avoid the morning rush of residents heading to work.

He's at his desk, smiling when he sees me. "Good morning, Miss Fallon. What brings you down here so early? Expecting a delivery?"

I lift the bag in my hand. "I made banana bread last night and wanted to bring you a loaf."

I cross the empty lobby and perch on the edge of Walter's desk, holding out the container of sliced bread.

"Thank you. This will go great with my second cup of coffee," he says with a grin.

"My pleasure."

Walter sets the bread aside, his gaze fixed on me. I bite my lip, glancing at the front door, second-guessing coming down. I'm sure the last thing he wants is to hear about my problems today.

Like he can read my mind, he pats my knee and asks, "Why don't you tell me what's bothering you, Miss Fallon."

"I'm fine," I say, but my voice betrays me, cracking on the last word.

I'm anything but.

Walter adjusts his cap, his eyes sharp with concern. "Oh really? So, you came to see me when you knew no one else would be around just for the fun of it? Because you look like you've got the weight of the world on your shoulders. I won't push you to answer, but I'm here if you want to talk."

I swallow the lump in my throat, trying to push down the emotions rising to the surface. Walter has quickly filled the role of the doting grandparent I've always longed for. It's still strange to have someone who listens, genuinely cares, and wants the best for me. Which makes it impossible not to confide in him now, not when he looks at me with patience and compassion, and I know he'll listen without judgment.

"Do you think I'm a failure?" The question spills from my mouth before I can rein it in.

He recoils, his expression hardening. "Why would you say that? If it was Mr. Stafford, I'll be having a serious conversation with him when he comes down later."

I shake my head, resting my hand on his shoulder. "Harrison wouldn't say that," I assure him. "I've just been thinking about what my grandmother said when she was here." I bounce my knee, glancing at the floor. "I gave up a steady career for what? A pipe dream of owning a restaurant and publishing a cookbook? Maybe she's right. I'll never amount to anything."

"That's not true." Walter's tone is firm. "I've been around enough people like her in my lifetime to know that woman spews nothing but lies, hiding behind her own misery and self-pity. She's just jealous of your confidence and desire to forge your own path. In simple terms, she's a bitter woman and her opinion is worthless."

I give his shoulder a reassuring squeeze, then place my hand in my lap. "You're a good friend, Walter. I'm lucky to have you."

"Likewise, Miss Fallon." He smiles.

He rises from his seat and heads to the coffee station in the corner to pour himself a cup.

"What brought on this self-doubt?" he asks.

He adds splash of hazelnut creamer into his coffee and stirring it slowly.

"I got a job offer from Theo, my old boss," I admit, finally saying it out loud for the first time since Theo and I talked. "He wants me to manage a new restaurant in London."

Walter nods thoughtfully, sitting back down in his chair. "It sounds like an incredible opportunity."

"Yeah, it is. The only problem is that it's not…" I hesitate, struggling to articulate my thoughts.

"Your dream," Walter finishes for me.

I nod. "Exactly."

"So, what's stopping you from declining?"

"With Theo, I'd have access to brand strategists, a PR team, and an experienced operations manager. With that kind of expertise, success is practically a sure thing." Walter taps his coffee cup thoughtfully as he listens. "If I venture out on my own, it'll be a big risk requiring a leap of faith."

Walter purses his lips. "Hmm. What does Mr. Stafford think you should do?"

Warmth rises to my cheek as I rub a hand across my face. "I haven't told him yet," I admit.

Walter blinks in shock, nearly choking on his coffee. I give him a light pat on the back as he clears his throat.

"Are you alright?"

He nods, grabbing a tissue to wipe his mouth. "Why haven't you told him?"

"We haven't defined our relationship. What if I pass on the closest opportunity I'll have to achieve my dream, and it turns out to be the wrong choice?"

"That's one way to look at it," Walter says, his mouth curling into a grin. "My Pearl used to say that every ending is just the beginning of a new adventure. What seems like a dead end is the first step on a new path you haven't discovered yet."

"Pearl was very wise."

He laughs softly. "Yes, she was. Have I told you how we met?"

I shake my head.

"I wanted to be a doctor, but I wasn't accepted to medical school. The rejection stung, especially since my parents were disappointed. It felt like there was no path forward, and I was so upset I almost said no when my friend asked me to go with him to New York for the weekend. We rode the subway to Central Park, and a woman sitting across from us caught my attention. She had hazel eyes and wore a yellow dress with a lace collar. I noticed she was reading *Oliver Twist,* one of my favorites, but I was shy and didn't have the courage to talk to her before she got off the train. I pushed it aside until the next day when we stopped at a coffee shop, and there she was, standing behind the counter. Pearl and I got married three months later and made a home in New York."

"Oh, Walter, that's such a sweet story," I say, resting my hand over my heart. "I wish I could have met her."

He gives me a fond smile, patting my arm. "She would have loved you, and I'm sure she'd have far better advice. All I know is that sometimes you have to take a risk, or you'll regret not trying."

The elevator chime has us both glancing up as a business-man in a pinstriped suit steps out, phone pressed to his ear and a briefcase in hand. A woman trails behind him, leading a Yorkie on a leash.

"Looks like the morning rush is about to start," Walter says. "Promise you'll think about what I said?"

I give him a parting smile. "I will. I'm heading upstairs to talk to Harrison now."

"Good, I'm glad."

He adjusts his tie and hurries to open the door for the residents leaving the building.

On my way up to the penthouse, I reflect on how much has changed between Harrison and me. We started as adversaries, both driven by personal vendettas, and now we've become the most important person in each other's lives.

It's made me realize that if I want this to work between us, I need to be open and willing to share my fears and dreams. He's shown that he cares and wants to support my ambitions—and now I just have to take a chance and tell him how I feel.

When I enter the penthouse, a shrill fire alarm pierces the air. I race toward the kitchen, quickly scanning the room, first landing on Cat sprawled in his bed, unfazed by the chaos. He must be de-sensitized from all the scary movies that we've watched. Maybe it's time to introduce him to cartoons.

A loud clatter draws my attention to Harrison standing by the stove. He's holding a smoking skillet with one hand, and moves fast, dropping it into the sink with a thud and turns on the cold water, sending a hiss of steam into the air. He lets the sink fill half-way before turning it off, exhaling sharply under his breath as he hops onto the counter to disable the smoke detector on the ceiling.

"Fuck, that thing is annoying," he mutters when there's fi-nally silence.

I walk toward him, thoroughly entertained. "Are you *trying* to burn down my kitchen?"

Harrison snaps his head in my direction, his eyes widening when he sees me. "I got off my call early and wanted to make you breakfast, but clearly, I'm hopeless in the kitchen. I can't even cook eggs without burning them." He jumps down from the counter, closing the space between us, and wraps me in a hug.

"Good thing you have me or you might starve," I joke.

"I'm definitely lucky." He smiles, pushing my hair back to give me a quick kiss.

His hands always seem to find me when we're close, and I can't get enough. "I'll make breakfast if you keep me company," I say, kissing him again.

Harrison rubs the back of his neck, a light frown creasing his forehead as he meets my gaze. "That sounds great, but could we talk first? There's something I want to tell you, and it can't wait."

A flood of possibilities crosses my mind, and while I'm anx-ious, this is my opportunity to address Theo's job offer and finally be upfront about my feelings, no matter where that might lead us.

"Yeah, I'd really like that," I say, shifting my weight from one foot to the other. "There's something I've been meaning to tell you, too."

A brief flash of worry crosses Harrison's face before he schools his expression. "Let's sit down, and you can share what's on your mind."

I nod, accepting his outstretched hand as he guides me into the living room. I appreciate him suggesting I go first. I've kept this all bottled up inside, and I'm afraid I might burst if I don't get it out soon. We settle next to each other on the couch, and I cross my legs, resting one knee against Harrison's thigh.

"Ladies first. What is it you wanted to tell me?" he asks, taking my hand in his, holding it tight.

I exhale deeply, gathering my courage. "Theo, my old boss, called yesterday and told me he's opening an allergy-friendly restaurant in London."

He shifts in his seat, blinking rapidly, a mix of confusion and concern in his eyes. "Are you okay with that? I assume you've told him that you want to open one of your own someday?"

Here goes nothing.

"That's the thing. His market research team found a growing demand for a restaurant specializing in food sensitivities. He wants me to move back to London and manage the one they're launching." I rush to explain, wanting to get it all out at once.

I glance over at Harrison. His features don't betray emotion, and the silence stretches between us. I'm not panicking because his hand is still firmly clasped around mine, his touch grounding me amidst the uncertainty. I'm tempted to give him more information, but I hold back, allowing him time to process. He'll ask questions when he's ready.

I let out a breath I didn't realize I'd been holding. It's only been a day, but keeping this from Harrison for even that long felt wrong.

He clears his throat before finally speaking. "Is it a good offer?"

"It is," I answer truthfully. "I'd have full control over the menu, a dedicated team to support the launch, and a state-of-the-art kitchen. Plus, I'd be involved in hiring the staff and overseeing the daily kitchen operations." Even as I speak, a knot tightens in my stomach.

"That does sound like an incredible opportunity," Harrison admits hesitantly. "Have you given Theo an answer?"

I shake my head. "He asked me to take some time to think about it and to reach out once I've made my decision."

Harrison scoots closer, his side brushing mine as he rests his hand on my knee. While his other hand remains wrapped around mine. "Can I ask why you didn't say yes right away?"

I frown, caught off guard by that question. "If I moved to London, we'd be on different continents." I state the obvious.

"Yes, but this is your dream. You've wanted this for so long, so why hold back when it's finally within reach?"

Now, I better understand his line of questioning.

The opportunity isn't as alluring as it was when Theo called me. On paper, it looks like a wish fulfilled, but I can't shake the thought that I'm trying to force a square peg into a round hole, settling for something close to what I want, but not quite right.

"My dream is to run my own restaurant, where I have control over every aspect of the operation. With Theo, I'd have to answer to him and his investors," I explain. "What I really want is the autonomy to make the decisions and create something that's mine."

It's not the financial success or prestige that drives me as much as the desire to build something that honors my mom's legacy. A tribute that reflects her kind spirit and the passion for cooking she passed down to me. Though she's no longer here, I want to make a space where her love for food and family lives on.

"What's holding you back?" Harrison asks.

I bite my lower lip, glancing out the window at the skyline. "My lack of resources. I've been saving, but it's nowhere near enough to cover the initial lease, let alone permits, licenses, renovations, and all the promotional costs, especially in New York City. Plus, I'm only one person. With Theo, I'd have a team to help support the venture."

Most restaurants fail within the first five years, and without a solid marketing strategy and financial backing, I wouldn't make it past one. It's a harsh truth to accept. In the past, I wore rose-colored glasses, believing that passion and hard work would be enough, but now I know I can't overlook the practical side of things if I want to make this happen.

Noticing my uncertainty, Harrison gently turns my chin to meet his gaze, offering me a reassuring smile. "You're far more capable than you give yourself credit for."

"I just wish there was a simple solution. It seems like no matter what I choose, there's a tradeoff." I breathe out slowly, releasing my pent-up tension. "Can we switch topics for a bit? Maybe it'll give me some perspective. Wasn't there something you wanted to tell me?"

"Yes, but before I do, I need to say something. I want you to know that whether or not you decide to accept the job offer, I'll be there with you," he vows. "If you want to move back to London, we'll find a place with a view of the Thames or Notting Hill. Or if you decide to open your own restaurant somewhere outside New York, we'll find a place with a sunroom for your plants and plenty of room for Cat to explore."

His willingness to put his own career second to mine catches me off guard. No one has put me first since my parents died, and it makes me see that I'm the most important thing in Harrison's world—just as he is in mine. I wish I knew what I did to deserve him, and I plan to spend forever showing him how grateful I am.

"Harrison, you're the CEO of the largest real estate firm in the country. You can't just move out of New York on a whim when this is where you do business."

He holds my gaze, making sure he has my attention. "I'd give up everything for you if I had to because you're all that matters," he states with unwavering determination. "Besides, what's the point of being the boss if I don't have flexibility in where I live? Now, back to the thing I wanted you to know about."

When he doesn't elaborate, I furrow my brow. "Well, are you going to tell me?"

He smiles. "I'd rather show you."

CHAPTER 33

Harrison

FIFTEEN MINUTES LATER, WE'RE STANDING IN FRONT OF A brick building, ivy crawling up one side and large glass windows covered in opaque film. I pull a key from my coat pocket, unlocking the black double doors.

I gesture for Fallon to enter. "Here we are."

Her eyes linger on the exterior before tipping her chin, curiosity written across her face as she steps forward. I follow closely, shutting the door behind us once we're inside.

A faint stream of light filters through the covered windows, and I flip on the light switch to give us a better view of the space. The building is in mid-renovation, but we have uninterrupted time to look around with the crew off today. Unfinished walls reveal their wooden frames, sections of the floor remain untiled, and the air carries the lingering scent of sawdust and plaster.

Fallon surveys the room with wide eyes, spinning in a full circle. "What is this place?"

"Your restaurant," I say, my lips twitching with excitement.

She stops short, turning around to face me. "My *what?*"

"It might not look like much right now, but it's yours," I repeat. "That is if you want it. Stafford Holdings acquired this section of the block last year, and this particular building has been sitting empty ever since. When you first told me about wanting to open your own restaurant, I immediately thought of this spot. It's in a prime location with the potential for an open floor plan."

Fallon's brow furrows, her lips pressed together as she processes the news.

I had planned to wait to bring her here until the construction crew got everything up to code. But when she told me about Theo's offer, I knew I had to show her now so she could weigh all of her options. I meant it when I said I'd support her no matter what she decides, but I'm not above pulling out all the stops to give her every reason to want to stay in New York.

She exhales, shaking her head. "I don't even know what to say. It's an incredible gesture, but there's no way I could ever afford a place like this. I'll be lucky to get a food truck or pop-up restaurant within the next couple of years. That's one of the reasons Theo's offer is so tempting."

Fallon's fiercely independent nature is her strength, and she's built her career from the ground up by sheer determination. So, it's no surprise that she'd assume she'd have to shoulder this burden alone. Soon enough, she'll understand that her dreams are mine too, and I'll be right by her side, even if she hesitates to accept it.

I gently touch her arm, my fingers lightly tracing the outline of her sleeve. "You're not alone anymore, beautiful. More than anything, I want to be your partner and stand by your side in every aspect of your life, including this one." I nod to the space around us. "I'm your biggest supporter and advocate, and all I want is for you to be happy and achieve your goals."

She glances up at me, her eyes filled with uncertainty. "What if things don't work out between us? I don't want to be indebted to anyone, not even you."

"The building is yours, with all related expenses covered for the next five years. It's been transferred to your name, giving you full control. The construction crew will make sure everything is up to code, but you'll have the final say on the design and layout." I draw her closer, her warmth grounding me. "I should've been more clear earlier. I want *everything* with you—to sleep in the same bed every night, wake up beside you in the mornings, and share a life through all the highs and lows. There is no future without you in it, trouble."

Fallon exhales deeply, her shoulders relaxing. "I want that too. So much." She gives me a tender smile. "I've been so scared that this was all too good to be true, and one day, you'd be gone. This is why I was afraid to let myself get too close, but I'm done letting fear control me. I'm ready to take the leap and give us a real chance."

God, hearing her say that is music to my ears. Since the truth came out, I was afraid she'd decided there was too much baggage between us and would walk away. Now, those fears have melted away, replaced with the certainty that we'll face the future together, stronger than ever before.

"I love you, Harrison," she declares. "You've shown me that my heart is safe with you, and that you'll always be there to catch me when I fall, and that you'll support me every step of the way as I achieve my dreams." She pauses, smiling at me with tears in her eyes. "And I want to do the same for you—to stand beside you, no matter what comes our way."

My heart leaps in my chest as a grin spreads across my face. Her confession settles around me like a warm blanket. I never realized how much it would mean to hear those words until she said them.

With a soft exhale, I place both hands on her face, my palms warm against her skin as I tilt her head slightly. Our foreheads touch as I breathe her in.

"Say it again."

Tears well in her eyes. "I. Love. You. Hotshot. More than I ever thought possible."

"That makes me so damn happy to hear because I love you too, trouble," I murmur against her lips. "No one else makes me laugh or challenges me like you do. You've transformed my cold, gray world into a vibrant reality filled with laughter, color, and a love I never saw coming. You're my past, present, and the only future I want."

Now I get why my mom was so determined for me and my siblings to find our own happily ever afters. There's nothing like finding *your* person—the one who sees you at your worst and still chooses you. Fallon has brought balance to my life when everything around me is chaotic. One touch from her, and everything feels right with the world again.

I nuzzle her neck, running my nose along her collarbone. "I love you so damn much, and whatever happens next, we're in it together." I lean back, gazing into her piercing blue eyes. "Now tell me, what do you really think of this place?" I nudge gently, hoping to make her feel more at ease with the idea that it belongs to her.

"You're kidding, right?" She snickers, clearly entertained. "It's amazing with a blank slate full of potential. The issue is that I'm not sure I'm cut out for a massive project like this by myself. I figured if I was ever able to venture out on my own, I'd start with a small space and grow from there."

"There's no doubt in my mind you could handle it."

"I appreciate your confidence, but my expertise is in the kitchen. What if I can't manage all the logistics of running a restaurant this size by myself?"

"For starters, you're so much more than a chef," I state. "Without your creativity and talent, this place is just an empty space. You're the one who'll turn it into a destination for incredible food and memorable experiences. If you need extra hands, you can hire an operations manager. And remember, you'll never be alone again. I'm here to lend a hand however I can." I brush a kiss against her forehead. "I may not be an expert in the food service industry, but I know how to create a business plan and keep it running smoothly. There will be roadblocks, but we'll figure them out together… if this is what you want. If you'd prefer, we can put the project on hold if you decide to return to work for Theo, or if you want to do this without my help, that's okay too."

Fallon brushes a strand of hair from her face as she steps out of my arms, moving across the room, her eyes darting over every detail as she surveys the empty space. She traces her fingers along the outline of a doorframe, her brow furrowed in concentration as if she's mentally mapping out the possibilities for the place.

I lean against the nearest wall, my heart swelling as I watch her roam, her confidence building with each step. She may doubt her ability to make this a success, but I know she's capable—a gift for creating mouthwatering dishes that leave people speechless and a rare ability to connect with anyone. I've been around enough successful entrepreneurs to know when someone has raw talent, and Fallon has it in spades. If this is the path she chooses, there's no question she'll turn this place into a must-visit destination with a waiting list at least a month long.

My family and I will be here, cheering her on every step of the way. She's now surrounded by people who believe in her and will remind her there is no limit to what she can achieve.

After she takes a tour through the entire space, she approaches me, her face lighting up with a grin.

"I want to stay in New York and turn this space into the restaurant I've always wanted with *you*." She holds a finger when I try to speak. "But I won't accept a handout, no matter how generous your intentions are."

I step in front of her, take her hand in mine, and press a kiss to the tips of her fingers, hiding my smile. "What do you propose, my love?"

"Will you be my first investor? I want this to be a partnership, like you said, not a charity." She squares her shoulders and extends her hand.

I tap my chin, pretending to think it over, though I already know there's no way I'll let her pay me a dime. This place was meant to be a gift and a way to honor her parents' legacy. But I understand she won't settle for anything less than an agreement to move forward, and I respect that.

"It's a deal, but I've got a condition." She eyes me cautiously, unsure where I'm headed with this. "We seal this one with a kiss."

She smirks, dropping her hand and sauntering closer. "I accept your terms, hotshot."

I rest my hand on the small of her back and the other on the nape of her neck. She tilts her head in invitation as I slant my mouth across hers. Fallon's lips are soft against mine, and I groan, losing myself in the sweetness. We've kissed countless times, but this one is different—it's a promise of a new beginning.

CHAPTER 34

Fallon

I WAKE UP THE NEXT MORNING WITH A SENSE OF PURE excitement. After years of working toward my goal of opening a restaurant, I'm finally one step closer to it becoming a reality. It wouldn't be possible without Harrison. When he said he had a surprise for me, I never imagined it would be a building, let alone one that I now have the freedom to transform as we see fit.

Admittedly, I was prepared to turn him down despite it being the perfect space. It felt wrong accepting such a grand gesture, especially since I've been adamant about doing everything on my own for the longest time. In the past, I refused help because I thought I had to prove I could handle things on my own. But recently, I've learned that relying on others isn't a sign of weakness but strength. It takes courage to trust someone implicitly and let them in to share the load.

It's still surreal that Harrison told me he loves me. I didn't think being this happy was possible, but he's proving me wrong.

After our conversation, it's like everything is falling into place as it should, and I'm ready to start our new life together.

I'm at the kitchen counter with my laptop, looking at design inspiration for the restaurant. I want the place to be a peaceful retreat amidst the hustle and bustle of the city. It'll include warm, earthy tones, natural wood accents, and vibrant greenery, including hanging plants, indoor trees, and fresh herbs that will be incorporated into the menu.

Cat trots over from his bed in the corner, nudging my leg with his head.

"Hey there, little demon," I say, bending down to scratch behind his ear. "You've already had breakfast, remember?" He meows loudly in protest. "Don't worry. I'll get you some salmon delight once Harrison leaves for work," I coo, ruffling his fur.

"I heard that," Harrison says from the doorway. "Remember what the vet said yesterday?"

We took Cat to his first vet appointment yesterday and were told he's in excellent health, but the vet recommended cutting him down to two meals a day to prevent any further weight gain. It seems I've been overindulging him.

I gently turn Cat's head in Harrison's direction. "How am I supposed to say no to this face?"

Harrison laughs softly, glancing down at Cat. "You're right, he is downright adorable when he's not attacking plates or knocking things over."

He maneuvers around Cat, leaning down to kiss me. He looks utterly edible in a three-piece navy suit. He got a haircut yesterday, styled in a tapered fade.

"I love you," I murmur.

"I love you too, trouble." He caresses my jaw, giving me another soft kiss. "Have a great day, and don't you and Cat get into too much mischief while I'm gone."

"We make no promises," I tease.

Now that I'm moving into Harrison's bedroom, we're working on converting mine into a sanctuary for Cat, complete with a climbing wall, a cat tree by the window where he can nap in the sun, and a scratching post in the corner to encourage him to leave the other furniture in the house alone. It's perfect timing, considering the new couch for the living room, and the dining room table and chairs we've ordered will arrive in a couple of weeks.

Harrison grabs his lunch from the fridge I made him earlier, and hugs me on his way out the door. "Can't wait to see you tonight."

"I'm looking forward to it. I love you."

"I love you too, beautiful. See you soon." He waves before heading down the hallway.

Before I go back to looking at design inspiration, I check my phone to find a message waiting.

Lila: I can't wait to fly out for the restaurant's grand opening and shower you with hugs!

Fallon: It'll take at least a year before we open.

Fallon: But have your hugs on standby!

After Harrison surprised me at the restaurant, I had to call Lila and share all the exciting news. Of course, I couldn't wait to tell my best friend that I've found the love of my life.

Lila: How did Theo take the news?

Fallon: He was very supportive.

When I told him what Harrison did and that I'm opening a restaurant for those with food sensitivities in New York, he confirmed that he's not moving forward with his plans in London. However, he does want to explore the possibility of investing in my business and expanding to Europe. It'll be a while before that's even on the table, but having his support is invaluable, especially when I'm ready for advice on the menu, marketing, and other aspects of the business.

Lila: That's amazing, babe!

Lila: I can't wait to meet the man who stole your heart.

Fallon: Back at you. I still need to meet Brooks.

Lila: Who would have thought we'd both find our Prince Charming!

Fallon: Well, obviously. We're amazing.

Lila: I know, right?!

An hour later, I step off the elevator to the lobby of the apartment building. Walter is standing at the concierge desk, sorting through a box of supplies filled with tissues, envelopes, and a package of extra key fobs.

He looks up with a smile. "Good morning, Miss Fallon."

"Morning. I brought you some chocolate chip cookies." I hold out a clear container, setting it on the counter between us.

"Thank you. I can't wait to try them," he says enthusiastically. "Mr. Stafford was telling me all about your restaurant on his way to the office this morning. I can't wait to see it."

"If you're free later, we could stop by," I suggest. "It's still a construction zone, but I'd like to get your thoughts on the space.

I have a call with an interior designer next week and need to finish putting a plan together before then."

"Let's go during my lunch break," Walter says as he pulls out another box of tissues. "Would you mind putting this in my desk drawer?"

I nod, grabbing the box and moving around Walter's desk to open the top drawer. I have to shuffle through pens, sticky notes, and old receipts to make space for the tissues. At the bottom of the pile, a blue collar catches my eye. Walter doesn't own a pet, so it's curious that he has one. Maybe it's from an animal that belongs to one of the residents.

I glance over at Walter, who's rushing to open the front door for a woman in a black blazer and pencil skirt, with a briefcase in hand, heading out of the building.

With him distracted, I grab the collar to study it closer. The small size and the bell attached suggest it's a cat collar. The only reason I know that is because I had to buy one for Cat. I squint to read the engraved tag: "Urban Tails Animal Shelter." That's the shelter where Walter volunteers. He's told me they primarily take in cats, which is a perfect fit given his reputation as the "cat whisperer." He's definitely earned the title in my book.

Cat was surprisingly at ease around him when Harrison and I left for Aspen Grove, and even now, Cat still gravitates toward him whenever he comes up to the penthouse, which is odd since he's still cagey around everyone else, including Harrison.

And then it clicks.

The day Cat showed up, the penthouse was hectic with deliveries for my catering events, and Walter made multiple trips upstairs to lend a hand to the couriers. I was busy in the kitchen and wasn't paying attention to him coming and going, but he must have brought Cat up at some point. Now that I've found this collar, it's the only explanation that makes sense.

My mind races, wondering why he would have left Cat with

me in the first place. I did mention the pranks between Harrison and me and how I was relieved that he hadn't pulled another one before he went on his trip. However, there was no guarantee that we would keep Cat or that it would bring Harrison and me together.

"You okay, Miss Fallon?" Walter asks, approaching the desk.

I glance up, holding out the cat collar. "Look what I found." I pause, watching for his reaction. "Is this Cat's?"

"Curious." Walter rubs his chin thoughtfully. "Wonder how that got in there."

I raise an eyebrow. "Am I to believe it's a coincidence that you have a cat collar in your desk, and I happen to have a cat in my apartment who showed up out of thin air?"

"Stranger things have happened." He shrugs. "I must've put the collar in my pocket after an adoption event at the shelter and forgot to put it back."

Except it's not.

I'm certain it was Walter who brought Cat to my apartment. No matter his reasons, I'm grateful to him. They've both become part of my family—Walter is like the grandfather I never had and is now one of my closest confidants. I'm grateful to have him looking out for Harrison and me. Cat can be a handful, but he's ours and I wouldn't change a thing.

I place the collar back in the drawer, and tuck the tissues beside it.

Walter watches as I approach him and I wrap my arms around him for a hug.

"Thank you for everything," I whisper.

"You're welcome." He draws back with a smile. "Are you happy, Miss Fallon?"

"The happiest I've ever been." I grin.

No truer words have been spoken.

A year ago, I never could have pictured this life for

myself—with a man who loves me unconditionally, a cat who shares my fondness for scary movies, and a strong support system in Walter and the Staffords.

Somehow, Harrison and I ended up exactly where we were meant to be. Funny how those closest to us always seem to interfere for the better, and I wouldn't have it any other way. Having people who care enough to push me toward happiness is something I'll never take for granted.

This is only the start of our love story, and I can't wait for what comes next.

CHAPTER 35

Harrison

Harrison & Fallon Sitting in a Tree

Dylan: I'm shocked you declined a 4pm meeting, Harrison. Are you sick?

Harrison: I'm taking Fallon on a date to the Mavericks game tonight.

Dylan: Good to see you making time for something other than work.

Mom: That's so romantic!

Cash: It's official, big brother. You're in love.

Harrison: I am. Fallon and I are officially a couple.

Mom: I've never been so happy. Do you think I should book the church in Aspen Grove next summer just in case you want to use it?

Presley: Ok Mom, calm down. They aren't even engaged yet.

Mom: Semantics.

<Cash has renamed the group chat "When is Harrison Proposing">

Presley: Dylan, you might want to go over and check on Mom.

Harrison: Cash, it's been 5 minutes.

Mom: I'm okay. Just so thrilled all my kids have found their perfect match.

Dylan: It's all thanks to you, Mom.

Mom: I have no idea what you're talking about.

Harrison: Regardless. We love you.

Mom: I love you all too.

<Cash has renamed the group chat "Harrison is Mom's Favorite">

I set my phone aside, scrolling through a résumé Cabrina sent me earlier. It's important that my brothers and I have quality time outside of work to be with our families. To make that possible, we're hiring a director of operations to handle the growing workload and streamline operations, with plans to expand our executive team once they're onboarded.

The change is a complete reversal of how I used to manage the business, where I took on a heavy workload and was reluctant to delegate. But it's the right thing to do to find a better balance in my life, and I couldn't be more pleased about it.

The rest of the day drags on, and by the time I reach the apartment building after work, I'm more than ready to see Fallon.

Walter opens the door when I get to the entrance. "Good afternoon, Mr. Stafford," he says with a tip of his hat.

"Good afternoon, Walter. How's our girl?"

"Miss Fallon had a good day. She brought me cookies this morning, and we toured her restaurant space during lunch. I've never seen her this happy." He beams proudly. "You're a good man for treating her right."

I clap him on the back. "She deserves nothing less. Thanks for always looking out for her, it means a lot to both of us."

"No need to thank me. Fallon is family, plain and simple. It's my privilege to be in her corner."

My heart swells at his sentiment. I know Fallon feels the same, and I'm glad they've become so close. Although it's a shame her grandmother failed to see how incredible she is, that's her loss. Fallon doesn't need that kind of negativity in her life when she has me, my family and Walter by her side.

Last week, I contacted the building manager to arrange a substantial bonus for Walter and to tell him it's from all the residents. I usually send him something during the holidays, but I want to go beyond that. He's an important presence in Fallon's life, and from now on, I'll make sure he's well taken care of. Whether he eventually retires or not—though I doubt he ever will.

I head for the elevator. "See you soon, Walter," I smile.

"You too," he replies with a wave.

When I get to the penthouse, I drop my briefcase off at the entry table, greeted by the rich aroma of herbs and spices with hints of garlic and onion. I follow the smell to the kitchen, where I find Fallon at the stove, dancing around to "What a Feeling." Her hips sway to the beat, and she holds a whisk to her mouth, belting out the lyrics, her energy contagious.

It takes me back to the first time I saw her dancing in the kitchen when my desire for her was waging a war against the resentment I convinced myself was justified. As I watch her, it's obvious how far we've come. The attraction that once caused conflict now fuels an unbreakable love that can't be shaken.

"I'll never get tired of coming home to this view," I say, speaking over the music.

Fallon looks back, a broad smile on her face. "You're home!"

I turn down the music off on my way to greet her. "Whatever you're making smells delicious." I wind an arm around her waist and bury my nose into the curve of her neck.

"It's beef stew. I figure we can eat before we go on our date to the Mavericks game."

Even though she refuses to take any more paychecks, she still wants to prepare our meals. Fallon doesn't trust anyone else to do it like she can and she says it's good practice. She might refuse to let me pay her a salary, but I'll make sure she gets the best equipment for her restaurant and every opportunity to make it thrive. It's the least I can do after everything she's done for me.

"Sounds perfect. I can't wait to try it," I say.

The stew begins to simmer, bubbles rising to the surface. Fallon turns, spoon in hand, stirring the pot as she leans back into my embrace. These simple moments are the ones I cherish the most. They remind me that everything I need is right here, and nothing else can compare to this feeling.

My world used to be a series of transitions, where every choice was a deal to be made. Focus and precision were my guiding principles, and I thrived on structured order. Now, I leave work early to be with my beautiful girlfriend. Our living room is bursting with plants, and Cat, our little demon, has woven himself into our lives for good.

Fallon turned my carefully structured life into a beautiful chaos that fills our house with warmth, laughter, and a love I never saw coming. With her, I've learned to slow down and appreciate what's right in front of me. I wouldn't have it any other way.

Getting a private chef didn't turn out anything like I expected, but now I know what happens when a CEO gets a second chance...

She becomes the love of his life.

EPILOGUE

Fallon

I DRAW IN A SHAKY BREATH AS I TAKE IN THE FINISHED restaurant. Large, black-framed windows span across the front, flower boxes nestled below. A golden glow spills from inside, illuminating the brick exterior.

The cold air nips at my nose as I wrap my arms around myself, reflecting on how far I've come. The journey here was long, marked by construction delays, sleepless nights, and countless hours perfecting the menu. Without Harrison, Walter, and the Staffords, I wouldn't have made it through. I'm grateful for them believing in me and cheering me on when I needed it most.

My heart swells seeing the vintage sign hanging above the entrance, *Catherine's Table*.

"We did it, Mom," I murmur softly.

She inspired this restaurant, and I like to think she played a significant part in guiding me here. As a gentle breeze stirs around me, I close my eyes, picturing my parents standing beside me, sharing this achievement with me. Their proud smiles are vivid in my mind, as if they were still here cheering me on.

Every struggle and triumph I've faced has played an important role in shaping who I am, leading me to this defining day, where all my hard work has paid off in more ways than one.

"Fallon?" My eyes flutter open at the sound of Harrison's voice.

He steps out of the restaurant and joins me on the sidewalk. He's dressed in his signature three-piece suit with a cobalt tie, the smell of his woodsy cologne reaching me before he does.

"What are you doing out here?" he asks.

"I wanted some fresh air and to take it all in." I smile softly, gesturing to the building.

Harrison takes my hand in his, intertwining our fingers. "It's remarkable, Fallon." His voice is filled with admiration. "These are for you."

He extends his other hand, revealing a bouquet of white tulips.

"Thank you," I say, bringing them to my nose and inhaling their sweet scent. "They're beautiful."

"You left the apartment early this morning, and I haven't had a chance to congratulate you properly today." He winds his arm around my waist, drawing me flush to his chest. "I'm proud of you, trouble." He tips my chin, his lips meeting mine in a kiss. "I love you so damn much."

I run a finger along the stubble on his chin. "I love you too, hotshot. This is your night as much as it is mine. Thank you for being there from beginning. I couldn't have done this without you."

We've come a long way—what started as a whirlwind weekend together, followed by mutual disdain, has blossomed into being head over heels in love. The past year has been pure bliss, and I thank my lucky stars for getting to wake up with him by my side. Even after a year, my love for him grows stronger by the day.

Harrison has hired several executives at Stafford Holdings, giving him more time at home. Our nights and weekends are spent in the kitchen, curled up on the couch with Cat at our feet, and enjoying walks through Central Park when the weather is nice. Our life together might not be filled with grand adventures, but it's proof that lasting love can be simple and still be extraordinary, and I wouldn't trade it for anything.

"Why don't we go inside?" Harrison suggests. "My family wants to see you before you go back to the kitchen."

"I'd like that. Lead the way," I say as I follow him inside.

Hand in hand, we step into the restaurant, immediately enveloped by the warmth. The air is filled with fresh basil and rosemary, with the subtle fragrance of mint from the plants around us.

Tables crafted from reclaimed wood are set up throughout the room, each paired with leather-upholstered chairs. Across the room, a bar stretches along the wall filled with top-shelf liquor, where the bartender mixes drinks with precision. Low wooden trays along the wall hold small clusters of herbs that we incorporate into the dishes.

I wave at Julie, the hostess, as we walk past. "You're doing great tonight," I commend.

"Thank you, Chef." She beams.

The place is packed with family and friends of the staff. Tonight, we're doing a soft opening to fine-tune the menu and service ahead of the grand opening next week. Lila and Brooks are coming to town for it, and I'm counting down the days. It's been too long, and I have a list of places to take Lila while she's in town.

The Staffords are at a large table in the corner, enjoying a sampler of appetizers, including stuffed mushrooms, sweet potato wedges, and smoked salmon cucumber bites.

As soon as Johanna sees us, she gets out of her chair and comes over to pull me into a hug.

"Sweetheart, this place is amazing," she praises, pulling back to look at me. "And the food is flawless as always. Mike and I couldn't be more proud of you."

Tears well in my eyes at her tenderness. "Thank you. I couldn't have done it without you."

I mean it. Since Harrison and I made our relationship official, Johanna has embraced me like her own daughter. She calls me every day, visits New York at least once a month, and is always available when I want to share a new recipe or simply talk. No one will ever replace my mom, but Johanna has become a close second, offering the guidance, love, and comfort that have helped me heal in ways I never thought were possible.

It's a stark contrast to the relationship I had with my grandmother. I haven't heard from her since she showed up at the apartment building last year, and I'm okay with that. I'm sure I'll have to face her again someday, but she no longer holds any weight in my life. What matters now is that I'm surrounded by people who lift me up and care about me unconditionally.

"Yes, the food is excellent. You've really outdone yourself," Mike says enthusiastically from his seat before popping a stuffed mushroom into his mouth.

"Fallon, when is the balloon maker coming?" Lola shouts from the other side of the table, sitting between Dylan and Marlow.

With so many kids here tonight, I wanted to make it special so a balloon artist seemed like the perfect choice to bring a little extra fun to the mix.

I glance at my watch. "He'll be here by the time you finish your dinner."

"Oh, goodie. This is the best day ever," she exclaims through a mouthful of potato wedges. "I want him to make me a unicorn."

Marlow leans in, softly touching her arm. "Lolabug,

remember what I mentioned earlier—talking with your mouth full isn't polite."

"Sorry," she says through a mouthful of food.

Marlow shakes her head, smiling softly as she leans back in her chair, resting her hand on her swollen stomach. She and Dylan are expecting a baby girl, and Lola is over the moon about becoming a big sister, telling anyone who will listen.

I hear a soft coo and glance over at Cash and Everly, who are next to Dylan, each cradling one of their twin boys, Teddy and Harry, in their arms. They flew in from London to be here and are staying at our penthouse. The last few days have been filled with cuddles, baby giggles, and tiny hands reaching for everything. It makes me excited for the future and the day I have my own kids. Harrison will be a great father, and our kids will have lots of cousins to play with, something I never had growing up.

"Fallon, this truffle aioli sauce is to die for," Presley gushes. "I think the touch of smoked paprika gives it the perfect kick."

Jack pulls her to his chest, kissing her forehead.

"I'm so happy you like it," I say, my voice brimming with excitement.

Over the past few months, she's visited the restaurant once a week for lunch, and I've made her a range of dishes to test out for the menu. We've grown close, and it's great having her and Jack in the city. They join us often for Mavericks games and occasionally come over on movie night. Harrison takes the flowers from my hands, setting them on the table. He's been incredibly patient and attentive tonight, allowing me to enjoy every moment without feeling overwhelmed. I'm the luckiest girl in the world to call him mine.

He leans in to whisper in my ear, "I can't wait until we're alone tonight. We're taking home some of that homemade whipped cream I spotted in the kitchen earlier."

A shiver dances down my spine at the promise in his voice.

"As long as we don't make as big of a mess as last time, I'm in," I say, my tone sultry.

I clear my throat when I remember we're surrounded by family.

"I better get to the kitchen before we start plating entrées. I appreciate you all coming," I say to the Staffords with a broad grin.

A chorus of thank yous echo in unison, and Lola frantically waves goodbye, her cheeks puffed with a mouthful of food.

Harrison leans in to kiss my temple. "I'll come find you when our family leaves."

"Sounds good."

I weave my way around servers and tables, the chaotic energy feeding my soul. As I pass the bar, I come to a stop when I find Walter folding cloth napkins. He came to dinner with a few volunteers from the animal shelter, and the last thing I expected was him to be helping out tonight.

"What are you doing? You should be enjoying your appetizers," I tell him.

He glances up, giving me a warm smile. "Your staff got busy and I noticed you were running low on napkins and I figured I could lend a hand."

I wrap my arm around him and rest my head on his shoulder. "That's so sweet, thank you."

He leans his head against mine. "Always, Miss Fallon," he vows.

No matter how many times I ask him to drop the "Miss," he just nods along but continues to ignore my request.

The sound of a dish shattering makes me snap my head toward the kitchen.

"You better get back there." Walter gestures at the back of the restaurant.

"You're right." I lean in to kiss him on the cheek. "Thanks for everything, Walt."

Over the past year, he's become like a grandfather to me, and giving him a nickname only felt right. He's one of the most important people in my life, and I think it means as much to him as it does to me.

I give him a quick hug before walking off. As soon as I step into the kitchen, I shift into work mode, ready to help with platting entrées and dessert prep.

Theo played a key role in helping me assemble a reliable team that I can count on to keep things running smoothly, even when I'm not around. He's flying in for the grand opening, and we've already begun serious discussions about opening a Catherine's Table in London next year. I've also been in talks with several publishers about my cookbook focused on allergy-friendly foods. It's another dream come true, but with all that's on my plate, I'll need as much help as I can get.

I never could have imagined that this would be my reality—my own restaurant named after my mom, a man who I thought I lost forever but has now become my everything, and a family who's given me nothing but love and support.

BONUS EPILOGUE

Johanna

TEN YEARS LATER

I T'S A BEAUTIFUL SUMMER DAY WITH THE LAUGHTER OF children filtering into the kitchen from the backyard. I'm just adding fresh mint leaves to a fruit salad when Harrison steps into the room, tucking his phone into his pocket. "Need any help, Mom?"

He has a slight crease around his eyes, evidence of a smile that never seems to fade.

As the CEO of Stafford Holdings, he still occasionally takes business calls, but he manages to keep work from dominating his time off. It helps that he has a reason to make every moment count and to remind him of what truly matters.

"Can you take the hamburger patties and hot dogs out to your father?" I ask. "The grill should be hot enough by now."

"Yeah, of course. I'll go help him too," Harrison says, grabbing the foil-covered tray from the fridge and balancing it in his hands.

"That would be lovely, sweetheart. Thank you."

I'm not far behind with the fruit salad. When I get outside, I put it on the food table Mike set up on the deck earlier.

Marlow, Everly, Fallon, and Presley are seated at the patio table nearby with glasses of wine in hand, except for Marlow, who opted for sparkling water since she's six months pregnant. It's bittersweet since I have a feeling this will be my last grandbaby.

She and Dylan have already blessed me with four granddaughters, and another girl on the way. Their house is filled with brightly colored walls, hair accessories and ribbons, and the constant sound of giggles and chatter, and they couldn't be happier.

A few years ago, they built a house on Harrison's property, complete with a studio in the backyard for Marlow. She only does one gallery show a year now, but I still watch the girls once a week so she can enjoy a few uninterrupted hours of painting.

"Mom, we're planning a girls' trip to Vegas next month to celebrate the opening of Fallon's new restaurant. Are you in?" Presley asks when she sees me.

I nod. "I'd like that, sweetheart, but who will watch the grandkids?"

Mike and I usually do it when our kids are away on business or vacation, and we always look forward to it.

"Our husbands," Fallon adds, shooting a smirk at Harrison, who's standing by the grill with Mike. "Apparently, they think the kids will behave better if they're all in one place, so they're bringing them all to Aspen Grove while we're away. We'll see how that goes." She laughs, shaking her head.

"I heard that," Harrison points out with a raised brow. "It'll be fine. Olive's an angel, so what could go wrong?"

Just then, the toddler in question dashes across the yard, giggling wildly, her unruly blonde curls bouncing as she runs. Her blue dress is covered in mud, and she's clutching string cheese in her tiny hand.

"Daddy, the doggies are chasing me!" she squeals at Harrison.

Muffin, Jellybean, Cheez-It, and Biscuit, the puggle Marlow recently adopted, bark enthusiastically as they follow after her. Waffles brings up the rear, not as fast as he used to be but still as energic as ever.

Fallon stifles a laugh, her eyes glinting with amusement. "You were saying?" she asks Harrison.

He shakes his head with a sigh, heading down the deck stairs. "I'll get her cleaned up."

"Thanks, hotshot. Love you," Fallon calls out.

"Love you too, trouble," he says over his shoulder.

From the moment I found them arguing in my kitchen during Cash and Everly's wedding reception, I knew there was history there. They just needed a little push to see what was right in front of them—second chance at love. Now, they have little Olive, who's beautiful and smart like her mother and already has a love for being on the ice, like her dad.

On the other side of the yard, Teddy and Harry are in the middle of a game of tag with Cash and their cousins. Cash is "it," and before he can catch up to anyone, the twins share a knowing glance, and spin around, taking him down in a surprise tackle.

"Man down," the twins holler dramatically.

"Boys, will you please stop tormenting your father?" Everly shouts from the deck.

"Looks like Cash is getting a taste of his own medicine for all the roughhousing he put me through growing up," Presley remarks, her voice full of satisfaction as she raises her wineglass to her lips.

"They do have their father's energy, that's for sure," Everly chuckles.

She and Cash still live in London, with Everly working at Townstead International and Cash at Stafford Holdings. I doubt I'll ever convince them to move back to the States. But now that the boys are older, they spend their summers and holidays in Aspen Grove. The boys are a handful, just like Cash and his brothers were when they were their age, and Mike and I love it when they come to visit.

Just then, Dylan comes out of the house with Lola hot on his heels.

"Dad, please say yes," Lola begs. "It's just a movie."

When he turns around to face her, she tilts her head, giving him that pleading look that still works wonders.

Her honey-blonde hair falls in soft waves past her shoulders, and she's wearing a faded band tee, ripped jeans, and white sneakers. While I love all my grandchildren equally, she holds a special place in my heart as the first one to call me grandma. It feels like just yesterday that she was a little girl wearing tutus and begging for her hair to be done in fishtail braids.

"It's not *just* the movies. You said Matthew asked you to go, which means it's a date," Dylan grumbles.

Lola lets out an exasperated sigh. "Dad, I'm seventeen, and I'll be in college next year. You won't have a say on who I go out with then."

"That won't stop him from trying," Jack interjects, patting Dylan on the shoulder before pulling up a chair next to Presley. "And I'm more than happy to back him up."

Presley shakes her head, giving him a pat on the knee. "Don't worry, Lola. If you ever need an alibi, you can always call me." She grins.

"Thanks, Aunt Presley, you're the best," Lola replies, giving her dad a sideways glance.

"I'll keep that in mind when Sutton is old enough to date," Dylan warns, nodding to Jack and Presley's daughter, who's on the patio coloring with chalk.

"Sutton isn't dating until she's thirty," Jack growls.

"That's what I said about Lola," Dylan mutters under his breath.

It reminds me of how Mike reacted when Presley started dating in high school. He was always so protective and scrutinized every boy who came around. Her brothers weren't any better, always right there to keep potential suitors on edge.

I'm certain Jack will be just as fiercely protective of Sutton when she grows up. They still live in New York, but make sure to visit at least once a month, which I'm grateful for. Jack's as busy as ever with his company, Sinclair Group, and Presley got promoted to chief marketing officer a couple of years ago. Though she enjoys her job, nothing compares to being a mom, and their weekends are spent taking Sutton to the park and museums.

"So, can I go?" Lola asks again, shifting from one foot to the other.

Dylan glances over at Marlow, who gives him a shrug.

He sighs, raking his hand through his hair. "Fine, but Matthew is coming here to pick you up, got it?"

"Oh, thank you, Dad," she exclaims, throwing her arms around him.

"You're welcome, ladybug."

A smirk tugs at the corner of my lips. I'm sure my sons and Jack will give Matthew the third degree before letting him take Lola anywhere, but at least she's happy.

I join Mike by the grill, who's taking everything in.

"You okay, Jo?" he asks with a hint of concern. "You look a little teary-eyed."

I place my hand over my heart, glancing at my grandchildren running around in the yard. "I'm just so grateful for a beautiful family."

"We did good, didn't we?" Mike grins as he flips a burger.

"Yeah. Thanks for sharing this life with me," I say, winding my arm around him, lifting on my toes to kiss him.

"Love you, Jo," he murmurs against my mouth.

"I love you too, Mike."

From the moment I met him all those years ago, I knew he was someone worth holding onto. It took some persistence and a few gentle pushes to get him to see it too, but now, looking at the life we've created, I know it was all worth it.

"Grandma and Grandpa are kissing again!" Teddy exclaims from somewhere in the distance.

"Gross!" Harry and the other kids groan in unison.

Mike and I pull back, catching each other's gaze. His eyes gleam with warmth as we both burst into laughter. I wouldn't want to share this life with anyone else, and I look forward to growing old together, surrounded by our kids and grandkids.

All I've ever wanted is the best for my family, and there have been times when I've had to nudge each of them in the right direction, even when they didn't ask for it. As I look around, my heart feels full seeing each of my kids with their one true love.

Now I know what happens when a mother takes matters into her own hands…

Her kids all find their own happily ever after.

What happens when a prank Fallon never meant to pull goes terribly wrong? Think shampoo, hair dye, and a high-stakes board meeting Harrison can't miss. Type this link into your browser to read the bonus scene for *If You Give a CEO a Chance*: https://dl.bookfunnel.com/kwcwg83eum

Thank you for taking the time to read *If You Give a CEO a Chance*. If you enjoyed this book, please consider leaving a review on your preferred platform(s) of choice. It's the best compliment I can receive as an author, and it makes it easier for other readers to find my books.

OTHER BOOKS BY ANN EINERSON

If You Give a Single Dad a Nanny (Dylan & Marlow)
A swoon worthy, single dad/nanny, age gap, he's grumpy, she's sunshine, banter-filled spicy small town romance

If You Give a Billionaire a Bride (Cash & Everly)
A marriage of convenience that starts with a Vegas wedding between a reformed playboy and his best friend's sister in a banter-filled spicy billionaire romance

If You Give a Grump a Holiday Wishlist
A small town, fake dating, one bed spicy workplace holiday romance.

When You Give a Lawyer (Dawson & Reese)a Kiss *is a standalone workplace romance between a grumpy billionaire and his new assistant in an age gap, banter-filled, spicy love story.*

The Holiday Claus (Brooks & Lila)
A holiday romance where a grumpy billionaire falls for his best friend's sunshine sister, wrapped in an age gap, only one bed spicy novella.

The Spotlight (Conway & Sienna)
A best friend's brother, opposites attract, dating in secret, spicy rockstar romance.

ACKNOWLEDGMENTS

There are so many people who made this book possible, and I can't thank you all enough for your love, kindness, and support. *If You Give a CEO a Chance* wouldn't have been possible without each and every one of you.

To Bryanna—You make the day-to-day of being a writer so much more fun and far less lonely, and I am grateful for your friendship always.

To Autumn—I'm so lucky our paths crossed. Thanks for your blunt honesty when I need to hear it and your dedication to helping me achieve my goals. I couldn't do this without you.

To Tab and Kaity—Words cannot adequately express my gratitude for you. Thank you for putting up with my endless DMs, questions, and concerns. Your feedback is invaluable and this story would never have made it down on paper without you cheering me on from the sidelines.

To Jess, Kenz, and Samantha—Thank you for helping to spread the word about When You Give a Lawyer a Kiss and for your creative input. Your ability to bring my vision to life always amazes me and I'm so incredibly grateful to work alongside each of you.

To Becky, Judy, Courtney, Stacey, Literary Sisters—I couldn't have asked for a better editing team. I'm grateful for your expertise and for pushing me to write a story worth reading.

To Caroline, Wren, Lauren Brooke, Jamie, Jessa Lynn, Hunter, Kat, Sammie, Tess, Annalena, and Alex—Your honest, detailed, and candid feedback drove me to create the best possible version of this book. Thank you!

To Sarah—For designing the most adorable cover for this book. It was love at first sight and it makes my heart so happy that my readers love it just as much as I do.

To Sandea, Roxan, and Randy—You taught me to believe in myself and to chase my dreams, no matter the cost. I love you always.

To Kyler—Thank you for supporting my insane work schedule while in the midst of moving across the world. Without you my dream of becoming a full-time author wouldn't have come true.

To my ARC team—Even before you saw the cover or read *If You Give a CEO a Chance*, you fell in love with Harrison and Fallon's love story. Thank you for all your thoughtful messages, posts, stories, reviews, and comments. Your endless love and support never ceases to amaze me.

Most importantly, thank **YOU**. There are so many incredible books to choose from and I'm honored you took a chance on my story. None of this would be possible without you! Every single tag, share, and DM means the world and motivates me to keep writing on the days I think this might be for nothing. I hope you enjoyed your time in NYC with Harrison and Fallon.

ABOUT THE AUTHOR

Ann Einerson is the author of enchanting contemporary romance novels that will keep you hooked until the very last page, complete with heroes who fall hard and the heroines who keep them on their toes. She believes sometimes the best family is the one we find, curiosity is good for the soul, and a good book isn't complete without banter.

You can find Ann surrounded by her ample supply of sticky notes ready for inspiration and ideas. When she's not writing, Ann enjoys spoiling her chatty pet chickens, listening to her dysfunctional playlists, and going for late-night treadmill runs. She lives in Michigan with her husband.

KEEP IN TOUCH WITH ANN EINERSON

Website

www.anneinerson.com

Newsletter

www.anneinerson.com/newsletter-signup

Instagram

www.instagram.com/authoranneinerson

TikTok

www.tiktok.com/@anneinersonbooks

Amazon

www.amazon.com/author/anneinerson

Goodreads

www.goodreads.com/author/show/29752171.Ann_Einerson